I0731243

UNDER

SHADOWS

After the Last Day, Book Two

By

Don Hayward

Reader reviews of the trilogy

"Awesome epic book. It doesn't just deal with a collapse, but follows society for several generations, from the viewpoint of multiple characters.

This is a unique story in that it includes people with disabilities, people of various First Nations, people who are immigrants, people who are visible minorities, and people of widely varying backgrounds, ethnic heritages, political views, and religions beliefs, and treats them as actual people with stories rather than background decoration. This gives so many more opportunities to develop the story, and the author fully takes advantage of it. After reading this, I realized how much it gets repetitive reading books where the same generic heroic man fights to survive, with kids and womenfolk only there to cheer him on. I think this is the first post-apocalyptic book I've read where more than half the narrative is from the viewpoint of women.

Anton Chekov wrote, "If you say in the first chapter that there is a rifle hanging on the wall, in the second or third chapter it absolutely must go off.". In this book, the wall would be destroyed by a train driving through it. The author keeps things interesting by setting up the story so you expect one thing, but then knocks the legs out from under it. For example, a community develops its own currency to replace the nearly-worthless dollar, using some old store coupons they found. The characters carefully sign each one, keep track of how many are issued, monitor the relative value of the coupons to available food resources, and secretly mark the coupons to prevent duplication. You expect that they will soon have problems with counterfeit coupons, or hyperinflation. But, just like real life, events take place that invalidate your predictions.
This is really, really, really good value for the money. A lot of good story for your dollar."

***

"Gripping story, and all too plausible. There are no plot points where one says "no, that isn't possible"; more like "OMG, that could really happen"...
...On the whole, highly recommended. Prepare to have your thinking about society provoked."

***

"The books are interesting to read. The narrative is for ordinary people, and the plot is credible."

This book is a work of fiction. Any resemblance to actual events or persons, living or dead, are entirely coincidental.
"Under Shadows: After the Last Day Book Two," by Don Hayward.
ISBN 978-1-7752459-4-0 (Soft cover)
Published 2023 by Don Hayward, 8 Huron Lane, Goderich, Ontario, Canada N7A 3Y2

©2023, Don Hayward. All rights reserved. No part of this publication may be reproduced, stored in a retrieval system, or transmitted in any form or by any means, electronic, mechanical, recording or otherwise, without the prior written permission of Don Hayward.

This book is a work of fiction. Any resemblance to actual events or persons, living or dead, are entirely coincidental.

Cover photo courtesy of Simedblack, Pixabay.com

Also by Don Hayward

Collapse
Book One of After the Last Day
ISBN 978-1-7752459-2-6

The End of Shadows
Book Three of After the last Day
ISBN 978-1-7752459-5-7

The Seventh Path
A follow on story to the After the Last Day trilogy
ISBN 978-1-62137-949-2

Journey's End
ISBN: 978-1-7752459-3-3
Sequel to The Seventh Path

Return
Science fiction sequel to Spielberg's Taken series
ISBN 978-1-7752459-7-1

Echo of the Whip-poor-Will
ISBN 978-1-7752459-1-9

Murder on the Goderich Local
ISBN 978-1-62137-993-5

Sherwood Green
ISBN 978-1-7752459-0-2

Contact Don with comments or to order books
https://www.danddhayward.ca/
haywardon@gmail.com

I dedicate this book to my children and grandchildren as they enter an uncertain future.

Acknowledgement: To Alex, who read the manuscript and made suggestions for improvement.

To my wife Diane, who patiently attempted to discover all of my technical errors, confusing text and provided many helpful suggestions.

All errors are the author's own.

Introduction

This is the second story in the trilogy set in southern Ontario during a global economic collapse, previously published in a single volume as After the Last Day, still available in its original form as an e-book. Those who have read the original version of After the Last Day will not find any significant changes in the story.

The trilogy version is physically easier to handle, improved, and updated. It would be best to read the trilogy in sequence, starting with book one, Collapse, but the books should satisfy on their own.

In Collapse, a global economic and climactic crisis that had been deepening for years exploded into widespread breakdown on a late September day. Residents of the small Ontario town of Weyburne, although shocked and despondent, began an effort to survive under the guidance of Warren Dunne, a man previously derided as a "doomer" and a little crazy.

The Canadian federation fragmented and the world collapsed into chaos, but the residents overcame plotting by local business people intent on profiting from other's misfortune and achieved some stability involving hard work and a life never far from hunger. The disappearance of almost 80 percent of the original local population in the first year, either by fleeing to cities in a search for work or through murder, suicide, hunger, and disease, made the task easier. As they made progress, a sinister threat developed from the local enclave of the former financial elite.

The progressive organization weakened as more members joined the elite camp, attracted by paid wages and the aura of strength and leadership. The influence of the elite increased in Weyburne through the efforts of a local contractor, Roger Smith, who used bribery, bullying, and murder to gather support.

As the fascist People's Liberation Movement took control of Ontario, local allies, under the leadership of Alphonse Angel, seized Weyburne.

A handful of progressive leaders confronted the reality of fleeing or being murdered. Five families fled north into a seemingly safer territory focused on Owen Sound and most of the former Grey and Bruce counties north of the Saugeen River. These refugees settled on a complex of three farms in the lower Beaver River valley and struggled under the shadows of their lost past. The threat from the racist dictatorship would colour their lives for the next several years.

Chapter One

Life begins anew. We know not where it leads, but for now, the way is smooth, and the sky is bright. The sun shines upon the valley, warming me as I sit in the open on top of the bags of seed. I am riding a hay wagon, rattling along behind a rusting yellow school bus, feeling content. I miss my Papa, Nan and Gran, hoping they are safe, and they will come this way with the rest of the family.

Our shadows, drawn sharply by the strong morning sun, chase us, sliding over the long, dew covered roadside grass. The road is running away behind me, away from my old life... our old life. What I wanted three years ago has gone. Being rich and famous has drifted out of my dreams. Now, being with my family, safe and fed, are the only important things.

The view forward around the bus is blocked. It is right. We should not know the future, and I love the present rolling past me like the sides of this road, new and full of surprise and wonder. I know we must plan and struggle to survive. It is nature's way. Like tree seedlings, we start our journey, hoping and planning to reach the sky. We will struggle through the ice storms, fire, drought, and the shadows of the forest. The shadowy path will lead us to our final outcome.

My hopes, fears, dreams, desires, and longings all ride high up here with me in the bright warming sun. I feel safe. I am near those I love, and I am happy.

From: "The First Days" (The Journals of Brandi Shadly Age 15, Vol. 3, p. 1)

The ride was not very long that first morning. I remember a motorcycle passing us, with Chester at the controls and Karen behind him. They waved as they passed, and before long, we slowed and then turned, with Karen and Chester guiding us, into a long, overgrown lane up towards the sun-drenched west slope of the valley. This was my first view of our future home.

From: "Conversations with Brandi Shadly" in the "Voices of the Founders" series by Erin Thomas, Mentor of Historical Ecology, Huron Ecology Institute (Kimberly Campus)

Author's note: "Voices of the Founders" series is available through re-enactment by the Truth Talker Players at the Southampton H.E.I. (Ojibwe) amphitheatre Saturday afternoons, May to October–ET

Sharon Shadly, washed in bright June sunshine, leaned against the wall where she placed stone, tired from the heavy work of handpicking the right piece, lifting it into place, grooming the surface for a steady fit and tapping it against the angle guide. The pieces seated firmly in place, and the wall cambered inwards. All stones sloped gently down so no rainwater would run back inside.

Almost a year had passed since they claimed this property, a year since they had fled from Dufferin County and the murderous Alphonse Angel and Roger Smith. Deciding to concentrate all the families on one farm required this first new building.

Stone and timber were the best materials and did not require a factory or diesel oil, only needing human workers using simple tools and animal power. The structure would last for centuries.

They used an old, simple design with two parallel dry stone courses forming a wall over two meters high. Each course of stone cambered in towards the other, beginning with a broad base and ending somewhat narrower at the top. Dirt pounded between the two stone faces, added draft proofing and strength. With Beaver Valley, the red clay from the escarpment shale provided superior filler material. They placed a course of longer header stones, about every forty centimetres of height, tying the stones together. The wall had already grown shoulder high and they would finish the stonework within the month.

Jim Handley fashioned windows, doors and the roof with material salvaged from a house on an adjacent farm. This abandoned building, once grand, but poorly constructed a decade before for a retired couple who had died in despair. It sat too far from the main farm operation, too close to the river in case of flooding and, with vaulted ceilings, too hard to heat.

The new structure would house three families that now lived in old recreation vehicles, making room for newcomers. The compound would need the space. They expected refugees from the Toronto area soon and the extra labour would be a help in working the farm.

Sharon removed her wide-brimmed hat and mopped her sweat-covered brow, carefully avoiding the red chaffing line. The crude straw hat took its toll on her skin. She expected some aloe plants soon and could treat the injury. Everyone suffered minor problems like hers.

Sharon peered down the lane, watching six figures approaching. Bill was due to return from his two weeks of security service; however, this group did not include her husband. She could make out Warren and Willard walking with Karen Lefevre, accompanied by three strangers.

The two men had planted trees near the bottom of the lane, and empty seedling bags slapped their thighs. Shovels rested easily on the men's shoulders. Sharon could see the sun glinting from work polished blades. The strangers struggled under the weight of large packs.

Sounds of horses drew Sharon's attention up past the old farmhouse towards the path from the stone quarry. Jeff guided a pair of massive Percheron horses into the farmyard. They pranced and snorted, tossing their heads, knowing the barn was near. The team drew a stone-boat heavily laden with limestone slabs. Two men, tired from a morning of teasing rock from the quarry wall, plodded behind Jeff.

Normally, they would work early and into the heat of the day, then a few hours of rest followed lunch. Often, during planting and harvesting, they skipped the rest period. Her son's arrival raised a loving smile and reminded Sharon of her hunger.

The farmhouse fly-door banged. Jani Coswell carried a plastic bucket of cool water down the steps. Her shape confirmed her seventh month of pregnancy. Jeff tied off the reins and hurried to Jani, taking the bucket and kissing her lightly. Their faces reflected their love.

One man managed a dry whistle, and everyone chuckled at Jani's reddening cheeks. The horses tossed their heads and snorted, impatient at the delay of getting to the barn. Tired workers crowded around, sipping cool water.

Brandi Shadly, splotched with red clay, appeared from inside the new building. She slapped leather work gloves against her leg, raising a small red dust-cloud. The young girl found the pounding of clay in the wall satisfying. Her arms ached, and a sweat soaked, dirt stained blue bandana held her hair in place. The physical work gave Brandi a chance to ponder life. She often thought about the past year in the valley and contemplated their future. Debbie Hunter followed Brandi from behind the growing building. She had been placing a cut stone on the interior wall.

Everyone dressed in simple garb: bib style coveralls over a variety of colourful shirts. The quarrymen wore only a singlet under their coveralls. All but Brandi had a wide-brimmed corn coloured straw hat decorated with bands and feathers. Everyone had deep tans from hours labouring under the sun. As a concession to the dangers of working with stone, stout boots protected everyone's feet. The men had beards.

"Hey, Clay Pigeon," Jim called Brandi with his favourite nickname. "What say we switch? You dig rock tomorrow."

"Naw, my brother and I would argue. Besides, you don't know how to talk to the dirt." Brandi's eyes twinkled. "You got to persuade it to do the right thing." The blossoming young woman smiled at her sparring partner. "Jim, you do better working with two-by-fours and a hammer."

"Yeah, I've seen you sweet talk the clay with that log." He mopped his brow. "I'll stick to my pry bar and hammer."

"Stop flirting with my sister, you old man," Jeff scolded. "We're saving her to marry the King of Huron."

"I thought he already had someone," Jim retorted with a wink. Karen Lefevre and the others drew nearer.

Jeff unhitched the stone boat near the new wall, and took the horses, prancing and skittish, to food and water in the barn. He would not remove their harness. They would work again in a few hours.

The change in everyone during this past year in the valley amazed Sharon. All looked strong and fit, perhaps underfed, but their positive attitude struck her the most. Optimism had grown through a year where they had fought cold and hunger, grieving lost relatives and the shadow of a lost life. They drew strength from each other.

The group's solidarity masked the sometimes-heated discussions about important decisions. After seeing some arguments, observers marvelled this group could work together at all; however, a deep bond had formed from struggle. The hardships of the almost four years since the collapse and fleeing from Weyburne to the valley made disagreement safe and possible.

"Lunch time," Jean sang out from the porch. She saw the group struggling up the lane and did not bother to ring the dinner gong. Her gaze lingered on Warren. A little girl about three years old followed Jean onto the porch.

"Daddy," little Kim cried and ran down the steps, racing towards Jim Handley. He scooped her up and hugged his daughter.

Sarah Handley stood beside Sharon and watched her husband and daughter. The two had been working together, lifting the heavy stone. Sarah was tired, happy to let Jim and Kim frolic. She suspected Kim would have a sibling before the year was out.

Children who tended the small animals and poultry came from the barn. An older girl carried a large basket of eggs. A small lamb, perhaps two months old, trailed after the group, bleating and nosing pockets for a treat while searching for the empty nipple-bottle in one of the boy's hands. Little Kim tore out of her father's arms, ran to the bouncing lamb, and hugged it to her cheek.

The strangers crowded into the yard, eagerly laying down their burdens. Willard hugged Debbie Hunter, collecting rock dust and clay on his sweat-soaked shirt.

Chester Amik had been to the farm several times; this was Karen's first visit in eight months. She last appeared the previous October, making sure the group from Weyburne had enough supplies for the winter.

Brandi stood silently, desperately wanting to chat with Karen, hoping there would be time later. She focused on the new people, wondering what their arrival might mean.

The two clean-shaven men wore baseball caps over short hair, in contrast to the scraggly beards and long hair of the resident males. The third, a tall woman had short, dark hair and sunken eyes. She seemed sad with a grieving look too familiar to the residents of the valley. Each stranger wore slacks and shirts as if out for a round of golf, but their running shoes had deteriorated to the point of being useless. The tall woman approached middle age and carried a "valley hat", wide-brimmed and made of rough straw similar to the ones worn on the farm. Brandi thought the older man was middle-aged while the other in his late twenties was more interesting. All looked underfed and were likely not used to physical work.

"These people have come from Toronto via Dufferin," Karen said, "and on the move since mid-winter."

"Lunch is getting cold." Jean reminded everyone and headed up the steps.

Farmers had built the stout brick farmhouse over a century before. It lacked modern features, with old-fashioned wooden sash windows, but it was large with lots of bedrooms. The living and dining rooms joined to accommodate meal times and meetings. Wood provided heat for cooking, and the summer kitchen, once converted to a recreation room, had now reverted to its former purpose of avoiding oppressive cooking heat in the main house during hot weather.

A water tap stood by the steps, and everyone washed their hands and splashed water on their faces. Towels hanging on the painted railing soon showed smudges of red clay and limestone dust.

The wastewater collected in a large bucket beneath the tap. Warren Dunne had dubbed this the "Herbert Bucket" regarding an old fiction writer who had created a world where collecting all water was essential. Even though they had no problem with the farm water supply, Warren said it would make them think about everything they did and used practice for a time when they would need it. Every day, one child took the bucket and watered the kitchen garden. The group followed Jean through the door. The newcomers hesitated until Walt Lefevre encouraged them.

"Don't be shy folks." Walt's voice was friendly. "We've enough for all. You'll earn it soon enough."

The hungry, thirsty, and tired trio eagerly followed the others inside, where Walt ushered them to the foot of the table. As usual, with large groups that ate together, everyone had their spot reflecting the parings of men and women. A vacant space lay beside Sharon Shadly.

All the men and women but Warren and Jean served two weeks of compulsory security duty. It was a custom at the farm to leave the missing person's place at the table vacant, ready to receive them home. Bill Shadly's spot would remain empty for a few more days.

Warren sat at the head of the table with Jean to his left. Even though time had been too short for traditions to develop, there was an honouring of elders. Dunne was such an important contributor to the innovations of the farm the others would have shown him respect.

Another empty place setting, its plate decorated with a single red paper rose sat to Warren's right, never to be occupied. It was in honour of Matt Long. The young man had sacrificed his life to save Warren, Bill, and Willard the night they escaped from Weyburne.

Jeff helped Jean bring two steaming pans of stew from the kitchen as the others passed around water pitchers. Several platters of rough brown bread, cut into thick slices, ranged down the table along with two large bowls of greens: early leaf lettuce from the garden, and a generous mix of dandelion leaves and other forest goodies the children harvested. A bowl held homemade dressing of oil, vinegar, and salt mixed with tomato sauce. Jean returned from the kitchen with another loaf of bread and laid it in front of her place, ready for the knife. Jani brought out additional place settings for the new arrivals. The mismatched dishes, flatware, and drinking vessels represented salvage from several houses.

The younger children had their own table with a pitcher of goat's milk. All the younger ones drank milk, as did Warren and Jean. Until production from the goat herd increased, the others would have water.

Five-year-old Megan Lefevre, who sat next to Kim Handley tried, with little success, to mother the younger girl. Karen had not seen her niece and nephews for many months and insisted on sitting with the children. With her knees touching the low table, the doting aunt settled in to enjoy lunch. At such times as these, she felt a slight pang at not having children of her own. She thought this explained why she had become a teacher, combining career and family in the best of ways.

They had no formality. Everyone dug in with helpings of stew and un-buttered bread. A pregnant Swiss Brown heifer stood in the barn, but she had not yet freshened to provide cow's milk or butter.

The newcomers were not aware of it, but the residents would take a little less than their normal portion to accommodate the extra mouths. An unwritten tradition of generous hospitality existed in the Huron region. Any violation of this custom caused much talk, with no one being shy about bringing a failing in hospitality to the guilty host's attention. It was also the norm to arrive at an establishment several hours before the next meal to allow time to prepare extra. Most visitors practised a custom of bringing some food offerings. Karen had not followed this courtesy since she had judged her charges needed rest and nourishment as soon as possible and the refugee camp at the 26 barrier had none to spare. The evening meal would be prepared to consider the four additional mouths. For lunch, the extra loaf of Jean's bread would make up the shortfall.

There was little talk as everyone concentrated on the meal. The newcomers, once they understood they were part of the crowd, ate with gusto. Their hunger would have made rougher fare enjoyable.

"It's nice to have visitors," Warren finally spoke through the sounds of eating. "Karen said you're from Toronto. There'll be plenty of time to chat later. Please introduce yourselves."

The trio glanced towards Karen, expecting her to make the introductions; however, she had abandoned the three as she mothered Kim and Megan and teased her nephews.

"I'm Kathy Nelson," the woman finally replied. "I'm from Mississauga, a Nurse Practitioner."

"Harold Kovalevsky," the older man spoke up, "I taught at the university campus in Mississauga. I have a doctorate in economics, for all it matters these days." The man sounded bitter, and the derisive groan directed towards his profession did not help his mood. While the educated group did not blame economists for the recent disaster, they had no respect for what they considered a priestly profession that had believed in infinite resources.

"I am John Bock," the younger one took his cue. "I sold cars, but was homeless and hiding after I ran away from the Western Defenders Militia, a bunch of racist murderers. They drafted me to carry their stuff. I got away when someone wiped them out."

John sounded matter-of-fact. His expression told of deeper horror.

"How did you meet?" Willard looked up as he sopped up the last gravy from his plate.

"The guys showed up at my clinic, needing a place to hide," Kathy said. "Several militias roved around and grabbed any able-bodied person they could. Hungry people eagerly joined any army, but many wanted to avoid dying." She sipped water.

"I lived in the clinic after a gunfight killed my neighbours in the condo building. They died trying to fend off looters. One gang protected me as long as I stitched up bullet wounds. I planned to get away, and then these guys showed up. I figured travelling with two men might make it safer. It didn't appear they wanted to rape me."

Kathy's expression suggested she had suffered a sexual assault. "We thought we would go west, maybe to Kitchener."

Everyone sat back, sipping water and paying close attention. Karen shooed the children out the door.

"Kitchener's as bad as Toronto," Karen drew her chair to the table, "good thing you came here."

Kathy glanced at Karen. "Yes, we headed west along the lake, but soon spotted a checkpoint. It was a few blocks away, so we dodged up side streets north to the rail line. No one used that track as it ran to Union Station. Gangsters have turned downtown Toronto into a wasteland. Nothing goes in there."

"We followed the track west, only walking at dusk and dawn so we would be harder to spot, finally reaching Erindale Station. Shipping containers surrounded it, guards everywhere, and lots of truck traffic. A bunch of people stood around the entrance, so we mixed in with them. It turned out trucks carried stuff from the old hydro jetty on Lake Ontario to the railway terminal. I'm not sure where the boats originated. It didn't look promising with all those guards carrying big guns, but the real danger was way east, near the old highway where most of the fighting happened. A guy came out and asked for volunteers to go north and do farm work."

John piped up. "Yeah, we figured anywhere had to be safer; it only took us a minute to volunteer. They didn't want Kathy, but when she told them she was a medic, they suddenly became eager. The guy said Mr Angel needed doctors, but she would do."

The Weyburne refugees stiffened at the mention of Angel. John looked at Kathy.

"I had to show them my kit to convince them. It appeared they would get a bonus for finding me. They searched us and herded us, and a dozen others, into a boxcar. Soon the train began moving north."

"We rolled along nicely for half an hour, freezing our asses off. After we left Brampton, a terrific crash sounded from the front of the train and gunfire. A couple of bullets hit the car. We flattened onto the floor. Boy, did it stink. I think they had hauled animals in there."

"We sat there for a long time but heard no more gunfire. Someone came to see if a bullet had hit anyone and soon we rolled on. A car smouldered at a crossing with a couple of bodies near it. It scared me. I thought perhaps I didn't want to work for Mr Angel if he had this much firepower and enemies to match. I would jump off at first chance. The boys have forgiven me for not letting them in on my plan. I had no time to discuss it and no idea if the others in the car were trustworthy. Most of them just stared blankly."

"My sister lived in Orangeville before we lost touch. I knew the area and jumped off well out of town." A shadow crossed her face at the memory of her lost sister.

"Living in fear for a few years can make you quick to act. I recognized Highway twenty-four when we crossed over. I knew it had to be soon. By good luck, the delay caused by the shootout meant night had fallen. I'm sure they had wanted to make the entire trip in daylight. When the train slowed climbing up the hill south of Orangeville, I grabbed my kit and jumped into a big snowdrift. Next thing I know, these two goofs are jumping too." She smiled. The trio had bonded on the journey.

"Yeah," the professor spoke up, "no way we wanted to be farmers; we figured we'd better jump too. Besides," he looked at Kathy with a smile, "it's hard to find a good doctor. We didn't want to lose the one we had."

Everyone laughed. The declining economy before the collapse created problems finding a personal doctor. They all understood the joke.

Warren ended the talk for the time being. "I think you'll be farmers, regardless of whether you like it." His tone was not vindictive. "Thanks for sharing. I hope you can give us the rest of your adventure soon, but everyone is tired and needs a rest." Warren noticed Jim and Jeff nodding off. "We go back to work in a few hours."

Dunne stood and walked back to the kitchen to visit with Jean. The others vanished, leaving Karen and the newcomers at the table.

"That's rude," Harold complained. "I've lost everything, haven't heard from my family, and they walk out."

"Let me tell you something," Karen flared. She had endured the professor's sense of self-importance all the way from the refugee camp. "These people have suffered, some worse than you could imagine. Several people here haven't heard from their family for over three years. Some had a husband and father murdered by people working for Angel. They've heard many stories like yours. Don't expect them to own your sorrow. They have a full plate of their own."

Karen had half-risen, glaring into Harold's eyes, and then eased back into her chair. Despite everything, the man's pain was deeply personal and real.

"I think you all should rest, too." Her tone softened. "I don't know how they'll fix you up, but for now, just find a spot to rest. They'll be starting work again about three o'clock, and even though you are all weak, offer to help. These people have been working hard for a long time. I'll talk to Sharon to see what I can arrange."

Karen followed Warren into the kitchen. The two men sprawled into big easy chairs in the living room. Preferring fresh air, Kathy claimed a soft patch of grass in the shade of a big maple. She rested her head on her kit bag and fell asleep, with a gentle June breeze comforting her; sunlight and shadows danced over her through the leaves.

Chapter Two

At first, Warren thought little of these three, our first new arrivals. We hadn't worked out any procedures. He thought they might be a burden and disappointed because we expected families, but having Kathy, a medical person, excited him.

We chatted with Karen in the kitchen, working out the details. Her enthusiasm picked us up. We had been suffering from boredom and incessant hard work. Surviving through the winter had been a near thing, so maybe that had us low.

From: "Conversations with Jean Bennett," in the "Voices of the Founders," series by Erin Thomas

I found Warren and Jean in the kitchen, looking tired and depressed. In those days, it was more hard work, but so much was new and innovative too. I helped with the dishes, and we worked out how they could fit the three new ones into the farm. Hard work right off was out of the question. The refugees were too weak.

I told them the council planned a dispersed system of medical care and Kathy Nelson would be at the farm to be part of it. This excited Warren. He said it seemed like progress. I remember Jean saying it would mean more visits from the neighbours and that would be good. Jean seemed to feel the isolation of those first few years more than most people. No one would pay for medical help. The farm would support Kathy, but she would do her share of work outside of her nursing job.

12

From: "Conversations with Karen Lefevre," in the "Voices of the Founders," series by Erin Thomas

*G*iggling? *Giggling?* The sound drifted across Kathy Nelson's mind. She awoke.

Who is giggling?

Kathy's eyes opened. Bright afternoon sun lit her face. She saw a canopy of tree branches and new green leaves. The giggles sounded again. She turned to the smiling faces of little Kim and Megan. The girls were kneeling on the soft green grass beside her, gazing into her face. Kathy smiled, and they jumped back, startled by her awakening.

She reached out and Megan, ever the brave little one, extended her small hand and gripped two of the woman's fingers. The girl stood, her bare feet firmly fixed on the ground, drawing Kathy into a sitting position.

"Hi, I'm Kathy," her words, gentle, crafted over many years working with nervous children in the clinic but coming from her heart. The nurse would forever miss her little nieces and nephew.

"I am Megan, and this is Kim," the brave girl replied. "We think you are beautiful."

Kathy smiled, and her cheeks reddened. She did not feel beautiful, with her dark hair unkempt and only having had one bath since arriving from the south.

When they reached the barrier on twenty-six, they walked a kilometre west to a rough camp and lived in tents for two weeks to make sure they did not have any diseases. They worked in the camp gardens. Kathy used her medical skills on other refugees and a few guards. This made her popular around the compound. The staff had given humane but basic care. Kathy had her last bath there, and her skin suffered from homemade soap.

Her ability as a doctor attracted interest. People at a higher level than guards interviewed Kathy. She related her story three times in those two weeks, partly because the crew guarding them had changed after one week. She guessed they thought she might be a spy. The interrogators were especially interested in the people who brought them to the Huron boundary. Kathy clearly saw that life on both sides of the border focused on three things: food, community, and guns. She felt safer than she had for years.

"Thank you, Megan." Kathy grinned. "How long have you been watching me?"

"Not long," the little girl replied, "ever since you fell asleep. We didn't want Lambypop bothering you."

Kathy noted from how far the sun had moved that the girls had been with her for a couple of hours. Time had a different meaning on the farm, and anything new fascinated the little ones. Kathy could not see any lamb.

"Could I please get a drink of water?" Kathy stood and the girls with her. They took her to the tap and handed her a tin cup from a nail fixed in a rough cedar post. Kathy paused, staring at the tap as her public health training kicked in. In the past few years, and especially on the trek to the valley, anything offered as food or drink could kill. Cholera flourished south of Lake Ontario, and in Toronto.

"It's safe," Jean Bennett watched from her seat on the porch. "We pump the water from the deep well with a solar power plant supplying the pump and a fridge and freezer. Our water is safe but full of lime."

Kathy took a long sip, giving her dry mouth comfort. No wine could taste as sweet.

"How long did I sleep?" Once again, she glanced at the sun behind the high trees towards the valley's western lip.

"Long enough for the bread to rise and put in the oven," Jean glanced at the doorway, letting her nose probe for the fine smell of baking bread.

A few more minutes, she thought, consulting a man's watch strapped to her wrist. *Then Ill get the wild turkey loaf in to bake.*

Hammering attracted Kathy's attention, Sharon and Tina Lefevre working on the wall of the new building. The unmistakable voices of the male refugees came from inside the growing structure. Brandi, her voice earnest and patient explaining the process to her apprentice helpers.

"You are the cook?" She returned her attention to Jean.

"Yum, Yum," exclaimed Megan and Kim and scampered away, bored by this adult talk. The girls disappeared into the barn in search of a new adventure.

"Stay away from the cow!" Jean's call trailed after them.

"I am the cook today. Tomorrow it's Karen's brother, Walt, and it rotates. Can you cook?"

"Not as good as you, but I can learn." Kathy said, in false modesty.

As a student, Kathy had lived out of the freezer aisles and junk food of the supermarkets, but as her training and understanding increased, she focused on healthy eating and became a fair scratch cook, but never a vegetarian or a fad dieter. Teaching people to eat healthy food was, in her mind, the biggest contribution she had made to their health. She would tell people: "Building a good car is more sensible than fixing a bad one." Occasionally, she wondered where her neat little red Toyota with the sunroof had ended up.

"Great!" Jean said. "We have little to work with, but this season should give us a lot more. We hung by a thread over winter. Come, let's check the bread."

The summer kitchen was huge and simple with a cook stove that was not as old as it looked, a present Chester Amik retrieved from one of the larger homes down the valley. The original owners had purchased the stove new only a few years before, when they considered everything that burnt wood eco-friendly and country chic. Now, it earned its keep cooking and space heating. Those who had to use wood understood it required hard work.

Two large, steaming pots of water sat on the stove, pre-heating for washing dishes and the potatoes to complement tonight's meatloaf. A stout wooden table filled the main part of the room with a freezer in one corner beside a small counter, stainless steel double sink, and over-crowded shelves. Everything looked new, and the fine joinery attested to the carpentry skills of Jim Handley, who in his words had "roughed it in".

The sound of an axe came from beyond the screen door. Kathy saw Karen Lefevre during a full overhead swing, smashing a heavy splitting maul onto a stubborn block of willow. They had harvested several of the big willows and Manitoba maples for fuel. Warren, the arborist, described them as "inferior for heat, but fast growing". Living branches and a few green twigs he had planted sprouted in otherwise unproductive soil. These shoots would provide a useful crop in fifteen years.

Behind Karen, the two Hunter teens, Don and Stephanie used a two-man crosscut saw to slice a log into stove lengths. Karen's oldest nephew carried the newly split pieces and stacked them. Kathy did not know wood cords, but the neatly stored piles seemed like a lot. A small open shed of post and beam construction with a rusting corrugated steel roof overflowed with split-wood, and well-piled rows marched away from the structure. The fresh-cut pieces would cure in the summer heat to be burnable in the coming cold. The settlers had burnt most of the handy dead falls the previous winter.

Willard and Warren planted aspen and birch twigs along the lane for this same reason and now worked down at the bottom end near the river, preparing a tree nursery for seed from the native species. The children would weed and water them.

Warren planned to use these seedlings for trading. One of the old orchard operating families survived and did Silva-culture, producing grafted fruit trees. Warren and Jean socialized often with this family.

"Take a break, dear," Jean called Karen inside and set teacups on the wooden kitchen table. "I get tired watching everyone work," Jean diminished her own efforts. "We can talk with Kathy about her new job."

Kathy cast a startled glance at Jean.

"Don't worry," Karen said, still breathing hard from her exertion. "You already know. We want you as the resident doctor. You impressed people down at the barrier."

"I like the idea. I want to contribute and earn my keep, but what support is there?"

"None," said Jean with a twinkle in her eye.

"She's just kidding, Kathy," Karen was not sure if Kathy appreciated the twisted humour of the Huron region's population.

"We're short of supplies, but the hospitals in Meaford and Owen Sound share a surgeon. There are few antibiotics, a shortage of anaesthetics and no sophisticated surgery, replacements, heart and so on. Only life-threatening injuries or broken bones get surgery. You'll go to Meaford to help for a bit and get to know Doc Adams. Safety and prevention are a challenge. We have a huge shortage of labour, so everyone's working too hard and tired, causing lots of injuries." Karen took a long sip of white pine tea.

"One thing," she looked sad, "most of the medically fragile people died. There are few chronic cases left."

Karen had nursed several of these doomed sufferers as they declined and died. "The principal work, after the injuries and emergency care, is midwifery, paediatrics and caring for ageing folks."

Karen glanced towards Jean. The busy woman did not notice as she extracted bread from the oven, replacing it with two large pans of wild-turkey loaf. A blast of warm air engulfed the room. Jean flicked a water drop onto the stove's cooking surface, frowned as it danced in its steam and inserted a stick of willow into the firebox.

"What about nutrition and prevention?" Kathy wanted to return to good eating practices. The past few years, she had eaten anything that would keep her alive.

"Right now," Jean returned to the table, "it's a matter of getting enough. We rely on starch, fat, meat and vegetables. It has been mostly carrots and potatoes, along with wild greens. We have apples up here, and this year's garden will provide for late summer and fall. White pine tea is popular for vitamin C, although you have to get used to the taste. How do you like it?"

"The taste is different, but I can drink it. Have you tried rose-hip tea? It's good for the same things and tastes better." Kathy sipped.

"We made it in Weyburne. There are rose-hips down around Heathcote." Jean looked forward to the taste. "I'll take some kids that way later in the summer. We'll start our own patch."

"I noticed milk for the kids, and you and Warren."

"That's raw goat's milk," said Jean. "It's tasty and the kids need it. Everyone says us old fogies needed it too." Jean was a dozen years younger than Warren, but extra calcium would do them both good. "We have a cow about to give birth. She'll soon have milk."

"Cow milk isn't the best," Kathy mused. "I would focus on goats."

Karen would raise the issue with Chester. Kathy echoed others who had questioned bovine milk, and smaller animals dispersed the loss if one died. Cattle required large resources; however, they had a growing demand for cowhide.

Huron faced many issues with no central authority to dictate solutions. Changes evolved with good ideas superseding weaker ones. Much of the population reflected this refugee farm, with want-to-be farmers struggling to become the real thing.

"So, how will it work for me?" Kathy's eagerness showed.

"You'll be available here to give medical care. We'll let the neighbours know. They can come and see you, or you go to them. There will be no fee. This farm will be your support, and when you aren't providing medical care, you'll contribute to the farm. Work all that out with Jean and the rest. Learn how to ride a horse. Fuel is scarce, and we walk or ride, if a horse is available."

"We have decided some of this," Jean spoke up. "John and Harold will sleep in the barn and Jeff will move out there as well. It's comfortable on the hay and straw even if it smells. You'll sleep in the room with Jani until we can arrange something else. The parlour will serve as infirmary."

"It's not fair displacing anyone," Kathy replied. "I'll sleep in the barn. We've been sharing for months. A little longer won't hurt. I'm used to Harold complaining."

The young woodcutters came through the screen door, tired and not too playful, looking for cool water. Jean gave each a big oatmeal cookie.

This ended the discussion. Kathie intrigued Stephanie Hunter and the new arrival was soon answering the young girl's questions.

Having sorted Kathy out, Karen headed to the construction site. She worried Brandi could use support. Harold had not impressed Karen. Her instincts proved her right.

"I still say you're wasting your time on this stone. Straw bale building is the way to go."

Harold leaned against the wall, lecturing as Karen arrived. It appeared he had yet to do any useful work.

"One of my colleagues had a place in Caledon, a million dollar property built of straw, snug and solid."

"Straw bale houses have great use," Karen pushed into the conversation, "but there's one big weakness you might not know about, not being a farmer, before now." Karen emphasized the "before now." Harold-the-Professor would have to accept being a farm hand.

"What weakness?" Harold flared. No one challenged him in the classroom. "I didn't see weaknesses with straw."

"It takes diesel oil to make the bales." Karen sounded matter-of-fact. "If you aren't aware, fossil fuels are expensive. We get little oil and gasoline. Most of it goes to the security forces."

"The results are worth it! We should bale straw for houses." The professor wanted to win, not admitting ideology held no sway against resource limits.

"We don't have the fuel or twine. It isn't an option."

"You see this building we're working on?" Debbie Hunter joined in. "We designed it to last for generations, perhaps centuries. Your straw house would rot away much quicker and have to be replaced, perhaps several times during the useful life of this place."

"Straw takes nutrients out of the soil. Warren told us everything we harvest represents soil nutrients, and we must replace them. Tying it up in buildings is not a good way to store fertility."

"You have a point," Harold said. "it isn't my area of expertise. What about log buildings?"

"Log is a great material if you're clearing land anyway," Karen took up the question, "but it's more valuable for heat and other things. Standing trees have more environmental value. We only want to cut them for good purpose. If you have no alternative, then build with logs."

"Another thing," Debbie interjected, "if someone attacks, it's harder to burn a stone building."

Harold grimaced at the reference to fighting and tired of the discussion. "What do you want me to do?"

Brandi handed Harold a shovel. John helped Debbie lift the stone and set the course. Karen saw the progress. They would complete the stonework before haying, and with any luck, have the structure ready before fall.

"Harold," Karen said, "they want to come up with a design using less stone and labour." Harold rested his empty shovel on the top of the wall.

"The way this place works, the way the whole territory might work one day, is for everyone to give ideas and opinions. The group wrestles them to the ground, and good ideas survive. Don't be shy about contributing, but be ready for tougher arguments than the one we just had. Remember, if they reject your idea, they won't be rejecting you. You'll have to be beyond hope for rejection."

"What is rejection?" The concept made Harold leery.

"If they think you aren't contributing and never improve, they will send you back to the barrier. We would give you one more chance with someone else. A second rejection would get you a few days' supplies and sent out the barrier. There's no appeal, and no trial. Living amongst us is the trial. You'll get a fair chance. Everyone here is a refugee."

Karen walked out of the gap in the wall. Harold jammed the shovel blade hard into the pile of clay, determined to do his share. He already liked this place and the people he had just met.

Chapter Three

I did not realize it, but Warren and Willard asking me to contribute to their project sent a message of acceptance. Years later, I had the privilege of leading the restoration of the piece we installed. Remembering the day we first raised the sign brings tears to my eyes.
From: "Conversations with John Bock," in the "Voices of the Founders," series by Erin Thomas

"John, please help Willard and me this morning." Warren took John Bock aside after breakfast. "We have a job down by the road and need some extra muscle."

"No problem. I'm not sure I could lift stones again today."

"Not to worry," Willard said. "We won't be working hard. We have holes to dig and poles to install."

The three men went to the equipment shed and loaded shovels, a pry bar, an axe and a ten-pound hammer onto a small handcart, joining a board wrapped in old grain bags. The carrier had bicycle wheels and looked like an oriental rickshaw.

As the trio started down the lane, the rest of the residents headed to work on the construction project. Jeff brought his horses from the barn, and Jim placed a water bucket on the stone boat. Handley's eyes followed the three men as they left the yard. He was the only one, other than Warren and Willard, who knew what was afoot. No one would rest after lunch today, but it would be a day to remember. Jeff called, and Jim hooked the boat to the whippletree.

"How are you doing so far?" Warren asked.

"So far, so good. This isn't hard to push."

"That isn't what I meant," Warren replied. "How do you feel about being here?"

"Compared to what I've been through the past three years, wonderful. I've been inside the barrier for two weeks and haven't gotten used to regular meals or feeling safe."

"Kathy left you in a snowdrift. What happened next?"

"When I hit the snow, I thought I was drowning. The snow went down my neck. I brushed myself off with bare hands, feeling lucky and an idiot at the same time." He chuckled. "Harold nearly landed on top of me. Then I hear Kathy telling us to stay down. We dropped like stones in the pitch-dark while the old caboose full of guards rolled past. The train didn't slow down."

The trio reached the end of the lane and unloaded the cart. Several squared timbers lay in the ditch. Willard grabbed a shovel and began the first hole.

"The train disappeared, and we looked to Kathy for leadership. I had no inkling of why she jumped, but Kathy was street smart and did nothing without a plan."

John took the shovel from Willard. The other men carried a timber to the far side of the laneway.

"Kathy explained the violence had made her nervous. She believed you couldn't trust men with guns."

John gasped for air, working the shovel deep into the hard ground. He finally resumed.

"She said we should find out what was going on before committing to anything. Kathy made sense. I was shivering; I had never felt so cold, and Kathy suggested we find shelter. We walked up the rail line to a road crossing, wanting to get away from the tracks in case someone came looking, but we left a trail in the snow right to an empty house. We couldn't do anything about our tracks, but had one of us on lookout once we got settled."

"The previous owners left lots of stuff. I found a nice coat, boots and mitts, and the others found warm clothes. No heat and electricity, but we made a tent in the living room to keep in our body heat. Kathy put a bucket of snow in with us, hoping it would melt and fix our thirst. We snuggled close to stay warm just as we did in Mississauga. Despite our intention to keep watch, we all fell asleep but woke up scared when a motor sled roared past. The wind had drifted snow over our track. The snow in the bucket melted, but man, we were hungry."

Warren inspected the hole and decided another foot would do.

"We need the same on the other side."

As the man dug, Willard and Warren laid the poles out and fixed the longer one to the end of the others.

"We discovered canned food in the basement along with matches, firewood and a few old papers to get it going. We desperately wanted a fire, but waited until nightfall to risk it. Eventually, we even burnt the mortgage for the poor folks who had the place. The worst thing, we found a dead guy frozen stiff in the garage. It looked like he had sheltered there and just froze, but maybe someone killed him. Sad case..." Bock paused for a minute, reliving a horrible memory.

"We stayed several days until the food was nearly gone, exploring every day but sticking to the woods. There was a village to the west with signs of life, so it looked safer heading north. At nightfall, we struck out staying well west of Orangeville along the old roads, stepping in one set of prints. Kathy went first. She had small feet. I went last with my size ten boots."

They completed the holes. John helped Willard drive wooden dowels through drilled holes, anchoring the capping timber to the uprights and fixed double angle mortised braces to solidify both joints. Jim had explained the technique to the men, but they wanted to do all the work. Their finished product impressed Handley.

"It was slow going," John continued. "Hiding out in abandoned houses, we found a little more food and made fires. All the houses had a wood stove, but we always suffered from hunger."

The men aligned the frame with the two dug holes. Willard retrieved the wrapped board from the cart and hung it from two chains in the centre of the cross timber without removing the bags, looping a rope around the crossing timber.

"John, you take the rope and head out towards the road. When Willard and I lift, start pulling." Warren took up a position beside one post and Willard the other. The lifting went smoothly, and the uprights slid into the holes. They pounded rocks and dirt firmly around the timbers and attached angle braces. It was a framed gateway with a large sack-covered sign in the centre, hanging high above the lane. A thin cord hung from the covering. Willard tied the string to an upright and declared it a fine bit of work.

"It's worthy of the Double R–Bar Ranch," Warren intoned. The others did not understand his reference to long-forgotten cowboy actors.

"I guess you're wondering," Warren spoke as Willard offered a jar of water and a sandwich from his pack. "You'll find out what it's all about after lunch, along with everyone else. It's a symbolic payment on an unpayable debt to an old friend. A man named Matt Long died to let us and Bill Shadly escape from Weyburne."

"Continue," Willard said. "You had me feeling cold."

"We worked our way past Orangeville. Kathy knew her sister would no longer be there and did not know where she and her nieces and nephew might be. I could tell she was sad. Places and distances were a mystery to us, but we made it about two roads north and a few west of the town. It was hard going in the deep snow. We didn't see signs of people, just desolate, abandoned farms and suburban houses. Big shacks sat empty and unlocked. People had not looted them all."

"Our packs became heavier as we found more supplies. We felt safe that far from town, so we holed up and rested in a big place with lots of stuff. It turned out to be a good idea. The weather turned nasty, snow and then blowing. I had seen nothing like it."

Willard and Warren exchanged knowing looks. One of those big Texas winter storms had hit and then the blow from Lake Huron behind it. Weyburne had a notorious reputation for horrible weather. They guessed from the past winter's storms the trio was in that house in late February.

"We would have died out in the open in that weather." John ate his sandwich. "The house had good camping gear, a cache of trail food and snowmobile suits that fit. Kathy looked like an orange penguin."

"Those folks liked the outdoors. Everything was brand-name. I do not know why looters left the place alone. Down in the city, they would have cleaned it out."

"We filled a toboggan with food and a tent. A big thaw hit on the day we headed out with bright sun and a nice warm breeze. Before long, we put the snowsuits on the toboggan as we dragged it through the slush."

Willard stood and impatiently checked the structure and the cord linked to the sign cover.

"Sorry about that," he said when he returned, "my bad back stiffened up. Lifting this thing didn't help, carry on."

"We came to a little village. I can't remember the name, but it started with an L."

The men had a good idea where John had been. Only one local village started with L.

"They abandoned the place with a gas station stripped bare. From a rise north of the town, we saw a couple of farmhouses with smoking chimneys. We detoured west, to another hamlet a few roads over on a little river. It seemed deserted and spent the night. It turned out some folks watched us. Next morning we took a road running north parallel to the stream. When we reached the top of the grade above the river, a bunch of armed and masked men and women jumped us. They didn't sound friendly, and I figured my life was over."

The lunch gong sounded.

"Sorry, it's getting exciting," Warren said, "but we're never late for lunch. You have us hanging, so be ready to finish the story. You're here. I guess things worked out."

Lunch was much the same as the previous day, with a roast of pork in place of stew. The newcomers were more relaxed and joined in the banter. In a few days, they might remember everyone's name.

"Willard and I have prepared a special something, with Jim's help and John's." Warren nodded at the newcomer. "Come down the lane for what we hope is a pleasant surprise."

Everyone, who only a few minutes before had been eagerly contemplating a rest, sprang to their feet. They would never ignore the promise of something to relieve the routine. Everyone asked questions, but Warren, Willard and Jim walked with silent smiles.

"You plan a hanging?" Sharon asked when they reached the new structure. "Do you have a Smith tied up somewhere?" The Weyburne survivors laughed, imagining Roger Smith, Stevie Hunter's killer dangling on the cross arm.

"Something better," Willard smiled at Sharon.

Warren began, "We've had sorrow and sadness in abundance the past four years. Everyone has lost loved ones, either dead," he looked at Debbie Hunter, who stood with her children and Willard's hand on her shoulder, "or missing." Brandi hugged her Mom, and Jeff held Jani tightly.

"There's one loss we all share, and someone to whom Bill, Willard and I owe our lives." Warren choked up slightly. He turned to the newcomers. "Matt Long died saving our lives when we fled Weyburne. I am sorry Bill isn't here. It's time to honour a memory."

Warren strode to the post and gave the cord a swift pull. The grain bag covering the sign fluttered to the ground. The signboard rocked gently. On it, Jim had inscribed the word "Longview" and carved the likeness of Matt Long from one of Brandi's sketches. The group stood in silence. Faint sobs rose from the crowd. Walt Lefevre's mouth organ wafted over the gathering. Picking up the tune, Debbie Hunter sang:

> *Should old acquaintance be forgot*
> *And never brought to mind?*
> *Should old acquaintance be forgot*
> *And old Lang Syne?*

The others joined in. The emotions were deep and real. Everyone hugged. The history of the group built a deeper bond, shared memories holding them closer with an unspoken promise to be worthy of Matt's sacrifice. They passed under the shadow of the sign and walked up the lane to their home, a home now called Longview.

Kathy Nelson lingered for a few moments, staring at the sign, grieving her own loss but wondering about the likeness carved sharply into the wood.

Chapter Four

Before I met Karen, I had not thought of my journals as anything but personal. Drawing and writing helped me cope with those first few years of calamity, especially when Roger Smith murdered Stevie Hunter. I couldn't talk about my feelings much, so I drew and wrote them down with my observations, only sharing them with my extended family. Karen recognized potential in my work and taught me technique, language, and the importance for me to tell our new story. She refused to teach me the theory of art, always telling me just to put down what I saw and felt and not to conform to some style or ideology. Some say that makes my work fresh and free; others say it's primitive. I just know I tried to be honest and accurate. She always told me: "you are drawing and writing history".

I cannot emphasize enough how much I grew to love her as my adopted aunt, sister and friend. Only my family, Warren, and Jean equalled her in my heart.

From: "Conversations with Brandi Shadly," in the "Voices of the Founders," series by Erin Thomas

(A self-portrait of Brandi done in oils depicting her and Karen Lefevre making that first journey together on the valley road hangs over the fireplace in the HEI Kimberly campus common room–ET)

"Sharon," Karen Lefevre opened the front door to the old farmhouse and stepped onto the porch, its boards protesting her tread. "I want to talk with you about Brandi."

Sharon Shadly slid over, making room on the roughly hewn wooden bench. She leaned her tired body against the maple-branch backrest. Karen sat and turned to face her friend. Crickets sang in the night air; she could make out a few stars shining between the porch roof and the shadow of the barn. Sharon remained invisible in the velvet darkness as a warm breeze wafted around them.

"You know, she has exceptional talent." The sacrifice she was about to ask Sharon to consider made Karen uneasy. "We need someone to record what's going on and tie it all together, to carry hope and information to all the remote places. It will be invaluable in the future." Karen could not make out Sharon's face. She had no clue about Sharon's reaction. "I want Brandi to come to Kimberly to polish her skills in drawing and writing and become that person."

Sharon stirred, and a sigh came from the darkness. The soft night wrapped around them. Karen waited.

"Karen, she needs that." Sharon finally spoke. "Brandi has worked hard here without complaint. She's important to our labour needs, but she's bursting to do more. She draws gentle portraits of everyone working and playing, sweet pictures of the children that the mothers treasure and hang over beds. I saw one picture in her book, a beautiful drawing looking down the lane, perfect in every detail, except the lane doesn't end but vanishes in the distance." Sharon slid closer to Karen. In the dim light filtering through the doorway, they could see each other's faces.

"I first thought it meant she was lonely. She's a teenage girl, after all. When I asked her, she said it wasn't loneliness, but she had no horizon here, only the steep green slopes and a cliff on the other side of the valley. She feels as though the valley has captured her and will never let her go. Her picture let her be free."

Sharon stood and leaned over the porch railing, gazing up at the brilliant stars hanging high above the valley. Her work-roughened hands gripped the weathered wood. The sound of an owl ruffled through the chirping of the crickets.

"I want her to go, Karen. Brandi will want to go. She'll thrive and be your scribe. The three people you brought us will more than make up for her work. I'll miss her deeply. We've lost many people in the past few years, but I know she's only down the road and we'll visit often."

Karen touched Sharon's hand. "I know the sacrifice you're making. I promise to take care of her like my daughter. We'll both come down to help with the harvest. I'll even get Chester to stook grain."

Karen giggled at the image of her partner heaving sheaves onto a wagon. Her hand squeezed Sharon's. The women stood in silence, drinking in the night, letting their hearts settle.

"Where's Brandi now?" Karen finally betrayed her eagerness.

"She has her bedroom above the tool room and likes to draw and write out there. She'll be drawing before bed."

Karen took a crank flashlight and headed across the yard. She wondered how long these devices would keep working. This technology would not survive long.

A well-fitted door accessed the addition to the barn, the tack shop where they made, repaired and stored horse gear. The icy light revealed leather straps, harness, steel chains, rings and pins for whippletree and other hook-up devices. Straw littered the floor; the space had the wonderful aroma of leather mixed with the faint odour of animals housed beyond the wall.

Jeff and Walt shared this domain and trained Don Hunter. The sixteen-year-old learned quickly. It was a learn as you go operation, and the men searched the valley to find someone to mentor them. In the meantime, they mimicked older harness kept as souvenirs by the former farm owners.

Bare wooden stairs with no handrail led to the room above. The treads sighed under Karen's weight. Her free hand steadied her on the rough barn board wall. As her head rose above the upper floor, Karen saw Brandi at a small desk near a window. Vegetable oil lamps illuminated the space in a pale yellow glow. Brandi's shadow danced on the wall above Karen's head.

"Hi, my dear, you have a wonderful little place here."

"Hi Karen, I hoped we would get to talk." She stretched. "I have finished for tonight. I rarely waste oil, but I wanted to complete this picture for tomorrow."

The drawing depicted the ceremony down the lane, with the crowd standing behind the structure. Brandi had drawn her father's face amongst the leafy branches of a nearby tree. Warren and Willard stood at the uprights. The sign dominated, perfectly rendered, with Matt's image drawn deeper and more clearly than the other figures. Like most of her work, this piece told where Brandi's heart lay.

Karen knew Brandi would be the truth talker, helping to tie the uneasy alliance of the region's people into a community, recording and sharing everyone's stories throughout the territory.

"Brandi, come to Kimberly to finish your schooling and polish your skills. You have a wonderful talent."

"Karen, I've wanted to ask, but was afraid to even think about it. They need me here." Brandi placed her desires behind the reality of Longview. "Everyone's working so hard with always more to do."

"I brought three people to replace you." Karen chuckled. "More will arrive. Come to Kimberly with me tomorrow. We'll return for the harvest. Does that sound workable?" Karen watched the struggle in Brandi's mind. The girl's deep sense of loyalty reassured Karen.

"Karen, I'll come; I want to come; I need to come." She hugged Karen, sobbing. "There's so much I want to say, so many things in my head and heart I need to get out." She stepped back and looked into Karen's eyes.

"I want to make it, so no one else has this sorrow. I miss my Gran and everyone and know they're dead."

Tears streamed down Brandi's cheeks. Yellow lamplight highlighted the anguish of her face. Karen could see Brandi's shadow, larger than life, trembling on the wall. Karen's heart broke. She shared Brandi's grief.

"When will we leave?" Brandi regained composure.

"After breakfast, I have to get back to help in the gardens. I've been away for a week. We need to get an early start."

"I'll be ready." Brandi hugged Karen.

"Good night, Sweetie. I'm so happy."

Brandi spent busy hours gathering the things she needed. When she entered the house, Sharon dozed in a big living room chair. Brandi pinned the drawing above the fireplace. It looked pleasing in the flickering light of a vegetable oil lamp. Brandi sat in a comfortable chair, spending one last night with Sharon.

"Good night, Mother," Brandi mouthed. "I love you."

Chapter Five

I stood in the lane, a rock hammer in my hand, watching Brandi and Karen walk towards the valley road, into the morning light, and the two dissolved into the land. My heart filled with happiness for her future, and sadness, my little girl making her way in life at such a young age. In my old plan for her, she would have been finishing high school and preparing for university. I could never have imagined she would receive a much different schooling, or this school would give her a life more important and useful than the one we had planned. When they faded from sight, I turned back to my work. Kathy and I lifted another stone onto the new wall.

From: "Conversations with Sharon Shadly," in the "Voices of the Founders," series by Erin Thomas

Karen and Brandi set a steady pace over the suffering asphalt of the old county road. A kilometre down, a young man on a bicycle appeared out of the morning mist. He regularly delivered messages along the main roads.

Mailboxes left over from the Canada Post days still proved their worth, and crossroads had a common drop box for everyone living off the major routes. The message run between Kimberly and Thornbury happened once a week.

The young man, who invented this job for himself, sometimes took three or four days to complete the return trip. He spent most of his travel time socializing along the way, always welcomed, and he could depend on a free meal and a place to sleep, including at Longview. People sought gossip and news as eagerly as any letter. Some of the gossip about him centred on the one or two places where winsome, available young women lived. It had become a game trying to predict which would be Mrs. Postie.

"Good morning, Ben," Karen knew Ben well. "You had an early start. Did you tire of walking?"

Although bikes were common in the valley, people saved them for when speed was important.

"Sure did, Ms Lefevre. I've got to get a message down to Thornbury quick. There's been trouble up on the number four barrier, some shooting."

"Is it serious?" Karen was concerned. It was a quick march from the barrier to Kimberly.

"I don't think it is. Chester took a few guys up there and then came back down in a hurry. I've got this message from him for Meaford base." Ben patted his pocket. "Chester said they're a bunch of damned fool drunks." Ben had dismounted from the bicycle but now swung his leg over the crossbar. "I have to get going. I'd love to talk, but I have to get down there quick." He sped off with a perfunctory wave, a long look back, and a smile for Brandi.

"I think he likes you." Karen smiled.

"He's nice," Brandi replied, "but has several girls on the string. I'm no fish."

Brandi's growing maturity and perception amazed Karen. She wondered how such a young girl had found so much self-assurance. In this tumultuous world, Brandi had found maturity. Perhaps she had grown up too fast.

They resumed their journey. The early morning shadow of the valley floor benefited the women as they walked. It would be a beautiful day and hot later on, but they hoped to be in Kimberly before the sun sapped their energy. The only sounds came from their footsteps on the crumbling asphalt and the urgent morning calls from the birds. Mist from the river and the dew-soaked fields gradually dissipated as the sun rose higher and stirred the first breezes of the day.

"You're smart about boys," Karen broke the silence. "There's time later. It's better to build your own life first."

"There wasn't any opportunity at Longview," Brandi replied. "This John guy is interesting, but I want to learn more and do things. I don't know if I should have kids."

"You remind me of me," Karen laughed. "I was a nerd. Few boys chased me. Most of them thought I would be desperate and easy to get into bed." Karen sighed. Brandi wondered if Karen regretted lost opportunities or remembered good times.

"I had a long, strange journey to get to Kimberly." Karen glanced at Brandi, checking for interest. Encouraged by Brandi's curiosity, she continued, "I graduated from university in history and then the teacher's college in Toronto with high marks, so I had no trouble there. I struggled to find a job. Even then, governments at every level were running out of money. I spent a couple of years teaching part-time, supply teaching and living with my parents." She paused for a few seconds. Brandi understood Karen remembered a lost family.

There are always these shadows crossing people's memories. Brandi thought.

"I finally broke down and took a job up in Weirton. It was a glorious life up there, and ten years flew by even though the winters were brutal."

The two travellers took a break, sitting on a bridge railing high above the little river. The sips of water and Jean's apple-jelly sandwiches restored their energy. They watched the water flowing beneath, absorbing the tranquillity of the morning.

Karen resumed her story as their feet once again found the road. "Every August, I went to the Powwow up at Cape Croker. I enjoyed the wonderful weekends, and I made many friends in the community. I met Chester there. He had returned from the city and worked as an assistant manager at the Kimberly ski resort. It was a torrid weekend," Karen paused, wondering how much she should tell, but then went on. "I figured, okay, the sex was wonderful, but that's the last I'll see of him."

"The next week Chester knocked at my door, wanting to take me for a ride and dinner. He didn't even call first. I thought he was one smug, self-assured bastard, but I liked him. We drove up to Tobermory, had dinner and ended up in a cabin for two days, sightseeing and, well, everything. He asked me to move to Kimberly with him."

Karen paused and smiled with a faraway look, savouring a long-cherished memory. She stopped walking and put her hand on Brandi's shoulder. Looking into her eyes, Karen said, "I hope you experience the thrill and wonderful feeling I had when he asked me."

"I told him I would try to get a job down here and find a place, but I had been on my own for many years and would not move in with him unless we were married. That was the best decision I ever made. It took a year to find a placement in Thornbury. I found the house in Kimberly. Chester spent a fortune on gas coming up to see me, but it had been a wonderful year. He lived at the resort, and I had the house. That was five years before the crash."

"Chester brought young people from the resort staff to me for tutoring. It amazed me how many struggled with language and math. We had a big family, though we postponed our own until we married."

"Humph," she muttered, "like that would ever happen. We were both too independent, but faithful. We never really lived together or planned to change that until the collapse, that is. Word got around, and I began tutoring, as well as my teaching job. Even today, we sometimes have several young people crash at our place or just visit. Most of them were local kids, and only a few have disappeared."

"What happened when the economy crashed?" Brandi wondered why the valley and Huron seemed to have done better than Weyburne.

"Lots of factors, but I'm not bragging, saying Chester was the key. The ski resort fired them all and closed. Chester convinced the owners they should let him stay there free, guarding the place. He soon had a dozen others living there and took in more. Before long, the old resort was the centre of our attempts to survive."

"My job went that October when the school board ran out of money. Chester realized everyone needed to work together. He travelled down the valley and over to Meaford, organizing." Karen caught her breath for a few moments.

"The mayor of Meaford was a progressive woman with many friends. The two soon had people cooperating. We saw some racism because of Chester being Ojibwe. Someone hit him. Chester became the leader of the valley by default. None of the politicians in Thornbury hung around or didn't want to try. Honestly, though, he's a nice guy, smart and a hard worker. Most were happy to have him doing it. Now we have the Huron Council taking some of the burden." Karen paused, lost in thought, trying to word her next statement carefully.

"Your group arriving last year caused a real stir. Many opposed having you here." She let Brandi think about that.

"I caught bad vibrations that first week," Brandi replied. "No one said anything directly to us."

"You can thank Chester and the other members of the Council. After your dad and brother first appeared, they had a big meeting, letting the opposition blow off steam. Some people had become tribal; Chester explained our labour pool and security forces were too small and we needed more good people."

"Over the past year, many eyes watched you, but now everyone is happy you're here. Even old Emma Wiseman likes you all. You'll find out she's the biggest busybody and gossip in the valley. Taking her to visit Warren and Jean last winter did the trick."

Brandi remembered Emma arriving on a snowmobile and spending a couple of days teaching baking, discussing gardening, and other things. Somewhere, she had a drawing of Emma, Warren, and Jean deep in conversation.

"Thanks to your arrival, people are more accepting of refugees. Everyone sees the advantage of good people replacing those who left or died over the past few years. You were the first large number of refugees." She hugged Brandi. "I'm glad you're here."

"The military commander is Roger LaFarge, down at the Meaford base. That's where Ben headed, I think. Chester and the rest of us depend on Roger's experience and training. He reports to the Huron Territory up at Owen Sound. The territory is a casual alliance and includes the valley, Meaford, Owen Sound and territory above the Saugeen over to the Beach and the peninsula. Your brother will meet Roger when he goes for training."

"When do I learn to shoot?" Brandi felt inadequate.

"Chester plans to teach you and other young people. He'll give you a bit of other security training too, but you won't be going to Meaford. They picked Jeff to become a leader. The rest of us just need the know how to shoot and have the guts to do it if necessary. I don't know if I could, and I sure hope I never find out."

Brandi thought the same thing; however, she thought she might like to hunt game sometime. She had only fired her mom's twenty-two rifle.

"Funny," Karen continued, "I was a pacifist and an anti-gun crusader before the crisis. I still think I was right in those circumstances, but now we have to defeat these evil characters. We had to kill a few racists below the Sound a couple of years ago. Some of the old local elite wanted to be dictators. We had no other solution. They wouldn't surrender and had murdered a couple of people. I think we'll need to do the same with these racist drunks up at the head of the valley. It looks like it might be soon." Karen thought of Ben's urgent message to Meaford.

The road meandered slightly and wandered away from the river. Brush and river willows obscured the stream. Brandi could now see the enormous cliff that dominated the village. Old Baldy reflected the late morning sun. She was glad that the walk was nearly over. They had exhausted their supply of drinking water.

"I want to get you reading and writing, Brandi." Karen switched to the task at hand. "I have some books that are especially important, I think. There's Kim, by Kipling; Who Has Seen the Wind, by Mitchell. Chester has a gigantic pile of native history and stories."

"Some of that is very entertaining, but a little off the rails, like Kinsella's stuff, although he wasn't a native. There's lots of serious native writing. We'll discuss the territory. Chester being a leader has helped us form a good relationship with the Ojibwe, fighting racism on both sides, but things show promise."

"Karen, I am running out of paper and am worried about supplies of paper, ink, pencils, and paint."

"We're going to solve the paper problem by learning how to make it." Karen smiled at Brandi. "I have information about papermaking in my library. We'll start by recycling old paper. There's lots of newspaper around as well as useless books. I understand from what I've read, we can use cotton and linen. We might have a product to trade or give away if someone needs it."

Karen's optimism encouraged Brandi. She had considered making paper, but did not know how to go about it. Brandi hoped there would be solutions for the other essentials. The sound of a whistle interrupted them.

"That's one of my students sounding the alarm." Karen chuckled as she peered ahead. She could make out figures scurrying about, and as they drew closer, several youngsters in the garden, pulling weeds. A young boy was hanging the wash on a line beside Karen's back door. Two girls perched on porch furniture, reading and talking.

"What a hard-working bunch you are," Karen called to the boy as she and Brandi crossed the unkempt grass. "Who was the lookout?" She laughed at the lad's discomfort.

"It was me, Karen." He responded. "We had the work all caught up and were having a break before lunch. You taught us well and scared us properly, too." He laughed in response to Karen's quizzical grin.

"Am I that mean, Jake?" Karen hugged the boy as she walked past towards the duo on the porch. "Get everyone in for lunch," Karen ordered. "I want to introduce Brandi."

Chapter Six

It is strange what goes through our heads sometimes. Suppertime, the day I returned from my security stint, I remember looking at Brandi's space at the table and thought of her thirteenth birthday with the partly eaten bunt cake. We joked about the missing piece. Thinking about it that evening, I remembered we had given Brandi an art kit for her birthday. Those tools became her preparation for her actual role in life, even though we hadn't known it. The gap at the dinner table represented another sharing, a greater sharing of our family with the world. Sharon's generosity in sharing that cake was now coming full circle. Somehow, that thought comforted me as if some grand plan was unfolding. Brandi would never again be a regular at our table, but I made sure her little loft above the tack shop would forever be hers.

From: "Conversations with Bill Shadly," in the "Voices of the Founders," series by Erin Thomas

At the evening meal, the day of Brandi's departure, Bill occupied the chair beside Sharon. His return diminished her sadness. They had only been apart for two weeks, but their smiles, little touches and quiet banter told how much they had felt the separation.

Bill had endured a long vigil. He and another man had patrolled two concession roads along the top of the escarpment east of the valley. Nothing unusual happened. The boredom and isolation hung heavily upon both men. Bill now had another good friend. The man's extended family was one of the several households living on the high ground. They farmed the frontier of Huron territory and were vulnerable. They should have evacuated down to the valley, but their farm hosted a large flock of sheep, with no suitable vacant farms for them in the valley.

A gift from Bill's friend made tonight's meal was possible. A steaming roasted lamb dominated the Longview dinner table. It was a treat that no one thought would be available for at least another few months, not until a male lamb reached slaughter weight.

"Randy promised me a new white-face stud ram for the fall." Bill said to Willard. "We can keep all of our female lambs and breed them to the new boy."

"Old Slam-dunk can still do the old girls one more time." Willard enthused. He was the designated shepherd of Longview since his bad back prevented heavy work. Willard called the old ram folks on the other side of the river had gifted them "Slam-dunk".

"We'll keep his girls again, and then we can turn him into mutton stew." Willard loved his sheep, but reality dictated they waste nothing.

"It looks like I missed the excitement." Bill glanced down the table at the new residents. "So fill me in." Sharon had made real coffee to celebrate Bill's return.

"Kathy left us hanging with them in a snowbank." Stephanie Hunter spoke up. The teenage girl had moved beside Kathy.

"John took us further." Warren gave a shortened version of John's story from the previous day.

"Who wants to continue?"

"It had better be me," Kathy spoke up quickly. "Harold will use too many big words," she smiled warmly in the man's direction. "John used to sell cars, so I'll be more believable."

"When the masked band jumped us, it petrified me thinking these were Angel's people or robbers. They ordered us to kneel in the snow, tied our hands and put hoods over our heads."

"Damn, it sounds like an execution." Tina Lefevre exclaimed.

"That's what I thought," Kathy continued. "I was shaking and crying. I figured that was it; however, they got us up and marched us along at a good clip. Not being able to see made it hard. I stumbled twice. Someone caught me. Their touch reassured me, not hostile, if you know what I mean. I felt better." Kathy drained her coffee; Stephanie made her another.

"We walked at least a couple of hours. By the warmth of the sun, we were going west. It got cloudy and cold, and I shivered. Our captors said little, but what I overheard, even though a few sounded like hicks, suggested they were relatively intelligent and disciplined, different from the punks I endured in the city. When we rested, they gave us water. I got the impression they worried more that the ropes hurt us, not about us escaping. I became optimistic and tried to tell the boys. A woman snapped at me to shut up."

Kathy stood and stretched. It had been a hard day lifting stone onto the walls.

"Finally, they led us into a big barn, warm and full of stale air. They removed our hoods and sat us in old living room chairs. A couple of masked people with guns stayed with us. They gave us water, but hunger hit me. John and Harold looked stressed, their eyes hollow and desperate. I suppose I looked the same."

"You looked horrible," Harold spoke.

"I reassured the boys I didn't think we were in danger, expecting the guards to tell me to shut up. They said nothing but listened. Sometime later, a masked guy came, grabbed my arm and told me to come along."

"We ended up in a well-lit room with a few hard chairs. A man interrogated me, taking notes. I told him the story you have heard so far. He asked me repeatedly what I knew about this Angel guy, and how I knew him, as if he thought I was one of Angel's people. The boys went in one at a time. It was obvious; they were trying to trap us in a lie."

Bill and Willard remembered Stevie Hunter interviewing the Quinn murder suspects. They did not mention it with Stevie's widow listening. Willard, in his own need, squeezed Debbie Hunter's hand.

"That was it. They gave us blankets, untied our hands and left us alone. There was no easy way for us to get out, although, given a few days, we probably could have made a hole. It wasn't a jail. We ate a hot meal with strange tea, this white pine stuff you like."

"We sat in darkness, chatting until we fell asleep. It had been a hard day. I remember waking when I heard Harold take a leak. We all used a bucket in the corner. Our sense of propriety had long since vanished. Later, someone showed us we were supposed to sprinkle sawdust into the bucket. This was our first experience with this sanitation system that you, uh, we use here."

Kathy glanced at Warren. She had learned the bucket sewage system at Longview was his idea. Brandi had pinned up a drawing in the kitchen depicting Warren hugging a tree. Warren puzzled over the mystery of who knew about composting poop.

"Am I boring you?" Kathy asked. "I feel like I'm droning." Head shaking gave her permission to continue.

"A woman came in with breakfast and not wearing a mask. She said they believed our story. She called herself Brenda and said no one should ask for last names, and the group had designated her to be our guardian and even though we talked with others, Brenda was the only name we ever heard, although everyone lost their masks."

"Days turned into weeks. Finally, they told they found a safe place for us to go, but it would take time to move us. They needed to do the spring work first."

"When the weather warmed, and the planting started, we helped, digging gardens, paying for the hospitality we received, going to the end of May."

"Several times in these weeks, most of the group disappeared, leaving us with the village folk. We guessed the others were fighters, since they always carried guns. We did not know where they went until one day, after she returned with new members and a stolen truck, Brenda told us they raided Angel's operations near Orangeville."

"They were hiding grain and other food because of Angel taxing the farms. His bunch would come and take a portion from everyone, maybe up to forty percent, so anything they could hide from him was a bonus."

"Angel was thorough and brutal about finding hidden stuff, punishing people who tried to hold out. Brenda said their group would take surpluses away, returning it as needed, keeping a small portion to supply the band. To distract Angel, they only carried out raids near Orangeville. I started calling them Robin Hood and his merry men. Brenda laughed and said Maid Marion and Friar Tuck lived in Weyburne."

"One morning before dawn, Brenda and another man took us north. At first, we made good time, but then slowed down as Brenda became cautious. We snuck up to every rise in the road. At all crossroads, we waited until they were certain it was safe."

"I reckoned we covered at least thirty kilometres. The longest wait had been at a main highway. All the direction signs were gone. I do not know the roads. There was some traffic on the highway. Brenda said there were patrols from Angel's crowd and led us through a culvert under the road, covering us in mud."

Warren called for a quick break. He needed to use one of his buckets. The talk of water had not helped. As the group re-assembled, the day faded into evening, but no one wanted to leave. The children scrambled noisily in the yard, the peaceful evening sounds of Longview.

"We camped in some thick woods just after crossing the road." Kathy picked up the story. "A fire might betray us. We slept under tarps in our wet clothes and snuggled to keep warm in the cool night. As the sky lightened, a stiff easterly breeze brought a cold rain."

"Before mid-day, Brenda brought us to a tree line behind an old snake fence. The other guy peered through binoculars at a small village in the distance with smoke from chimneys. We gave the place a wide berth."

"We found an empty house complete with beds and built a fire in the fireplace. Once we evicted the mice, we had soft places to sleep. We finally dried out and spent a wonderful night compared to the previous one."

"Brenda had relaxed. She said we were north west of Weyburne and the gangsters, as she called them, hadn't come that way yet. They don't have enough people to repopulate the area. Many of Angel's fighters had died the past year, and he had a labour shortage."

"Two days later, we reached the top of a high hill and saw the lake stretching to the horizon. The road dropped over the edge and disappeared into the trees."

"From this point, we were on our own. They knew you would treat us well. Then Brenda said something funny: Say hello to everyone you meet. They might be some old friends. I do not know what she meant. They disappeared. We headed down the hill and arrived at the barricade."

"We didn't know someone organized opposition to Angel." Warren sounded encouraged.

Jani sobbed in the corner. Kathy had mentioned the casualties in Angel's forces. Her father and brother were probably dead. Jeff hugged her and held her tight. Their hands rested on her pregnant belly.

Chapter Seven

"When it is evening, ye say, it will be fair weather: for the sky is red. And in the morning, it will be foul weather today: for the sky is red and louring."
The Christian Holy Book, authorized version

The rain came overnight, a light summer rain that soaked the ground and enhanced the green of the grass, giving life. An east wind blew the showers in as dancing curtains of mist. The federal weather service had disappeared. The propaganda radio from Toronto gave weather forecasts but obviously had no actual information. Longview relied on guesses based on the wind and the movements of a cheap barometer hanging in the dining room. It now rose, promising fair weather.

Work continued on the new building even though the clay needed protection from the rain. The tool shed saw a flurry of activity, preparing scythes for cutting hay. Longview had no mower, but a horse-drawn side-rake sat ready. It would be another year before they found a repairable mower. This year's harvesting would seem advanced compared to the struggle of the first summer at Longview.

As promised, the sun shone, and the wind went to the north-west. Bill, Walt, Jim and Jeff headed into the nearest hay field at first light, swinging the scythes in unison, following clockwise around the damp field. They paused for water and, occasionally, to run a wet stone over their blades. It became a routine mechanical movement. The men were relieved for brief spells by Sharon and Tina, and even Harold tried. Little children sat on the side, watching in fascination until boredom took hold and they ran off. Older youngsters carried water to the work crew. Don tried his hand at the cutting while Jeff drank.

The warm sun cursed and blessed. The heat helped make the hay quickly; however, the workers laboured in the sun, soaking their clothes in sweat and drinking much water. A little smoked salt-pork helped restore their bodies. Everyone wore stout gloves, but hands that seemed work hardened became tender and blistered. Kathy bandaged the wounds, allowing the work to continue. That evening, she would work on every hand that had touched the tools.

Through pain and fatigue, the crew worked until dark, abandoning the normal rest period. After the second day, almost ten hectares of hay lay flat, making in the sun. The next day, they would rake and gather the cuttings.

Jeff, who had laboured hardest the day before, had the privilege of riding the horse-drawn rake. As soon as the sun had dried the dew, one of the big draught horses easily drew the rake over the ground, with the hay rolling into neat windrows behind. The other Percheron followed, pulling the hay wagon between the rows. Two crews working each side forked hay onto the wagon bed. The sound of the women chucking to the horses and banter from the loaders filled the air.

The ground yielded a good crop and shortly, the moving pile of perfectly green tinged hay was too high to accept more. An old-fashioned hay loader would have made the work easier, but there seemed little possibility of one being available soon. The younger folks rode the wagon, struggling to move the load higher. Soon the wagon, loaded to the limit of the great horse, had to break off and head for the barn, with two of the youngsters atop a high load of hay, enjoying the view.

This first trip was an adventure of unloading. They found it easier to fork the load off at the barn door and carry it inside while the wagon headed out for more. The crew kept the pace all day, with only a brief pause for lunch. At day's end, half of the hay safely rested inside the barn.

During the night, everyone received a lesson in the frustration and heartbreak of farming. Jeff woke to booms of thunder followed by flashes of lightning. He stood on the porch, protected by its roof, watching the driving rain in the flashes of light. His mood became as dismal as the thunderous onslaught. The rain would ruin half of the hay they had laboured so hard to cut. Bill came through the door; his footsteps lost amidst the thunderclaps.

"It's frustrating," Bill spoke to his son. He could not stop the thunder and the pounding rain, no matter how much he wished. "This is farming Jeff. We have to roll with it."

"I know Dad," Jeff sighed. "My hands still hurt from the cutting. It's hard to accept it was for nothing."

"We have to cut the field over in the next place now," Bill stared through the rain. "It would be nice to have had some warning, though. This means it's going to get hot."

A brilliant flash of light and a loud clap of thunder shook the house. Shrill sounds of a frightened child came through the door. The horses cried out from the barn.

"We can probably get another cut off this field, Dad." Jeff tried to be optimistic. Briefly, his face shone pale, reflecting another flash from the sky.

"I agree, son," Bill turned towards Jeff. "We'll be at Longview a long time. This won't be our last setback. We just have to work on through. It'll be too wet to cut today. I'll get a crew out weeding the oats, and you guys can get back to construction for one day. Remember, you're going up to Meaford for training at the end of the month. For you, it will be about six weeks, so you'll be back just before the grain harvest."

"There's still a bit of windrow from yesterday. We'll gather that up after it dries and use it for the toilets. The stuff lying flat will rot into the field and not hurt the grass. Get some sleep, son." Bill gave Jeff a fatherly hug, and they returned to their beds.

Bill organized Kathy, Jean, Willard and the older children to walk through the oat field, pulling out the wild mustard, milkweed and other intrusive wildflowers. The grain had not yet headed up and resembled long grass. The wet from the storm quickly soaked everyone, and mud was everywhere as the gang spread out and worked methodically.

"Pull everything that has big leaves. Don't worry about getting them all," Bill said. "We want to increase the yield as much as we can."

They had not double harrowed the field this year, so Bill saw more weeds than he would have liked.

"Bill," Kathy Nelson worked the line beside the man, "I've been thinking about diet and what we could do better." She paused as she found several weed plants within her reach. "Flax is a great plant to grow. The seeds have Omega three and high fibre content, and the seeds and oil have other uses. We would get stalk fibre and make linen. If we have seed, we can grow shoots as greens for salad."

"Sounds like you own a flax-seed company," Bill said dryly. "I'll defer to you, Kathy. Warren has seed, but we didn't use any. I'll check to see if there is time this year to get a crop off. Mention it tonight at supper."

At day's end, Kathy's back was stiff, as were those of the whole crew. They had walked through about ten hectares of grain. Fortunately, the heat Bill predicted came later in the day. They finished the work an hour before dinnertime. Everyone looked forward to resting.

"Mom," Don Hunter interrupted Debbie as she and Sharon lifted a heavy tie stone onto the wall, "we're going to take the little ones to the river for a dip."

Debbie Hunter burst out laughing at the mud-caked boy smiling back at her. "I'd say you need it," Don's Mom chuckled, "make sure the little ones are safe."

"No problem, Mom." Don tossed the answer over his shoulder as the group that had already assembled, not expecting a no, hurried down the lane.

The river bridge sat a five-minute walk away on the farm side of the old county road. The best swimming hole lay just up from the Longview lane and became the main recreational spot for the residents in the summer months. Even little Kim began to doggy paddle with confidence. The children raced away, laughing and teasing.

Debbie gazed after the happy little group, struck by the ability of her own older children to find happiness. The younger ones, with no actual memories of how things had been, ran carefree. She savoured the joy, letting it push away the shadow of her husband's murder.

Chapter Eight

"In the time of that abbot, while they were rooting up the walls and other things that hid in the ground, the diggers broke up the foundations of a splendid palace in the middle of the ancient city. While they were marvelling at the remains of such massive buildings, they found a hollow place like a sort of chamber... that hid in the ground..."
Matthew Paris. - Gesta Abbatum (13th century) - From the private library of Erin Thomas

The huge, black Percheron stallion pranced around the corner from the old county road and drew the hay wagon up the grassy lane. Jeff stood on the wagon bed, holding the reins loosely. He loved to give Billy Boy his head and let the horse stretch his legs whenever the footing was safe.

In the papers for the horse, the beast's official name was "Georgian Valley Boy Ironman" out of Georgian Elizabeth Glenelg, but no one cared about official bloodlines. Billy Boy was a big, strong four-year-old whose muscles rippled as he moved. The horse's eyes shone, bright and intelligent. Jeff did not know who enjoyed this more, Billy Boy or himself. After the work of haying and hauling stone, this seemed like a vacation.

The rig came to a quick stop beside a pile of lumber and framed windows. Sharon and Debbie added more salvaged lumber to the pile. Don and his sister Stephanie appeared from behind the structure carrying a double-glazed window, framed in wood with plastic trim. Some of the salvaged assemblies were sash types, but most were of the hinged crank design prized by Warren and Jim.

"Wow, Mom, you've been working hard." Jeff dismounted and tied Billy Boy to a handy porch railing.

"No flies on us, Son," Sharon smiled, wiping her sweaty brow and swatting at a deer fly with her straw hat. "We've salvaged some wallboard, but Walt isn't sure where we would use it. There's a gigantic pile of insulation in a back bedroom, so we leave that watertight for now."

Jeff loaded the two-by-four sticks onto the wagon, crossways. He noted the holes where Walt had carefully removed the nails. He hoped they had used real nails here and not the inferior air driven variety. Jeff soon caught up with the work of the others and slipped away to scout around the garage, looking for anything useful.

As he walked through the grass, he spotted a big fox snake slithering away in fear. He smiled, remembering. A month before, little Megan had stuck a smaller one into her father's rain boot. Walt's shout and kicking off the boot was a genuine laugh, but little Megan's innocent comment would forever make the story worth telling.

"Oh, Daddy," she had cried out, gently retrieving the frightened reptile. "You have scared Mr Smithers."

She had cuddled the writhing creature and then set it free beside the porch. The sly little smile she directed back over her shoulder to the laughing crowd suggested she knew what she had done. From then on, everyone called Walt "Grandpa Smithers" behind his back. Megan herself spoiled this game when she asked Walt one evening at dinner why everyone called him Grandpa Smithers. Everyone's shoes had received a good stare as all tried to hide their smirks. Walt's roar of laughter eased the tension.

Longview embraced the richness of these little stories. It was a testimony to the hardship, struggle and grinding routine of their existence that most of the memorable stories raised laughter. Only a few of these early memories would summon sadness and a tear. Laughter seemed to come easily and stick. Sadness had to be deep enough for the tears to earn their way into the shadowy legion of tragic memories.

Jeff found nothing of value. Four years ago, looters had snatched what they thought was valuable. Organized salvage by the valley committee later claimed anything useful.

Frustrated, Jeff climbed up on the bench in the garage to search the rafters. The gloom inside the structure made it hard to see. He reached up to feel for a handhold. His fingers touched cold steel, the barrel of a rifle. Someone had laminated the beam using three pieces of two by six. Just above the bench, the centrepiece had been dug out to create a deep groove. Someone hid the rifle in this groove along with two boxes of cartridges. It was a Savage 110, 30-06 heavy hunting rifle. This common calibre would make ammunition easy to get. Finding nothing else of value, Jeff headed back to work.

"Now Jeff, you know I don't like you playing with guns," his mother sounded serious but had a mischievous smile. Sharon had become a decent shooter during her stint of security training. "Where did you get that beauty?"

Jeff relayed the story as he checked the chamber and carefully stowed the weapon into the wagon.

It took an hour to build a load Billy Boy could handle. Standing amongst windows, with a good pile of lumber behind him and straddling his new rifle, Jeff swung the rig around towards Longview. As he drew up the lane, he could see men standing on top of the new structure.

"We need to get the roof on first," Jim explained to Harold and John. "Then we can work inside in the rain." Jim Handley stood on top of one of the thick, stone walls surveying the accuracy of the protruding, hand-carved pieces of limestone that would tie the rafters to the walls, anchored in the hard clay, designed to hook over and tie down wooden beams along the top of the stone. They would screw rafters to these timbers. The roof would not survive a tornado but could resist strong winds. Jim drove a wedge beneath the first timber, fixing it tightly to the stone. The other two men steadied each end. Jim checked his level and went on to the next wall.

"I don't understand why you made this back wall so complicated." Harold gasped as he forced a timber to butt snugly at right angles to another. "Why didn't you make this thing a rectangle?"

"Don't you like a challenge?" Jim smiled and focused on finding the right shim and wedge while watching the bubble of his level. "Give me a minute, and I'll explain." He called, "Hey Kathy, can you please hand me up some of those birch wedges?"

There was a flurry of activity on the ground where Kathy and Sarah worked to level the dirt interior to prepare for floor stones.

"This alcove," Jim stood and pointed as Harold gingerly walked along the top of the wall, "has stone all around at the foundation level and the floor sunk a meter. It's divided into three sections."

"It's complicated. Is that a kitchen?" Harold asked.

"Nope," smiled Jim, "the other end of the process, the pooper," he chuckled. "We are building a system to compost our waste. This is just a bigger version designed to eliminate the buckets we use. It's a direct deposit into the compost bin." Once again he laughed, enjoying the idea of everyone having an intimate relationship with their waste.

"The three bins should each hold a year's worth of deposits." Jim's grin grew large. The other two men thought their mentor had a strange sense of humour. "Then we switch to using the next one and let the first sit. After another year, the third one is in use and just before that is full, we open up the back entrance to number one and shovel it out. By then it should be sweet compost. Each bin gets between two and three years to break down."

"Isn't human crap dangerous?" John looked a little doubtful. "Television ads told us waste could kill."

"What about all the controversy over spreading sewage on fields?" Harold questioned.

"I'm no expert. I'm just a carpenter," Jim replied. "Warren has the book on it. He would love to explain it. One other advantage though," Jim now looked thoughtful, as if trying to understand the idea himself, "these composters get pretty warm as they break down the stuff. We are hoping we can use the heat to help warm this building in winter. It won't replace wood stoves, though."

"I bet they will stink," John was doubtful.

"Not if you do it according to the rules." Jim was feeling like a tree-hugging hippie. "Notice the buckets don't stink, well maybe a slight odour, because we cover the stuff with sawdust or leaf mould after we use it. If you go out by the compost piles, you will notice little smell unless we dump the bucket. We cover that with straw or spent hay. It keeps the smell down and creates air gaps for the right bacteria to work. These critters make a lot of heat and cook all the bad stuff, even weed seeds. Talk to Warren," he finally tired of lecturing. "Let's get this ready for the trusses."

The men had set the last timber when Jeff and Billy Boy rolled up. Jeff stashed the rifle in the tack room and helped unload the wagon.

"We need heavier stuff for the rafter trusses," Jim spoke to Jeff. "Walt needs to get going on the roof."

"We need more people at that end." Jeff leaned against the empty wagon. "It's tricky on the roof and we need a hand to take the screws from the steel sheets."

All the men rode the wagon back to the salvage site, leaving the women to organize the delivered material. Jim wanted to make sure no one took any chances. It was dangerous on a steel roof. Minor injuries were critical, with a small cut being dangerous. Working safely had to be the method. Kathy already had too much first aid work.

Chapter Nine

"The thing that impressed me the most, the day we arrived at Longview, was the wide open space and the sun shining over the valley. I had spent so much time inside, slaving at the carding table, that all the open spaces, even after several weeks on the run, held a wonderful appeal to me. When I saw Warren and Willard talking to Chester, I simply felt safe."

From: "Conversations with Joseph of Longview." in the Voices of the Founders series by Erin Thomas

Willard and Warren stepped aside for the wagon on its way to the salvage house. The two men stood down the laneway from the farmstead.

"The Shadly boy has fun with the horses." Willard watched the wagon run down the lane.

"Yes, he does," Warren agreed, "but it is hard work. He'll be leaving for training soon. Walt or Jim will replace him for the second haying."

"Young Don is learning. I think we should make sure he helps Jeff with the team. He has big muscles, and I have a hunch Jeff will be away a lot." Warren turned to face the new structure. "Willard, I love the design, but this thing took too much work."

"Yes, cutting stone and ramming the clay was too hard. What can we do? We don't have a contractor down the road willing to work for his supper as we do."

"Willard, we need to make mortar so we can build single walls with field stone. It would reduce the quarry work."

"What do we do?" Willard did not sound hopeful. "We have to bake limestone, and there's no coal or natural gas."

"Let's walk," Warren headed down the lane towards the river. "I have an idea. We need to make charcoal for the smithy and other things. Why don't we build a charcoal kiln and use the heat to cook limestone into lime?"

"Will that be enough?" Willard was sceptical.

"Not likely, but it would be a start. I'll check into it. I'm not sure how hot it would need to be."

The two men arrived at the bridge where the Longview lane crossed the river. The water flowed three meters below. Trout flicked about in the swimming-hole downstream from a smooth rock bottom. The low summer flow rippled over the limestone with eddies, and eventually disappeared into the calm water of the swimming hole.

"We could build a stone weir on that limestone bottom and rig up a turbine to power a rotating lime kiln and rock crusher. It would make enough for our own use."

"The spring floods would take the turbine out." Willard examined all the issues.

"We can design something to remove in the fall. There is a guy down in Thornbury who has experience with micro-hydro and turbines. Let's take a day and find him."

Warren sat on the bank watching the flow in the soothing, warm sun.

"If we can't keep manufacturing parts, eventually turbines, generators, and so forth, will disappear, or we'll make them from wood and stone."

An approaching small truck rattling up the river road, bouncing on the frost-heaved asphalt, attracted their attention. It stopped at the turn into Longview.

"Hello, Warren." Chester Amik slid from behind the steering wheel. "I have a young family to live with you."

A little face peered around the side of the cab, staring wide-eyed at the men. A pair of bright shining eyes with large whites stood out from a chocolate face. The little boy seemed scared. Chester escorted the men to the rear of the truck. In the pickup box, they saw two younger, under-fed girls, perhaps three, with the boy a few years older. Hugging the two girls, a gaunt young woman, perhaps thirty years old, stared back at them with vacant eyes. She might have been beautiful once. The little boy's legs seemed odd. Kathy would later explain the impact of rickets on the human skeleton. The mother, Willard assumed, seemed too tired and spent to care.

"Gentlemen, this is Ellen, and the girls are Grace and Hope. This fine young man is Joseph." Chester tousled the boy's tightly curled hair and smiled warmly.

The boy squirmed away but seemed to enjoy the attention.

"They've had a hard time of it, almost starving and running for their lives for two weeks before they made it to us. We worked on them for three weeks down at the twenty-six barrier until they were strong enough to move. We need Kathy Nelson to nurse them."

The mother's listless response to their greetings troubled the men. Chester explained it as post-traumatic stress disorder compounded by starvation. Warren and Willard simply saw more suffering humans who needed kindness. The three men climbed into the cab. Chester drove up to Longview. The rare arrival of a vehicle attracted a gathering in the farmyard. Megan's eyes grew wide when she saw Joseph struggle down from the truck.

"I'm Megan." She extended her hand in a formal greeting. When Joseph did not respond, she took his hand in hers, her childish enthusiasm not yet muted by adult restraint. "What's your name?"

"Joseph," the young boy whispered, and then smiled. There had been no kids at the camp. Megan drew him towards her playmate.

"This is Kim." The older girl was still formal; however, Kim spotted Grace and Hope and rushed past the two, flying headlong into a hug with the two girls. Kim's bold attack bewildered Grace and Hope, but they squealed with delight.

"You're a different colour than me," Megan said to Joseph. "I have seen no one your colour before." The innocence brought a smile to Chester. *If only,* he thought.

"Come on, I'll show you Lambypop," Megan pulled a reluctant Joseph toward the barn. He looked at his mother, pleading.

"It's okay," the frail woman said, mustering a faint smile. These were her first words since she had arrived. Joseph went hesitantly on protesting legs, half dragged by the energetic girl.

"Kathy, nice to see you again; this is Ellen. She and the kids arrived down on twenty-six about three weeks ago. They need nursing. Did you see Joseph's legs?"

"Hello, Chester." The nurse replied. "It looks like rickets. How have they been eating?"

"We've been giving them small portions, trying to build them up. At first, they couldn't hold any food down. We gave fluids, then oatmeal porridge. We had a few vegetables but got them going on apples. They haven't had bread or meat."

"I have some vitamin D," Kathy replied. "The little guy needs it for sure. I'm not sure we can get his legs back now, but we'll see. How are you, Ellen?" Kathy took Ellen's hand.

"Fine, fine... I'm fine," the woman's appearance denied her words. She was obviously not fine, suffering, but brave. Kathy led her to the wooden bench on the porch. The young woman's hand felt frail and cold. Ellen's wrists were shockingly thin. Kathy examined the woman without bothering to ask permission, normally an affront, but the medic understood assuming control would be reassuring. Ellen had suffered abuse for a long time.

"Are you hungry?"

"I guess so," the response was listless.

"Sarah, see if Jean can muster up nice warm tea and something semi-sweet like a couple of her cookies? Get some for the kids, too."

Kathy checked her thermometer and felt Ellen's pulse. The nurse's frown deepened. She retrieved a warm blanket, wrapping the suffering woman snugly, even though it was a warm day. Kathy wanted to raise the patient's temperature.

Kathy turned her attention to the two girls. They sat beside their mother, staring with wide, innocent eyes. It pleased her to discover they were in better shape than the suffering Ellen and did not show Joseph's deficiency symptoms. The little girls had played in the sun outdoors while Joseph, even at five, had spent his waking time inside, forced to card wool for an overseer. None had an adequate diet, but Ellen had shared her portion with her children and suffered greater starvation.

It pleased Kathy to see Megan dragging her new friend about in the sunshine. The girl showed Joseph, Mr Smithers, whom she had confined to a box. The young boy smiled but appeared to be afraid of the snake as Megan gleefully held it towards him.

Kathy had been a city kid, wary of the creatures, and had empathy for the little boy's feelings, but liked the fact the sun was full upon him. As for the captivity of the animal, Kathy knew Warren planned to discuss it with little Megan, hoping to get her to understand wild creatures should go free. However, Warren did not want to stifle the girl's wonderful thrall with nature. He saw in her a little Warren Wallace Dunne and wanted to encourage her.

"We need to get protein and fat into these people," Kathy spoke to Jean, who had just delivered warm tea and oatmeal cookies. "I saw people like this in Mississauga. They soon disappeared. Either they found food, or they died. Ellen and the kids arrived just in time."

Kathy turned back to Ellen, who was gingerly sipping the pine tea with tentative bites of cookie. The nurse knew there was much more to her condition than the physical problems. The woman's frightened eyes flitted here and there like a feral cat.

The little girls ate their cookies with gusto. They did not seem to enjoy the tea as much. Both finished their cups. She called Joseph and Megan over for their portion.

Jean returned from the kitchen with small bowls containing a few bites of ground goat-meat mixed with boiled barley. Kathy gently spooned that into Ellen's mouth, leaving the children to devouring their portions while sitting at their mother's feet. Jean would give them similar fare for supper and a nutritious snack before bed.

Kathy spent a restless night with them in the infirmary. All the family, but especially Ellen and Joseph, passed a night filled with waking dreams, crying out often and seemingly in anguish. Kathy knew the road to recovery would be long and painful. She faced a much bigger challenge than soothing hand blisters and scraped shins. Doctoring Ellen and the children would give Kathy a renewed sense of satisfaction and purpose, displacing years of frustration and sorrow.

Chapter Ten

I stood with Jeff in the warm morning air. I remember it was July 1st under the old calendar, but that date was not widely celebrated even then, only four years after the collapse. Jeff had his pack on his back with about eighty pounds of provisions. I didn't want to keep him standing under that weight, but I didn't want to let him go. His mother had said her goodbyes inside the house and did not come out.

I wanted to say something profound to Jeff, some wisdom from his father. What could I say to my boy leaving home on an adventure, perhaps to die? Could I say keep your head down and your spirits up? I simply hugged him and said "be safe and work hard". I had a tear in my eye, but did not want to cry in front of him. We hugged again and told him I loved him.

He headed down the grass-covered lane towards the valley road and the Meaford training ground, stopping at the bottom gate, under the new Longview sign to wave back at me. It looked as if he had saluted Matt Long, acknowledging the sacrifice required of us all. He was just then beginning his long road to sacrifice.

From: "The Last Conversation with Bill Shadly" in the Voices of the Founders series by Erin Thomas

It seems strange now, but I was nervous and scared the day I left for camp. My pack was heavy because I had two weeks' rations with me. We had an extensive discussion about Huron needing to produce enough surplus food and other things to afford the security forces. Dad convinced me not to take the rifle, your rifle, as it was heavy and he said they had military-class stuff at Meaford. I'm glad. The rifle was much more useful to you.

A letter from Jeff Shadly to his sister - The Brandi Shadly Archives

Jeff followed the county road parallel to the river. The frost-damaged asphalt made for difficult walking. He was not a poet like his sister, so he did not frame his surroundings with any conscious description, but he enjoyed the pandemonium of nature around him. Birds flitted about, calling and arguing as they looked for their morning food before seeking roost in the heat of the day. The roadsides were a jumble of grass, weeds, and small bushes, some already flowering in the earliness of summer. Grass seed heads were bobbing in the light breeze.

Jeff's feet kept their course, plodding on, following his shadow north toward the lake. He found places where they had pried up the asphalt, revealing the gravel below. Mostly, the material was missing, but in a few spots, small piles of pavement blocks sat, black and greying on the roadside.

An industry had developed to salvage the asphalt and extracted the bitumen. This material waterproofed boats, roofs and the planking of docks. It was a polluting activity. Jeff knew the councils all around Huron were working to reduce the problems. Where the pavement lay intact, he could stride smoothly. He stumbled on rougher ground, beneath his heavy pack, and raised protests from his muscles. He took many water breaks.

Jeff reached Thornbury several hours after leaving Longview. He found a shady spot by the river, near the harbour, where he could have lunch and rest. He laid his boots aside, letting his feet breathe in the brisk lake breeze.

The stream had dug a deep course into the surrounding limestone, but in its low mid-summer flow, wandered quietly towards the bay. A centuries-old dam blocked the river. It, the harbour and later the railway provided the original purpose for the town. Jeff munched bread and cold chicken, with young snap beans and immature peas.

Men laboured along the dam and in the streambed. They had laid a pipe about thirty centimetres diameter from deep in the water to a point above the dam. The pipe tied into a small, handcrafted turbine assembly. A shaft stuck out the top of this, and another pipe dropped into the pool of water below the dam. Jeff had paid enough attention in a physics class to recognize a siphon system. Warren and Willard had asked about this work and planned to consult one of these local experts.

Eager to reach Meaford before nightfall, Jeff shouldered his pack, ready to take twenty-six west.

"Are you headed for the Meaford camp?" The voice startled Jeff. He turned to see an older man smiling at him.

"Yes, I'm off for my first training."

"I'm too old for more than picket duty, so never took the course, but I do a little freighting for them with my boat. Would you like a ride over by water? We're about to cast off. With this east wind, we ought to get to Meaford before it rains." The man wore a battered sea cap and a khaki jacket.

"It would be great," Jeff responded. "This load's heavy."

"They call me Captain John," the man stuck out his right hand. Jeff felt a firm grip. "John David, but don't get confused with my last name being a first name." The man chuckled. "It used to be fun back in school."

For a brief instant, John David's eyes seemed to look far away, and a frown crossed his face. Jeff recognized an all too common shadow from a remembered loss. Everyone he knew had similar shadows.

They reached a small sailing boat which copied the dishevelled appearance of the man's hat. When aboard, Jeff realized the boat's condition only reflected a lack of maintenance supplies. Other than the peeling deck paint and threadbare hand stitched sails, it was in immaculate trim. A woman's face popped out the gangway amidships.

"Welcome mate," she smiled.

"This is Delores. She is the admiral. I'm just the captain." He clicked his heels together and saluted in a lame imitation of the Italian Navy.

"My real name is Jane. He calls me Delores because we planned to sail this tub to the Caribbean to retire. He said he needed a Spanish girlfriend, but the economy sank before the boat could." She relished in her humour. "I call him Long John Silver. Believe me, that's not a physical description. He has no silver either."

Jane burst out laughing. She had been waiting for a new audience for her jokes. Jeff recognized the innuendo and the two people who seemed able to share fascinated him. All survivors of the last few years of tragedy had to have this self-preserving sense of humour.

"Hey Delores, my sweet conquistador, help young Jeff here stash his duffle in the cabin and we can get underway." John began loosening the lashes that held the sail to the boom.

Down below, Jeff found wooden crates and bags tied to the cabin floor. He set his back with the freight.

"This is our cargo," Jane stooped to secure her guest's duffle. "There's still a lot of salvage, and up at the base, they need food and stuff. We get a lot locally, but there's a growing trade from Collingwood. Another boat, a nice guy too, comes several times a summer, bringing cargo. We trade food for it. They haven't organized as well as Huron. He says there are bad people all around, so they are always short of food."

Jeff walked along the wharf, pulling a rope running from the bow as John and Jane used poles to ease the craft along the wall towards the narrow harbour entrance.

"We have no fuel for manoeuvring," John explained, "so we have to do it this way. The wind is going to pin us against the entrance wall, so I'll set the jib to drag us. I hope these old tires will always be available."

Car tires hung as side bumpers on the boat, replacing the long since worn out commercial fenders. The boat slipped around the corner of the seawall. Jeff leapt aboard as the jib filled with wind, dragging the little craft forward at increasing speed. He nearly fell overboard when they cleared the wall, and the boat suddenly heeled over.

John deftly spun the wheel, taking her off the wind. Suddenly, they were near upright and gathering speed across the waves, riding the sharp, fresh breeze. The prow lifted and settled as they cut through the water, getting a good distance clear of the shore before John and Jane ran up the mainsail. The boat surged forward. Jeff had the exhilarating feeling of lift as if they were climbing out of the water. He decided he enjoyed sailing.

"Still got your lunch?" John laughed.

"So far, so good," Jeff replied. "This is fun."

"That thrill is why we started sailing in the first place," Jane responded. She gripped the cabin roof rail against the pitching under her feet. The little crew was all smiles and settled down to a satisfying ride, with the shore sliding by to port as they headed west to Jeff's temporary home. The little craft sped into Meaford harbour at suppertime. Just before the narrow entrance, John dropped the mainsail. It seemed to Jeff that brakes had applied. He stumbled slightly forward as his novice sea legs betrayed him. Jane struck the jib. The vessel drifted deliberately through the channel, and the freshening east wind pushed them sideways into the wharf with the experienced crew easing her into the last few feet on their poles. Snubbed to bollards that could have held a craft dozens of times larger, the boat came to rest, bobbing gently in the well-protected harbour.

"We can have a bit of supper up at the house." Jane issued an invitation. "We have to wait for whatever transportation the camp sends down."

The trio climbed onto the dock and headed along the concrete promenade towards what had once been expensive condominiums.

"We wanted to winter on the boat, but without electricity, we couldn't do it. Instead, we have," John chuckled, "a nice fancy five-star condo. No power, but the water is still running from the town. We cook outside in the summer and have a wood stove in the winter. The owners would not like the pipe stuck out the kitchen window."

Jeff spent a pleasant evening with his new friends. They told a story typical of many and not too different from the one the Weyburne refugees had lived. John and Jane had been together for many years and were about to retire when the economy crashed. All of their dreams vanished. They had lived two years of hardship in Meaford. Focused community activity built a strong local organization similar to the one Jeff's parents had begun in Weyburne. The David's absorbed Jeff's stories of Longview and the danger to the south.

His friends had turned their love of sailing into a business, servicing remote villages all the way to Weirton in an easier way than long overland routes, at least in good sailing weather.

Chapter Eleven

Vigilamus pro-Te (We Stand on Guard for Thee)
Motto of the old Canadian Army

One of the most beautiful qualities of genuine friendship is to understand and to be understood. - **Lucius Annaeus Seneca**

Jane shook Jeff awake. Early morning light barely penetrated the room. He had fallen asleep on the carpeted floor with his head on his pack. Neighbours had visited after the evening meal and talk had gone on well into the early morning hours, lubricated by hard apple cider and decent homemade wine. The young man's head did not respond well to the rousing. Jeff had never drunk much alcohol and had not expected the hangover.

"Rise and shine, soldier boy." His head disliked Jane's cheerfulness. "The army boys are here. You got to go."

Jeff slowly gathered his wits and became mobile. He splashed cold water on his face, easing the throbbing in his head. Jane thrust a breakfast sandwich of egg and back bacon on brown bread into his hand.

"You have a few minutes. Meet us down at the boat. We'll be loading the stuff onto their wagon. Don't dally, my boy. You don't want to walk if you don't have to."

By the time Jeff reached the dock, they had loaded the wagon, a long affair of recent construction, on a steel chassis with pneumatic tires. A pair of smaller dark-brown workhorses stood ready, attached to the vehicle with a strong harness and a box-steel double-tree. As an experienced horse handler, Jeff appreciated the setup. Two men in military uniforms chatted with John and Jane. Jeff introduced himself and they examined his handwritten orders over Chester's signature.

"Come back soon. If you ever need a new mother, look me up." Jane hugged Jeff, and John's firm grip gave his hand a parting squeeze. The recruit clambered onto the load in the back of the wagon. A chucking sound sent the two sturdy horses forward, ten kilometres up the hill. At the walking pace of the team, they would be there for lunch.

Jeff's head ached. He resolved never to do anything to make him feel this miserable again. The two men on the seat directed questions towards the recruit. Jeff responded in short, unenthusiastic phrases. The men laughed. Both soldiers knew the symptoms too well. The occasions were now rare in a world of shortages. Happily, the sky was cloudy and comforting. Jeff dozed in the fresh morning air until spitting rain woke him with the camp in sight. Two more men and a woman sat on the back of the wagon, reporting in the same way as Jeff when the wagon saved them from walking the last kilometres.

Rain pelted as the rig passed through the camp gate. The brisk east wind suggested it would last for some time. A uniformed man stood on the guardhouse porch cradling a rifle with his left arm and waved them through. The wagon stopped in the pouring rain opposite a large building.

"Go in and see the Commander."

The recruits hurried over the remnants of an asphalt drive and up the stone steps. The splashing of horse-hooves faded as the doors swung shut. Subdued light filtering through the windows revealed the sparse interior. The bewildered four dripped water onto the floor. No one greeted them.

"I'm Jeff Shadly," he extended his hand.

One man came from Thornbury while the others lived in Meaford. They rested their packs and had relaxed but tensed to approaching footsteps. A large, middle-aged man emerged from a darkened hallway. He strode with purpose, erect and disciplined, a military man. Army camouflage tunic and pants barely concealed his muscular frame; hard boots echoed on the terrazzo floor. His long greying hair and beard did not look as martial as the rest. He stopped directly in front of them, feet apart and hands behind his back.

"I am Captain LaFarge," his French accent softened his words. "I'm in charge here."

The four stiffened and tried to stand a little straighter.

"You can relax. We aren't the Canadian army, and we don't salute, march or polish officer's bums. Maybe one day, if there is a standing army and we all get bored, we'll do those things to fill in the time. I'm ex-army, a commando, but now I am a civilian like you. I just know more than you." He smiled and stuck out his hand.

"Welcome to the Meaford Training Camp. You can call me Roger," he pronounced it in the French manner, row-jay.

"I resigned my commission and removed my Canadian insignia after the coup in Ottawa. I swore to uphold the law and wouldn't be part of it. Besides, they had forgotten about us out here, so we had to fend for ourselves. Most of the officers took off to Ottawa."

"Too many racists, real Nazi types, joined over the past two decades. Even the generals in Ottawa are like them. In your barracks, you'll see pictures and souvenirs of men and women who fought the original Nazis. What's going on in Ottawa is a betrayal of them. You'll learn some of that history."

"There are a dozen of us deserters. Most farm but come back to help. I'm the only full-timer, although my family and I mostly farm here on the base."

Jeff had heard of Roger from his dad but was unsure of what to expect. This friendly giant put him at ease.

"Even though we don't do all that military ritual, I expect you to obey my orders. I have my authority from the Huron Coalition, to which your local groups belong. They get my reports, and everyone agreed to contribute people."

"Remember, you volunteered to take this training, and your local councils sent you. You won't get any parenting from me. You shape up because you want to do it, or you get relegated to the irregular forces, but you don't get out of serving. I want you all to learn how to soldier well and learn the skills, especially how to lead. Eventually, you will teach this to others under your command. I'm patient, so don't worry if it takes a little practice to get good at it. You'll need a lot more learning beyond these six weeks."

The four volunteers formed the first cohort of a well-trained and active militia. They would not be on active duty at all times, but would train every month and be on call at no notice. These recruits would lead the irregular forces assembled for operations more than routine picket duty and would rotate command at the barriers. They would be on duty for at least three months of the year. Current threats would make them much more active.

"We expect forty of you today. About a dozen are already in the barracks. I'll send you over there, and you can settle in. There's a central kitchen and gardens and a barn. You'll be working in those between training sessions. Fitness is essential. Shadly," he looked at Jeff, "I see you have a bit of muscle and tone, so you should be okay, but the rest of you look underdeveloped. I want all of you to do your time in the weight room and gym. Every morning, we do a ten-kilometre run." They gasped. "Don't worry, we'll go easily to start, but in five days, you will be running. Remember, when you get into a tight spot, many things can get you killed, but you don't want your body to let you down. Before you leave, we will have done a hundred kilometre hike, and a twenty kilometre run a week."

Jeff grew strong from farm labour, but the running would be a new thing. He looked forward to the challenge.

The group hurried through the downpour to the officers' barracks. They found a roomy reception area lined by comfortable chairs. A woman in her thirties sat at the desk, and another in one chair.

"Welcome to Camp Where the Hell Are We." The women laughed. "We heard you got all soft and had a ride." Her teasing reassured.

"Yeah, we are so important they sent a limo for us," the female recruit joked. "It was a nice one, two horsepower and all."

"I'm Helen Niemczyk," the woman rose, "if anyone calls me numb chuck, I break their arm." Her grip said she had the strength to do it. "I'm the Master Sergeant and hand-to-hand combat instructor."

No one dared call her "numb chuck", not even behind her back.

Helen ushered the recruits into a long hallway. Photographs and other memorabilia hung between many doors. These dated back to when the Canadian army used the base. The ex-soldiers left them hanging as a reminder of the effort and sacrifice that the Canadian military had made over the years. This respect persisted even though Helen, Roger and the others had little regard for the remnants of this once proud force huddled in Ottawa and across the crumbling Canadian federation.

Everyone had a small, comfortable room. The washrooms worked, although they lacked hot water.

"You keep your rooms and the common areas clean," Helen said, "and we are sticklers. Routine and dedication might save your asses someday."

The four went into the dining hall for lunch. Being new, Helen assigned them clean-up detail after the meal. By the end of the day, all but two of the new trainees had arrived. The stragglers, who had come down from the Bruce Peninsula, arrived early the next morning, completing the group wearing army fatigues, boots and caps. A store of basic supplies left in camp would last for some years and outfit a force of several hundred, leaving only the problem of finding good people to fill them.

Training began with fitness. After every morning run, they devoted several hours to shooting, horse riding, and hand-to-hand combat. Once they mastered the basics, the forty split into two squads, with one reviewing and practising in the morning and the other in the afternoon. When not actively training, each group worked in the gardens or barn and prepared the next meal. The food consisted mostly of vegetables and meat, but the volume offset the lack of variety. Some recruits were squeamish about slaughtering farm animals.

"If you can't shovel manure and gut a chicken," one of the regular army trainers asked, "how can you learn to stick a knife into an enemy? There ain't any servants here. If you want to eat, work."

Soon everyone performed all the tasks, if not eager, at least with resignation. After two weeks, Roger deemed everyone fully competent in the basic skills and fitness, rewarding them with a morning ten kilometre run under a twenty-kilo pack. Training changed to tactics and strategy.

"I am a tactics guy," Roger had said at the start of the new direction, "hand-to-hand, door-to-door, rock-to-rock and tree-to-tree." The impact of this opening suffered from the group's giggling at the man's pronunciation of the word tree in his French accent. Roger tried to glare at his unruly students, but the toothy smile leaking through his bearded face betrayed him. Roger was well aware of the laughter frequently caused by his accent. He had always taken it in good humour, while eagerly waiting to pounce on careless English speakers using "ain't" and double negatives. What he lacked in pronunciation, Roger made up with impeccable English grammar and vocabulary. His students' reaction pleased him. He could see bonding and comradeship developing, not a minor accomplishment in just a few weeks. They had enough confidence to risk his displeasure.

"For strategy," the man finally continued, "all I know is, split them up and confuse them. By the way, that's good tactics too. The most important rule to save your life, and maybe those of your friends, is not to hesitate. If the other guy has a weapon, he will use it. Always have a plan before you engage or back up a bit and see if you can figure out the enemy's plan. If someone surrenders, make them strip naked, even in the winter. If they won't, well, you know what you have to do." He made a pistol shooting motion with his hand, giving a depressing introduction to the seriousness of what they were training to do.

The third and fourth weeks comprised classroom discussions relieved by running about with rifles kicking in doors on some of the unused buildings, doing searches, learning to cover each other's backs and feeling like they were playing a serious game of soldier.

They spent days sneaking through bush and open fields, learning how to use cover and apply forces to distract, flank and overcome an objective.

Part of their time involved doing grid searches, working away from the main compound into the old live ammunition practice area. Here, they did actual work, looking for unspent rounds and marking them. Roger alone removed anything dangerous and carted it off to an open bunker well away from the compound. He intended to blow it all up at the end of the session, using military explosives as part of the trainees' demolition course. This work trained them in checking for land mines while hoping hostiles would not have that terrible weapon.

The weeks sped past. After a month, Jeff still did not feel like a commander, but he had developed more confidence. He looked forward to completing the remaining two weeks and return in time for the harvest. Jani and the coming baby filled his mind. He showed everyone Brandi's sketch of beautiful Jani.

In the second last week, emphasis shifted to commando tactics, camouflage and living off the land. They learned about local edible plants and setting snares. The reward for being successful in trapping was to eat your catch raw. After some discussion, the group agreed rabbit was preferable to racoon, skunk and mice.

To develop stealth, everyone hunted. The large base had healthy deer, grouse, coyotes and wild turkey populations. The trainers were excellent hunters. Recruits paired up with an old hand and spent a day in the back areas, eating off the land for the day while trying to bring a deer or bird back to the camp. In the years to come, whenever the group met and reminisced, they would recall this hunting week with fondness.

"You have done well," Roger said one evening at dinner on the last weekend. "You are no way as well trained as a regular force. We spent years learning this stuff, but you will be better trained than most enemies. I don't expect you will fight any regular army. What you will meet will be a bunch of poorly trained psychos forcing groups of untrained reluctant conscripts to do the dangerous fighting. You'll discover, if you separate the conscripts from the leaders, they will surrender but shoot the brutes." He let that sink in and then continued, as if he had been discussing gardening or some other innocent topic.

"We'll celebrate tomorrow and next day, march down to the barrier on twenty-six for a week of live experience."

***

The next day, as the majority worked to prepare the graduation events, Jeff and two other trainees drove down to Meaford harbour in a three-ton diesel truck, following Roger, who manoeuvred a military one-ton over the deteriorating asphalt roadway.

"This thing handles like a pig," Will Sullivan snorted as he tried to keep up with Roger. Jeff, from his position beside the passenger window, glanced at the driver. The other trainees did not like Sullivan. He was demanding and full of himself. While most of the trainees talked about themselves, Will remained tight-lipped. He lived south of Owen Sound. The Owen Sound council had recommended Will; Jeff was not so sure.

"Glad the roads are good," Will grunted as they bounced over a pothole. Will had demanded to be the driver. He drove as if he were angry.

"Hope that wasn't too big a bump for you, Sniffles." Will sneered. The young man in the centre seat grimaced at the nickname. His embarrassment did not escape Jeff's keen eye. Sniffles' real name was Theodore (Ted), Macedo. "Sniffles" had been the nickname Helen gave him because of his unfortunate nose he had broken as a youngster. His family lacked the money to have it repaired properly. The public plan would have paid for the surgery and other medical issues, but the family could not afford the travelling and hotels to go to the hospital in Toronto.

Ted worked hard and excelled in hand combat. Helen used the label with respect; however, Will bullied Ted.

At the edge of Meaford, Will backed up to a storage building. The three clambered onto the dusty ground.

"What happened to your nose?" Jeff thought talking might help. Will sucked up to Roger out of earshot on the far side of the vehicle,

"I broke it playing baseball," Ted trusted Jeff. They had trained together. "I played right field, and a kid hit a high fly ball. I didn't know how to play and put my glove in front of my face and couldn't see the ball. Then I moved my glove to look. The ball got me square on the nose. You should have seen the blood. Mom thought I was dying. It took weeks to convince her to let me play again. Anyway, it ruined my good looks." Ted chuckled. Jeff thought he had come to terms with his nose.

"It was hard in school. The kids called me Piggy. That hurt, especially when Becky, a girl I liked did it and laughed at me. Some teachers said it too."

Ted frowned, recalling the embarrassment. Jeff resolved never to call him anything but Ted. They began a lifelong friendship and would share danger. Jeff would always say he had no fear because Ted kept him safe. Then Ted shared a secret that cemented their friendship.

"I am in love with Helen," Ted said it so matter-of-fact it caught Jeff off guard. Ted needed to tell someone.

"Muscles are sexy, eh?" Jeff teased if only to gather his thoughts. He did not know Helen's marital status. Ted had just said he trusted Jeff.

"I know, it's impossible," Ted continued. "She's older than me and has a guy here in town. Just the same, I love her. She told me I was her best student and asked permission to keep calling me Sniffles."

"I hate Will, and don't trust him. He hates me too, I'm sure. Once, when he and I were one-on-one, practicing hand-to-hand, I put him down hard twice to pay him back for calling me Sniffles. It made him mad. He started rushing and cursing me, so I gave him a good throw to end the match. He swore to get even. You weren't there, but he lost it. Helen stepped in and told him to take her on. He kept glaring at me, but couldn't say no. She took his rush and flipped him down hard. Then she leaned down and said 'never lose your temper' loudly enough for all of us to hear. She stood up and winked at me. That's where Will's hate comes from." Ted glanced at his nemesis sucking up to Roger.

"Have you said anything to Helen?" Jeff didn't know where to take this conversation.

"I did," Ted seemed relieved, "and she smiled and kissed me and told me to look her up in a year. That was that." Jeff gave his friend a punch on the shoulder, and they went to join the other men.

The four men worked hard, with Roger doing his share standing in the truck's bed stacking heavy bags of grain carried from the darkness of the warehouse.

"What's this grain?" Ted asked Roger during one of their brief rests.

"It is mostly barley and a bit of wheat and oats, part of the grain tax everyone pays."

Roger felt the effort. Even though fit, he found it hard to keep pace with these young stallions.

Jeff remembered the discussions at Longview last winter as they scrounged one bag of oats to send on the collection wagon. It had made them tight for food in the spring. The explanation the grain paid for security made sense but did not lighten the burden. Willard had pointed out that everyone had to produce some surplus for collective good. Today became a learning experience in how the contribution helped.

They followed Roger to Meaford harbour, and pulled up on the concrete wharf beside a large, steel-hulled ship. The David's small sailboat moored behind exaggerated its apparent size.

"Stay in the truck." Roger seemed confident. The commander walked up to a bearded man at the gangway. The stranger wore two open holstered pistols. Four big men stood cradling rifles on the boat. None looked friendly, but after a few minutes of conversation the man with Roger smiled, shook his hand and signalled the others to relax. The bearded man examined the load in the vehicles and Roger's list. After a few minutes of discussion, the men once again shook hands.

"Okay," Roger returned to the truck, "Get this load onto the boat."

Boatmen carried crates and wooden boxes from below and manhandled them over the gunnels onto the wharf.

"This is a snug little harbour you got here," one man spoke to Jeff in an American accent as they passed.

"Where're you from," They paused for a brief rest.

"Bay City, I worked in a car plant."

"How're things there?"

"It's hard," the stranger frowned, "people died or just walked away leaving lots of stuff. There're too few people to do much with it. We have trouble growing enough food, not enough farm hands."

"That's not good," Jeff said, "How do you survive?"

"We scrounge scrap and anything we can trade. You guys want guns and ammo. We have lots, and we can trade downstate for more. They got a shooting war down there. Weapons are cheap. There aren't enough people left to use them all. We find guns inside houses up our way. I think I know of every hiding place that people thought of."

Jeff remembered his discovery of the rifle. What had seemed ingenious at the time was probably ordinary.

"You trade food for the guns," the man went on. "We'll be taking what you don't buy on down the lake. We have other customers there, but they don't seem to have as much food as you do. They try to pay with your Canuck buck." He laughed at his rhyme.

Jeff thought it had to be the hostile bunch in the former Simcoe County dealing through Collingwood. *They must be short and paying heavy taxes like Kathy said Angel collected.*

"Hey, get back to work! I ain't doing it all by myself!" Will's harsh voice ended the conversation.

The four soldiers leaned against the truck, tired and aching from the rush of work. They watched the ship chug out of the harbour; its straining diesel engine belching black exhaust. It needed maintenance.

Some plain wooden crates and boxes filled the back of the trucks, but others had US military markings. They contained a mixture of standard military issue rifles and ammunition, plus heavy hunting rifles and a few dozen AK-47 Russian assault rifles. The ammunition was even more mixed with thousands of rounds of 9 mm, .22, .30-06 and a few less common hunting calibres. Crates of military explosives with the necessary fusing and detonators added to the load, including four steel drums, three of diesel oil and one gasoline. Roger seemed pleased with the load and relieved the exchange went well.

"They'll sell some to the bad guys," Roger spoke in his French accent. "There's nothing we can do about that. We can't afford to buy it all. These gun runners don't care about our politics. If it comes to a fight, discipline and training usually matter more than guns."

Roger paused, thinking about the threat they faced. He wished he could show the recruits how discipline defeated numbers.

"Where did they get the fuel?" Jeff wondered.

"There's a refinery near Chicago. It took half of our grain to pay for those four barrels. If we didn't need it for security, we wouldn't buy it. Guns are plentiful and cheap."

The over laden trucks roared away from the dock.

The regular staff had prepared a feast of venison, chicken and wild turkey with all the trimmings, including cranberry sauce with wine and beer as a treat.

The demolition of the collected unexploded rounds highlighted the evening. Trainees had installed charges and learned how to set and arm explosives. A raffle decided who would get the honour of destroying the pile. The lucky woman caused a spectacular blast with the sobering effect Roger LaFarge expected. It made their training real. They were not playing a game.

Chapter Twelve

Forty newly minted soldiers swung through the main gate onto the county road under an overcast sky, although the freshening southwesterly breeze hinted at hot weather. Eddies of dust swirled from the marchers' feet, and the drumbeat of stout boots rose from the crumbling asphalt. The cohort moved easily under thirty-kilo packs and shoulder-slung assault rifles. Web belts held ammunition, pistols and water bottles.

A three-ton truck preceded them towards Meaford, laden with food, belongings and extra ammunition. Helen drove, accompanied by two of the trainers. They would stop in Meaford for a mid-morning break before heading to the barrier on highway twenty-six east of Thornbury where they would learn protocols from the volunteers guarding the border barrier and deal with actual problems.

The training programme made the security effort more professional and gave Huron an aggressive capability. The number of refugees arriving at the border had increased. They expected organized, hostile forces to follow. The new comers' disturbing stories suggested factional fighting over most of southern-Ontario was coming to a head with bloody battles, and the victors would be formidable and hostile.

The well-conditioned trainees reached the outskirts of Meaford, passing an abandoned residential neighbourhood. As they arrived downtown, spectators appeared. It would have been breakfast time in the old days, but now people rose at first light to eat the morning meal. Most onlookers were older women and children under the age of eight with a few old men. Some of the latter stood stiffly and saluted the soldiers in an echo of days long gone. A cohort of children trailed the squad. These gradually became brave enough to mingle with the troops. The pace slowed as the young men and women savoured the attention, enjoying the children and feeling important. It gave them an understanding of why they had trained so hard and the import of their role.

This wonderful collection of old and young marched down to the town harbour. In the parking lot by the water's edge, the truck crew had set up a charcoal cooker and had a breakfast of bacon and eggs waiting, with dark whole grain toast. The smell was delicious, drifting up the road on the freshening morning breeze.

When the cooks spotted the enlarged contingent, they added more food to the pans. No matter how much food people might have eaten at their last meal, it had become common to eat at any opportunity. Added to this custom, the regular trainers were friends or relatives of many of the civilians. The disciplined military contingent degenerated into the chaos of laughing folks sharing food.

The townspeople drew reassurance from the confident and well-armed troopers. Roger LaFarge stood near the truck, observing. No matter what lay in the future, the existence of the fighting force was contributing positively to the morale of the population. The commander would suggest more of these morale-building events to the Huron Council.

All too soon, the spontaneous gathering ended. The platoon shouldered packs and headed up the street, turning east. Similar enthusiasm greeted them in Thornbury at a rest and water break.

Several Thornbury townsfolk accompanied the group to the barrier a few kilometres east of the town. They only parted when, in the early afternoon, the soldiers turned off the road into the bivouac compound that doubled as a holding area for refugees. The border lay two kilometres down the road.

"Jeff, how did you like the stroll?" Ted ambled over from his just completed tent.

"No problem," Jeff looked up from his seat on a large rock as he eased his boots off, other than sweaty feet. "Who's on duty first?"

"Helen is taking a few down there soon," Ted eased onto another rock. "Roger is bringing the other snipers and me to do some shooting. You get kitchen duty, you lucky stiff." Ted was grinning.

"You get to pay for that," Jeff retorted, "and eat my cooking."

LaFarge's whistle took Ted, leaving Jeff to his own devices.

"Hey mister," Jeff looked up to see a boy staring at him. "Do you have food?" The lad asked with no embarrassment.

Jeff had erected his tent close to the roadway dividing the camp. On the other side stood a collection of A-frame structures with a large cook-tent. A steel stovepipe protruded from this structure, and wood smoke wafted into the still air. A crowd around the entrance waited for lunch.

"What's your name?" Jeff found bread and cold pork.

"Jimmy," the lad replied, accepting the food. "Thank you, sir." Food in his mouth cut off his polite response. The boy ate ferociously.

"Lunch is soon, but I'm hungry. Dad says we are going to live on a farm with animals and lots of food." He sounded eager. As he talked, he slipped some of the food into his pocket, hoarding it for later. The backs of the boy's hands had scars and red welts.

"What happened to your hands?" Jeff looked closely.

"The man hit them." Jimmy sobbed as if recalling pain.

"What man?" Jeff glanced over the road looking for someone close. His hand went to his pistol.

"The man who made me work," the boy sobbed, "before we came here. I took food. He hit me."

Jeff rubbed his fingers over the boy's skin. The wounds were old. Although Jimmy acted like a five-year-old, he seemed older. Shadly was wondering what to ask next when a fatherly voice from over the road interrupted.

"Jimmy, stop bothering the man!" A tall, underfed man approached.

"I'm Jeff Shadly." Jeff extended his hand.

"Jim Smithson," the grip felt tentative. "I hope my boy wasn't bothering you."

"Not at all, he's a polite young lad." Jeff did not realize how imposing he appeared in his camouflage combat fatigues, forage cap and stout boots with a heavy handgun hanging on his belt. He contrasted the run-down man in front of him. Jim's clothes were threadbare with worn-out shoes tied with twine. He had no hat.

"Come along, JJ." Jim turned abruptly, afraid of anyone in uniform.

"He can visit anytime," Jeff sounded reassuring. "You can too if you would like to chat."

Jim retreated without acknowledging Jeff's invitation. Jimmy glanced back as his father pulled him along. Jeff headed to the cook-tent.

Jeff had the short end of the duties that day. He drew midnight watch at the barrier under the direction of Richard, an old hand with little formal training but experience.

"We don't expect action," the Richard said. "Refugees are usually smart enough to arrive in daylight and when the sun's out of our eyes."

"Have there been any attacks?" Someone asked.

"So far, no, but we had trouble and shot a couple of bad guys a few weeks ago. It's the same story at the other barriers, especially the twenty-one along the lake at Southampton. They put fighters from the south there to guard the nukes. Some of them get frisky, but no shooting."

"Don't fire without my order but shoot in self-defence."

They paired up and rotated in one-hour watches over a four-hour shift. Replacements would arrive five minutes early to ensure overlap.

"No smoking, no talking, no sleeping, no noise. Make sure you know your target. There are patrols, but they won't come this way. They work the flanks and return around the ends. The password is Nancy."

Despite the order for silence, whispered conversations took place at the cycling of the watch. Otherwise, everyone lingered in their thoughts. Jeff constantly thought of Jani. He did not believe he could love so deeply. The quiet ended during Jeff's third stand down.

"Safeties off," Richard's voice hissed from the darkness. "Stand ready. Watch that left flank, Shadly."

Jeff leapt to the barrier behind a double wooden crib, filled with fieldstone and sloping away. He could not see much beyond the edge of the wall in the moonless blackness. They stood stone still, listening.

"Crack,"

To the left, Jeff brought his rifle to his shoulder, resting his right cheek on the wooden stock, his finger on the trigger guard to prevent accidental firing. Once the finger touched the trigger he would be shooting. Jeff's chest heaved. His heart wanted to fly out of his chest.

Damn, he thought, *did I set it to manual or auto?* Training dictated they set their weapons for a single shot unless ordered otherwise. "We don't want you wasting bullets on tree stumps," Roger had said.

In the oppressive blackness, Jeff heard his partner's excited breathing. The man shared Jeff's fear. They strained to hear the approaching enemy, silently cursing the incessant crickets.

"Crack!" the sound was unmistakable. *Yes, just to the left!* Jeff's thoughts raced as he trained his weapon towards the sound. *Can I shoot someone?*

Another crack sounded from the darkness. Did he hear a low curse? His gun slightly lowered as his grip hardened and the trigger finger itched for action. All thoughts of hesitation had left. Jeff focused on finding a target.

"BANG," Richard's loud voice startled Jeff, "YOU ARE DEAD!"

"Damned twigs!" a familiar French-accent came from the darkness. "Nancy! Don't shoot!"

"Stand down, safeties on!" Richard said. "Good work, lads! Come on in LaFarge. We got you this time."

Several figures emerged from the darkness. Richard went from defender to defender making sure they had set safeties properly.

"I knew, with Roger here, there would be fun." Richard laughed.

"It's a good thing I didn't send a second wave." LaFarge emerged from the darkness. "I knew I had better take it easy on you, old man."

The two old friends had a good laugh. Shadly and the other rookies leaned against the cribbing trying to calm down. Jeff's hand shook. It was their best lesson yet. The weeks of training had never put them when they thought they faced an actual enemy.

"Those dry twigs work well." Roger peered into the dark. "My boot snapped one, and I knew about them." He sounded disgusted with himself.

"Who's the old man?" Richard teased. "You're losing your touch, Mon Ami. Okay guys, back to your posts!" Richard led the attackers to the rear laughing with LaFarge.

The night passed with no more excitement; however, everyone kept keen senses in the remaining watch. Dawn had broken when Jeff fell into bed. He never had thought the camp cot could be so welcoming.

Jeff woke to the sounds of laughing children playing across the way, carefree and being children. He emerged from his tent and found some water to splash away his lingering drowsiness. From the look of the sun, it was late morning.

"Finally, out of bed I see," Helen passed with a bucket of water. "I heard you had fun last night."

"It scared the hell out of me," Jeff responded. "It didn't seem real in Meaford. I sure thought it was bad guys."

"Good," she replied, "I'm always scared in an actual situation like the Ivory Coast. We're going to get action here soon. We had better be ready."

Helen wandered off towards the mess tent. Jeff followed and ate a breakfast of eggs, chops and fried bread washed down with raw milk. He sipped rose-hip tea as he washed the dishes and tidied up the mess.

"Hi Mister," the familiar voice came from beside Jeff as he sat tying his boot, wondering what the schedule was for the day. JJ had silently appeared from behind the tent.

"Hi Jimmy," Jeff smiled and this time the boy smiled back, "you sure are a quiet walker." Jeff reached into his pack and produced some bread before the boy could ask. "You would make a good soldier." This remark brought a greater smile to Jimmy's face.

"I want to be," Jimmy responded, "I had to be sneaky back home."

"Where was home, Jimmy?" Jeff made room for JJ on the big rock.

"Toronto, but the last couple of years we were over by Lake Simcoe near Barrie. We worked making stuff or in the fields." Jimmy spoke well and seemed older than he appeared from his skinny frame and sunken eyes.

"How old are you, Jimmy?"

"Twelve." The reply shocked Jeff who expected ten years at the most. Joseph's arrival at Longview had unsettled, but Jimmy's sad condition upset Jeff more; however, the lad appeared to have some strength. All youngsters seemed to be resilient and better off mentally than the suffering adults. Jeff realized older people grieved loss while younger ones might have fewer shadows on their hearts.

Damn, he thought, *I am thinking like Brandi, but that isn't a bad thing.* He smiled at the thought of his sister.

"In four more years, you too will become a soldier, Jimmy." In the back of his mind, Jeff hoped they could hold out for four years against whoever threatened them. Perhaps Jimmy would become a fighter at an even younger age. "How long have you been here?"

"About four weeks. We arrived with a bunch of people. Some were sick and died, over there," he pointed to the far corner of the camp at a fenced area. "They put the worst ones in there, and almost no one ever comes back out. Billy and Mary-Jane are still in there." Jimmy sobbed slightly, but his tone was matter-of-fact. These had not been the first deaths he had witnessed. Jeff did not know who Billy and Mary Jane might be, but he hoped they would survive. "Dad says we will move soon to live on a farm. I hope so. I like farms."

Jimmy's family had done forced labour for over two years. The farm they finally escaped from had been a better experience with more food. The freehold farm sold produce to some of the fighting forces further south. JJ's family worked for room and board but fled when the army they had supplied, in retreat and on the verge of defeat confiscated the farm and shot the owner.

A shrill whistle pierced the morning air. Helen came running past.

"Get your weapons and ammo," she called out as she passed. "Something's happening at the barrier!" The woman vanished. Jeff grabbed his rifle.

"See you later, Jimmy!" Jeff joined the force in a quick jog to the barrier. So far, there had been no shooting.

"Ted, what's going on?"

"Damned if I know," came the reply, "but if Helen says jump, I'm already in the air."

"She has you well trained." Jeff joked.

It took the contingent ten minutes to reach the barrier. Richard and Roger stopped the group a hundred meters short of the roadblock.

"I want two sniper squads, one to each flank. You saw the positions yesterday."

Ted and Roger plus three other soldiers headed to the left flank between the barrier and the lake. Helen dispatched the other group to a position towards the escarpment. Ten fighters went directly to the barrier while more headed out on each flank. The forty trainees augmented twenty from the volunteer force.

Jeff joined the group at the barricade. The empty highway beyond disappeared into the sunlit distance. In this dead still summer day, not even a lake breeze disturbed the leaves.

"Is this another drill?" Jeff asked one volunteer.

"Not this time, buddy," the man focused on the road. "A bunch with guns is coming down the road."

"Okay, guys," Richard's shout carried all along the fortification. "Hostiles are approaching. They will be desperate folks needing help. At worst, there will be shooting, and remember," he paused for effect, "no shooting unless I give the order!"

They pulled the bridge back from the central gap and placed heavy logs across the far entrance. The passage zigzagged in two sharp angles before the gap and then once afterwards. A pedestrian passage lay to the south of the main one, and it too had a serpentine design with a controlled passage made from an old cattle crate.

The leading sides of all barriers sloped up at a forty-five-degree angle to deflect the blast from an explosion on the far side. Dangerous vehicles could not get closer than about one hundred meters. A blast at that distance might kill those directly exposed and not protected by the barrier.

Slit trenches and camouflaged bunkers, the winter accommodation for the guards, staggered to the rear fifty meters to each side, and out of the way of an air attack. Hostile aircraft would use the roadway to guide them.

Roger checked the sniper positions. Shooters had an open line of fire from the barrier to about a kilometre down the road. A cleared, fan-shaped area extended in front of the barrier, and dry branches and round glacial stones would impede the advance of attackers as well as betray them in the dark as had happened the previous night.

White-painted stones with black crosses formed a fan pattern that retreated away from the barrier in fifty-meter intervals, giving the snipers ranging marks. Armed fighters manned the edges of the fan. These emplacements formed a jagged defence in depth that extended to the lake on one side and the scree slope of the escarpment on the other.

Patrols watched the top of the escarpment. Two mobile forces of ten members each waited behind the line to deploy anywhere along the line. To Jeff's newly trained eye, it seemed formidable; he would later realize the flimsiness of their defence.

A light flashed far down the road. Rapid flashes came from a spot to the right of the old highway, Morse code.

Helen leaned on the wall with her binoculars.

"Tango thirty-nine," her voice broke the silence. Another trainer stood at her side recording her words. "Mike twenty-two, Whiskey twelve, and Charlie five." None of this made sense to Jeff. "Papa Alfa thirty, Romeo Foxtrot twenty-five, Hotel Golf thirty, and Alfa-Alfa-Alfa," Helen turned and handed the glasses to a guard.

"If you see anything," she said to the woman, "call me."

Richard approached Helen.

"This group has lots of guns. There are thirty-nine of them, twenty-two men, twelve women and five children. There aren't any heavy weapons, but they're carrying twenty-five rifles and thirty handguns."

"They're fighters of some sort." Richard took the paper from Helen and stared at the numbers. "There are too few children and too many guns. We must expect the worst." He felt lucky to have the training contingent available. Richard passed along the line, admonishing everyone to wait for orders. His hand signal released the snipers to Roger's command. From that moment on, they could shoot anyone who aimed a gun. The guards stared down the crumbling roadway to where it vanished in the haze.

"Here they come," the woman with the binoculars broke the silence. Tense fighters checked their weapons. Safeties clicked off.

Dark shadows, wavering as if part of the air, then solidifying into humans as they emerged from the haze. The distant figures approached with painful sluggishness. It reminded Jeff of stalking game, waiting for the prey to wander close for the fatal shot.

Women and children, the youngest perhaps five years old formed the leading cohort. Their short legs set the pace; however, some adults limped.

The pathetic vanguard shielded the majority, men and women, clutching rifles and warily watching the trees. Two figures trailed behind, perhaps in charge but more afraid of their entourage than enemies lurking in the trees.

Jeff saw fear and desperation. The barrier looked formidable from the far side; with weapons threatening over the wall, it made a fearful sight. Jeff dreaded the next few moments.

"Stop right there!" Richard's voice boomed as the vanguard reached the first obstacle. "Lay everything on the ground."

The first group dropped their bundles. Frightened parents hugged crying youngsters. Everyone's clothes rotted off their bodies. None had a hat. The trailing group stopped with the leaders remaining further back.

"Drop your weapons!" Richard commanded. Several armed people put their rifles on the ground, but the majority hesitated.

"Who's asking?" demanded the male leader. The man and woman seemed fit and well fed in sharp contrast to the rest of their party.

"We aren't arguing, drop your weapons."

"You aren't telling us what to do," the man shouted as he and his companion strode to the front. "No one tells us what to do."

As they passed the scraggly vanguard, the man yanked a little girl free of her mother's grasp. There were gasps from the watchers on the barrier. He intended to use the little girl as a shield. The woman grabbed another child from his mother and wrapped her arm tightly around his neck. The mothers stood silently with anguished faces listening to their children's terrified cries.

"Hold your fire," Richard reminded his forces. "Only shoot on my order. Pass it on."

A murmur went down the line. The commander stepped back one pace and pointed to the snipers with each hand. Richard returned to the barrier and without hesitation, raised his rifle and fired a shot over the heads of the arrivals. Everyone dropped to the ground leaving the defiant leaders standing, glaring at the barrier, brandishing handguns and twisting the children in front of them.

"That wasn't too smart!" the man yelled at the barrier. "Shoot again, and this kid dies."

Two shots rang out from the left flank. The two holding the children seemed to stand still for an instant, hostile looks frozen on their faces, then collapsed to the ground, dead. Blood oozed from a neat hole in each of their temples. For an instant, there was no movement and no noise. The sudden violence froze everyone, including the barrier guards. Then the sound of metal and wood on stone mingled with crying, as the visitors' threw their guns away. Distraught mothers retrieved their children, the boy from beneath the dead woman's body.

The mothers felt relief and horror at how close their loved ones had come to lethal bullets, but these were not the first killings the motley group had witnessed. Richard would apologize to the mothers, but he could not have let the dead pair take the initiative. He had to trust Roger and his sharpshooters. It had become a brutal world.

These were the first killings Jeff had ever seen. His trembling hands gripped his rifle tightly, safety off, but his eyes remained focused on the cowering group on the road.

"Women and children come forward to the next barrier," Richard called out. The group of twelve women and five children made fearful progress to the next point. Richard called two guards.

"Get blankets and stand by the gate." The pair hurried off. "I want two volunteers to take the blankets out to the end of the walkway."

Jeff stepped out of the line with no hesitation and joined one woman.

"Now strip," Richard's voice boomed.

Loud protests came in return, but the commander would have no discussion. Reluctantly, the women and children complied. Most had little in the way of undergarments. After four years of crisis, fighting and turmoil, many had lost irreplaceable necessities. Several had rags for underwear; some none. Modesty was not a big an issue in this depraved world. All accepted their fate; just another degradation.

One more handgun appeared from a woman's rags and she openly kicked to the side.

"Wait there," Richard no longer feared concealed weapons, "and we will put blankets out, then walk up and cover up."

Jeff and his companion walked through the cattle gate and twenty meters from the barrier. Even in this short distance, he felt exposed and insecure. He still had his handgun but felt naked without his rifle and the safety of the stone barrier. They deposited their burdens and retreated. Jeff resisted the urge to run, trusting the snipers' vigilance.

"Okay, come on and pick up a blanket." Richard scanned the approaching figures. All eyes searched for any hint of concealed weapons with no voyeurism.

Richard assigned ten guards to the entranceway and commanded the group to walk through. The guards took the mothers and children to a large tent and put the women with no children under the shade of a tree. Guards distributed water and left them to their thoughts.

The remaining men, huddling beside the bodies came through in groups of five with the same ritual of stripping and donning blankets. No one had expected such a large group of arrivals. The last of them wore sheets they had stripped from guards' cots.

The barrier contingent stood down. A small force separated the discarded clothes so that each refugee could dress before interrogation. They evaluated each person's needs. They would provide essentials to anyone accepted as a refugee. If rejected, they would send them back through the barrier with their original possessions but no weapons. They confined the former fighters as potential criminals pending investigation.

Jeff led the recovery group. Shadly had never been this close to a corpse and felt numb. The dead woman was a little younger than his mother was. As head of the group, he searched the bodies. Both wore large, well-honed knives, battle fatigues in good condition and stout boots.

The pockets yielded a trove of interesting information. Each carried a card identifying them as citizens of North York and designating them as commanders of the "Free Forces of North York". Written orders allowed them to conscript anyone and to use whatever force necessary to "achieve the protection, freedom and prosperity" of the region and its noble leader. It was a blank cheque allowing any crime.

Jeff found a personal letter written by the dead woman's husband, dated a year previously. It ranted about the superiority of the white race and arguing for the extermination of a diverse number of groups from "Wogs, Niggers, Pakies, Jews, Injuns and perverts". The dead man beside the woman's body was not the letter writer.

Jeff stared at a stash of handmade currency bearing the seal of North York, reminiscent of Centrebucks. Jeff did not like this reminder of his mother's job issuing the local currency in Weyburne. Roger watched the work, swearing quietly in French.

Roger took all the items recovered from the bodies back to the interrogation bunker. Jeff's detail carried the bodies to an abandoned apple orchard beside several mounds of fresh dirt. They stripped the bodies and dropped them into the newly dug pits, marking the graves with a piece of numbered limestone. Huron Territory would keep the number at Owen Sound, matched with the names on the dead fighters' identification. One day, someone might look for loved ones. On this day, no one cared. Reducing these killers to numbers was more honour than most innocent casualties of the collapse had received.

Jeff accompanied a trembling, teary-eyed Ted back to camp. Ted's bullet killed the man. He had never taken a human life before. Ted staggered to a tree and threw up, taking some minutes to recover.

"Who else fired?"

"Roger shot the woman," Ted shuddered, "I think he knew it would be too hard for me. After the shot, Roger rested his cheek on his rifle butt for a few seconds." Ted paused in thought. "Even Roger found it hard."

Jeff remembered Roger's vigil over the bodies and understood. The old entertainment industry used to depict fighters without feelings. In the real world, even those trained to kill, suffered trauma when involved in violence and death. He rested his hand on Ted's shoulder.

They walked in silence with heavy hearts. They had come of age, bloodied as the old hands would casually put it, but the two had painfully shed their youth in the stark reality of a shattered world. A motorcycle came to a sputtering, dusty stop in front of them at the camp entrance. Chester looked grim.

"Hello Jeff," he smiled and glanced towards Ted.

"This is Ted Macedo," Jeff made the introduction. "He's a crack shot and my best friend." Ted shook Chester's hand with a warm glance towards Jeff, delighted by his status as Jeff's friend. He had not had a genuine friend in years.

"Jeff, I'll talk to you later. You have a family to take up to Longview at the end of the week."

Chester gunned the bike and roared off towards the barrier where he would conduct the interrogation.

Jeff collapsed onto his cot and passed the rest of the afternoon in fitful slumber, waking often with memories of horrible dreams. Chester's noisy motorbike roused Jeff from a deep sleep.

"Hey Jeff, wakey, wakey," Chester's head poked through the tent's entrance. "Come have a coffee." Jeff followed Chester to the mess tent.

"We have an additional problem; these arrivals are leftovers from a gang calling itself the government of North York."

Chester sipped his drink. Real coffee was a luxury, a reward for those serving on the barriers. Supplies would soon run out as the shipments coming through the USA and Chicago had stopped. Coffee took much buying power away from essential items such as guns and fuel. Huron took the luxury off the official trading list.

"These people survived the last battle. That group in Toronto defeated all the others and has them on the run. Your enemy, Angel, in Weyburne is part of them, the People's Liberation Movement."

"How did they get past the Weyburne crowd?"

"Their army lost a battle at Oak Ridges. They turned tail, retreated to Lake Simcoe and Barrie, and finally swung over this way fighting all the way. They lost people between here and Toronto. According to some we interviewed, there are more bands of them. We've sent out patrols along the lake and up east of Maxwell. They have a mean streak, as you saw today. If these refugees are right, several other defeated armies are on the loose. I hope they hurt each other before any bother us. One other thing," Chester seemed even more saddened than before, "a family here escaped a massacre by this group on a farm near Barrie."

"I met a boy and his Dad. They told me the story."

"Jim and little JJ, you'll get to know them better. I'm sending them to Longview with you. Jim might identify murderers in this bunch, but we think the two we shot are the killers. Some women and children came from that farm, working as serfs like Jim's family."

"Once we sort out the innocent from the rest, we'll accept them. Just because someone fought in some punk army doesn't mean much, but we don't want cold-blooded killers. If we trust them, we need fighters too."

Jeff understood the practicalities. Any serious enemy would out-number the small Huron population. They saw every honest refugee as a positive. The last four years had smudged standards of morality and guilt.

"How can we accommodate more people at Longview?" Jeff switched to other issues. "Ellen and her family have stretched us and won't contribute for months."

"I know these folks are weak and in need," Chester sighed, "but Jim can work. We can get Longview extra supplies for the winter. Everyone thinks what you're doing there is important, maybe a model for others. We want you to succeed. No one else can nurse these needy people but Kathy."

"Apparently, I'll be helping with your harvest." Chester broke into a broad smile. "Karen and your sister cornered me and gave me my orders. Karen has me mesmerized, I couldn't say no." He winked as he rose.

"I have to get back up to the barrier. I won't see you again until September." Chester left Jeff with the luxury of a second cup of coffee.

Thankfully, the rest of the week was uneventful. Jeff continued to draw night duty and twice patrolled beyond the barrier. They went several kilometres out from the border, almost reaching Collingwood. Once, they escorted refugees to the barrier. When the week ended, the training contingent said their goodbyes. Jeff tried to get Ted to come to Longview, but he was eager to return home to his mother. She struggled to survive alone, running a small farm and a yeast making operation. In only a few weeks, the pair would answer a new call to action.

Chapter Thirteen

Jeff guided JJ's family to a Longview finishing the second hay crop. Word of the extra mouths to feed preceded them, and they would harvest many more hectares of hay. The valley committee donated more grain, sheep, and goats to help in Longview's care for needy refugees. The feed would carry the new animals to slaughter time. Longview would not make a tax payment this winter. Overall, debilitated refugees imposed a burden on Huron Territory, draining resources, with the newcomers contributing little for some time.

Jeff hardly had time to kiss Jani before he went to the field, helping to fork hay onto the wagons and putting in a stint on the scythe. Nature smiled on them, and the hay came into the barn in excellent condition. Warren and Walt smiled as they evaluated the legume content and full seed heads. This would be excellent fodder.

Jeff was less enthusiastic as he and Bill wandered back from the far edge of the last cut field. He looked over the healthy stands of grain rippling in the wind and turning golden in the sun. The fields stretched down to the river. Jeff contemplated days of aching muscles and sore hands as he swung the scythe through the crop.

"It was pretty rough, I hear." Bill put a hand on his son's shoulder. Bill had heard an enthusiastic and embellished account of the confrontation from young JJ, somewhat changed by Jim Smithson.

"It still feels horrible," Jeff said. "I saw no one shot before or been near a dead body." Bill shuddered in empathy, remembering Stevie

Hunter's body on the Centreville jail floor. He had not seen someone die. Jeff had travelled a bit of life's path Bill could not share.

Bill looked into his son's eyes. "I can't imagine it, and the world is going to get a lot uglier before it gets better, if it gets better."

"The grain will be ready soon." Bill's eyes swept over the fields. Neither man would speak of the shootings again.

"Brandi and Karen will come next week to help harvest. Chester should arrive soon after. These new folks are weak, but they are helping with the hay. Harold and John have come along, but Ellen and her kids are rough. Kathy's positive but says to be patient."

"I worry about JJ," Jeff felt like an uncle. "He's weak and angry."

"Maybe Kathy can get him to talk."

"There's other help to come." Bill looked down the valley as the pair reached the rail fence at the kitchen garden. "Do you remember the folks from Heathcote we gave food to last March taking IOUs for labour? They will send several people to help."

With no regulated currency, people developed informal solutions with direct bartering and trading of goods, and as with Longview, people gave commitments of labour for future payment. Few had anything else to offer. The value came from the existence of potential buyers, but the things most people had, most other people possessed in adequate amounts, eliminating any market. Shortage made food the highest value, but most people did not have any surplus. They only had labour to trade, and the decimated population made workers valuable. This would evolve into a more formal currency. In the beginning, the casual arrangement between people depended on mutual trust.

Gifting to the needy became the norm.

***

Longview now had too many people to sit together for a meal. The situation upset the original founders, and they made plans to renovate the interior kitchen, dining room, and parlour into one large room. Everyone could not interact as before. Longview had reached its maximum for adult residents and needed a new governing structure.

They replaced the meal meeting time with more formal decision-making. This would evolve as Longview transformed into a village. Between haying and the grain harvest, they tried these new things and got to know the Smithson family.

A hot August evening became the backdrop for the first after-dinner gathering. Everyone carried a chair into the yard. Warren, assuming the role of patriarch, placed his wooden armchair beside the front steps. Light banter murmured about the yard. Jean, Bill and Don Hunter finally came down the steps after finishing the cleanup. Jean sat beside Warren. Her work-roughened fingers touched the back of his hand.

"Jim Smithson's been telling me interesting things about happenings in the city." Warren raised his voice, and the group fell silent. "We've only heard bits and pieces, but Jim is the closest we have to an insider from the city. Please tell your story."

Warren turned towards Jim Smithson and shared the crowd's eagerness for stories that broke the hours of hard work and boredom.

"Walt, go get the popcorn!" Tina Lefevre sang out, raising a laugh.

The end of television is a good thing. Warren thought. *This is nice.*

"Thank you for taking my family and Billy and Mary-Jane." Jim Smithson sounded formal. Bill and Warren recognized the corporate tone.

"When you hear about our past, you'll think we are the last people you would want on a farm." Jim tried to smile, dreading failure with this group. He and his family felt safe for the first time in years. It took an effort to believe in the reality of that safety.

"I was a banker." He expected a hostile response. Many times in the past few years, he had heard bankers blamed for the calamity. The Longview group had long ago stopped blaming anyone for the disaster.

"I worked in Toronto, as a vice-president with a pleasant office on the fortieth floor looking over the lake." He paused, recalling good times.

"When the crisis first hit, we tried to fix things. We struggled to free up money and get credit available, but everyone was afraid to lend even between banks. You all know the rest. What you might not know, the bond sale disaster finally killed us. Until that terrible week, those of us who thought we had power had hope. My boss killed himself the night of the bond collapse." Jim paused for a few seconds. "Every bond issuer owed enormous amounts, and since we couldn't sell new bonds, we had no cash to pay off the old ones."

"Sounds like my credit cards." Walt snickered relishing that the banks suffered the same fate.

"Sort of," Smithson responded, "except the bondholders had a lot more clout than the banks." Jim swiped at a deer fly and mopped his brow in the warm evening air. "When the bonds defaulted the Bond Investors Group filed lawsuits in Superior Court. The courts had collapsed.

Missed payrolls made the staff stay home. The Province had not paid the judges.”

“The bondholders outflanked the banks and found cash to pay the judges. I do not know where they got the cash, but there was so much stealing going on some bank employees could have been providing it. I know branch managers had cleaned out their vaults and disappeared. One of my friends told me the bondholders expected the crash and hoarded cash and gold over a few years and allied with organized crime.”

“They called their organization ‘BIG’ and got to the courts first. To hide their involvement, they hired some of the administrative employees, paying cash, and had them funnel money to the right judges, so the courts ruled the bondholders could foreclose on the banks. That was in the middle of November, but by then the banks only existed in name. These money people held the actual power. They ordered the disastrous attempt at mortgage foreclosures. I administered bond sales at my bank and had contacts in BIG. They found a role for me, overseeing the foreclosures and building connections with politicians.”

“We didn’t have it easy.” Jim’s wife sounded defensive, “with little food and dangerous streets in Forest Hill. We had to do something.”

“What Beverly is saying,” Jim continued, “I worked full time with the provincial politicians. These people were self-serving and smug, but I don’t think they were cruel or criminal. All that started later.” Jim tried to rationalize his past.

“No one at my level, the upper-middle-class, had any cash. We had used plastic for everything and didn’t have currency. A friend of mine used a coin collection at face value to buy food, but that didn’t last long.” The non-reaction from the old hands of Longview puzzled Jim, but they had almost forgotten about cash.

“As insiders, we got food and protection. They bought the police as they had bought the courts, but many cops went to drug gangs and gangsters. We called in cops from the province and fired the few who didn’t obey orders. Cash attracted most, and we all enjoyed getting some.” Jim noticed his audience looked at Debbie Hunter whose murdered husband, Stevie, was one of the fired cops.

“The provincial government collapsed, and our group took over. Again, money talked. We gathered in the university, west of the legislature, fortified with shipping containers with about three thousand police and us. The widespread violence kept the cops busy.”

"At first, supplies came in easily with a police escort, mostly opposed by street gangs that could not defeat the cops who knew there would be no legal repercussions for using lethal force. Cash incentives encouraged successful operations with a bonus for dead enemies. This lasted about a year. Supplies gradually tightened, and conditions worsened. We used helicopters to get in and out safely."

"The outside gangs sorted things out and the big ones aligned including bikers and ethnic gangs. A former provincial cabinet minister led us and he sent out cops to get rid of this alliance. The police died to a man, and he lost the support of the security force."

"Unknown to us, the cops had organized themselves. They built a powerful group of former Metros, OPP, and RCMP. These guys had friends in some of the elite families in the bondholder organization. One day, they arrested everyone working for the former leadership. It scared us; however, they only locked up the real insiders, the old politicians. The rest of us worked for the cops."

"One of the wealthy families ran things, and the commissioner of the provincial police was number two. This group assassinated many others. We didn't think things had become that brutal, but then, none of us wanted to know. I became a small fish in their organization, only important because I administrated payments and supplies, a low-level job."

Jim glanced nervously about the group. Kathy Nelson thought Jim downplayed his importance.

"How did you get your supplies?" Kathy was trying to fit Jim's story into her own experiences.

"We created a safe corridor from the university and Queen's Park down to the lake, including the island airport." Jim gave Kathy a questioning look. "The water access and airport helped us survive. Some suggested we retreat to the lake, but the leader wanted to remain in Queen's Park."

"He said when they took over completely the population would look to us as the rightful authority. The guy spent a lot of time designing flags, posters and other stuff. His motif was a broken red maple leaf with a black bar running through it, representing healing a broken Canada. While we struggled to stay alive, he had totally out of touch dreams of glory, but he had invented the public face of the People's Liberation Movement."

"Canada had fallen apart by then. As far as we could tell, five regions had formed. Quebec had gone on its own and taken northern New Brunswick and a little of northern Ontario with it, but it was too big to run.

The Canadian military had ousted the central government and pretended that Canada existed. All they did was send the occasional missive out telling us they were in charge and asking for money. Except for military skirmishes with Quebec, they were doing nothing. Ontario remained in chaos with fighting and gang violence all the way to Niagara. The people on the Niagara River fended off attacks and refugees from the USA and fought each other."

"A few boats attacked Toronto, but they were more pirates than military. Our forces captured an old USA coastguard boat, and so had a navy with one fighting ship. There was fighting over the rest of southern Ontario from Windsor to Cornwall, and several powerful groups emerged. I heard they aligned with the group in Toronto."

"We desperately wanted to keep the power supply working, so we formed alliances with people to maintain transmission corridors including the old Hydro One and OPG corporations. These, along with the remnants of the police became the backbone of the People's Liberation Movement. On paper, it looked good, but every day was a struggle to keep it working amidst the constant fighting. The hydro corridor into the downtown saw real fighting for a few months. I think it still does."

"I don't think so." John Bock interjected. "The gang that kidnapped me was one group fighting for that line, and I think your bunch wiped them out in a bloody massacre. I was lucky to get away alive." John trembled. "I think the fighting had stopped by the time we left."

"A year ago the fighting along old 427 Highway cut the city off before we fled."

"That was two years later," Jim responded. "My family and I had already fled out of the city. I am not sure of the exact situation, but the central enclave survived. The influence of the PLM is wide. The people you are fending off on the other side of the barriers are part of it. Up here, this man Angel heads it, but he's small potatoes and gets his orders from the PLM in Toronto. Angel is an outsider to the big guns, but he's useful. The PLM needs his fighters to defeat the hostiles in old Peel. Angel has forced out everyone else locally."

The Longview founders scowled at the memory.

"The real rich folks have an armed camp in the middle of old King Township and are running things from there. You can still see their helicopters and planes flying in and out. There is contact to the USA across Lake Ontario, although the situation is impossible to follow. They get supplies from there."

"The rest of Canada, out west, is in at least two parts made up of everything east of the mountains on its own and British Columbia. Ontario had a deal to keep natural gas flowing. It still seems in effect. BC broke up into isolated places. Someone said Chinese forces had landed on the west coast from Mexico to Alaska, but I don't know for sure."

"How did you escape?" Bill enjoyed the first-hand news but wanted to get to the end. The sky was golden over the western valley lip. Purples of dusk crept from the east. Chores could not wait much longer.

"It became too dangerous and wasn't comfortable living in the old dormitory. We got out. A good friend in the security detail, an ex-OPP superintendent got us a helicopter ride to the OPP stronghold in Orillia."

Jim worried people might think it was cowardly. He did not know everyone at Longview had made the same decision.

"We didn't hang around Orillia. Refugees from up north in holiday country crowded it. Once the economy collapsed, there was nothing up there to support a large population and most had headed south. Many went to the city to fight. Some were involved in vicious, racist fighting with native bands. They called it the Indian War. They outgunned and out-manned the Natives and they had mostly fled by the time we arrived."

"I didn't want to be a soldier, so we ran away to the Jones farm. Jones wasn't too bad a guy, although he hit JJ for stealing. It wasn't JJ's fault. I was angry and told him off. Jones and I waged a kind of cold war until those gangsters attacked the farm and murdered Jones."

For the first time, Jim showed genuine emotion. His wife, Beverly began sobbing, and Sharon put a comforting arm around her.

"Jeff dealt with some folks who attacked Jones. They seemed to have lost most of their fighters after we fled as only twenty-five arrived at the border. They kidnapped the women and children from Jones' farm."

"It was horrible," Jeff said. "They used kids for shields."

"That's common." Jim continued. "They would have killed those two and grabbed more. They deserved what they got. Those two tortured Jones."

"Thank you," Warren stood and stretched. "We hope you work out here and get to stay. You're the last ones we can accommodate and now have enough labour to farm all the land. I think you'll be happy here."

The group scattered. Mothers took the younger children yawning and complaining to their beds. The night fell swiftly, and no one wanted to waste lamp oil or candles. The Hunters now occupied one unit in the new building with Tina and Walt Lefevre in the middle and the Handleys in the third space, leaving room for Ellen and her kids in a mobile unit. Jim Smithson and his family slept in the old school-bus.

Don and Stephanie went with Ron and Walt to set the animals for the night. When they finally left the barn, a waxing, three-quarter moon cast shadows over the yard. Human sounds faded. The natural rhythms of nature's night music persisted, and Longview drifted into peaceful rest.

Chapter Fourteen

The grain harvest occupied every waking moment. Workers filled the oats and barley fields, labouring in warm September sun. Scythed stalks stood in neat, hand-bound stooks of sheaves in rows spiralling around the fields. They had placed a horse-drawn binder on the list of equipment needs. Only a mower had a higher priority.

"You work well for an old man." Karen teased Chester as he threw sheaves up to one of the Heathcote labourers. The man interwove each bundle so the load would survive the trip up to the barn.

"Good thing you are over there, teach, or I'd throw you up too." Chester wiped his brow keeping sweat from trickling into his eyes.

"Hey Karen," Brandi stood on the wagon helping with the stacking. "This might be a good time to get Chester to agree." She winked at Karen.

"Agree, what have you two cooked up?"

"Calm down, dear. Brandi and I want to formalize the school and get community support. We need to replace the dead school system."

"We've been concentrating on survival," Chester replied. "If we don't survive, none of the rest will matter."

"You have it wrong, dear," Karen heaved a sheave up to Brandi. "If we don't build something good, there's no reason to survive."

"Karen," Chester sighed, "You know I agree, but it's too soon, and there are no resources."

"We only need approval. If Council supports us, we can restore some basic education, catalogue peoples' skills and spread the best ideas."

"That's ambitious. I don't think you can do it all." Chester swung the last of the grain up to the wagon and walked around to hug Karen. Brandi jumped down, waiting patiently.

"We won't do it all at once, Chester." Brandi finally got their attention. "We plan to start with basic home schooling and do the rest as skilled people can help. It would be nice to get extra food and supplies."

"The students at my house," Karen said, "are making good progress. My star pupil here," she hugged Brandi, "is helping with the younger kids, teaching English and art and arithmetic. We plan to put together a teaching kit and support so places like Longview can home school."

Karen leaned against the wagon collecting her thoughts. "The next step is to decide what skills and information we should spread around and find people who know, carpentry, weaving, cooking and even farming. Teaching those would help us survive."

"Longview needs new skills and ideas," Brandi piped up, "with the basis for something good. We should spread the Longview approach."

"I like the long view. What do you need? I'll take the idea to Council."

"We want a letter from the Huron Territory to show people we contact, designating us as mandated to establish education and cultural connections everywhere."

"That, I can get approved." Chester doubted Karen had finished.

"I've drafted a letter. It would be good if Council contributed some basic food supplies and help establish a supporting farm in Kimberly, including a couple of horses with wagons and horse gear."

Chester gulped at the enormity of the request. It would take a lot of persuading to sway the representatives. The letter would be easy. The Council would have a major problem providing resources. "I'll look at the letter and see what I can do. I can't make any promises."

Brandi climbed onto the wagon and with a flip of the reins started the patient horses towards the barn. Karen and Chester watched her confident handling of the team.

"It's as if you have a daughter." Chester hugged.

"Yes, I love her like she's mine," Karen smiled still staring after the wagon. "She's smart and talented. Brandi doesn't know where she got her artistic ability. She said Sharon and Bill always let her be free as a child, to explore and play, drawing was an everyday thing."

"I'm reminded of a spirited racehorse waiting to be set free to run. There is little more I can teach Brandi. I can only encourage her to keep doing and put more polish on her writing. She's my teaching partner, not my student. The younger ones love her."

"Brandi will help me get the centre going, but I don't think she'll be in Kimberly long. She wants to explore and we should encourage her. We need something to tie all the isolated places together and give hope. Brandi's wandering around would connect people and gather useful knowledge to share with everyone."

Chester kissed her. They stood silently, enjoying the brief break from the hard work of the harvest.

***

Warren and Willard stood by the gate into the first grain field. The stooks of oats were dry enough for the barn. It was a race against time, trying to get as much in before the next rain. Some moisture would not hurt the grain but would delay gathering and threshing.

The two men were constant companions. Their outlooks meshed well; however, their physical limitations also dictated their companionship. Warren was becoming older, and Willard's back injury limited him. Their effort during the harvest was to evaluate the yield and choose plants for seed. Warren had a growing pile of sheaves separated for recovery.

The two men helped unload the wagons, but they could not do heavy tasks, working alongside the children. Little Joseph, although restricted by his deformed legs, had sat on the wagon handing sheaves to Willard.

Joseph now stood with the men beside the gate, holding Willard's hand, feeling proud and important. He could not remember his father whose hand he had never held.

"It sure takes a big crew." Warren gazed over the field at its cover of bristling golden stubble and an ever-decreasing spiral of stooks.

"We were lucky this year, having the newcomers and those promissory workers." Willard watched a small formation of Canada geese noisily flying down the valley. The "V" formation of their white breasts reflected the lowering sun. Joseph's hand felt good in his. Willard wondered if he had any grandchildren of his own.

"Those folks from Heathcote were a mixed blessing." Warren turned towards his friend. "They're good workers except for the one guy. I hated sending anyone away, but he wasn't worth feeding let alone working off his debt. Lucky for him, his sister volunteered to stay a couple of extra days. The guy huffed a bit, but I could tell he was happy to get out of the work. But she's a smart, tough one. I wouldn't want to be him when she gets home. His stomach might be empty this winter."

The two men laughed. Joseph looked up smiling, not understanding but happy to be sharing.

Megan's persistent calling drew the boy away. She was excited about the threshing operation outside the barn door. Jim Handley had rigged up a device from an old bicycle mounted on a solid plank. Don Hunter occupied the seat, peddling at an easy pace while his sister fed the heads of grain stalks between the spinning spokes. As they dragged against the frame, the seeds stripped away, falling into a pan below. Jim stood beside the device listing improvements. He looked up as Warren and Willard arrived to watch.

"This is a lot easier than a flail," he was smiling at his success, "but there are a lot of ways we can improve it." He put a hand on Donald's shoulder, "mainly improving the power source, sorry Don." Jim chuckled. "It's easy peddling, but after a bit, your legs will get worn out. For now, we can take shifts. I want to get wind power doing the threshing. I'm going to add paddles that will blow the chaff away and a chute to bag the grain."

Jim wrote notes and dimensions on a small board. He had worn his pencil down to a stub, sharing a common problem with Brandi. They needed to replenish writing implements.

"I like the re-using of all this stuff." Warren watched as Stephanie fed another handful of grain stalks into the spinning wheel. "Our descendants will need new solutions, but for now we can take advantage of salvage."

A load of grain arrived with Brandi at the reins. A crew waited at the barn to unload and stow it inside. John Bock stood ready with the handcart to take high heavy loads of sheaves to the back. He eyed Brandi speculatively. Willard hoisted Joseph onto the wagon. He and Brandi, along with Jim and JJ Smithson, soon had the load off. She jumped down and holding Joseph on her hip headed towards the water bucket.

"Your turn, Don," Brandi threw the comment over her shoulder, "they want one more load off before supper. We'll get it all done by dark."

Don tried to be calm, guiding the snorting team back into the field. Inwardly, he was full of joy, wanting to shout. The young man admired Jeff and his ability with horses and was eager to learn. Jeff's return as a soldier had reinforced this desire. He deeply grieved his father and often looked at the picture of Stevie in his full OPP uniform. Jeff was the living memory of his Dad, and Don longed to follow both examples. For now, he would be content to share the horse work with his friend.

Brandi peddled a bicycle furiously past Don and the team and arrived at the group near the stooks. Jeff peddled back at an even faster pace and cleared two steps of the old farmhouse before the bike hit the ground. The door slammed. Jeff reappeared and ran to the water tap, to rinse his hands and face before repeating his mad dash inside.

The group from the barn gathered around the steps. The commotion puzzled and frightened the youngest. A scream of pain from inside, followed by Kathy Nelson's quiet, reassuring voice. More screams and Jeff's deep, excited voice joined Kathy's quiet and calming. Soon, the cries of a newborn baby wailed through the screened doorway. The adults cheered and hugged. Jeff appeared in the doorway, with a small bundle.

"Meet William Allan Matthew of Longview," Jeff smiled proudly, stumbling over the unfamiliar name. "Jani is fine, so is Little Bill."

The tiny bundle stirred, as if this baby, only minutes old, recognized his name. Another loud shout of congratulations followed Jeff into the house. Brandi, in hot pursuit followed Sharon and Bill towards the house. Hugs, kisses and tears made for slow, smiling progress through the gathered friends, but soon they too disappeared inside. Little Bill was the first new baby at Longview and the couple's first, all too early introduction to grand parenting.

Work had to go on. The field crew kept loading the seasoned stooks until the barn group stowed away the last load of the day with the bicycle thresher working flat out. Walt's two boys had taken over the threshing, with the older pumping the bicycle peddles furiously as his brother gingerly fed heavily laden oat stalks into the spokes.

The crew made a dusty retreat to the yard just before sunset, leaving another three days' work in the field. Everyone was eager to visit Jani and Little Bill. The dining table returned to the old parlour which only hours before had been a birthing room. Jani and Little Bill rested upstairs, away from the loud laughter. Stephanie Hunter hovered inside Jani's room.

Out on the porch, Kathy Nelson sat alone, tired from her efforts as a midwife. Jani had been in labour for almost a day. Tears of happiness streamed down her cheeks. It was a long time since she had a truly wonderful medical experience. Little Bill's birth satisfied and restored.

Chapter Fifteen

"I hope this becomes a tradition." Warren leaned close to Chester, raising his voice above the din of the after-harvest party. Chester nodded and took a sip of something a local described as beer. The brew was the pride and joy of one boy from Thornbury, busily filling assorted cups from a plastic pail. More pails waited on the floor.

"I guess we'll like the taste, sometime," Chester raised the glass towards Warren. "It has a kick."

Warren quietly sipped a hard cider, observing the enthusiastic crowd filling the Heathcote hall. Willard and Sharon had organized the harvest party, along with friends from Heathcote. Word spread magically as if telephones existed. Self-invited guests came from as far as Thornbury.

Longview had completed the harvest the week before, just after the anniversary of the collapse. Sheaves were safely in the barn, and a good fraction threshed. They brought bags of oats and barley to Heathcote to pay the labourers who worked off debt. Some had earned extra grain. Most farms had completed their harvest all along the valley; everyone was eager for socializing.

"I need some air." Warren headed to the door with Chester following into the cool calmness beneath a cloudless evening sky.

"We only have flax left standing," Warren spoke, watching the bright light of Jupiter hanging high to the south. "It's all headed up, and if we get another week or two before a killing frost, we should get a crop of seed.

The frost-free season is getting longer each year. I think we will get away with the late planting."

"I like this flax thing," Chester replied. "There are lots of uses for it."

"Kathy Nelson got us moving." Warren turned. "We hadn't bothered to plant our seed. She reminded me of its benefits, so we put in a half hectare, hand-cast at the end of June. I hope the seed is useful. The old stuff might not germinate." He took a sip of cider. "Sorry for the lecture."

"You're the expert," Chester replied. "There are a few more like you with expertise in plants and crops, but most are conservative, unwilling to experiment. We hope you can light a fire in their pants." He laughed at his joke. The homebrew was strong indeed. "Your Weyburne buddies respect you. I've heard people say, we must talk to Warren so often I lost track."

"I have training and experience," the older man responded, not feeling the need to deflect the compliment. "I had too many years tending shade trees. This is a challenge and much more important. I love doing it, despite the tragedies that have made it necessary." He stared at the darkening sky, awed by its timelessness.

"I admire your hard work," Chester sipped his beer. "I talk like a worker and work like a talker." He laughed a little too loudly, staring at his glass. Chester decided he would switch to juice.

Warren smiled. "No one works harder than Chester Amik."

A loud burst of cheering and applause drew the men back into the hall. Sharon had called one of the Heathcote locals to join her at the front. A guitarist, a local fiddle player, Walt on harmonica and a woman from one church on piano paused for the formalities.

"We're happy to have the chance to be together," Sharon raised another enthusiastic cheer. "Beth and I just put the word out, and here you are." Another loud response swept the hall. "Before we go any further, I want to introduce our newest family member, my first grandson." Sharon beamed with love. "Jani, come up, please?" The young mother walked gingerly to the front of the hall, holding a small bundle snugly in her arms. "Everyone, this is Jani who joined our family last year and here is her son, Little Bill." Jani presented the bundle to the audience. The baby's red face peered out. His big grey eyes opened. He did not cry. Another cheer echoed through the hall. The birth filled everyone with hope.

Jani slipped away, embarrassed by the attention, but feeling a thrill of attachment and belonging, accepting best wishes from friends and strangers as she made her way to Jeff's side. Her new life as a mother displaced some shadows of grief. She would be the mother of many, and most who would call her "Mom" would not be her own and not yet born.

Taking a cue from Sharon, several people shouted news of births, marriages and sadly, deaths.

People resumed dancing in an eclectic display varying from old waltzes to some tribal swaying and stomping.

Sharon and Bill spun about the floor. She hugged him and said it reminded her of the first Christmas in Weyburne after the crash.

Brandi danced with Jeff and Don and even had a turn fighting off Ben the Postie during a slow dance. John Bock had one turn with the young girl and concluded their age difference was too great. Brandi's dancing culminated when she and Stephanie Hunter, imitating the standard practice at an old-time school dance, left the boys standing and staring as they danced together, wild and free, both of them remembering shadows from their past, of school dances that were long gone and hours spent in bedrooms dancing to CDs.

The younger children frolicked in pairs or threes and even by themselves. Little Joseph stood and swayed beside his mother's knee; his bright eyes fixed on the musicians. His fingers gently tapped out a perfect beat on his mother's arm.

The players, once they saw the youngsters on the floor, improvised a rendition of a more recent tune, the last recording by Lulu Barry. Carefree fun filled the evening.

Warren and Jean danced together. Warren's eyes closed. He held his love tight, lost in the music and memories, savouring his present happiness. The crowd formed a silent circle, honouring the pair as they shared such a special moment. Warren blushed deeply, and Jean buried her face in his chest in embarrassment in the moment of profound silence. Someone clapped, and the room filled with applause as the band broke into a subdued version of "They Could Have Danced All Night."

Jean looked into Warren's eyes and smiled with her heart full of love. She knew the tribute had been his and felt honoured he shared so much with her. Throughout the rest of the celebrations, people reached out, squeezed her hand, and gave Warren a pat on the shoulder or a handshake. Later, she told Sharon it felt like their wedding party. Sharon had smiled and kissed her.

Little children buzzed about between the adults' legs, exploring under the stage and chairs and having fun. Little Joseph hobbled about in pursuit of Megan and the others. Each child haunted the goodies table and like sponges, absorbed raspberry punch.

An older lady from the town, long separated from her grandchildren, relished the children's untamed enthusiasm. She stood behind the table beaming as she happily doled out treats to the youngsters. Gradually, the little ones tired and one after another sought parents' laps, eventually finding snug spots in piles of blankets in corners where they slept soundly despite the adult revelry about them.

Older children drifted in and out and sat talking on the steps and front yard of the centre. Teens paired up and wandered a little further into the night's shadows. There had been little chance of socializing in the past year, and normal yearnings and desires demanded attention.

Ben had somehow convinced Stephanie Hunter to take a walk with him. If he wanted to take advantage of the girl, she would disappoint him. Nurturing adults at Longview surrounded Stephanie, and her mother Debbie, as well as Kathie, Sharon, Brandi and Jani, had educated her in the realities of the world. Poor Ben was well short of having an advantage on the girl. She was; however, not averse to kissing, hugging and "fooling around", as Jani put it.

The pair's walk led to a more serious upset when they reached the bridge and listened to the water bubbling below. A few minutes of kissing passed with Stephanie frequently fending off the boy's roving hands. Suddenly, she pushed him away.

"Stop!" the girl screamed. Ben thought he had upset her with his insistence. "What's that smell?" she continued in shrill disgust.

"Ugh!" Ben had been too intent on his passion to notice the stench. Stephanie's outcry brought him to reality. "It smells like someone crapped in their pants."

"You're right," the girl giggled. "Did you?"

"I didn't do it!" replied a horrified Ben. Darkness hid his blush.

"What's going on here?" Jeff's angry voice came from the darkness. Heavy, quick steps sounded on the bridge.

"Are you okay, Steph?" The formidable young man crowded into their space, prepared to defend his adopted sister. "Ugh! What's that smell? Ben, did I scare you that bad?" He laughed, but his voice seemed menacing to Ben.

"I think it's the river." Stephanie had calmed. "That's disgusting. I'm out of here." She ran to the hall.

"That stink's bad," Ben was not sure if Jeff was angry with him. "I've smelt nothing like it."

"I have," Jeff leaned on the bridge railing trying to see the water in the darkness below. "When the sewage treatment plant failed in Weyburne, the stench was unbearable. The crap made the creek stink like this and worse. As bad as this is, it is nothing."

"Where did it come from?" Ben relaxed as Jeff focused on the river and not Ben's tryst with the girl.

"Only one place for that," a voice came from the darkness, startling Ben. Jeff calmly turned to the sound, "it has to be from up the hill, from Flesherton."

"Chester, you need commando training," Darkness hid Jeff's smile. "I hope you weren't sneaking up on us."

"I'm not wearing my moccasins," Chester liked the Shadly boy, "and Roger tells me your enormous feet sound like a bear in a berry bush." Chester leaned on the railing.

"It's time to deal with these jerks up in Flesherton. I will make the rounds tomorrow and get it going. This river is too valuable to have it destroyed by drunken idiots."

"When do we go?" Jeff was eager to get another chance to test his fighting skills.

"Slow down, soldier boy! Go home tomorrow and wait for orders. We've been working on a plan since the gunfire three months ago. People have to be contacted. Be patient."

Chester's mind was sharp and focused. He was happy he had not drunk too much high-octane brew. The sounds of laughter and music drifted through the night. It sounded safe and normal contrasting with the pungent smell of reality surrounding the two men. The evening had much fun left, but the call of duty would soon unite everyone in more desperate work.

Chapter Sixteen

"The start of that first military campaign was innocent enough. Chester sped off in his little truck towards Thornbury. The rest of us, in various stages of recovery from the wonderful party, found a place on the wagon returning to Longview. Soon, Brandi and I were climbing off, to begin our second walk up the road to Kimberly. The footfalls of the horses and the farewells from the people on the wagon faded up the Longview lane as the two of us turned to walk up the valley. The wind was chilly that morning, and my head hurt. It was not a pleasant walk."

From: "Conversations with Karen Lefevre," in the "Voices of the Founders," series by Erin Thomas

"Hello in there!" Sharon Shadly called through Karen's front door. "Is anyone home?"

"Hi Mom," Brandi replied from the classroom, helping a youngster learn to shade. "Karen's in the kitchen. What are you doing here?"

It had been a busy, worry-filled week since the party at Heathcote. Brandi stepped into the entranceway and stopped short. Her mother had dressed for hunting, with a peaked cap, heavy bush jacket, trousers and work boots. The .22 rifle hung over her shoulder.

"You look like a mountain woman!" Brandi smiled, but the sight unsettled her.

Out front, most of the Longview adults unloaded well-filled backpacks from a hay wagon. Don Hunter stood on the wagon holding the reins of the pair of Percheron. The horses contentedly lapped water from buckets; their dark, sweat-soaked flanks glistened from the effort. Jeff, dressed in military fatigues, his pistol on his hip and rifle slung across his back gently ran a hand along the heavy neck of the nearest beast.

"You look formidable." Karen surveyed the force. They exuded strength and purpose. The resolve and unity of Longview included several people from other farms. "What's going on?"

"The army's on the march." Bill sounded light-hearted. "We're meeting some others to liberate Flesherton."

"I bet you didn't think you'd be a general," Karen assumed Bill was the leader.

"You got the wrong Shadly," Bill replied. "There's the boss." Bill pointed to Jeff.

"At your service, mam," Jeff clicked his heels together and pretended to salute in the best British fashion. "We're waiting for Roger LaFarge's group from Meaford. They have the plan, and then we'll get on with it. More are on their way from Heathcote and Thornbury."

"The team's yours now," Jeff spoke to Don Hunter as he stowed the water buckets on the wagon. "Walk them back easy and rub them down well before you bed them."

"Good luck," Don shook Jeff's hand. "I'll try to treat them like you do." He snapped the rains. Don guided the team in a sweeping turn through the parking lot of the long-derelict ice-cream parlour. Tufts of grass, pushing through widening cracks in the asphalt, bent under the worn pneumatic tires. They swept past Jeff towards Longview.

"Hey, Sis," Jeff appeared from the late afternoon haze. Brandi toiled in the remnants of the vegetable garden.

"Hi, Jeff," Brandi threw a handful of dying bean vines into the barrow and stretched her back. "Is everyone settled? I hope Mom and Dad can eat with us tonight."

Jeff carried two rifles.

"We'll be there," Jeff grinned. "I miss your cooking, but we have something to do first. Things are dangerous right now and going to get worse. I want you to know how to use this." Jeff handed her the Savage 110 from the abandoned garage. "I don't need this one, and it has good firepower. If you learn to use it, you won't need to get close to a target."

At the far end of the field, a split-rail fence separated the property from the dirt and brush-covered clay foot-slope of the escarpment. It provided a safe backdrop for shooting. Jeff set up various sized bits of punk birch trunk as targets along the top rail. The white bark provided contrast at a distance.

"The telescopic sight is tricky." Jeff adjusted the weapon, and they retreated 100 meters. He slipped a cartridge into the chamber. Gripping the stock to his right shoulder, Jeff paused and squeezed the trigger.

The report startled Brandi. Her mom's small-bore rifle hardly made a sound. The blast echoed from Old Baldy and down the valley. Jeff grunted, adjusted the scope slightly and spent another round splitting one of the smaller bits of birch in two.

"I think that's good now."

It took a few attempts for Brandi to hit the largest target. The sound and kick from the weapon scared her, but after a half dozen tries, she felt comfortable, and an hour later, she could hit the smaller targets.

"Not bad," Jeff patted her on the head. "You learned quicker than I did, and your rifle is more accurate than this AK assault rifle. You need to pull the bolt each time to reload. The magazines are small, but I hope you never need over one or two shots. I'll show you how to reload."

They sat on the dry grass as Jeff loaded a small magazine with bullets. He then gave an empty one to Brandi and guided her in the effort.

"I have more magazines when you are in Longview. Carry them filled and a good bunch of loose rounds. There are at least a hundred bullets in this bag. You should always be prepared, if you are somewhere dangerous, keep it close and ready but the safety on until you decide to shoot."

"This is your rifle," Jeff said. "Think of it as all those birthday-presents I never gave you."

They headed to the house. Brandi proudly carried the weapon, rubbing her right shoulder. She forgot to snug the butt properly before taking a shot.

A contingent of thirty well-armed men and women arrived from Thornbury. The barrier on twenty-six had fewer guards. Stripping the defences was a risk but signified the importance of this operation. Along the river, the lingering odour of sewage motivated.

Those not suitable for the fight stayed at home, armed and ready. At Longview, Willard was the leader of several adults with light weapons. They could deal with all but a large and well-equipped threat.

Around midnight, Roger and Helen arrived with a larger contingent from Meaford, including a hundred volunteers, the army trainers, and part of Jeff's training company. All carried AKs, hunting rifles or 12 gauge shotguns. Roger took the leaders through the plan.

"We'll form two forces." Roger spread a map out on Karen's kitchen table. "A group split off from us and headed over to Rocklyn. They're coming down the road towards ten." His finger traced a line on the map. "We don't know what's up there, so it's a recon and clean up."

"How are we going to be organized?" Jeff still felt like a greenhorn.

"I'm leading one force and Roger the other." Helen peered at the paper. "My group will go down thirteen, join up with people from Maxwell and take Road Four towards Flesherton."

"The other group will follow me," Roger said. "We'll head along the bottom of the valley, past the generating station and follow the road along the Boyne towards the town. We'll come onto their Road Four blockade from behind. They're disorganized amateurs. We're more afraid of accidents than real fighting."

"What if the Rocklyn force flushes bad guys down off the hill?" Jeff saw that there would be a long, exposed flank along the west side of the valley.

"We'll leave a force here, about ten people," Roger showed the place where the two roads split about a kilometre before the hydro-electric installation, with one going west up the western slope of the valley, "to stop anyone coming down this road. Your parents and several other volunteers will be the rear guard and leave the hard marching to you youngsters."

"Once we deal with the barrier east of town, we'll plan our next moves. It's a bit of a mystery how they organized behind the barrier. I would rather capture them. Shooting will be the last resort. Most of these folks are people, maybe off the rails, but they are people and might join us. Just remember, if we have to shoot, we shoot to kill."

The murmur of agreement hid the unease of the inexperienced fighters. To them, life was getting too real; however, none of the force could know what was going through Roger's mind at that moment. Even though the woman he shot at the barrier was not the first enemy he had killed, it haunted.

Damn, he thought, *why did they have to grab those kids? Maybe we could have talked them down.*

"Turn in now," Roger did not betray any doubt. "We're leaving at sunrise to be in position by noon."

The troop slept fitfully and stirred before daylight, boiling water on newly built fires.

"Let's go!" Roger commanded as the first rays of sun hit the far valley top. Roger's group turned onto the valley road. The first few kilometres of their march would be flat and level. Helen's force faced a long, steep climb. Bill Shadly glanced up the hill, remembering walking with Jeff a year and a half before and glad he would not do it this time.

"Take care, Sniffles, and do me a favour, don't get shot. You won't be any good to me dead." Helen smiled and slapped Ted on the shoulder. Only she, Jeff and Ted knew the significance of her teasing. Ted assumed the best in her meaning. Jeff had doubts, but he had to admit Helen seemed to care. The two men exchanged glances. Ted's feet felt lighter on the pavement that morning.

"How do you feel?" Sharon asked Jeff. The family was together near the head of the line moving at a steady pace.

"I'm great, Mom," Jeff looked at Sharon from the far side of the road. They moved in two lines, on opposite roadsides, a spread out target against a surprise attack.

"You look professional, Mom. I hope nothing happens, but you'll do well." Jeff had seen his parents survive many trying situations. His mom had impressed him in bringing their convoy safely through the barrier into Huron. He felt proud of his parents and hoped he could measure up.

At the intersection Roger organized the rear guard.

"Put logs on that bridge, not too high so someone can hide behind but to stop a vehicle. Bill you're in charge. If you get through today with no fighting, you should be okay. The force coming down from Rocklyn will pass the other end of this road by suppertime. Stay on guard overnight and then come down the road towards Flesherton and find us. The password is pooper scooper."

The older people laughed.

The primary force headed south, towards the fight. The early October sun wore on them, and the road climbed towards an unknown end.

Roger sent out two scouts. The Flesherton crowd had a watch post on the road, but it had never been much. This end of the valley had little agricultural use with few travellers and a casual border.

At the watch post, they found the scouts seated in stuffed chairs deteriorated by weather. An old grizzled character cradled a small-gauge shotgun and shared his whiskey with the two scouts.

"Isn't this comfy," Roger muttered. "It's a funny way to fight a war."

The old man stared wide-eyed at the large force. "You guys hunting turkey?" Dirty teeth peeked out through an unkempt beard.

"Is that what you call the punks running Flesherton?" Roger gingerly retrieved the man's gun and found it not loaded.

"Looks like you folks mean business." The guard responded. "I take it you've had enough from us."

"Yes, we have," Roger said.

The elderly watchman smiled.

"If you don't mind, I'll just go on home and take care of my chickens and lambs. Most of the people are out retrieving the bit of grain they planted. You won't get much fight from many; they'll mostly welcome you, but there are a few tough skunks. Don't be turning your back on them. They've been scaring us all."

The geezer carried his shotgun west. The force headed east.

"Rick," Roger turned to one scout. "I know you have been with me crawling around the hills in Africa, but that was a gigantic risk you took there? That could have gotten you killed."

"Look, ma mère," Rick grinned, "we cleared the gun, and when the old guy said it had been his pappy's best shotgun and he wanted to keep it, we gave it back. Sorry if we scared you."

The force walked towards the main road. At a slight bend, they slid off through the trees to a roadside ditch. In the far field, people loaded grain onto a wagon. A house sat at each corner of the intersection.

"Jeff," Roger whispered, "Take four guys to the first house, clear it and try not to be seen by the guys in the field."

Jeff tapped Ted on the shoulder and selected three others. They crab-crawled up the ditch, slipped through the decorative cedars behind the house and ran across the yard. Jeff and Ted squeezed against the wall on each side of the back door as two of the others checked each side. One remained in the trees for covering fire. Jeff nodded. Ted pulled the storm door open with a loud squeak. Jeff burst through, rifle ready, followed by Ted. There was no sound in the gloomy interior. Jeff moved cautiously through the kitchen, peering down the main hallway.

As he travelled down the passage, Jeff could just make out a low, somehow familiar sound. He first thought the living room was empty but then noticed a tattered playpen in the corner emitting low gurgling sounds. Jeff eased across the room, weapon ready. He found an unhappy sight. A baby, dirty, emaciated and making bubbling sounds, perhaps a few months older than Little Bill looked up at him. She smiled. Jeff teared up.

"Ted, make sure the place is clean." He could barely speak.

Jeff gathered the emaciated body to his chest, talking in low, reassuring tones, ignoring the unbearable stench coming from the little bundle. He could find no clean clothes for the baby. He located a relatively clean sheet and a bucket of water and cleaned the baby as best he could. The rawness of the little girl's buttocks sickened, but Jeff persevered until a dry diaper covered the wee frame. As he worked, he gave the fragile creature sips of water from his bottle. The baby accepted the liquid, obviously used to drinking from a cup.

The rest of the force secured the crossroad and rounded up the workers in the field. The captives thought the baby's mother had gone to the village. As the old man had promised, they found the field workers docile and friendly and a source of information. They would have to fight, but so far no hostiles knew a battle had begun.

"I hear shooting," Ted reacted to the distant rattle of rifle fire.

The roadblock was about half a kilometre to the east near a gravel pit where a creek passed under the roadway. If things had gone to plan, Helen had set up flanking attacks and occupied the gravel pit. A small force would fire from directly in front to attract attention while the flanking forces closed in to attack from the rear. The Huron barriers prevented encirclement, but the forces up here had poor leadership and fewer resources. Roger organized a squad to support Helen's force. His job had been to secure this crossroad to cut off reinforcements, but he had plenty of troops to augment Helen's attack.

A motorcycle sped from the direction of the fighting. Roger stepped into the road and put up a hand. The man slowed slightly, trying to aim a rifle. Half a dozen shots rang out. The rider flew off as his bike flipped into the ditch. His body bounced to a stop in the centre of the road about twenty meters from Roger.

"Damn, why did he have to be a hero?" Several men and women cleared their weapons. "Someone get the body off the road."

Jeff comforted the baby that screamed in fright from the loud gunfire. More shooting came from the barrier.

"Hold this position," Roger left a squad to guard the intersection. Jeff left the sobbing little girl in their care and jogged towards the shooting.

"Hit the ditch, north side!" Roger led by example.

"Where's the wind, Shadly?" Roger unhooked a smoke canister from his webbing. "They pinned Helen down behind the gravel pit southeast of those guys. It looks like all the bad guys are in this north side ditch. Our guys are up on the ridge east of their barrier and have a good look down on it, but they can't get direct fire into the ditch. We need to get behind them. Damn, the other flanking squad is late."

"Wind is light, out of the north-west." Jeff interrupted.

"Okay, I am going to throw this smoke out into the field, so it drifts between them and us. Shadly, take five guys and head into the creek on the other side. Slide up so you are northwest of them. If they come at you, let them get to about 100 and shoot. You shouldn't be in line with any of our fire, but don't take a stray bullet. We're going to fire directly down the ditch."

Roger pulled the pin and heaved the canister twenty-five meters into the field. Smoke drifted downwind between them and the hostile force.

Jeff's squad took off at a run. He could hear rifle fire from Roger's group as he ran low and hard towards the green line of the creek bed. It seemed a long way off, but he knew the open field would only expose them for about thirty seconds. Suddenly, he heard a whizzing sound as a bullet passed near. Then another one missed. There was a sound of an impact and cry behind, but following their training, they kept going. Five of them reached the ditch.

"Cameron got it," someone said. "I thought I was a goner too."

Jeff peered back from his spot in the creek. Water covered his legs and boots, but the rest was on the dry bank. Cameron lay in the field, not moving.

"Let's get this done quick so we can help him." Jeff looked towards the road. From this vantage, he could see six armed men crouching in the ditch. "Let's go!"

Jeff ran up the creek closer to the hostiles. Sustained fire erupted from Roger's position. A sharp cry rose from the enemy. A bullet had hit.

Suddenly, heavy fire erupted to their left from over the swamp. The other flanking group from Helen's force had finally gotten into the fight. The cries from the enemy confirmed accuracy. Jeff saw four men in the road ditch stand up with their hands in the air. A red flare rose from the far side of the road above the gravel pit.

"Cease fire," Roger's voice came from the distance. A shot rang out from Jeff's left. One of the surrendering men fell to the ground.

"I said cease-fire," Roger sounded angry. A second red flare arced high into the sky. All shooting stopped. Jeff's group closed on the surrendering men, slowly; rifles ready. One person writhed in pain on the ground. Two others lay silent. Roger's group ran up the road.

"Get your hands behind your heads, on the road and down on your knees!" Jeff barked the command.

"Good work, Jeff." Roger was calm and businesslike. "We saw Cameron get hit. Sue and George are over with him. Who the hell took that last shot?"

"I'll go help with Cameron," responded Jeff. He was trying to control his shaking after the rush of the fight.

Jeff headed to where his comrade lay. They could do nothing but gently carry the body to the road and cover it with a tunic. The bullet had passed through his chest. Cameron had died instantly.

Helen's group arrived along with the flanking party and the force from the barrier. A runner raced off for medical help. One of Helen's fighters had suffered a broken hand when splinters flew up from a bullet hitting a rock. Ted joined a grieving Jeff on the side of the road.

"I feel horrible." Ted began. "Cameron volunteered, from Meaford. I liked him." Jeff nodded. The two remained silent until a shadow fell over them. Helen gazed down with sympathy.

"It's never easy to lose a friend." Helen crouched. "I've seen too many deaths, and it doesn't matter if it is the first or the most recent. It rips your guts out, and you cry."

"Is it worth it?" Jeff stirred. "I've seen too much killing."

Helen's face darkened, "if we don't do this, a lot more will die and maybe a horrible slow death, starving, abused and all that. I saw a lot in Africa. I'm sad guys die to protect other criminals." She jerked her head towards where the dead hostiles lay. "People get far off the rails and can't think straight."

She squeezed Jeff's shoulder. "Never stop feeling bad about it, but don't let it stop you. You are a good soldier. More will die under your command, but fewer will die because you care."

Helen turned to Ted. "I know you have been on the other end of killing." She took his hand in hers. "I hope you never start feeling good about it." She leaned forward and whispered something in Ted's ear, then abruptly walked off to help process the prisoners.

"What was that about?" Jeff stood in his waterlogged boots.

"She said we could meet at her place in Meaford, if I wanted to discuss it more. What does she mean?" Ted followed Jeff to his feet. Jeff managed a smile.

"She whispered it. That should tell you everything."

Kathy Nelson and Stephanie Hunter arrived in Sharon's old red van, brought up from Longview White circles painted on the doors and roof left a red cross in each circle. Stephanie, shaken and pale, had never seen a corpse. The grisly scene in the ditch horrified her.

"It's horrible," Jeff put his arm over her shoulders "I'm bummed out."

They stood silently, and then Stephanie found some strength and went to the soldier with the broken hand. She gingerly explored the damage and slung up the arm, supporting the hand. Kathy had transformed her into a competent nurse.

Kathy examined the wounded captive. The nasty bullet hole in his side had spared anything vital. She replaced the crude dressing and placed him in the van beside Cameron's body. The man with the broken hand climbed into the front. Kathy sped off. The surgeon from Meaford had arrived at Kimberly. The victim would have to suffer. Painkillers were in short supply and saved for more severe cases. These men had drunk some whiskey. It would ease the pain for a short time.

"The booze in him will help." Roger's watched the van disappear down the road. "Probably being drunk made these guys into heroes."

"Come here, Shadly." LaFarge sounded gruff. He was upset by the deaths and second-guessing his decision to send Jeff's squad across the field. If he had known the flanking force was going to show up, he never would have exposed his men, but with work to do before dark he had no time for remorse.

"Helen's taking the primary force down Road Four. These guys," he jerked a thumb towards the prisoners, "told us most fighters are in town."

Roger spread his map on the crumbling asphalt. "Shadly, you and I are going to the left, down that side road." His finger showed the direction. "I'll take the first road over to highway ten and head back to town. Helen and I'll flank them. We expect the guys from Rocklyn and the others from the west to connect the other side of town this afternoon. We have them in a vice, and the only place they can run is to the south. It might be good if they all run away. We can't count on it."

"Helen, you send two pairs with AKs off to the left through these trees. I'll put three more below them. They will set up positions at the creek so they can stop anyone coming out, just in case these guys know how to fight and try to flank us. We'll be coming down the highway. I worry about the school, motel and arena."

He looked at Jeff. "Shadly, this is your second command. You didn't get to do much last time." He flashed Jeff a thin smile. "You'll continue to the second crossroads, to the highway and then left to their barrier on ten. Last we heard they only have a couple of guys there. Go slowly and decide on tactics once you see how they're set up. They might have heard the gunfire. The ones in town know all about us by now."

Roger paused as Helen organized her force. "Helen, leave that one with me," he pointed at Will Sullivan whose shot had killed the already surrendered defender. "We have business to discuss."

He turned back to Jeff. "Once you have taken the barrier, go past it to this road and south over to the next one then back up towards Road Four. When you get there, secure the intersection and wait. Watch for us coming out of town. The guys from the Sound will come down the other way. Be ready for any birds we flush out, either on the road or in the bush. If we're tied down in the village, you come in behind to outflank them."

"What about the other roads and farms?" Jeff saw a lot of countryside to cover with his small force.

"I think they forced the people to work and they will be friendly like that first lot. Watch your back." Roger stood. "Let's go! We want it done before dark if we can. Rick, you and Bobbie take the prisoners to the slaughterhouse and come back to the crossroads."

"Come on you three," Rick growled at the prisoners. "Get your asses in gear." Rick was a middle-aged man with long hair and an unkempt, greying red beard. Being a volunteer from Thornbury, he was happy to be out of the developing fight. He pulled the nearest prisoner to his feet. All had their hands cuffed behind their backs. Stout rope bound them together about two meters apart.

"What happens if we make a break for it?" One captive was defiant despite his bonds.

"Well then, buddy," Rick drew his words out, and his lips curled into a smile that peeked out from his scruffy beard, "I'll shoot you. These two won't drag your body far," Rick snicked his rifle bolt, bringing a cartridge into firing position. The prisoner said no more.

Jeff organized the twenty men in his squad. He made sure Ted walked at his side in front of the hodgepodge of trained recruits and volunteers.

As they waited for Roger, Jeff called out to Helen. "They have a baby at the crossroads. Its mother is probably in town. If you come across someone asking about the baby send them to the corner."

Roger's bunch started out on the right side of the road, and Jeff's on the left. Roger turned down the next road. The last Jeff heard was Roger, lecturing Will Sullivan.

"Why did you shoot? The guy had surrendered. Why were you late? It cost Cameron's life."

Jeff's contingent reached their objective with several hours of daylight remaining. To their advantage, the sun shone from behind them.

"Ted, you and Turtle go to the edge of the bush where you can get a clear shot." Jeff pointed. Turtle had gotten his nickname because he was invariably the last one to arrive at almost everything during training. After Ted, he was the best sharpshooter of the group.

"We're going to capture that house. It might be the barrier HQ. If there are more than those two on the road, they'll be in the house. We'll take the house then rush the barrier. If I fire a shot, take the two out."

Everything went smoothly. The squad occupied the empty house. Jeff's platoon sprinted the sixty meters to the barrier. Once the pair saw nineteen fighters approaching with rifles levelled, they raised their hands. Their weapons leaned against a derelict car, carelessly out of reach.

Too easy, Shadly thought.

"Hit the deck!" Jeff cried out. A table had three place-settings. "Look sharp! There's another one somewhere."

Both captives glance towards the trees on the far side of the road. Jeff twisted around for a better look. The creek wandered away to the north, lined with a small stand of birch. A breeze rattled the yellow leaves. Jeff studied the scene, searching for a sign, a movement or a familiar shape.

There! He calmly raised his rifle and put a slug into a birch trunk about forty meters away. A woman jumped up; her hands stretched high beside the bullet-scarred trunk. Her red bandana had betrayed her.

"Hey boss," Ted and Turtle arrived from the woods. "I'm glad I'm smart enough to know your shot didn't mean for me to shoot." He chuckled; happy he did not have to kill. "You'd look funny with a bullet up your ass."

The company roared with laughter, tension released, and they relaxed.

Jeff felt confident as commander and selected four to guard the barrier and prisoners until relieved. With no time for niceties, the captives would endure bound discomfort until after the fighting.

The force hurried off. Two fighters formed a rear guard, following the main body by a few hundred meters.

"Why are we women always being left to cover your asses?" Jeff had chosen the only women in his group.

"Well, this is a cleanup position, and that's woman's work." Jeff appeared to be serious.

"You're a chauvinist bastard!" One of them exclaimed, but then she added, "Don't you have a sweet little woman back home who tells you what to do? Oh yes, it's that Jani girl you keep bragging about. I'll chat with her and the rest of your life will be hell." The women chuckled.

"Okay, okay," Jeff surrendered. "Jane, I know you two are good shots and will stay alert. If someone tries to ambush us, I expect you will deal with them. At least warn us. You can come down to Longview anytime and visit. Jani will have us all hoeing potatoes real quick."

The force worked back towards Road Four. If anyone had heard Jeff's shot, there was no sign of it. Workers laboured in several fields, but they simply stared at the group of armed fighters. The setting sun in their eyes caused the worst problem requiring them to move cautiously. They reached the intersection just as the sun dropped behind a wooded hill. They had heard sporadic gunfire, but it faded to silence. Jeff deployed his force in a defensive arrangement. With darkness falling, he did not want anyone wandering around risking an accident. Jeff knew Helen and Roger would go to ground for the night. No one wanted to risk moving in the dark in unknown enemy territory. Jeff organized watches, and everyone found places to sleep. Jeff selected a spot amid his force and lay down beneath a leafless tree.

Jani, hug Little Bill for me, he thought as his tired body crashed, and he drifted into a fitful sleep.

"Shadly... wake up!" A female voice came from the darkness.

"Jani, it's too early."

"Not the right gal, lover boy," Helen chuckled. "You don't qualify for more sleep."

Jeff stood, trying to get his bearings. Helen, looking tired in the pale dawning, had a job for Jeff.

"A few bad guys escaped," the woman continued. "We don't care but want to make sure they went far enough. It would be inconvenient to get shot in the back." Shadly did not appreciate her macabre humour before sunrise.

"How are things?" Jeff's squad moved about in the half-light, trying to warm up. A blazing fire suggested safety.

"They put up a good fight at first." Helen offered Jeff a sip of water. "We traded heavy fire on the way into town, but they were disorganized and incompetent with no fire control. We soon had them on the run. These guys are just a bunch of gangsters, not an army or even a decent militia.

They had bullied defenceless people; when they saw our firepower, most gave up." She paused for a drink.

"Just like at the barrier, the ones with a bit of booze in them were the worst, too drunk to surrender. Most of those are dead. We have a bunch tied up at the intersection. Chester is on their way to sort out the real bad ones. We want to release the rest as soon as possible."

"Is there any word on my dad, mom and the others?"

"We didn't hear of any fighting. The Rocklyn group arrived just before dark, herding a few more into the bag. They didn't see a hostile until they hit the outskirts of Flesherton. We sent a runner down the valley to meet your parent's group. It would be good to send them straight home, but we need people to occupy the town."

"Once Chester starts, we think there will be a lot of information to follow up. It might be a few days before we can start releasing the volunteers. You can count on at least a couple of weeks up here." The pair wandered over to the fire, surrounded by eager listeners.

"What we don't know," Helen continued, "is what's beyond here, down to Priceville. We want you to check it out. It's about seven kilometres, and it would be best to get there before sunrise. We guess there will be no opposition, but we want to know. The Owen Sound force only went down to Irish Lake. Somewhere below is the People's Liberation Movement. If you come across them, you are to stop and not rile them up. We aren't ready to take them on."

Someone gave Jeff a warm drink. He retrieved a makeshift breakfast of bread and smoked pork from his pack.

"What are my orders, if I find any of these goons?"

"Open orders. You decide what you have to do on the spot. We would prefer prisoners. If you have to shoot, then do what you need to do. Sorry, I can't tie it up nice and neat for you. We're inventing as we go." Helen smiled and yawned. Jeff wondered if she had slept at all.

"Okay, I'll take Ted and ten others, enough for a recon."

"You sure like having Ted around," Helen observed. "He's a handy guy."

"I trust him," Jeff replied, searching the woman's face for any sign of her intentions. "He's honest, smart and willing to think and keeps me straight." He looked directly into Helen's eyes. The last thing he wanted was for her to mislead Ted.

"I agree," she whispered. "Get going and try to be back before noon. I'm retracing your route to the barrier on ten to collect the prisoners."

She walked away. As far as Jeff could tell, she had not talked to Ted. He finished his meal and looked for the people he wanted. Jeff would not take the volunteers. He felt they had served enough.

Five minutes after Helen left, Jeff's force was on the road hurrying towards the smaller town. An hour later, they crested a hill to see the lifeless village spread out below. The sun had not risen, and the dwellings slept in shadow.

"What do you think, Ted?" He swept the valley with his sniper scope.

"It's quiet," Ted began and then paused. "There, on the right, in a shadow, a man, unarmed. I don't see anyone else."

"Okay, we are going ahead, keep looking." Jeff un-shouldered his weapon. The force made their way slowly down the hill in a staggered line. About fifty meters from the man, Jeff rushed to close the gap.

"Come out here," Jeff commanded, his rifle menacing. The rest of the squad checked alleys and alcoves on both sides of the street. Ted used his scope to check windows and the far end of the street. All remained quiet.

"Don't shoot, mister. I ain't got a gun." The man stepped into the strengthening light. "I saw you coming. Could've run; I didn't."

"What's your story?" Jeff frisked the man. He had no weapon.

"I guess I'm the greeting party," he fidgeted and stuffed his hands into his coat pockets. "When we heard about the fighting, we gathered in the old church, six families, everyone left in town."

The man led the way up the street towards the spire of an old brick church. Even before the crisis, this crumbling house of worship had become an oversized reminder of better times. With no heat for several winters, the mortar cracked, and bricks had fallen off. Peeling paint and windows, opaque from dirt, completed the picture of decay.

The sorry condition of the half dozen families cringing inside blended with the squalor of the building. Jeff gathered them on the fragmenting concrete church steps, ten sobbing children and fourteen adults. Jeff asked for people's names and everyone volunteered bits of the story.

Many people left or died during the past four years. It was an all too familiar tale. The mob from Flesherton came and demanded payment. The gangsters used guns and killed one man who resisted. Jeff made a note for later follow-up. As Helen had said, they wanted to sort out the real criminals from those whom they could rehabilitate. After the killing, everyone complied. They farmed and paid a tax that left them short, but able to survive.

"What's down the road?" These people were not a threat. Jeff wanted to decide how far to take his squad before turning back.

"There's a roadblock." The man from the shadows spoke up, "with a tough bunch protecting the hydro line. They leave us alone, and we ain't had no trouble, as long as we don't cross into their territory."

"Take me there. I want a look."

Jeff returned within an hour.

"Okay guys, let's get back." Jeff did not want to rest. "We need to get to Flesherton. The blockade on the road is a danger."

Jeff left his people at the crossroads. The force from Owen Sound had arrived and guarded the road to Irish Lake, following the Huron Council's directive to secure the Saugeen watershed boundary.

Once the population realized the invaders were friendly, the people, who had lived through several years of oppression, showed relief and gratitude.

Jeff arrived in Flesherton to various pieces of good news. He could hug his parents and Stephanie Hunter dressed his foot blisters in the makeshift infirmary, where he found a connection to Weyburne.

"You're Brandi's brother, aren't you?" Jeff turned to a dishevelled middle-aged woman with a blood-soaked rag covering a painful hand wound and waiting her turn as Kathy tended to Jeff.

"Yes, I'm Jeff Shadly. Do I know you?"

"I'm Samantha James. I taught Brandi at Weyburne, in the church basement."

"Oh, yes!" Jeff exclaimed. He remembered Samantha, but she was almost unrecognizable. "Brandi loved you. How's Mr James?"

"Better than I am," she winced, waving her injured hand towards Jeff. "We've been here almost a year. How's my star pupil?"

"Brandi's working with another woman, teaching and learning to write and draw. She might be up here soon." Kathy checked Stephanie's dressing on Jeff's blisters. He moved, allowing Samantha to take her turn.

"How did you do that?" Kathy asked.

"When the shooting started, I was on the street and had to take cover. I broke a window and cut myself on the glass." Kathy gingerly removed the old rag, revealing a nasty, deep cut. A small amount of blood oozed. The nurse set about cleaning the injury and applied a dressing.

"How did you get up here?" Jeff asked.

"We stuck it out for a few months after you all left. You badly hurt the Smith boy at the jail and caused a violent reaction. Roger Smith seized the high school, trashed everything, and they harassed us, even the Reverend." She winced as Kathy finished tying off her bandage.

"In September, they tried to conscript every able-bodied person for their army. The first people they took either died or just wore out. We hid in Reverend Wright's house for several days and then headed here. Unfortunately, we stayed too close to Highway 10, and these thugs grabbed us. It wasn't pleasant working for them but less dangerous than going to war for Smith and Angel."

"Two of my friends ran for it about the time we left," Jeff said, "maybe I'll find them here."

"There's no one else from Weyburne, but people grateful you freed them. Around here, it looked like an amateur night at the feudal castle with us as glorified serfs. These guys were incompetent but brutal."

"You'll find us a lot better." Jeff smiled. "Our people will want to interview you. We need to know about the threat from Weyburne. Mom and Dad are here. They'll love to see you. I'll tell Brandi when I see her."

Jeff hoisted his rifle and headed for the door. He hugged Stephanie as she fussed over a baby.

"They found this little girl on the edge of town," Stephanie frowned. I think we can save her.

"I'm the one who found her. She was a mess. I cleaned her as best I could and left her with the rearguard. Is there any sign of her parents?"

"You are a softy, new daddy!" Stephanie smiled, "I hope I catch one like you. We haven't found them yet. It's strange; a mother should be desperate to find her baby."

Jeff frowned and stepped out the door. Samantha James' stare followed him.

So young and so grown up and mature, she thought, feeling sad, *and living in a world where he's a boy who has to carry a gun.*

***

Jeff leaned against a railing in front of the dilapidated high school serving as the Huron force's headquarters. The surroundings gave Jeff a flashback to Weyburne.

The building had suffered weather damage. The pipes had frozen and burst. Many shattered windows reflected the gangsters' penchant for drunken shooting. Salvage teams would likely dismantle the structure, but it would do for the required few days.

A barking dog startled Jeff. He had not heard a dog anywhere for several years. They all disappeared in Weyburne in the first year of the crisis. Most had probably starved to death, but he knew desperate people had eaten some. The sound of the dog gave hope. Jeff pondered going in search of the animal.

Chester's little pickup truck sped into the parking lot, squealing to a stop on its deteriorating brakes. Chester and another armed man hopped out. Brandi leapt from the truck box and rushed to hug her brother.

"I am happy you're alive." She squeezed him tight. "I saw Mom and Dad in town. Chester wouldn't stop." Brandi hugged him again.

"Hey," Jeff smiled, "leave some for Jani." There had been little family time the past few months, and he knew the future would be the same. Jeff hoped the family would be together for at least this night.

"I never came close to dying." Jeff deliberately left out the episode when Cameron died. "How were things in Kimberly, and why are you here? Not that I am unhappy seeing you, my little twerp."

Brandi gave her brother a hard punch on the shoulder. "You aren't the only big shooter in the family." Brandi teased. "I've used the rifle."

"What!" Jeff exclaimed, suddenly serious. He had not heard of fighting towards Kimberly. The rifle slung over her shoulder with Brandi's journal case. "I didn't know about shooting down there."

"Lighten up, Brother," Brandi enjoyed his concern but wanted to tell her story. "It was nothing serious and no bad guys. A big white-tailed eight-point buck wandered into the garden behind Karen's house to eat leftover cabbage. I took the trusty Savage, and we have venison curing in the shed. Karen's handy with a knife. I was shaking too much after I shot it. She bled it, and we hung it from the rafters. I didn't want to shoot; it was beautiful," Brandi looked sad. "It will give us some winter protein."

"My sister the hunter," Jeff hugged her again, jealous; he had not gotten a deer up at Meaford.

"Brandi, can you come in, please?" Chester called.

"I'm here to document this. It's my first actual job." Brandi headed off. "Get Mom and Dad here for supper."

She disappeared past the broken door into the gloom.

Brandi spent the afternoon recording Chester interviewing captives. They accused some with crimes of slavery, rape and murder. Chester had an impressive list of complaints, and only a fraction of the population had made statements. It would be a sad, hard task to sort the evidence and find the guilty. They wanted to salvage as many people as possible. No one knew how to punish the real criminals.

The Shadlys shared supper with a war council of Chester, Roger, Helen and representatives from Owen Sound and Meaford. The group gathered around a fire in front of the high school and ate rations from their packs. Brandi sketched furiously.

"You've done a magnificent job," Chester gazed around the circle. As daylight faded, the dancing light of the flames bathed everyone in a cheerful glow. "I know it was hard, and we'll mourn Cameron forever, but we've freed a lot of good people from oppression."

Chester's words reflected satisfaction and the sadness. They could see other campfires in the darkness. Small groups of fighters had settled for the evening. The faint strains of a harmonica warbled through the darkness as Walt and the rest of the Longview group bedded down.

"We have to make some decisions," Chester continued. "We border a more serious threat. Jeff, you found an outpost out on Four, I believe."

"There's a barrier on the road west of Priceville." Jeff glanced around the circle. "I saw six guards on it, and they seemed alert. They're stronger than this garbage we just rounded up. It's a well laid out operation. My guide claimed they are allies of the PLM in Toronto, guarding the transmission line from Bruce Nuclear to the city. He couldn't tell me how many people they had, but he had never seen six on the barrier before."

"They patrol the line down to Dufferin," said one man from Owen Sound. "We have shortwave radio contacts telling us they're guarding a swath about twenty kilometres wide with the transmission line in the middle. There's a strongman down in Dufferin, and his force takes over there. They'll likely defend the line to the death."

The news reminded the Shadlys of Smith, Angel and the sad memories of Weyburne.

"Our force went beyond Southampton and ran into a defensive position." Another of the strangers from Owen Sound spoke. "We stopped there and withdrew to the bridge over the Saugeen. It seems quiet. The locals say the force is friendly enough and guarding the nuke plant, not expanding territory."

"We have a problem," Chester seemed tired. "I think the PLM liked this bunch of gangsters running things here. They weren't a threat and were a buffer. Unless they have spies in Huron, they wouldn't have known much about us. Now they know we're a competent force and a threat."

"Why don't we just take out their forces around here?" Jeff was eager. "They don't have many troops."

"Hold on there, General," Helen laughed. "We could probably whip the bunch here, but once Toronto found out they would muster a much larger force and would defeat us. We don't know what weapons they have or how many fighters."

Jeff felt silly for suggesting it.

"I would propose," Chester said, "we don't go too far from highway ten and 21. We should put observers out but make sure we don't start trouble. Did we liberate any reliable people out that way?"

"I already set it up down to Markdale and out to Chippewa Hill so we can just fine tune." The man from Owen Sound consulted a map. "A few isolated groups are farming southwest of here near Irish Lake. We should set them up to be spotters like we have on the high ground east of Beaver Valley."

"Take out culverts to block roads." Chester leaned over to check the map. "The PLM will see we are making a defensive perimeter and not attack. Jeff, you'll be looking after the work down near Priceville. See if you can get a message to the barrier guards to let them know we've no intention of attacking."

"These people are way behind with their harvest," Sharon spoke up. "How can we help?"

"How about you and Bill see what they need. Can some of us spare a week of labour? The prospects over winter are bad for these people."

"We'll try." Sharon did not think a week would be sufficient but wanted to be home with Jani and her grandson.

"HALT!" A loud challenge came from one of Chester's bodyguards at the road.

"We're the James. We know the Shadlys." Brandi hurried toward Samantha James' voice, and they appeared walking arm in arm.

"Do you want to come down when we return home?" Sharon asked Samantha.

"We've made friends up here," the teacher replied. "Brent and I discussed it and decided we would stay here, at least for the winter. It wouldn't be right to abandon them, and we want to start a school."

"We'll make sure you get whatever we can spare," Bill replied

"We can support you from our school in Kimberly," Brandi relished working with her former teachers.

The exhausted group faded away. Only the Shadly family and the two teachers remained to watch the fire die. Sleep soon overpowered everyone.

Chapter Seventeen

Jeff walked up the lane to Longview near the end of October. Smoke rose from several chimneys. Flurries hung in the air. The new residence dominated the entrance to the farmyard. A structure, planned for the opposite side of the lane would create a walled village.

Sharon rushed down the lane to greet him, while Jani stood on the porch with Little Bill in her arms. Jeff felt the wonderful peace of a soldier coming home.

"We're so glad you're back," Sharon hugged him tightly. "We've had enough excitement for this year. Everyone hopes for a quiet winter."

"It was rough, Mom," Jeff smiled and looked beyond to his own family. "I just want to have a nice Longview meal and a soft bed. I hate digging and sleeping on the ground in October."

Jeff held Jani in a lingering embrace. Sharon cradled Little Bill, gently cooing and smiling. Finally, Jeff let go and took Little Bill, holding him to his chest, rubbing his bearded face against the baby's cheek. The little one struggled and fussed but looked into his father's eyes and smiled. For Jeff, it all seemed worthwhile.

At the midday meal, Jeff teased Willard about being commander of Fort Long. Someone suggested Jeff could use a good bath.

"I am going to have to make a quick trip in a few days," Jeff told the throng, looking solemn.

"You just got home!" Sharon and Jani exclaimed in unison. "Get Chester on the phone!" The laughter softened Sharon's pang of sorrow.

"Don't worry, Mom; it'll be good. I have a letter for Warren and Jean." Jeff smiled and handed the paper to the couple. The pair remained silent as they read the letter. Jeff talked about Flesherton.

"We'll need to donate food. Chester reckons they don't have enough until next harvest. We don't want to move anyone off suitable land. On the bright side, we've added good citizens to Huron. Drunkards released the crap from the broken sewage plant. People had switched to outhouses, but the old stuff was the problem."

"We must get the composting system spread all over," Warren said nothing about the letter.

"Anyway," Jeff continued, "the James set up a little school, and there's a lot of excitement."

"That's good news," Warren said, "and related to this letter."

*Finally, p*eople thought, *he's going to let us know.*

"This is from Chester and Karen." Warren lifted the letter. "They have asked Jean and me to go to Kimberly to help Karen and Brandi build the learning centre. They think we have something to offer."

Warren's attempt at modesty failed. Everyone at the table respected his knowledge, insight and imagination. He deserved the privilege and would be a profound influence on developing a sound education system. Everyone jumped to their feet, shouting and clapping. Little Bill cried. The other young ones joined in, unsure why the grownups were excited.

"Don and I'll take you up to Kimberly in a few days." Jeff raised his voice above the din. "Thank you for everything you have taught me and for the encouragement back in Weyburne." Jeff nearly said "back home," but caught himself. Longview was home. Many choruses of "me too," and "yes you did," rose around the table.

Kathy leaned over to Ellen and said, "We have a big family here."

The frail woman watched her enthusiastically cheering children, their faces radiant, and a tear came to her eyes. She squeezed Kathy's hand and felt growing peace. Little Bill wailed, and Jani took him to the quiet of the kitchen. Jeff's gaze followed them through the doorway.

Don Hunter stood silently, knowing Jeff had just given him responsibility for the horses. He had much to learn but felt like an adult.

***

A snow-covered team of horses and a wagon pulled up in front of Karen Lefevre's gate. Tarps covered a pile of belongings as well as two individuals huddling against the cold beneath the canvas. Don and Jeff sat together on the front of the wagon, covered with their own blankets of snow, their legs hung above the tongue.

"This makes us men!" Jeff slipped from his perch and shook snow from his clothes. "I don't think the boys like it." The horses tossed their heads, snorting loudly.

Karen and Brandi rushed out to help Warren and Jean into the house.

"Will you stay for a bit?" Brandi asked.

"Sorry, Sis, we have to get back. The team is wet and cold and need the barn. It'll be over two hours to get home even with the wind behind us. We'll go as soon as they finish their water."

As he rubbed down the horses, removing snow and slush, Don watched Brandi and Jeff talking. He had a crush on the girl, but sadly, her future no longer lay at Longview. There were no other suitable girls at home and even fewer chances to meet ones off the farm. He had met a couple of nice girls at the harvest party, but they were in Thornbury. Don wished Jeff would stay, but the new father wanted to get back to Jani and Little Bill. They called goodbyes as Don guided the team past the house. He held the reins loosely, letting the team have its head. The horses moved briskly knowing a warm stall and food waited.

"We put you in this back bedroom." Karen showed the couple around the house. "This is your house now. You needn't ask for anything, but if you move the furniture let me know, so I don't crash into it in the dark."

Karen felt as if several generations of a family shared the house with Warren and Jean the grandparents, Karen a daughter, Brandi a granddaughter. She embraced the wonderful sensation with all her heart.

The next few days had cool clear skies, and Warren and Jean explored the hamlet. Several older residents welcomed new people their age. Warren listened more than he spoke and mostly asked questions. He and Jean soon had a decent understanding of the town. The list of resources and skills was impressive. They befriended one young man who excited Warren.

"Here's my shop," the man held the door open. "I don't have electricity to run the machines, but I can build anything with hand tools."

A wooden sash window illuminated an inspiring collection of saws and other woodworking machines, with shelves of hardware and an extensive collection of hand tools.

"I'll see what I can do about electricity," Warren said. "Would you be willing to conduct woodworking classes?"

"I would love to do it."

The man and his wife had hung on in town hopeful things would improve. They helped their neighbours with repairs and raising food.

Most of the people in Kimberly helped on neighbouring farms, working for grain as some had done at Longview. Everyone had substantial vegetable gardens and chickens. It encouraged Warren and Jean.

"I'll tell you what I need," Warren sat with Jean, Karen and Brandi around the big pine kitchen table, "a sunny acre or two for seed plots so we can work on improving the varieties. A greenhouse would be great. Do you think we could get something rough for next spring?"

Karen took notes. Warren listed a workshop for repairing and making implements, space where they could experiment with new ideas for technology and try to reverse engineer old equipment. He soon converted the list into a detailed plan.

"We first need to organize." Warren thought of when they created the Emergency Aid Committee in Weyburne and found fresh energy.

"Whoa!" Karen exclaimed. "We first need to put together a general plan and get Chester to take it to the Huron council. They have approved what we are doing, but we need resources to make the ideas come to life."

"We need a mandate and a mission." Jean remembered the formation of the Centreville council and the Emergency Aid Committee in Weyburne, "and we need a name." She brought the others back to basics.

"What should we call ourselves?" It excited Brandi.

"The Beaver River Institute," Jean loved the river.

"It's too limiting," Karen replied, "but I like the word Institute. It sounds official. Maybe Huron Institute because we want to serve the whole Huron territory."

"Hold on," Warren raised his hand. "We need to define our purpose and mission before we can pick a name. I like the Huron and the Institute, but it is incomplete. It sounds like we're organizing strawberry socials. What do we want to do?"

The group sat in silence for a few minutes. Brandi served hot tea.

"I have been thinking about this ever since you asked us to come here. I hope you don't think I'm trying to take over, Karen," Warren looked at her with a wise kindness.

"Never, Warren, I'm happy you are involved. What are you thinking?"

He took a piece of paper from his pocket. "Our mandate should be:

To provide support for home-based schooling

To identify mentors and spread key skills throughout the territory

To evaluate the skill levels of operators and farmers to determine what support they need

To create bonds to improve morale throughout the territory

To sustain the health of local ecology."

"Two things," Karen said, "I would add the words: 'and to operate a learning centre at Kimberly' at the end of the first one. Also, we need to work your sustainable ecosystem reference into our name. That will be our real legacy to future generations."

Karen's intelligence and wisdom impressed Warren.

"The Huron Ecology Institute," he said the name for the first time. The others nodded. It sounded right.

They converted Warren's plan into a proposal for Chester to take it to the Huron Council and appended a long resource request, including bringing electricity from the Eugenia Falls generating station to Kimberly. Brandi created an official document in fancy lettering with the title: "Charter of the Huron Ecology Institute".

Chester pretended horror, but he felt Council would approve the document.

Issuing a charter impressed the Council. From then on, it would use charters to mandate many decisions. Brandi would have steady work creating documents, culminating in Huron Territory's own charter.

"There's one thing before you head to Owen Sound, Chester," Warren said. "I think we should organize the territory based on watersheds. The sewage in the river warned us. The basic political unit should be the watershed so the Beaver River watershed would be a township; every stream valley would be a political unit. Huron Territory should not be able to dictate building anything in a watershed. Final approval must be the people at the bottom, not the top."

"We need a larger organization for security and coordination of resources," Chester replied.

"Yes," Warren spoke, "that should be the role of the territory. We have to come together for higher needs, but Owen Sound cannot tell Beaver Valley they will polluted us, or even to grow a crop we don't want. We will find it complicated."

"The Huron Territory will have the power to stop an activity harmful to Lake Huron. We are all at the bottom when it comes to Lake Huron. We should make it clear; the top level can only stop a harmful activity but force nothing onto a watershed."

It made sense. Chester kept Ojibwe respect for the land and embraced Warren's thinking. He knew it would be a hard sell to the Huron Council. A few were power hungry and liked the idea of being the boss. Most active people had grown up in top-down political organizations. This idea of Warren's would be unfamiliar. It would take time and necessity to get it approved. He would bide his time.

"Warren, it might come down to a referendum." Chester mused. "I like your idea, and many will agree, but some won't. You might have to come up to Council and sell this. If it comes to a territory-wide vote, campaign."

Why do I shoot my mouth off? Warren wondered to himself. *I hate public meetings.*

Chester returned with the signed charter. A wooden engraving appeared in Karen's kitchen above the doorway. It read: "The Centre for Advanced Speculation." Brandi hung a drawing portraying the creation of the Institute, the four of them at the table with faces of children peeking through the doorway, a distant sunlit horizon visible through the window.

Chapter Eighteen

November and December remained cold but drier than normal. The big November storm hit, then everything melted, and bare ground lasted until the end of the year, encouraging the residents of Longview to quarry stone to prepare for the next building. Several of the men built an ice rink, carrying buckets of water to flood a spot in the main garden. Despite milder spells, the children and most of the adults skated; overcoming the boredom of winter. Jim fashioned hockey sticks from dried maple; they added factory versions retrieved from abandoned properties along with skates and pucks.

A shortage of skates led to a successful search in Thornbury. They tried to pay by trading but received a surprising response.

"You folks at Longview have contributed lots. We have way more of these than we can use and they will only rot, so we are giving them to you. Put together a hockey team, and we will take you on."

Gifting had become an important way of sharing goods along with barter and trade. Longview had accumulated social capital, and the refugees discovered how well the community accepted them.

All the young spun about the ice. Sharon held Little Bill, now heavier in her arms, leaning against the gatepost watching the action. Jeff had never skated much and struggled, slow and clumsy. Don and Stephanie had both taken part in organized hockey and were adept, spinning about, gliding and stopping with ease. Jani skated well and teased Jeff as she effortlessly glided past. Older ones patiently helped the smaller children in tentative push and glide.

Chester's truck turned into the lane and sped towards the farmstead. Sharon's heart sank. The man's appearance usually meant bad news. The vehicle squeaked to a stop. Chester slid out from behind the wheel.

"I have to get the brakes fixed," Chester smiled. The joke did not hide his serious expression.

"The kids sure enjoy themselves." He stood beside Sharon and clucked his tongue at the baby.

"I have a present." Chester nudged his head towards the truck. The back held a large shape covered with a tarp and tied down with ropes. "It's a piano from an abandoned house. They tell me it's in tune and includes music and lesson books." He smiled.

"What's the bad news, Chester?"

"Damn it, Sharon, can't I at least feel good for a minute?"

"We need Jeff for a job. He'll be away for a few weeks. I'm sorry." Chester watched the skaters, the thrill of his gift lost on a mother facing more sacrifice. "He kept his beard," Chester said. "He looks grown up."

Movement caught Sharon's attention as Ted Macedo left the truck's passenger seat. It would be a serious mission. Helen told her at Flesherton, Jeff and Ted was the best pair they had for hard jobs. There would be little time for goodbyes.

"He's competent and important to us." Chester reached for something positive. He saw a tear on Sharon's cheek.

"I know," she whispered. "He's important to me too." She hugged Little Bill more tightly.

Jeff spotted Chester and Ted and skated over, clutching the fence to stop.

"What's up, Boss?" Jeff smiled, but he knew duty had called him much too soon.

"You skate like a girl," Ted laughed, "but not like her." He pointed to Stephanie, speeding over the ice dodging amongst the smaller kids.

"Yeah, and she can shoot a puck better." Jeff laughed.

"We have a problem requiring field time." Chester had a deadline. It was mid-morning, and Ted and Jeff had to be on the road before noon.

"Yesterday, a helicopter attacked the training base at Meaford." Chester let the reaction die down. "They didn't do significant damage, and they didn't hurt anyone. The helicopter dropped a couple of firebombs on the old hanger, but the fire quickly burnt out."

"That makes the barriers more dangerous." Jeff saw the implications.

"We think it was just a show of strength, not the beginning of an invasion. There's another helicopter flying around up near Southampton, not coming into rifle range but obviously wanting to be seen. Can we get this piano off the truck?"

"Are you bribing Longview?" Bill asked.

"I don't think of it like that," Chester paused as he opened the truck's door. "Jeff… you all have earned this. We know you support him in the field, and you contributed big at Flesherton. I got this free except for the council's fuel, so it isn't much payment. You folks are trailblazers, and we enjoy feeding you new opportunities."

He backed the truck against the porch steps. The instrument had a wooden soundboard, and they easily moved it into the parlour, placing the fine-looking piano beside the hospital gurney. Kathy smiled at the double promise of healing both spirit and body. Chester reluctantly accepted a hot tea. Even in his hurry, he could not ignore courtesy.

"There are other developments," Chester sat at the big table. "We're part of a short-wave network. A few of them suddenly went off the air two days ago. One of them was in Orangeville. We think the PLM captured them. It seems too much of a coincidence that they all went out at the same time." Chester turned to Jeff.

"I am sorry there is no one else to send. We have to keep more experienced people just in case."

"You mean we are expendable." Jeff frowned.

"Not at all," Chester flared. "You did well up at Flesherton. We know you can do it. If we didn't have you two, Roger and Helen would go. Can you be ready in twenty minutes?"

"Twenty minutes!" Jeff looked at Little Bill in Sharon's arms. He took the baby and went to find Jani.

"The last reliable information we received showed the fighting has died down. The People's Liberation Movement seems to have won. They sound progressive, but they are a bunch of cold-blooded killers." Hatred crept into Chester's voice.

"We've heard of atrocities and slavery, not only from our short-wave network but refugees. Almost a thousand migrants arrived this week, mostly from defeated factions. We had a full-blown shootout at the twenty-six a few weeks ago and placed a much larger force there." He finished his tea, eager to leave. "The PLM has a radio station. Have you heard it?" Chester wasn't sure if Longview had a radio.

"We tied in a radio to our solar electric system," Willard responded, "but we gave up listening a long time ago. There was no news, just garbage from south of the border and propaganda from Toronto."

"The PLM uses radio to solidify their power with propaganda, and what they call: music of the collective, ban anything individualistic, and play a lot of marching music and atrocious songs about the homeland aimed at rallying the population. They dredged up some old Canadian pop stars to sing. They don't allow creativity. It's real fascist stuff."

"We need to find out what things are like in the hundred kilometres outside of what we control. No refugees are coming from the direction of Orangeville or south of the Saugeen, so we are blind. Ted and Jeff are going to probe towards Weyburne and beyond if they can. We're sending two more pairs south from Priceville and Southampton. If they are going to attack, we need to know where and when."

Jeff reappeared and a teary Jani hugged his arm as he cuddled Little Bill in the other. Tears filled their warm goodbye. Finally, Jeff shouldered the AK. He hugged Jani and kissed the baby's forehead.

The truck sped off in a swirl of snow and dust. Sharon buried her face in Bill's chest shivering from cold and sadness. Jani clutched the baby with her feet planted on the porch deck, watching the vehicle disappear. Her tears had dried, but her bruised heart remained. Jeff would have their love to sustain him. Jani had grown, accepting theirs would be a life of sacrifice and separations. Jani felt she had to mimic the limestone cliff: stoic; silent; enduring. In these hard times, she had no choice.

A young, black finger exploring the promise of the new piano sent soft, hesitant musical notes, made sad by circumstance, through the doorway, to float away on the icy December wind.

Chapter Nineteen

Ted and Jeff leapt from Chester's truck at the Maxwell barrier. Jeff last visited the day his Mom led them through the checkpoint. He now knew the price of peace and security. Chester shook hands and wished them luck then sped off with a wave behind the closed driver's window.

"Hello, Shadly," a man in his late forties extended his hand. He had commanded the barrier the day they arrived from Weyburne. "How are your mother and the baby?"

"Oh," Jeff shook the man's hand. "Come down to Longview and see for yourself. Everything's fine."

Jeff blushed, remembering Sharon's fake pregnancy to smuggle Al Wright's money. It seemed worthless and hidden away at Longview. He hoped to be there when his mom would have to wiggle out of that one.

"This is Ted Macedo," Jeff changed subjects. "He's a crack shot and my best buddy. We plan to go down Road Two here and take Road Nine over to Dundalk." Jeff showed the commander his map, "spend the night there and tomorrow take Road Eight down to the old highway."

"We have patrols all over this area watching the zone from Highway Ten over east a few roads and curl up towards Road Four. We work hayfields out there, but no one lives between here and county nine or in Dundalk. I heard you guys did a great job at Flesherton last October. We've had a couple of volunteers from there. Those folks are thankful, and we sure need the help if those buggers down to Weyburne decide to come our way." He stood and stretched, stiff from cold.

"I'll give you some white monkey suits. The snow isn't much now, but you might need them later. They'll fit over your sledging suits." He went off to a small shack nestled in the trees.

Jeff looked around at the fortifications with slit trenches and log cribbing running out from the major barrier. It was like what they had done on twenty-six. The swamp and bush were too thick to clear, but he could see cut trails to channel attackers into the easier paths and ambush. Jeff knew they built firing positions located to turn those paths into killing zones. Of course, any decent commander would try to outflank all of this. There would have to be more surprises, patrols and many more fighters to defend the place. They needed more people. A few hours warning would be helpful, and this highlighted the importance of their mission. Hopefully, what they found would provide that warning.

Ted and Jeff passed through the serpentine passage onto the old road that ran southeast. Jeff remembered when he and his Dad walked through the gate returning to Weyburne. They stuck to the road, walking easily and felt no reason to fear enemies. A challenge from the bush startled them.

"Teeter-totter," Jeff replied. Satisfied by the password, four fighters emerged. One was from Meaford training.

"Jack, how are you doing?" Ted was smiling.

"Damned cold here!" the man replied. "We can't have a fire, and our relief won't be here until dark."

Daylight would soon fade. Ted and Jeff headed east.

"Jack was a great guy," Ted spoke as they walked. "I remember him moving us all back and risking himself the time we found a hot round on the firing range. He cares."

"Yeah, I like him." Jeff looked at Ted. "Chester rounded you up quick. Did he drive to Weirton?"

"I was in Meaford." Ted blushed and stared straight ahead. "Helen invited me down for Christmas."

"Darn, Christmas was fun." Jeff tried to make things easier seeing Ted's discomfort talking about his love life.

"Did you have a good time?"

"Sure did," Ted found the courage to look at Jeff. "She's a wonderful woman. She's tough on the outside but soft inside; she knits and draws."

"What happened to the guy she had?" Jeff worried Ted had gotten in too deep.

"Oh, he's a nice guy." Jeff's looked puzzled. "He's a combat engineer, an electrical technician. He moved to Kimberly to help with the power station. Helen said he has a new girl he met in Flesherton."

"So what happens now?" Jeff was hopeful.

"I don't know," Ted said. "She's older than me. One day at a time, but I don't think she wants anything permanent or us living together. She thinks times are too scary to plan, and she's too old to have kids."

It was a widespread view, and Jeff had heard it before. Most people were considerate, but some had obnoxiously asked how he and Jani could consider having a family with this danger. He could not answer. He loved Jani and Little Bill and that was what mattered.

They turned towards Dundalk. Past the empty fuel-depot, the pair entered the deserted town. Dundalk seemed eerie in the fading winter light. A house on a side street offered a welcoming bivouac. The place gave shelter from the wind with double brick walls offering protection from bullets. A bedroom on the second floor with a window covered by a heavy curtain allowed a clear shot at the stairway. Body heat would add some warmth to the small room, but they dared not light a fire. The smoke could betray them. They settled down to a meal of pemmican, washed down with water.

An easterly wind chilled them the following morning. Low grey clouds scudded in the sky, and the bit of snow on the ground swirled at their feet.

"Storm's coming," Ted muttered, glancing to the east and feeling the chilly breeze on his cheeks. "The wind will be behind us to Road Eight, then worse from the side."

By noon, they reached a point well down County Eight and found a secluded spot for lunch where a creek crossed the road. Trees offered protection from light snow riding on the freshening wind.

A hundred meters down the road, they crested a slight rise and hit the ditch. A kilometre ahead, visible through the flurries, smoke rose from a farmhouse chimney.

"I wasn't expecting anyone way out here." Jeff trained his binoculars on the farmyard. "I can't see anyone."

"No wonder, in this weather," Ted peered through his sniper scope. "I see a couple of horses by the barn, but no people."

"Okay," Jeff had a plan. "Let's go into those woods and get behind them, then decide what to do."

The trek through the bush was difficult, but it kept the wind off, and little snow penetrated into the trees. After an hour of labour, they reached a cedar rail fence at the farmyard. There was no sign of a dog. The horses contentedly munched hay.

"They're inside staying warm." Ted decided. "I can get to the door without being seen."

"That's my job," Jeff insisted. He twisted around, confirming no one lurked in the barn. "I'll sneak past the combine and tractor and then run the few meters to the door. Cover me."

"What are you going to do when you get to the door?"

"Knock, like I am supposed to." Jeff chuckled. "I'll be standing to one side in case they think shooting through the door's a good idea. I won't have my rifle. It's staying with you. If they get me, at least they won't have it, only this popgun." He tapped the Glock, still in its holster.

Ted watched Jeff scuttle up to the dead machinery then briefly lost to view beyond the hulking yellow combine, reappearing a few meters from the house. Ted tensed. Jeff pressed flat against the wall. Ted slipped the safety off and framed the door in his scope. If anyone pointed a gun, they would die. Jeff rapped on the door leaving Ted a clear view of the entranceway. Ted exhaled slowly, calming his body, his finger slipped to touch the trigger lightly. The door swung open, cautiously. Ted heard muffled voices, and the face of a woman appeared in the cross hairs as she leaned out for a better look. Jeff held his hands in front of him, palms up in a friendly gesture.

The woman smiled, stepped out the doorway and shook Jeff's hand, glancing nervously around but not spotting Ted. He slipped the safety on and rested his finger on the trigger guard. Breathing again, Ted waited. Jeff beckoned towards the fence and shouted for Ted to come forward. Two more figures emerged from the building as Ted approached. They were soon in the warm kitchen. Jeff and Ted shivered from their lingering chill and the tension of the past few minutes.

"You say you're from Beaver Valley?" the woman seemed in charge. "What're you doing all the way down here?" She did not sound suspicious but implied she would like a believable answer.

"We're on a spy mission," Jeff made it as bluntly as possible. He was not completely comfortable with these strangers but trusted the ability of Ted and himself to handle three adults. They would have to worry about anyone beyond the inner doorway if a problem arose.

"Our community is afraid the dictator at Weyburne might be a threat. We want to find out what's going on down here."

"Bad guys are running the show." One man spoke up. "If they get their act together, they'll be dangerous. Have you two eaten lately?"

"Only cold rations," Ted spoke up.

"We can give you something better," he placed a large iron skillet on the hot stove, "How about eggs and pan-fried bread?" Not waiting for an answer, he had a scoop of lard sizzling, followed by a half dozen eggs.

"You two look formidable," the woman asked, "soldiers?"

"We're fighters," said Jeff, "trained by ex-army people, but we aren't the Canadian army. We have seen fighting." Jeff savoured a new aroma. "Is that real coffee?"

"Yes," the man chuckled. "We liberated it from the bad guys. What fighting have you done?"

They described the liberation of Flesherton. It sounded impressive enough without embellishment. Steaming mugs of strong, black coffee, laced with floating grounds warmed their hands. Thick slabs of dark brown bread landed in the pan and fried up quickly. Soon the two men were eating heartily and feeling at home.

"You took a chance knocking on the door. What would you have done if I had a gun?" The woman glanced at their rifles leaning against the wall.

Ted looked up from his feast. "You would not be here to ask," he said, taking a sip of coffee.

"I'm sorry there's no bacon," the woman frowned, giving Ted's sniper-rifle a second glance. "We're going to build a smokehouse this summer, aren't we Peter?" she shot a glance at the cook. He smiled back. "Where're you headed from here?"

"We plan to get to Highway 89 and head towards Weyburne." Jeff washed down his meal with cooling coffee. His host refilled the mug.

"Not a good idea." The quiet second man spoke up. "It's dangerous that way. I'll take you to people who can help. Maybe you can help them."

Several children appeared with a young woman Jani's age. Jeff wondered at the relationships. The men were middle-aged, much older than this girl was. The little ones stared in awe at the impressive strangers. Before long, they were sitting on laps, accepting the visitors as if this was an everyday occurrence. In reality, the family suffered from isolation. The strangers relieved the dull winter routine. The storm closed in ending any possibility of going anywhere for two days.

On the third morning, sunshine greeted them. One host escorted the visitors from Huron through piles of snow. Drifts made walking difficult, but they turned west onto a road blown open by the strong westerly wind that bit into their faces. The footing was easier with only the occasional hummock of snow grabbing at their feet.

As the road passed through tangled, swampy woods, Ted nudged Jeff. With his right hand, he clinched his mitt-covered fist three times and his left twice. Jeff nodded. Three armed figures lurked in the jumble of cedar, aspen and tamarack to their right and two to the left. Jeff and Ted quietly followed the guide.

Chapter Twenty

"It was a short walk made longer by the wind. Ted and I worried about the armed men and hoped we weren't walking into a trap. I had no suspicion of the joyful surprise in store for me. Other than Little Bill being born, this one event convinced me your previously infuriating optimism was justified. Soon after I stepped into the house, I believed all would be well."
From: A letter from Jeff Shadly to his sister - The Brandi Shadly Archives

Jeff, Ted and their guide topped a slight rise in the road. The bitterness of the wind increased, but they had reached a large farmhouse. Several bungalows sat on either side of the old, yellow-brick building. The front door banged shut as they entered a gloomy, once elegant parlour. Ted and Jeff's eyes tried to adjust to the dim light.

"Here they are, boss," their guide spoke into the gloom. "We think they're what we hoped for."

"Welcome," a shadowy figure stepped from behind a desk. His voice sounded strangely familiar to Jeff. "What are your names?"

"This is Ted Macedo, and I am Jeff Shadly." Jeff peered at his host. He was about Jeff's height, but his hair and beard were scruffier.

"I'll be damned! It's Bill and Sharon's kid grown into a soldier." He was not sarcastic and extended his right hand, then thinking it not enough wrapped his arms around Jeff and hugged him tightly.

"I'm Matt Long," He hugged again. Jeff was speechless.

"I never dreamed we would see any of you again." Matt stepped back and called out, "Billy, go get Brenda!"

"We thought you were dead." Jeff finally spoke, choked with emotion. "Everyone will be thrilled. We had you dead, buried, and all cried over." It was Jeff's turn to hug the long-lost hero.

A woman entered the room with a puzzled expression. She was tall but not as tall as Jeff was and gave the impression of strength and confidence.

"What's the big deal, Stud?" The woman looked at the two visitors.

"I bet you can't guess who this is?" Matt smiled looking like a kid who just found a quarter.

"Sure, it's the Shadly kid and some other guy I never met." She winked at Jeff and chuckled. Matt's jaw dropped.

"How the hell did you know?"

"Because I asked Billie who was here." Brenda laughed. She hugged Jeff even tighter than Matt.

"We have a lot to talk about." Matt had a permanent grin. "This is encouraging. We sure need encouragement."

"How did you survive?" Jeff wanted to race to Longview with the joyous news.

"First, I need to know what's happening up your way. Then, I'll tell you our story from the night your Dad escaped. Come into the banquet hall. This calls for coffee and goodies."

The group trooped into a dining room that resembled the one at Longview, and the dishes had a common ancestry. "You can leave your rifles over there with ours." Matt pointed to the corner gun rack holding a half-dozen rifles and shotguns. Matt admired the AK and the sniper rifle. They did not have any of the Russian weapons but had liberated a few Canadian military issue rifles with superior accuracy. Mugs of coffee, cookies and muffins appeared.

"Okay," Matt began. "Tell us about Huron."

"Matt, I have to tell you first, your memory has been an enormous influence on our group. We live together on a big farm property. Wanting to be worthy of your sacrifice has given us more strength. It hasn't been easy, but no one ever complained." Jeff paused, remembering Warren and Willard's gateway. "We call our place Longview, mostly to honour you, but to remind us we have to think far down the road and be willing to make a similar sacrifice." Brenda had tears on her cheeks. She loved Matt and felt the honour more deeply than he did.

Jeff outlined their adventure from the barrier all the way to the battle of Flesherton. When he talked about more refugees, everyone at the table nodded. They had noticed the change and more bad people from the losing sides were showing up. Most were in graves. They found it a chore to sort out the good from the bad.

"We've been sending the good ones up your way," Matt explained. "We can't risk having strangers here in case a squad of goons shows up. There are spies everywhere. Most of the locals blow with the wind. They want to be on the winning side."

"We have three you sent living at Longview," Jeff replied. "Do you remember two men and a nurse, passed through late last winter?"

"Sure do," Brenda piped up. "I guided Kathy and the boys up to the escarpment near Craigleith. It's ironic they got to your place. We would have kept them here if we could. We had to move just after they left."

"That's our story." Jeff carried on. "We're not strong militarily and are hoping for more good refugees. It would help if the bad guys kept fighting each other longer."

"We hoped you might be strong enough to attack," Matt seemed deflated. "Angel is more active and has solidified the territory from Weyburne to Orangeville. They're part of the PLM crowd. We aren't sure they won't expand from Weyburne and attack us." There was a murmur of defiance around the table.

"So, what happened that night?" Jeff wanted the actual story. His father had described a hero's sacrifice.

"Well, it sounds better in your telling," Matt leaned back in his chair, thinking back, so much had happened in a year and a half. "When Willard gave me the handgun, I didn't think; I just acted."

Brenda moved her chair closer to Matt. He had bad dreams about this.

"I crept towards the voices. Something tipped them off because I heard a rifle bolt and a whisper, so I challenged them." Matt struggled with the memories. "Your dad and the others made a break for it, and the bad guys opened fire. Their rifle flashes and light from the house doorway silhouetted them. I fired a few pistol shots chest high. One guy screamed, and I hit the ground. I must have hit my head on a rock. It stunned me. Next thing I know, a big dog is growling at me, not a foot away. I fired the Glock and passed out." Matt trembled. Brenda took his hand.

"I woke just at dawn, damp and cold, lying where I fell, and the pistol still in my hand. My head hurt. When I struggled to a sitting position, I saw the dead dog beside me and the three bodies. Even in my daze, I knew they were dead." Matt paused and gulped his cold coffee.

"Seeing them brought me around. It horrified me. I had killed no one before, let alone three at once, and for all I knew, these were innocent men protecting their own. I staggered over to make sure. They had a couple of heavy rifles and a .22 and stank of booze. Why is it people get drunk and then want to fight?"

Jeff thought of the poor misfits of Flesherton who had died, probably because they were drunk.

"The bodies were stiff. Lucky shots, but one had died slower and crawled a few feet." Matt trembled again.

"I sat beside the bodies wondering what to do until a woman's voice scared the hell out of me. I hadn't heard her coming behind me and jumped and pointed the gun. She yelled at me not to shoot but asked if they were dead and seemed scared of the bodies. Later, I learned she had feared them for so long the reaction was automatic, even when she knew they were dead. She dabbed my head with a hanky. Wow, it hurt, but there was fresh blood from where my head hit the rock. A couple of other women hid in the house. You met two at the farm. The other one ran off."

"They washed dressed my wound, and I felt better," Matt rubbed his head, recalling the pain.

"These women had been slaves, everything from cooking to sex. They couldn't thank me enough. They even offered to sleep with me." Matt paused looking at Brenda. "I refused, and that won them over. It seems sex stopped them from being beaten."

"How did you end up here? What happened since?"

"We had to move fast. Angel's men came regularly expecting sex and food and had the three men watching for us. Smith's people would be back."

"We buried the bodies deep in a manure pile, and loaded their horse with food, the guns, and the women's stuff. We headed down the paved road to hide our tracks then turned towards the old highway. The third woman said she was heading home to Orangeville and kept on south. We haven't seen her since. The little berg of Colbeck turned up. We hid there for the night. It turned into a year before they forced us to run here." Matt fetched more coffee. A man in winter camouflage and carrying a rifle came in the back door.

"The bastards are up to something. They sent a plough out 89."

"Any sign of them coming this way?"

"Nope, it raced off, west. We's timing it on the way back to guess how far. Whatever's going on, it's worth their wasting the diesel."

"They're worried about the transmission corridor, the high-voltage lines from the Bruce nuclear facility." Matt explained. "They want to keep the road open. Let the watches know and send a patrol to watch the Dundalk road." Matt returned to the table.

"I know him. He's Bob who ran the Xpress."

"Yes, Angel seized their truck a few months after you left and tried to force them into his army. Bill and Bob brought their families this way, trying to reach your territory, but when they found us, they stayed. We're glad they did, and they had a cache of weapons for us. You can see how things go here." Matt looked at Jeff and Ted. "Normally, it's quiet, but occasionally we have to go on alert. The hydro line is why we had to move from Colbeck. It was too close. Towards the end of this spring, Angel sent a bunch of toughs to check the transmission line. The PLM has branched out around Orangeville and Weyburne and has enough forces to go out further. I think someone found a whole warehouse of OPP uniforms. They looked like cops."

"We knew they were coming and disappeared into the swamps. The legitimate residents hung back to make things look normal. They're a brave group down there."

"There are a lot of brave people everywhere," Brenda spoke up. "It's scary but still better than living under Angel and the PLM."

"They're the same thing," Matt added. "The PLM rules and appointed Alphonse Angel local governor."

"He's no angel," someone added. No one laughed.

"Anyway," Matt resumed, "they harassed folks on farms near the line and took inventory so they could squeeze more tax out of everyone. In late spring the PLM checked on planting. Last fall they sent out squads with trucks rounding up grain and animals as a tax. No one has any money. They tipped their hand in the spring, so we hid a bunch of grain and stock from the farms."

"Last year everyone suffered," Brenda joined in. "but this year, we hoped to have a surplus, until Angel stole it. We'll distribute what we hid when it's needed."

"We know they're still weak," Matt continued, "because they haven't come north of 89 west of Riverview. Our source in town tells us their orders from Toronto are to guard the power lines at any cost, so they used most of their resources in patrolling it."

"Where do they get their fuel?" Jeff could still feel his feet and would love to have been riding. "We have little, and we reserve that for our security force."

"It comes in by boat is all we know. For us, it's horses and walking. We have vehicles, but we keep them for emergencies."

"We're still building. When we fled Colbeck, we found this area mostly abandoned. The few decent farms here had a mix of old timers, Mennonites or those who thought they were rich. Most left or killed themselves. Some farmers stayed, but we had to get rid of a few who wouldn't cooperate. Some thought they would get their neighbour's abandoned property, so it was dog eat dog. I have persuaded several to help us, although I don't trust them. We shot a couple when they tried to out gun us." Matt did not look happy at this bit of the story. "So here we are." Matt finished his cold coffee.

"What's the plan now?" Jeff asked.

"If Angel doesn't get any stronger, we'll get more people under our protection and try to kill him." Brenda sounded determined.

"What's your mission?" Matt asked.

"We're worried the PLM might attack us soon," Jeff repeated the story of the helicopter attack. "We want to find out about Angel's forces so we can estimate the threat."

"Okay," Matt replied. "I planned a patrol to Weyburne and Orangeville. You can replace a couple of my people. We're spread too thin, so that will help."

Jeff experienced other joyful reunions. His old friends, Tommy and Kelly had joined Matt's group. Matt found them in Colbeck with the girl's aunt when he arrived. A familiar aroma in the garage alerted Jeff to other old friends. Gary and Sally, the marijuana experts, had also found the group of freedom fighters. Gary had used his stockpile of Mary Jane to bribe some watchers, allowing Gary, Sally and their families to flee Weyburne. Having experienced the genuine horror of the PLM, they became the most dedicated fighters.

Roger Smith had forced Gary into Angel's army and sent him to Peel. Good fortune spared his life during the brutal, bloody campaign, and Gary got back to Weyburne on a visit. Angel was desperate for fighters, forcing young girls into the depleted army.

"They threatened Sally," Gary said. "It was hard to sneak out of town. There were watchers everywhere. Many of the families of people in the army had joined the PLM, spying on neighbours. They threatened some while others supported who they thought were the winners. The PLM held rallies to support the troops, just like a hockey game. Dying fighting against Angel seemed better than dying fighting for him."

Chapter Twenty-one

The twenty-five-kilometre trek to Weyburne took place with little excitement, following back roads and working through the swamp north of Weyburne, fighting only snowdrifts.

"Look there." Matt pointed at houses with smoking chimneys beside the old arena. "Lots of people are using wood heat now. Angel cut off gas and electricity to some folks and is using energy as a threat to keep people in line." The group lay at the edge of the woods north of town.

"We'll go down the road ditch and follow the creek past the sewage plant." Matt retreated into the bush and headed east. An overpowering smell engulfed them.

"Good god, what's that?" Ted gasped.

"The sewage plant," Jeff and Matt responded in unison. "It broke down a couple of years ago, but the sewers are still running. The crap is just flowing straight into the creek. That's why I came this way. Angel's guards don't want to be in the stink."

They into town, past the sewage plant to trees behind an abandoned strip mall. To their relief, the west wind blew the odour away.

"Have you seen any people?" Jeff peered down what remained of Main Street.

"Nope," said Matt. "The fighters have gone somewhere. They only have a skeleton guard, relying on spies and fear. No one has ever troubled them here. Orangeville is the hot spot, and we've caused trouble there as well. It keeps Weyburne quiet, better for us."

The winter light waned, chilling the tired force.

"Let's find a unit in the mall to hole up for the night."

Matt pushed open the door to one of the central units. The wind rushed into their faces. The front window was missing. They had better luck at the next. A wall separated the storage space from the front. It would do. They strung a tarp over shelving. The igloo effect would trap their body heat. Guards would spell each other every hour.

"I'll be back." Matt headed to the rear door. "If I'm not here by seven in the morning, leave without me." He disappeared into the night.

"Where's he going?" Ted was curious.

"It's best not to know so you can't tell if tortured."

They settled in with cold rations and water. Matt returned about midnight, took his watch at four in the morning and roused the others before daylight.

"Can you tell me where you went last night?" Jeff asked as they followed the creek out of town.

"Visiting old friends, they had lots of information, but the best is there is no threat here. They sent all the recruits to fight south and east of Dufferin. The casualties have been heavy. They killed or scared off the townsfolk. People are angry, but they're hiding it because Angel has terrorized them."

The team followed the abandoned railway, then a concession road south, reaching a hill above Orangeville about the middle of the afternoon. A light breeze stirred the snow beneath a cloudy sky with the temperature hovering below freezing.

"I think we've another storm coming soon." Ted had a keen eye for weather signs. Since his sports accident ruined his social life, he had lost himself in many trivial interests. Now, some of these became assets. "So far the wind is west, so we're okay."

"I want a good look, but we start back before dark." Matt crouched behind a fence, watching the town with a pair of hunting glasses. "I wish there were something we could do to hurt them before we leave," Matt grunted as he stowed his binoculars. "I saw a train locomotive shunting at the crossing, but little else."

"Where do those power lines run?" Ted searched around. "The ones they guard so tightly."

"Two lines go to Milton, but another one comes in here. There's a big switchyard over the hill," Matt pointed.

"Let's look." Ted had a plan. "Maybe there's something we can do."

From the top of the hill they could see the huge electrical compound of large transformers and circuit breakers. Barracks stood near a chain-link fence that surrounded the place. Guards patrolled the perimeter.

"It's well defended," Matt pointed out the obvious. "There's nothing we can do about it."

"How does it work?" Ted concentrated on his scope.

"This is a hub. It ties in lines from the north and Bruce nuclear to one to Toronto. What do you have in mind?"

"Can we get away fast when all hell breaks loose?"

"The snow's deep." Matt consulted his map. "Yes, if we head back the way we came, we will hit tree cover and can go west, but it'll be hard slugging."

"Okay," Ted checked his rifle. "I'll shoot out an insulator." He slipped a cartridge into the chamber. "Which one do you want?" Ted looked for potential targets. "What'll hurt them the most?"

"We don't know. The line from the northwest is from the nukes. If you knock that out, they might shut the plant down for several days."

"Okay, I'll try. The biggest ones will be the most effective I think. I would love to hit two, but if it's one they won't suspect sabotage." Ted warmed his hands in his coat.

"They are paranoid, but it might take a few hours to react, time enough to get away."

"I've changed my mind." Ted had looked once more. "Look at where the guard barracks are located, outside the fence, beside a big transformer, underneath those drooping wires. I bet there'll be a big arc and explosion when I hit it. Maybe the transformer will blow and take out the building. I'll shoot that one."

"Your choice," said Matt. "I want to see it. I don't think anyone can make that shot."

"Ted will," Jeff said, remembering Ted's head-shot at the barrier.

"It's about six hundred meters." Ted adjusted his scope, allowing for the wind and estimated the distance from the height of the men near the fence. Ted rested his rifle bi pod on a solid boulder. The others stood quietly, watching the target expectantly.

The rifle spoke. An instant later, a huge flash burst below the damaged insulator. The cable had dropped and struck the steel fence. The roar reached them a second later. Several of the guards fell to the ground while more ran from the already smoking building. Everyone slapped Ted on the back and shook his hand. Matt jumped up and down like a kid.

"Let's get out of here," Jeff headed down the hill.

They ran to the concession road. Clouds added to the fading daylight, and gloom engulfed them. Light from the fire reflected from the overcast. Orangeville had gone dark except for vehicle lights rushing towards the burning complex. No one waited to enjoy the view.

"It'll be snowing soon." Ted grinned, satisfied with his aim and excited by the result. He had doubts he could make the shot and had allowed three bullets.

"Snow will cover our tracks." Matt still smiled.

The group walked all night, sticking to the roads to make better time. They saw no other traffic and before daylight reached a large abandoned house some distance north of the power line. Exhausted, they slipped inside as the first flakes from the new storm drifted to the ground.

They waited all the next day. The storm was not as big as the previous one. An icy wind blew in behind the snow. During the boring vigil, Matt and Jeff made a plan.

"See that plane?" Matt looked out an upstairs window at a metallic glint in the sky. Jeff had not seen an aeroplane in years.

"They started flying patrols over the line about two weeks ago, not every day and at irregular times. They have thermal technology from the OPP. This plane went out two hours ago and is returning. I think he went all the way to Bruce, but they don't fly at night."

"What can we do to help?" Jeff sat, cleaning his rifle.

"We want to delay the PLM as much as possible. Keep them fighting ghosts." Matt turned from the window and sat on the floor with his back against the wall. "The fighting in the city has saved us."

"Do you want explosives; maybe a sniper?" Jeff asked.

"I don't want to stir them up too much." Matt smiled. "Yesterday was a tremendous blow. We'll have to see what the radio is saying. Maybe we knocked the useless station off the air for a few hours. We could use medical help. There's little medicine and no doctors. Most of the medics are in the Angel camp, either willingly or by force. So far, they don't realize we exist. They think face isolated troublemakers; we would like to keep it that way. Few know about us as an organization."

Jeff agreed to provide medical supplies and perhaps someone to train medics. They created a password for anyone crossing into or out of Huron.

Three days later, Ted and Jeff passed through the barrier on the Maxwell road and walked to Kimberly. In his eagerness to tell about Matt, despite Ted's protests, they made the journey in record time.

***

The news of Matt's survival burst upon Longview like a bomb of happiness, almost surpassing Sharon's joy at Jeff's safe return. The dining room filled in a spontaneous get-together. There had never been so many smiles not even after Little Bill's birth.

Ted joined the merriment, enthralled by the deep emotion. He saw Jeff's elation the instant they had encountered Matt, but he had not realized the reverence the Longview founders felt for the man. Matt had been their symbol of sacrifice and now their flame of hope.

The scene at Longview contrasted with Jeff's quiet celebration of the news with his sister when Jeff and Ted had stopped in Kimberly. Brandi had sat quietly at the kitchen table and cried tears of happiness. A shadow had disappeared from her heart.

"Tell us about your trip," Bill asked Jeff, and the room fell silent. Everyone looked towards Shadly. The water for tea had not yet boiled. Tina and Harold, on kitchen duty, stayed in the room.

"I want to tell you how I felt this morning, walking under the sign." No one in the room had to ask which sign. "Before, I always felt sadness, remembering and thinking the worst. Today, I felt happiness and now connect that joy and with a stronger belief that we will succeed."

"When did you become so wise?" Sharon teased her son, but he would have none of it.

"The day you brought me into the world… you and Dad have taught me all of it."

There had been a growth in him on this trip. Jeff had stepped over a threshold into adult life and now loved his parents as friends.

Bill's thoughts drifted back to that first meeting in Weyburne with the Mennonite trader, David Koch. *We listened to our fathers*; he had said. Bill realized there need not have been any great spoken wisdom, but simple example and guidance, a caring love from a father for a son. Bill felt completeness in his life with his son standing beside him as a man.

Jeff related their adventure, making Ted blush with a glowing account of the "impossible" shot.

"When can Matt and Brenda visit?" Tina was excited. She had worked with Brenda, clerking at the Weyburne discount store.

"They can't come soon." Jeff saddened. "It's too dangerous down there. They would abandon their people. Much of the surviving population supports them. Those people fear the dictators and only cooperate as much as they need to stay safe."

"Matt claims most of Angel's troops would desert if they weren't afraid of being killed or their families murdered. If Matt needs to flee here, then we'll be in trouble and time might be short for everyone. We would lose. We aren't yet strong enough to win." Jeff's blunt assessment stunned the group. His reminder of their vulnerability weighed heavily.

"To hell with all this gloom," Walt leapt to his feet. "Let's celebrate our hero's safety and his fight for freedom." Longview put aside all but routine chores. They seized this precious excuse to party in mid-winter. Walt's harmonica leapt to life, playing happy old tunes.

Quiet sounds from the piano soon joined the playful notes from the mouth organ. Walt made his way to stand beside the piano. The room quieted once more. Little Joseph, the boy with the crooked legs who had just turned six, had followed along with Walt, one hand mimicking the melody and occasionally the left adding an embellishment.

Joseph's round black face filled with an enormous smile as he looked up to Walt, listening to his lead. Everyone stood in dazed wonderment at Joseph's untutored skill.

For the rest of their lives, everyone would retell the story of that day of joy; the day Joseph of Longview first revealed his genius.

Chapter Twenty-two

Jeff stood on the steps of the old church in Maxwell, surveying his troops. The quiet winter after Jeff had met Matt and the routine of spring planting gave way to military action. He commanded a platoon of two hundred fighters including three-quarters of those who had trained with him at Meaford. One noticeable absentee was Will Sullivan who would be in Roger's force, on a scouting operation below the escarpment. The commander wanted Sullivan under his close watch.

Jeff would advance along Road Four to Singhampton and the edge of the escarpment and secure the highway to the scarp where the road dropped to the low ground. Paralleling forces gone east on roads through the centre of the high ground. They planned to take a census of the local population and to convince them to join the Huron territory and the Beaver River entity headed by Chester Amik.

The Huron Council conceived the operation after they received Jeff and Ted's report of their trip south. This would secure the high ground and the last section of the Beaver River watershed, out-flanking the PLM.

Jeff's force had a secondary assignment, to mimic the efforts of Matt's group and offer a place for residents for people living above the Noisy River to hide surpluses from Angel's taxation. It would thwart the dictator's roving gangs of extortionists. Huron believed, if they befriended everyone, it would buffer an attack from below.

"Let's go!"

The stirring fighters raised dust in the June sunshine. Jeff disliked the early morning sun in their eyes, but they had a timetable to meet.

"Ted, get them into two staggered lines on each side of the road?" Ted went to organize the force. Jeff went forward between rows of impatient fighters to murmurs of greeting and the occasional wisecrack.

"Remember who your mommy is." Jeff spun on his heel and glared.

"Mom, if you embarrass me, you'll peel potatoes in Singhampton."

He smiled, winked and continued his walk. Sharon and Bill had volunteered for Jeff's force. Roger had been reluctant to let them be under their son's command. He gave in when Sharon threatened not to invite him to the harvest party. Chester's effusive accounting of last year's gathering had attracted requests for invitations from many outsiders.

In fact, no one expected real fighting. Bill and Sharon split off with ten volunteers to help local leaders in Feversham. The people there, already closely allied with Huron, would organize defensive patrols, an effort repeated in centres as far east as Singhampton.

"I'll see you back at Longview." Jeff shook his Dad's hand. A hug for Sharon brought catcalls and whistles from the rest of the force.

"On the way home we're going to go down past Randy's in Kolapore," Bill told his son. "We want to invite them to the harvest fling and get them to bring a nice spring lamb to trade for a ram lamb out of Slam Dunk. They need a new stud line up there."

"See you soon, Dad." Jeff started his force east.

"Pick it up, double pace," he barked. Jeff wanted to see if the platoon would still follow his instructions after their reaction to his family farewell. He slowed to a walking pace after a few hundred meters.

"What do you think of the plan, Ted?"

"It makes sense." Ted furrowed his brow. "Matt Long's group doesn't have this option and has to be secret. We can work in the open. It should make it easier for folks, especially those towards Weyburne. Even if Angel knows they have brought stuff up here for protection, he has no option short of an invasion. For now, they are too weak to attack."

"That's the thinking of Council. I don't expect resistance. Some crazy guy might take shots at us, nothing more." Jeff checked his rifle by reflex.

It turned out to be such a smooth operation people would derisively call it, "The Battle of Mad River." There were obstinate and contrary folks here and there, but no one pointed a gun. By noon, Jeff established his headquarters in an abandoned motel in Singhampton.

His force had thinned as sections split off to secure side roads. A squad of ten went down the main road towards Weyburne. They would only go to the Noisy River and explain their mission to residents. This force would withdraw and build a debris roadblock in a rock cut just below Singhampton. They built similar blockades on every road heading south and manned by Meaford trainees getting command experience.

A force of twenty-five went out the highway to where the road dropped towards Collingwood. They blocked the road at the top of the hill, and a patrol checked conditions as far as Duntroon.

By mid-afternoon, a steady stream of visitors kept Jeff occupied. He had not expected so many slovenly, destitute and desperate residents. Jeff saw signs of rickets and thought of little Joseph. The squad struggled to treat minor ailments. Most physical issues were due to lack of hygiene and food. The stench from some was terrible. One of the first treatments involved a trip to the river. With homemade soap, a soaking in cool water made a difference. It puzzled Jeff that people had not taken better care. Hopelessness had paralysed this isolated population.

"Where's Turtle?" The depressing flow of desperate people exasperated Jeff.

Jeff took Turtle aside. "Go find Helen. Kathy Nelson is with her. Tell them we need medical support. It's a disaster here." Turtle hurried away.

The desperate flow lasted all day. An exhausted Jeff found a few hours of sleep. The faint light of dawn filtering through the dirt-caked window roused Jeff, stiff and sore from a fitful slumber. His sleeping bag had not cushioned the concrete floor. Ted stood over him.

"Turtle's back with Kathy and Stephanie; Kathie wants a word before she rests."

Jeff groaned as his body protested. He splashed water on his face, soaking the front of his shirt and shuffled onto the front porch.

"Sorry it took so long, Jeff," Kathy seemed to think that her rushing over in the night was not fast enough. "Good news delayed Steph and me. Sarah Handley had her baby yesterday. It's a little boy, and they're calling him Steve. They thrilled Debbie at the honour," Kathy smiled.

"We have a squad following with supplies." Early morning shadows hid her sad eyes but not her heavy voice. "How many are in need?"

Jeff gave her a number that was large for even these hard days.

"I'll try to treat the superficial stuff beginning in a few hours. I need some sleep. Maybe you can have something set up for us. Steph is already sleeping. It's much worse over here than nearer the valley. As we came east, we found that those who had never been in touch with us in awful shape. The ones here will be the worst." Kathy found a place to rest out of the morning sun.

Jeff returned to his makeshift office. He ate a cold meal and tried to organize his day. As the morning progressed, the activity rose to a fever pitch. The supply convoy arrived, comprising a three-ton army truck and a pickup. A field kitchen prepared hot rations for the troops and the needy. Kathy took charge about mid-morning and comforted the sufferers. Stephanie triaged and tended scrapes, superficial infections and rashes.

The more troublesome cases went on to Kathy. At her insistence, anyone who appeared to be suffering vitamin D deficiency rested in a sunny spot. Dietary solutions would come later.

"Jeff," Ted drew Jeff away from interviewing a local. "The Noisy River patrol returned. They have someone who claims to know you."

Ted stood aside to reveal a trembling, dirty and dishevelled woman. Jeff could not tell her hair colour.

"Hello, Jeff," the familiar voice faltered. He strode around the table, standing confident and healthy in his army fatigues, towering over the cowering woman.

"Maud, Maud Dillingham, is this you?" This apparition was a frail shadow of the confident, well-groomed operator of Maud's Café.

"Yes," she whispered, "I escaped from Weyburne."

"You look terrible," Jeff was in shock. While his reunion with Matt Long had been happy, he was not sure how to approach the lover of Roger Smith, Stevie Hunter's killer. Maud fainted into Ted's arms.

"Get Kathy, quick!" Jeff commanded a nearby soldier.

Kathy took charge and placed Maud in a comfortable, shady spot. She decided Maud suffered from fatigue and hunger and let her sleep.

Maude's eyes opened, and she burst into tears. Stephanie noticed.

"You're awake, what can I get you?" The girl smiled.

"I know you," was the shaky reply. "Who are you?"

"It's Stephanie, Mrs Dillingham... Stephanie Hunter." Steph held Maud's hand, ignoring the grime and sores.

"Hunter... Stevie's little girl?" Maud wept harder, remembering Stevie, convinced she was complicit in the murder of Stephanie's father, remembering Roger Smith ranting about how Hunter had deserved it.

"It'll be okay; you're safe. They can't hurt you now." Stephanie wrapped her arms around the woman, comforting her. Stephanie teared with the memory of her father. Maud trembled in the young girl's arms.

"We need to get you cleaned up and food into you."

Stephanie took Maud to the river and helped her bathe in the cool, restorative water. Camouflage fatigues hung loosely on Maud's wasted frame, and a tin plate of hot food and a cup of apple cider ended up in her hand. The cooks in this camp had a different idea of good food, but in her hunger, she ate heartily, accepting the food as the best she ever tasted.

Jeff watched his people work with Maud. Unlike most of the refugees from Weyburne, he had a positive opinion of her and less judgement. Jani had liked her former boss and said nothing but good things about her, with sympathy over Maud's predicament with Roger Smith. Jeff would interview her after she gained strength. There was no hurry. For the time being, Jeff had bigger priorities than Maud Dillingham.

Chapter Twenty-three

"Maud, this is Karen Lefevre." Bill opened Karen's screen door.

"Welcome, Maud," Karen flashed her customary smile. "We have a room ready for you." School tables and chairs, rearranged for dinner crowded the living room. A couch and easy-chairs lined the sides.

"Lefevre sounds familiar." Maud sat on the couch beside Sharon Shadly.

"You know her brother, Walt, from Weyburne," Sharon replied. "We all live down the valley."

Maud seemed dazed but regained some strength during the two weeks she had been in Huron territory, although Maud looked frail. She had lived in fear and guilt for so long; she struggled now to embrace a new reality.

Jeff had kept her in Singhampton for the two weeks while she recovered from the physical effects of her ordeal. Her body responded to food and rest; her mind remained fragile. She convicted herself of many crimes.

Moving Maud to Kimberly had required waiting for transport in Chester's pickup after he had crisscrossed the newly gained territory trying to understand the strengths and needs of the population. Someone told Jeff the exaggerated story Chester had spoken to every adult and most of the children from the Beaver Valley to the Devil's Elbow. Truthfully, he had been to most of the area and talked with many people. When he understood the territory, he felt free to drive Maude to Kimberly.

Sharon and Bill Shadly travelled from Feversham to Singhampton to help with Maud. Jeff had debriefed Maud only to be certain of the situation north of Weyburne. Although he wanted to hear Maud's story, Jeff had not seen Little Bill or Jani for three weeks.

Jeff hugged his parents. Brandi emerged from the kitchen to kiss her brother.

"Give kisses to Jani for me."

Jeff disappeared out the front door. His road-weary feet hurried over the roughening surface. It would be after dinner when the homesick soldier arrived at Longview.

"Do you feel up to talking, Maud?" Bill wanted to hear about their Weyburne friends.

"It might help you, my dear." Warren's kindly smile reassured Maud.

"Thank you for helping me." Maud hesitated. "I thought you might hate me too much." She teared up. Sharon gave Maud a handkerchief.

"We never hated you, my dear." Warren once again gave gentle reassurance. "We understand your ordeal. It would have been better if you had come with us, but too many thought you supported Angel and Smith."

"I was stupid... I was stupid but never meant to hurt anyone. Roger cornered me and threatened me. Soon, I was in too deep and couldn't get out. He's dead."

Maud revealed the fact for the first time, disguising her conflicted joy and anguish. It startled the others who had not imagined Smith being dead.

"What," Bill wanted Smith on trial and convicted. Smith's death denied the satisfaction.

"Angel's men murdered him and his youngest son a few weeks ago in the office where they killed Stevie Hunter. I think they were lucky. The goons shot them cleanly. I would've made the bastards suffer." Maud snarled her words, vehement.

"They dragged Roger from the café right in front of us to the police-office. They wanted to scare us, and it worked. Angel had no more use for the Smiths and made them expendable. The other kid, his oldest, had gone off to fight, all strutting and proud. He never came back. Roger said he had a glorious death, but it shook Roger."

"So the kid didn't die the night we escaped?"

"No, but you hurt him badly. A few hours after you left, he staggered into the café with a goon. Roger came barrelling in and organized a posse. The jerk left me tied up for another hour. He yelled at me like it was my fault, hit me a few good ones too." She sobbed. "I hope he rots in hell."

The listeners felt empathy for Maud.

"What else happened after we left?" Sharon feared the worst for many of their friends.

"They figured you headed to Mennonite country, so they searched west looking for you. They found the truck abandoned out that way. I knew better but kept my mouth shut and enjoyed their running around in the wrong direction. Roger posted a reward. Most of their bunch had gone south, so they didn't have many people. Weeks went by, and they gave up. Roger went ballistic when he found his other truck missing from the pit. He blamed Ron for stealing it and vowed to kill him."

"We stole the truck; Ron came with us," Sharon added. "He's at Longview."

Maude gave Sharon a warm smile.

"Roger took over the EAC. At first, the regulars there didn't want to work for Smith, but right off they killed the Centrebuck, making them all broke. Then he paid them a few Canadian dollars to be there, way below what they needed to live, and so they didn't work hard and stole whatever they needed. Eventually, they fired your friends and put in their goons. These guys did not know how much physical effort it took. Some animals starved to death. It ended up a big mess. The surviving animals went to Roger's insider friends on farms."

"Roger used to repeat something Angel said: make them want you; make them need you and then make them fear you. When he cancelled the Centrebuck, he said it would make the people need him. Roger thought he was in charge. The folks in the hills thought of him as a dupe. They used his ego like a puppet string. I enjoyed watching. The fear came soon enough."

Brandi brought in a large platter of chicken. Roasted potatoes followed along with some late asparagus. Green onions in water glasses completed the feast.

Jean and Sharon flanked Maud. Warren sat opposite with the others randomly arranged including four students.

"This is impressive," Maud fingered a white serviette, "real linen."

"You're special," Jean smiled. "Besides, paper napkins don't exist. The plates don't match except for Karen's original few that didn't break."

"The Second Law at work," Warren mumbled.

"Brandi," Maud finished her meal, and dabbed her lips with a napkin, "I remember you as a young girl. You've grown up and have a following."

"Mrs. Dillingham, I'm both a teacher and a student." Brandi's formality caught the attention of her young protégés, used to the casual. They made fun of "Miss Shadly" until Karen made them stop.

"As unlikely as it seems, these brats are our future leaders. I'm pretending to be like Karen and my parents."

"You'll get here soon enough," Karen laughed.

"I have more to tell," Maud said, "but should I talk in front of the young ones?" Maude thought of her missing daughter.

"Maud," Warren's frowned, "everyone grows up fast these days. These kids have heard some awful stuff so more won't hurt. They need to know who we are fighting."

"People resisted," Maud picked up her story, "and did little work. A few sided with Angel and Smith, more dodged and pilfered to stay alive. Angel forced cooperation. He cut off all the electricity and natural gas and only restored it to those who swore loyalty. They even cut off their supporters. Roger said to remind them who's in charge. Most pretended loyalty, leaving a handful of holdouts. Then, they played their big card. Angel was in with the power brokers in Toronto who controlled the surviving banks."

"We have an ex-banker at Longview," Bill said. "He had a conscience and ran away with his family."

"I wouldn't trust any of them." Maud flared. "The café was never my property in the first place, but Smith came in one day with the original defaulted mortgage on the building and the deed signed over to Angel. He told me he could throw me out anytime, but if I was nice to him and his friends, he might sign it over to me. I don't know why he kept threatening me. Maybe he knew I hated him." Maud paused and then burst out, "God I hated him!"

"The only place I could find peace was visiting Al Wright and Ester. They still ran the prayer meeting, a way for us to comfort each other."

"How's Al?" Jean loved the Reverend and his wife.

"He isn't too good... in mind anyway. He's feeling guilty that he couldn't save more people."

"What do you mean?" Warren had hoped the Wrights would somehow make it to Huron.

"Smith and Angel threatened the Wrights. They said they knew where Al's children were, and if Al didn't cooperate, there would be a price to pay. Al said they showed him proof. Worse for Al, Kevin DeSantos remember the other preacher in town? He and his family disappeared. Al believed Angel murdered them." Silence claimed the table.

"I saw lots of bad things." She paused once more, "a lot of the women lost their families, their husbands and many children. They conscripted everyone over fourteen. Most never came back. Jani's father...," her voice choked, ".. Jani's father and brother never returned home. Some women who lost husbands joined up. They had no way to support themselves. People joined to find their families, most never returned. Jani's mother didn't go fight, but the last I heard she was living up on the hill with one of those goons. Or maybe she's a hooker up there. I don't know. People are desperate and have been doing desperate things."

Bill looked at Sharon. They would not tell Jani.

"Angel used the mortgages and defaults to seize all the property." Maude changed the subject to a safer horror. "They even claimed title to the land their friends like Bob Spencer farmed and said if they lived and farmed there they would get it back. I don't think they intend to give anything back. Spencer is just a tenant farmer."

"I remember his loyalty to Smith disgusted me," Bill flared, "especially on the posse and then betraying Warren before we fled. Sometimes people get what they deserve. I won't forgive anyone who followed Smith." Bill rattled some dishes as he banged a fist on the table.

"One night," Maud continued, giving Bill a nervous glance, "Roger was drunk and in one of his better moods. I think Angel had patted him on the back for something. He would ramble on when he was drunk and told me Angel's thugs killed the Quinns. He wanted the farm because it was next to his. The Quinn's wouldn't sell so they threatened them. It got out of hand when Quinn grabbed a gun. The thugs murdered him. Since the family saw it, they killed them all. Those three we arrested were just a lucky diversion. Smith broke them out of jail to keep them looking guilty. They were lucky. Angel needed labour and made them slaves. As far as I know, they're still working for the bastards. Roger said he was proud of the way he helped Angel cover it up." She paused again and gulped. The detail gave her story credibility.

"Roger and his boys did the jailbreak. They figured Stevie wouldn't fear them until it was too late, and they killed him deliberately. Stevie thought the three were innocent. Smith didn't want him convincing the rest of us."

"It's a good thing they're dead," Bill said. "I would kill them myself." A chill gripped Brandi as she relived her grief for Stevie.

"Do you know the thugs who murdered the Quinns?" Chester had known none of the people involved. "You'll have to make a formal statement. If we get control, these killers will pay for it."

"I don't know who did it," Maud said quietly, "just lynch them all."

"They might hang," said Warren, "I hope the rule of law survives."

"It's worse," Maud replied. "They made up a list of all the defaulted property owners and posted a PLM law that said everyone in default was a criminal and indentured to the title owner. Of course, that was Angel. If people farmed, they could earn title to their land. At least those guys had a chance. Anyone who just had a house became a debtor condemned to servitude. These folks could barely make enough to survive. It's a combination of feudalism and the company store. Angel runs all the food distribution. No one can ever get out of debt and will be slaves forever. They posted the names of everyone who had defaulted but were missing. All of you are on that list. There's a reward for helping capture or kill you."

"Why don't they run away?" A young student asked.

"You don't understand," Maud replied, "they have everyone scared. One family in town resisted; they publicly shot the father and mother, and the kids disappeared. After that, no one dared resist. Besides, no one knows there's a free territory anywhere. The only news comes from Toronto radio, and it's all lies. There's a rumour about a band of robbers helping people. Angel is working hard to find them. They blamed this mysterious outfit for the power outage we had in the winter. Roger said it was sabotage, and they shot two guards at the Orangeville yard for letting it happen. We didn't have any electricity for over a week and nearly froze to death. Ice damaged a lot of things."

"Someone, out of spite or desperation denounced Evy. Through all of this, she stayed at the town hall, the last of the old guard. They said Evy passed on information to these nameless bandits. One day, they dragged Evy and her husband into the police station and tortured them, trying to make them talk. I could hear the screaming from the café. It was horrible."

Maud broke down, crying as hard as she had ever done. The listeners shared her horror. Jean comforted Maud until her tears subsided.

"They kept Evy alive until April but killed her husband weeks before. I only guessed she died because the screaming stopped around Easter. If it hadn't of been for Al, I would have killed myself. As it was, I thought Al might do the same thing. He blamed himself for not saving Evy."

"I made a run for it after Evy died. I figured I had nothing to lose and tried to get an idea from Roger what was around us to see if there was a safe-haven. He mentioned troublemakers near Georgian Bay. You did something last fall to get their attention."

"Yeah, we cleaned out the racists up the hill here," Bill said. "They'll want to fight us now we have taken Singhampton."

"I was trying to decide when to leave, waiting for nicer weather. Angel decided for me when they dragged Roger out of the café. I thought they would torture him. Then I saw them bring in his son. Soon after, there were two shots." Her lips curled into a smile.

"I ran to the church. They would kill me next to tie up loose ends. Al hid me in the basement. The goons came looking for me. Al said he thought he saw me heading west out of town. He later said the Bible says not to bear false witness against thy neighbour, but he reckoned it was okay to bear false witness for your neighbour."

The refugees from Weyburne laughed, recognizing the "Wrightism". Al called his interpretation of the Bible the new, New Testament.

"It was too dangerous for Al and Ester to hide me. They gave me a bit of food, an enormous sacrifice because they had little. Al told me to head north and not stop until I reached the lake and hide in the daytime. I slipped away at night and wandered for over a week. Hunger drove me crazy enough to walk up the old highway and Jeff's people found me."

Maud sipped water and held her face in her hands. Her sobs continued for a long time. Everyone sat in silence, mending troubled hearts.

Chapter Twenty-four

"Warren told me the restoration of electricity encouraged him. He knew industrial technology had damaged the Earth's ecosystem to the point of failure, but felt we had become too dependent on it to give it up quickly. He hoped we would have several generations to work out something new as our old technology declined. Warren knew there had been a horrible collapse in the human population. He felt using leftover technology would ease the suffering of the survivors. I just enjoyed having some lights and the use of the water tank. It let us move the Institute to the old ski resort."

From: "Conversations with Jean Bennett," in the "Voices of The Founders," series by Erin Thomas

"This is awesome!"

One of the young students flicked the lights on and off. Electricity had come once more, but only to Kimberly and Eugenia.

"This will start industry at this end of the valley." Warren smiled. "Shortly, there will be a metalworking and repair shop for the generating station. We plan to make components for micro-hydro turbines and generators, and distribute them to the locals."

"Will they teach those skills?" Karen expected that development.

"We need technical people," Warren said, "labourer apprentices. It's planned to have a heavy sawmill near the generating station. This is the only site we have in the territory able to produce enough power for big motors. We only run about six hours a day when there is water, more hours in spring, less in summer and winter."

"How do we pay for this?" Maude knew everything had a cost.

"This is a strategic project. Huron Council made the military engineer manager. He gathered electricians and a technician who once worked at this site. The team will live there full time. The territory will subsidize them with food, but those of us who benefit from the power must contribute. We will give food and labour, at least one person-day of food each day. Having electricity will be the same as having another mouth to feed."

"Can we do it?" Brandi spent much of her day in the garden or barn.

"This's getting costly." Karen's enthusiasm for electricity waned.

"The region has to confront the issues of money and internal trade." Warren tried the light switch. "We must avoid currency, using barter, trade and gifting only. Fiat currency is open to manipulation. If greedy people took control of the money supply, they would end up running everything. For now, perhaps for all of our lifetimes, this electricity will be available. What happens after that is a question. We have to build a solid region, politically and economically. It will only be possible if we defeat the PLM."

"We must be environmentally sustainable. It's unknown how much environmental damage occurred during the past six years on top of the previous disaster. The climate is changing. I can see it in the trees. Maybe we can't recover. We can only try locally and limit technology and cannot afford industrial pollution. I think it's fortunate that the collapsed world depleted most of the cheap resources."

"Jean and I plan a trip upstream to Eugenia." Warren spread some maps on the table. "We'll look at the watershed to decide what is farmable and what we should reforest. The larger the treed area, the more reliable the water-flow. Eugenia will get power. The folks up there need to see a benefit from it, and we need power for the head gates of the penstocks. Trees are my speciality, so I am looking forward to this trip. Jean and I have never been camping." Warren smiled.

While Warren and Jean surveyed the upper watershed, Jim Handley analyzed the condition of the old resort. It needed repairs, but he deemed the building safe. The lobby area, dining room and other public rooms were the first he renovated, to provide cooking and dormitories. Most staff and students moved to the larger facility. Warren and Jean became the adopted parents of the resident students.

Karen and Brandi remained in the old house, and Karen's kitchen remained The Centre for Advanced Speculation. People gathered at Karen's for evening tea and a long discussion.

Maud flourished, in charge of the school kitchen and the administration and record keeping for the whole of the HEI. Maud had run the planning office for the Ministry of Natural Resources in her life as an Ontario civil servant. The familiar work restored her. Maud had not been this happy since her first months in Weyburne.

Jim surveyed the site of the generating station to build living quarters and shops and repaired a nearby vacant house to accommodate the first operators. Even though it was the mid-summer agricultural season, a crew of a dozen workers appeared and brought two pole structures from adjacent farms to make the shops. Lacking concrete and steel for proper foundations, Jim dug the timbers deep below the frost line, completing the work in record time with some machine shops operational before harvest. Jim Handley earned a reputation for building quickly and with quality.

***

Karen and Brandi laboured on the front lawn of the old resort planting mid-season beets, onions radishes and greens. The sound of horses' hooves, many horses' hooves, complete with whistling and calling attracted their attention. A small herd of horses swept up the lane, wrangled by a middle-aged man and woman, both astride lively quarter horses. The little mob spun to a halt in front of the women. Streamers of sunlight filtered through the flying dust.

"Are you in charge here?" the man spoke quickly, excited by the just completed trail drive.

"We have a proposition for you." The woman spoke without waiting for an answer.

"I am Karen Lefevre. Yes, I am in charge of the Institute. You made an interesting entrance."

The pair dismounted. Both newcomers wore Stetson hats, flamboyant western shirts and well-worn high-heeled boots, nearing the end of usefulness. Bowed legs told of a lifetime astride horses.

"I'm Jake, Jake Costello, and this's my wife, Maureen." The newcomers had firm country-honest grips.

"We heard you were looking for horses and people to teach," Maureen said. "We have horses, a few more than these and know a thing or two about riding and harnessing. I'm a master farrier."

"Yeah, we have worked a lot with horses, riding and wrangling. We can teach harness making and farrier work." Jake stumbled as his horse gave him a firm nudge.

"You got any water we can give these critters?" He patted the horse's neck and scratched behind its ear, letting the coarse mane pass through his work-roughened hand.

Brandi retrieved buckets and helped Jake draw water from the nearest tap. With electricity flowing, they could pump water and had full plastic barrels for the frequent episodes when the power failed. Maureen strung a rope between several of the trees and tethered the ten horses, western roundup style. The unkempt lawn provided fine grazing.

"We hadn't considered this so soon or so big," Karen and the others sat at a glass-topped patio table. A student appeared with cups of water.

"What do you have in mind?" Karen felt overwhelmed.

"Chester Amik dropped by last week and said you would like some horses. He explained what you're doing. We thought we could help." Maureen sipped cool water.

"We have a ranch towards Maxwell. We have too many horses. It's a struggle to grow food for them and us. We're offering them free, just board them nice. We would teach about horses."

"We thought people could come up to help and learn as they worked." Jake looked at his wife. "Maureen is a good riding instructor. I make harnesses. Our kids, Little Jake and Muffin, can teach too. You get four for the price of none." Jake laughed loudly at his joke.

"You drive a hard bargain," Karen said. "I need a second to say yes."

"Where can we put them?" The problem overwhelmed Brandi.

"I saw a barn just up the road," Jake responded, "and good pasture there too. When the gaffers get here, we'll go check it all out. Where are those slowpokes?" Jake turned in his chair, looking out to the road. "You would think they were carrying the horses. They were right behind us at the start."

Karen and Brandi already liked this pair of cowpokes. Sophistication lay beneath their down-home style. Both had graduated from the University of Guelph. When anyone visited their ranch house, they would see frames of ribbons won at most horse competitions in Ontario from the Grey Quarter Horse competition to the Royal in Toronto.

Maureen came from an old, local farming family. Jake was the brash upstart, originally from Windsor, but sounding as if he had oozed out of the local dirt. After the crash, they lived between the Flesherton mob and Huron, surviving and keeping their horses safe.

"There they are!" Maureen stood, looking towards Kimberly. The sound of horses and the crunching of steel-rimmed wagon-wheels came down the road. Two wagons loaded with hay and horse gear pulled up to the building. Jake and Maureen Costello had expected a positive response. Tandem teams of Belgian crosses stood quietly at the front of the rigs. A large young man and a slight young woman leapt from the wagons.

"This is Little Jake, and that's Muffin." Jake made the introductions. When Brandi shook the boy's hand, she had to tilt her head back to look into his face as he towered over everyone. Little Jake stood six foot six inches and every bit of two hundred and fifty pounds of muscle. Muffin had a natural beauty, a duplicate of Brandi except for flaming red hair.

"Well, he was little once," Jake laughed. "Maureen's potato salad grew him big. He sure loves that salad."

Brandi would post a drawing of her and Muffin standing on a bale of straw looking Little Jake in the eye and lecturing him. In the picture, the young man had an expression of defeated resignation.

The Costello's easily fit into the Institute, as if they had always been there. The old barn proved suitable, and the paddock and pasture were perfect for the herd. Jake and Maureen stayed two nights and then returned home with Little Jake.

"We'll leave one set of Belgians and the wagon," Jake told Karen, "these are nice and quiet. The other pair is younger and uppity. We'll keep them back. There's a couple of Canadians we're training to harness. We'll bring them down soon with a combination wagon. They'll be handy for running about to the supermarket and the doughnut shop." He chuckled, savouring his wit.

"Those old fogies over there would find it easier working with the smaller beasts." He nodded at Warren and Jean talking with Little Jake.

Muffin stayed for several weeks, teaching everyone but Maud, Warren and Jean how to ride. The latter trio learned to drive a wagon. Everyone enjoyed the horse training and dropped all other activity except tending to the gardens and livestock.

Maud complained about the lack of help in the kitchen. In reality, she did not mind the extra work. Being busy took her mind away from haunting memories. The most dreadful part of her day was returning alone to her bed. The bed itself reminded her of the old suffering. Many nights she could not endure the mattress and slept on the floor.

"Which one do you like best?" Muffin and Brandi leaned on the paddock fence watching the horses graze. August haze lingered in the valley. A warm breeze funnelled down the old ski slope.

"You're a decent rider now; you should pick your horse. It's best to bond with one. You just can't take mine." The girl pointed at her dark-brown filly with a white blaze running from her eyes to the nostrils.

"I like him." Brandi pointed to a big, light-brown gelding. "He's gentle. I think he likes me. I enjoy riding him best."

"It's no surprise." Muffin smiled. "I was watching you on Dodger. You do the best with him under you. Sometimes, a horse and rider belong to each other."

"Where did he get the name, Dodger?" Brandi stared at the horse, her horse. He seemed to know they were talking about him, lifting his head and turning towards the girls.

"He tries to get the easy work," Muffin laughed. "He's always dodging."

Even though Muffin was younger than Brandi, she had a lifetime of experience with horses. As a parting gift, Brandi presented her mentor a drawing of Muffin on her filly, both looking confident and proud.

"You make me look like I'm bragging." Muffin said.

"No, I am bragging for you. You are the best!" The girls hugged. Muffin swung onto her mount.

"I would like one thing from you," Muffin looked down to the older girl, "I want you to teach me to draw. Mom and Dad will let me come down in the winter. You know so much more than I do. Maybe we could talk and stuff." Muffin felt she had said something important. Brandi's smiling agreement made her happy.

"Come down for the harvest party at Longview," Brandi called after her. She understood the desperate isolation Muffin must have endured on the remote ranch.

Chapter Twenty-five

Karen and Brandi stood in the Longview barnyard, cinching their saddles. Willard called the farmyard "The Plaza". Longview now resembled a little village. They had already laid the foundation for the next housing structure, running west from the lane, creating a gateway between it and the first stone building.

Residents filled the plaza to say farewell. Having come down from Kimberly for the harvest party, the two women were leaving on a pre-winter survey, searching out people with skills and spreading the news about the Institute.

"Take care of yourself." Jani urged Brandi.

"You had better more than me," a new baby was bulging in Jani. "Better still; tell that lug of a brother of mine to take care of you."

Jani shifted Little Bill on her hip and smiled.

As if on cue Jeff appeared, walking beside the stone boat as the team of Percheron drew one more load of cut stone down from the quarry. Don Hunter guided the team, the reins easily fitting into his hands. His confident manner reflected his progress as a horseman. Don would go to the Costello ranch for more training before winter and then Kimberly for some "book learning" as Willard put it.

"I can't call you Dad," Don had said to Willard, "but I'm glad you and Mom have hooked up. Dad would be happy she has found someone nice." Willard turned away so Don would not see his tears.

In one of the happiest social changes at Longview, Kathy Nelson paired with Harold Kovalevsky. Kathy insisted someone had to take care of Harold, and she was the only one with enough patience. "Besides," she had laughed, "every woman needs a good man to boss around, and Harold is a good man. He has the papers to prove it."

Harold grinned, "PhD means: Pretty Happy Dude'"

Harold would go up to Kimberly for a few weeks before Christmas to learn how to teach young children. His previous experience only made arrogant first-year students humble before his brilliance. Now, he needed to find his humility in the face of the trusting enthusiasm of the young. Put simply; he did not know how to teach.

Sitting high in their saddles, Karen and Brandi guided their horses towards the lane. The smaller children ran beside them to the corner of the building and waved goodbye. At the end of the lane, just after the bridge, they passed the newly completed charcoal kiln and the beginnings of a limekiln and the waterwheel they would install after next spring's flood. Jim Handley enjoyed the challenge of fabricating the mechanism.

Following them towards Heathcote, Walt peddled an old tandem bicycle with Joseph clinging to the rear seat. They were on their way to the boy's piano lesson. "The piano-playing church lady", as Joseph called her, was teaching him how to read music. In return, Longview donated food and repairs to her house.

Joseph had given a greater payment by tuning her piano. She had thought the instrument was fine, except for "that one D note". Even though he did not understand it Joseph had a perfect ear for pitch. Without a reference pipe, his slight frame almost disappearing into the inner works, he adjusted every string on her old Baldwin. She had never made better sounding music.

At the end of each lesson, she let the little boy play whatever piece he wanted. Walt would sit in her parlour listening to the lesson. When Joseph sat on his bench, legs too short and twisted to touch the peddles, his mentor would sit back, eyes closed and smiling as her little student, lost in a world of happiness, filled the room with a sweet, sincere melody. They absorbed Joseph's musical genius.

Leaving Walt and Joseph at the edge of town, the women walked their horses along the main road. They passed the old hall where the second harvest celebration had overflowed the place. Perhaps five hundred people had gathered and spent a fine September evening spread over the yard and roadway and down past the bridge.

The sight of Ben the postman being led about under close control by a sweet young lady amused Brandi. The young man carried their newborn son in his arms. His conversation seemed to comprise, "yes dear".

"We were lucky it was a pleasant night," Karen looked towards the building and yard, trampled by many feet.

"There has to be a change next year." Brandi looked back at the hall. "Maybe we can have it up at Kimberly."

"It's a long way for people to come." Karen was doubtful. "They had a bash in Flesherton. Every place needs to have their own." Brandi nodded. The territory was evolving.

They had no schedule. First, they visited the fiddle player who crafted his instruments and had told Karen he was interested in teaching violin.

The man was running out of steel fabricated strings and needed to find someone to teach making gut strings. Karen and Brandi had another skill to find.

By late afternoon, the pair arrived at the orchard run by Warren's friend and wanted to convince the orchardists to spread their knowledge of Silva-culture, fermentation and vinegar making. Deeper issues related to the economy and social life of the region confronted them.

"I see nothing in it for us," Les Young leaned back in the kitchen chair and rubbed his chin. "We have a good trade going. Folks want our products."

"Why create competition?" Mary Young added.

"You're the only ones in the valley," Karen replied, munching on Mary's apple cobbler, "but there's room for more producers up on the top and over towards Huron."

"If we expand, we can trade up there." Les was adamant. Karen puzzled over the problem.

"Look at it this way," she finally spoke up, "people will come here to learn and contribute labour and trade goods in return for the training. We will expect no one to donate anything free. You have some basic products like the mother of vinegar and spliced tree stock. You'll certainly have an expanding market for those, at least as long as you are creating new producers."

Les Young thought for a long time. "We could use more help," he said. "This would be a way to get some. Mother of vinegar would be a source of trade. God knows, we struggle to get food and need tools. They wear out. The guys in town need to live too."

"How do people pay you?" Brandi had taken part in discussions in Longview about trade.

"We get grain, meat, tools and some labour," Les said.

"How much can you use?" Brandi remembered this conundrum at Longview.

"We can trade one for the other, but yes, I see the limit. We always have needs so haven't really hit that problem yet, but I can see it coming."

"Then you need a balance for a stable, comfortable life and enough to pay the security levy and have a cushion for hard times." Karen had had discussions with Warren Dunne and others about this. "You can't transport your produce far, limiting your market. If another producer doesn't overlap, then it will all fit, be stable with no competition."

"You make sense," Les suddenly brightened.

"Another thing," Mary said, "our kids need schooling. We've tried to teach reading and math, but we don't have books, and neither of us was good at school."

"Come to the Institute for a week this winter." Brandi said. "We can teach the kids, and Karen can teach you how to teach. The Institute wants to support home schooling."

"Reading, writing and arithmetic would be good for them… help run the farm." Les focused on basic needs. "I don't want them to go off though. We need help here."

Les' attitude was common, but the Young's agreed to take part, setting the pattern for almost every encounter.

The women stuck to the main roads from Thornbury to Meaford, visiting the military training compound and then south to Kimberly before the weather turned nasty.

Their recruits included metal working folks in Thornbury and a wool spinner and weaver. They had carried some flax fibre, the first produced from the Longview crop. It had excited the woman to explore new material. Jane and John David volunteered to teach sailing for deck hands, and so new people to hear their stories. Brandi was Jeff's sister, sealing the deal. The sailors loved Jeff.

Before the pair descended the county road to Kimberly in the last days of October, they had filled a complete roster of trainees for the winter. Families, desperate to teach their children would make the trek to the Institute. They would leave with the children helped and the tools to carry on. Home schooling would become the method used to educate young children. No one could imagine a return to centralized education.

Brandi made a huge impression on everyone. The young girl had a flair for storytelling. She fascinated their hosts with tales of Weyburne, their escape and life at Longview. She filled her portfolio with drawings and notes. Many more images of families hung in their hosts' houses.

The sailors had a breezy picture of themselves on their boat, sails bulging in the wind and Jeff Shadly hanging on for dear life. The irrepressible couple would tease Brandi's brother every time Jeff visited.

The David's introduced Brandi to wine with similar results to Jeff's first encounter. She had never seen a brandy glass before and signed her work with a stylized brandy glass. Even though people appreciated Karen, they would remember Brandi Shadly with fondness.

Brandi did not realize it, but the October trip signalled the beginning of her career as wanderer, recorder, scribe, and storyteller for Huron and beyond. She would always spend much time at Kimberly teaching and learning, but she would become more familiar, and more comfortable, travelling the back roads of Huron Territory.

Karen and Brandi perfected papermaking and spent the winter creating a fresh supply. It had taken her some practice to work with the unfamiliar material, but Brandi soon found her stride in both pencil and ink.

Chapter Twenty-six

From that day I left home, the road was beckoning, demanding; its joy; its sorrow; its loneliness; its community, always before me, leading to a retreating horizon. I have never found the end of the Longview lane.
- Brandi Shadly Archives, from a letter to her mother.

Brandi swung onto Dodger and turned him down the lane. Karen walked at her side, prolonging the farewell.

"Take care of yourself. I wish I could go with you again." Karen looked up at the rider. The Savage rifle in a scabbard at the girl's right leg displeased her. She did not find it reassuring.

"Thank you, Karen. I know you could use my help. I have to go."

"It's your life's purpose, what I trained you to do." Karen patted Brandi's leg. "Bring back wonderful stories and drawings."

She watched Dodger and Brandi make their way towards town. Brandi now fulfilled her dream, but Karen's eyes grew moist. She felt the anguish of Sharon's heart the day Brandi first left Longview.

Brandi would first stop in Flesherton. She had outlined an intended route, but had no timetable. Interesting encounters and helping people would add time. Karen hoped Brandi would be back before fall.

The territory seemed safe. Locals had dealt with troublemakers during the first years of the crisis. Friendly people lived in the newly gained areas and happy to be in the Huron fold. Chester warned Brandi to give the

Saugeen River a wide berth. While the patrols reported all quiet, he feared the enemy would see anyone wandering too far as a spy.

Brandi led Dodger into the front yard of an old brick house in Flesherton. The unkempt grass, tended by a few goats provided nice fodder. A little girl about two years old scooted around the dilapidated porch, skidding to a halt in front of Dodger.

"Hello, little one," Brandi knelt to meet the child's eyes. "What's your name?"

"I'm Steppany," she said proudly and then suddenly shy, stepped back, staring at the immense horse.

"Stephanie, who is it?" A woman's voice came from the front door.

"Hi, Mrs James," Brandi reverted to her classroom respect. "It's Brandi Shadly."

"Do you remember Steph? She's the baby your brother rescued. We named her after the Hunter girl. She cared for this one so well and loved her so much."

"The mom never came?" Brandi smoothed Steph's hair.

"We think Steph was the child of rape. Her mother must have run away. No women died in the fighting. Brent and I have adopted her. Even if someone shows up and claims to be the mother, she won't get her."

Samantha James' eyes flashed, and her face showed deep resolve. Brandi had no issue with the idea. The James' would be the only family the little girl had ever known. All the same, her heart ached for the nameless woman who had given birth to this sweet little girl.

"Where's Brent?" Brandi could hear children nearby.

"He's helping with planting out of town. He'll be here for dinner. I have a few students out back, supposedly learning poetry. I need to get to them. Won't you come and join in?" Samantha headed into the house.

***

A warm clear evening ended a busy day. Brandi sat with Brent and Samantha on their front porch. Stephanie played at their feet, occasionally running to stare at Dodger, resting comfortably beneath a big maple.

"Brent is the chief magistrate." Samantha smiled at her husband. "He got the job because the locals felt an outsider might be fairer. His assistant is the guy who used to own a used car dealership. He's from an old local family, but he risked a lot to oppose the thugs. People trust him."

"Two families caused all the trouble," Brent extended the story, "They used the economic collapse to seize control, bullied folks and got more brutal over the years, using fear and murder to get their way. Only about a quarter of the population was actively involved; the rest were too scared and disorganized to resist. Everything changed with our liberation. The last of the perpetrators have almost finished making restitution."

Brent retrieved his adopted daughter from her precarious perch on the porch railing.

"Most of the hardcore ones died in the fighting. I guess they knew we would execute them. A couple disappeared. We assume they went south to the PLM." He tousled Steph's hair and set her on the porch floor.

"We've had trials for the rest. Two of them were guilty of murder, and we buried them with the rest." The casualness of his words masked the deep trauma.

"It's too expensive to jail folks, so we worked out a system for the others who had killed no one. They have to confront their victims, if they are still here, and reach reconciliation and restitution. Believe me; those sessions have been hard. We still have a couple of unresolved conflicts involving rape and enslavement." Brent's face grew dark. Brandi could see him struggling with the horror.

"Before you leave, I want you to meet a person who helped release the sewage into the river. His punishment is to apologize to everyone down the valley as he gets the chance. He has already met several."

"These guys have to do various amounts of repayment. I was helping plant today watching several guilty ones working in the fields. They must keep me happy to count the hours. It seems to work."

The sun slid below the horizon and following custom, everyone went to bed. Even though Brandi was eager to explore, she lingered in Flesherton for an extra day. She especially enjoyed the company of Samantha's students. Stephanie had warmed to her, melting Brandi's heart whenever Steph called Samantha, "Mommy".

They duly paraded the sewage villain in front of Brandi; however, it turned into a tea party with everyone sharing stories. Brandi saw the wisdom of drawing offenders back into the community instead of isolating them and sowing seeds of bitterness. She resolved to reinforce this approach wherever she went.

Brandi said goodbye and guided Dodger out of town. Samantha returned to the kitchen to clear the breakfast table and found a portrait of the couple and Stephanie, looking into the distance, seeking a future beyond their vision. The woman stared at the paper for a long time. The uncertain future played on her and Brandi's hearts.

Brandi and Dodger followed a side road west at a leisurely pace in a pleasant day. Many fields lay abandoned, but farmers had worked a good number. The spring crop was in, and fields of winter grain showed green.

By mid-morning, she reached a small collection of farm buildings on a prominent ridge. The view was satisfying, with the road falling away to the west between planted fields and hay almost ready for cutting. Trees swayed in the brisk breeze. Shades of green melded together towards a mist-shrouded horizon.

"Hello there." Brandi slid to the ground beside a man labouring over a horse-drawn mower. "I'm Brandi Shadly."

"You don't look like you're from the south." The man glanced up, suspicious. He straightened and spat into dandelion puffs at his feet.

"I'm from Kimberly." Brandi smiled.

"Guess you're safe enough," he returned the smile but glanced nervously at her rifle in the scabbard.

"Do you get many visitors from the south?" Brandi leaned against the rusting seat of the mower, watching the man checking the sickle blades.

"We don't get many visitors," he replied without looking up. "We see some from down there, patrols like your folks. They come by too. We aren't sure who's watching whom." Brandi remarked the man's good grammar, obviously more than the country bumpkin he appeared to be. The farmer decided to trust Brandi.

"Come in to meet the wife and have a bite." He straightened and stretched his back.

"You can put the horse over there in the paddock. There's a water trough, hay too. Don't mind the dog. He won't bite."

When Brandi entered the house, the aroma of roasting pork greeted her. Six adults and two pre-teen children shared the table. They ate before mid-day. They began working before dawn and would rest before doing more in the afternoon.

Another similarity with Longview, Brandi thought.

Everyone ate silently. Boiled potatoes, carrots and brown bread supplemented the roast, washed down with water. Brandi noticed the younger man staring at her.

"I know your brother." He said, just as Brandi became uncomfortable. "We trained together at Meaford."

The connection broke the ice. Brandi learned they ran a real farm operation, but with the one young couple part of the forward guard. If the PLM attacked, they would take the news to Huron. Some posts rotated guards, but the couple lived here permanently. The family gave them a cover story. The woman came from the second cohort at Meaford.

"We see patrols once in a while. They don't seem to be too keen on war and just want to make sure we will not have a go at them. The ones we've met seem decent. We tell them we see patrols from the north once in a while and that satisfies them."

"I think they're mercenaries." Jeff's friend added. "Maybe one day we'll find out if they're decent or not."

"Is there a chance of them finding me here?" Brandi realized she might be a risk to the operation.

"Not likely. They came last week and probably won't return for a month. Will you stay the night?"

Brandi helped with the barn chores. The wind was out of the east, so they waited for the rain to pass before haying. They had a few sheep and goats. A couple of pigs snuffled in a fenced yard with a small shed. The swine cultivated next year's garden expansion before they became the winter meat supply. A large chicken coop and chick hatchery dominated the farm. It impressed Brandi.

"Extra labour will come from Priceville to help with the hay and the harvest," a woman said, "payment is in grain, live hens and eggs. They're looking for people to work neighbouring farms, but so far, with no luck."

The requirement for so much labour to operate a farm meant several families had to live together in the Longview manner. The reduced population made compatible people scarce. Refugees might be the answer.

As she lay snug in her blanket in the hayloft, waiting for sleep to come, Brandi thought about how empty the land had become. Many thousands of previous residents disappeared. As she slipped into slumber, Brandi thought of her own family now separated by circumstance.

May all be safe, she thought as sleep claimed her.

Chapter Twenty-seven

"That's a large bunch." Matt peered out from the sumac grove. His binoculars followed a gang labouring on the railway right of way five hundred meters away.

"I see about a hundred workers clearing brush and two bosses and only two guards." Jeff swung his glasses along the old roadbed.

"I'll be damned!" Matt exclaimed. "Look again at those at the front, the ones being guarded." Jeff shifted his focus. Ted followed suit with his sniper scope. "Check out the guy with the machete."

"Wow!" Jeff exclaimed. "It's an escapee from Weyburne jail. I last saw him in Angel's orchard."

"At least one is still alive." Matt examined the guards. "The goons seem casual; I guess there's no threat of escape. No one's working hard."

A small crawler-tractor smoothed the gravel behind the forward group. A dump truck backed along the right of way and emptied near the crawler. The truck bore the logo of "RS Construction".

"They haven't bothered to hide the fact they took over Roger Smith's assets," Jeff spat. "The driver worked for Smith. Money and fear at work."

"I could take these guys out." Ted glued his eye to the sniper scope.

"Don't!" Matt exclaimed. "It would cause trouble."

"I was only kidding," Ted smiled, "but anytime."

Jeff looked at Ted. He knew He was not a hardened killer. If ordered to shoot, he would, but it would haunt him after. They often discussed the incident at the 26 barrier.

"Those two guys with the transit and the paperwork are in charge," Matt said. "I wish we knew their plan."

One supervisor began walking toward Orangeville. He would have to pass their position if he headed to town. They had no cover here, but to the south, the roadbed disappeared into trees.

"Let's grab him," Jeff enthused, "and find out what's happening."

"Will he talk? What'll we do with him after?"

"We can take him back." Jeff gasped. "He looks important. It might delay the work." They hurried into the bush and set up an ambush in the scrub. They could hear track-laying about a kilometre south.

"I hope no one comes up the line to screw this up," Ted whispered. "Here he comes."

The man seemed to enjoy the pleasant afternoon. He occasionally stooped to examine the fresh gravel. Although clean, his clothes were rough and suited for work. He was in his forties with a neatly trimmed, greying beard.

"Stop right there!" Matt leapt out. Jeff and Ted surrounded the target.

"Who're you?" The voice squeaked from a suddenly dry mouth. He resigned himself to his fate, ashamed he could not muster more courage. Over the past half-dozen years, he avoided dying several times. If death came now, at least there had been several reprieves.

"No names," Matt replied. "Who're you?"

"Barry Young," His voice calmed. *With thieves, I'd already be dead.*

"What's your job here, Barry?" Jeff patted the man down. Barry noted Jeff did not act like a thief.

"I'm the engineer for this railway construction. Moving dirt and pouring concrete is my forté." His well-educated voice strengthened.

"We won't hurt you unless you make us," Matt said. "We want information. Get into the trees."

Jeff and Ted half-dragged Barry by the arms, and Matt found a comfortable clearing out of earshot of the line. Young briefly considered trying to escape but realized he would have not gone far before dying.

"What's the story on all this work?" Matt asked.

"Things are settling down in Ontario." Barry thought the province still existed. "The Movement eliminated most of the opposition, and we are improving things. We need heavy industry, and we have fired up the steel mill in Hamilton. There's lots of scrap, but we need iron ore. That's where the railway comes in. Can I have a drink?" Ted produced a bottle.

"Fighting has blocked the Detroit River. The PLM doesn't want to take on the Yankees, so we need rail to by-pass Lake Erie. Owen Sound is the only port that still has adequate docks for big ships. Collingwood destroyed theirs with housing and a sunken ship is blocking Midland, so we are pushing the rails north."

"How do they plan to get past that hostile territory up there?" Jeff tried to appear local and wanted to see what Young knew about Huron.

"Toronto says they are a bunch of criminals who are weak and it will sweep away in one glorious attack," Barry smirked. "The PLM is strong and will win. We eliminated all the enemies down south."

Barry glanced at the faces of his captors, judging their reaction. He did not know who these men were. They could be agents from the PLM testing his loyalty. Young did not want to sound unpatriotic. Having an opinion could get you killed. Looks of genuine pain suggested these three opposed the dictatorship. He risked honesty. If the PLM wanted to trap him, there were easier ways to do it.

"Once they take Owen Sound, the PLM plan to take Sudbury and Sault Ste. Marie within the year giving us, uh them, a route west. They are hoping to get coal from Alberta."

"When do they plan to attack Owen Sound?"

"I am not sure, but soon." Barry tried to sound truthful. "We've surveyed the route to Dundalk and will have the track laid by autumn. It all depends on when we get rails. They can't make rail in Hamilton yet. Someone is rebuilding the extrusion mill, but it won't be ready for a year. They're stripping branch lines and shipping the rail here."

"Why rush the rail line before the attack?"

"Transportation is difficult, especially for sizeable amounts of anything including people. They'll bring troops and supplies up to the starting point. Orangeville is a big army camp with at least a thousand troops there, waiting to move up the line. My boss is an army officer who isn't too smart and talks a lot. He told me we'd set up a command in Weyburne, and I'll live there. The troops won't move until we can get them to Dundalk and then attack before the bad weather. Apparently, they have aircraft, old civilian stuff that can drop makeshift bombs and scout things out. They want to win before winter makes flying hard."

"So the attack will be in October?" Jeff seemed shaken. Huron was not prepared.

"If we're on schedule, we'll be to Dundalk about the middle of September. Give them a few weeks to bring up the army and get set, yes, in early October. From what I hear, they'll have a couple of thousand troops here and about the same at Collingwood and Kincardine." Barry guessed his captors came from the hostile territory and willingly committed treason.

Jeff and Ted exchanged glances. Huron could muster three thousand fighters, mostly made up of slightly trained volunteers of men, women and teenaged children armed with a mixture of the military and sports grades and limited ammunition. They had to avoid a head-on fight.

"What's their plan?" Jeff felt ill.

"My mouthy friend says they will attack up old highway ten. The force from Collingwood will move along the bay. The western force will be defensive and protect the generating station at Bruce. It's too hard to supply them because there's no railway past Goderich. They have their best troops in Toronto and along the Yankee border but are sure the operation here will be easy and short."

Matt wanted to discuss the information with Ted and Jeff, but not in front of Young who did not know who they were.

"You're a problem." Matt looked at Barry. "Now we have you, what do we do with you?"

"I won't talk." He said, suddenly fearful. "You can trust me." He had relaxed, but being a liability to his captors scared Young.

"I've heard that before," Ted scoffed. "I don't trust anyone."

"So what do we do with him?" Jeff asked.

"Please, I am not a supporter of the PLM." Barry begged.

"Don't worry; we will not kill you, but how can we know you won't talk? We'll have to take you with us."

"I think," Barry said after a moment's silence, "I can solve your problem. I can give you my son as a hostage."

The three men glared, horrified by the despicable suggestion.

"It isn't what you think," Barry spoke hurriedly, desperately. "It would solve a problem I've been struggling with for months."

"Too many mouths to feed," Jeff sneered.

"No," replied Barry. "Brian's twelve and they'll draft him at thirteen. I don't want my kid dying in that goofball army. Promise me you won't make him fight for you." Barry glanced at their weapons.

"If he came with us, he would decide for himself at sixteen, if we survive until then." Jeff's heart weighed with thoughts of Little Bill and pregnant Jani.

"Let's take him with us." Jeff pointed at the captive.

"You can't!" Barry yelled. "They'll think I ran away and make my family slaves."

"Calm down!" Ted hoped no one heard the outburst.

"Okay," Matt finally said. "We will take the boy, and he'll go with you two." He nodded at Jeff and Ted. "We can't baby sit, and nearer home the kid might run away."

"Where's he now?" Matt asked.

Barry led the men to a comfortable house in the heart of Orangeville. It took most of the morning. Bypassing the track laying gang, they strode boldly down the rail line. The PLM army had random uniforms; the three outsiders posed as Barry's bodyguard. With many new people wandering around town; no one worried about strangers.

Barry's wife was shocked and sceptical, suspecting the strangers might be slave dealers. Jeff produced Brandi's drawing of him, Jani and Little Bill. Love and happiness radiated from the page and calmed her fears. Jeff talked about kids and told stories of the baby and convinced Jennifer their oldest child had a chance for safety.

Brian did not want to leave but wanted to die in a PLM uniform even less. They had to leave quickly. Barry decided they could take a work train and drop off before the work site halfway towards Weyburne.

"Would you be interested in sending us information?" Matt tested Barry's willingness to betray his masters.

"I'll do anything to defeat the PLM."

"We need to know their plan," Matt said. "There's no guarantee we can win, but the more we know, the better our chances."

"When are you moving to Weyburne?"

"The rails will reach there in five days; We'll move up soon after."

"Do you go to church?" Barry's responded with a sheepish smile. He wondered if Matt was a religious zealot.

"No, we don't," Barry replied. "Most of the congregations are PLM supporters. They drum up the Christian angle. It helped when they were wiping out all the racial gangs, calling them the devil's coloured helpers. It made it easier to kill them."

"I want you to go to the United Church in Weyburne. You'll like the reverend. Sit in the first empty, centre pew from the front near the right-hand aisle. I'll show you code in a moment. Leave coded messages in the first hymnbook in the pew at the place of the first hymn you sing. On your way up the aisle, pick up the second hymnbook from the first pew to the left. If there are any messages for you, they'll be in it."

Ted and Jeff looked puzzled.

"The code is simple," Matt spread a sheet of paper on the table. He printed the alphabet along the top and then the second line with it offset one character so that "z" was at the beginning. He quickly filled in the rest of the matrix.

"This is all you need to remember. Each line shifts one character to the right of the line above and the front filled in with the leftover characters. You can make a new copy every time if you need to. There're a few simple rules. Substitute the plain message letters with the corresponding one on one of the other lines. Drop the e out of every word before you code it and do not use words like the; and; and pronouns. Let the decoder figure those out."

"Now remember this, group your coded letters into groups of five but do not leave spaces. Make one long string of letters on each line. The first letter in each group of five will be the first letter of the line you used to code the next four characters so we never need a key word. Repeat this using a fresh line at random for each five group. Only the four characters will form part of the message. If the last group is not five long, just add random characters but no repeating letters. This code won't be hard for a professional to crack, but most people can't. Let me show you."

Using this matrix, Matt quickly coded the message: "Your son will be safe." Jennifer gave him a thankful look. They understood the method.

"How will you be certain they haven't grabbed us, and someone sends false messages?" Barry was practical. The thought upset Jennifer.

"We won't," Matt replied. "If you're being forced, you'll have to include a warning, something subtle like using the same code line twice in a row for the blocks of five. If someone else is coding, we'll have to rely on the telegraph key method."

"What's that?" they all said in unison.

"When sending Morse code, every key operator has a slightly unique style. Experienced receivers get used to it, and they can tell the sender. We'll rely on the fact you'll have your unique way of saying things, probably a bias with which code lines you choose more often."

"How the hell do you know all this?" Jeff asked.

"The years in the Scouts are paying off." Matt laughed.

"We have to go." Barry stood. "This is the last run of the afternoon. The engineers are friends and won't see anything on purpose." Jennifer hugged Brian and cried. Jeff remembered a similar hug and tears from his mom.

"We'll tell your sister that you have gone to help on a farm." Jennifer sobbed. Brian tried to look brave, but his eyes glistened.

"We'll meet again in safer times," Matt comforted. "Be careful."

He looked at Jennifer and thought of Evy.

They made their way to the rail yard. Barry's status took them past security guards with no question. Jeff, Ted and Matt did not conceal their weapons. Most people gave them a wide berth. The soldiers wandering around seemed to be no older than Brian was.

The four jumped off the train on schedule. Barry rode to the end of the line. His partner would expect him on the last run, and they would ride back together. Barry did not want to make the devoted PLM supporter suspicious.

"I have to split off, here," Matt rested his pack in the dusty intersection of the 30 Sideroad and the 6th Line. "I need to set up Brian's dad's drop box."

Brian sniffled. He suffered severe homesickness and any mention of his family upset him.

"We'll head west here," Jeff relaxed and stretched a sore shoulder. He looked down the side road towards the fading sunset. The waxing quarter moon hung above the trees and would light their path for a few hours.

Handshakes followed in the fading light. Matt followed the road to the 4th Line and then angled through the swamp into Weyburne. Guards would be on the roads.

The back door into the nave squealed in protest as Ester Wright entered. Her morning ritual involved making sure the daily search party that hounded the Reverend and Ester would find no surprises.

Matt Long stirred in a corner pew, startling Ester.

"Sorry," he said making his way forward, "I got here about midnight and didn't want to scare you both."

"Hurry," Ester's agitated voice echoed in the hollowness of the great space, "someone might barge in anytime. They search every day and we leave the doors unlocked so they aren't suspicious. Hurry," she repeated.

"I only saw a drunk on Main Street last night."

"There are lots of drunks, but Angel has recruited some to watch everywhere but us in particular. It's hard to tell if one is just a drunk or a spy."

"They started that before we left town," Matt laughed.

"Al and I tried to help the drunks, but with little luck. The spies don't want help. Angel pays them in booze and food. They set up Maud's café as a sort of soup kitchen and flop house and the drunks are too comfortable to want anything better."

Matt only had time to outline the procedure that the Youngs would follow once they reached Weyburne before Al Wright hustled him into the basement, past the Sunday school rooms to the furnace room door.

"Hide in there, behind the furnace. They don't always open this door, but sometimes. We don't follow them around so I don't know what they do now."

Matt realized the floor was dusty, and his first step left a betraying mark. As Al closed the door, Matt walked to a bench against one wall, turned and walked back to the doorway. Then he walked backwards to the bench. A long step to the left took him behind the furnace where he sat against the wall, clutching his rifle with the safety off. He would not die without a fight.

The darkness pressed down on his gloomy mood.

Even in his nervous state of readiness, the opening door startled Matt. He raised his rifle and had flashbacks to the night at Riverton he shot three men. Several light footsteps sounded and a shadow from the doorway light fell against the wall. The rifle rose in readiness.

"Are you here," Ester's voice sounded calm and did not signal danger. Matt slipped the safety on and clambered to his feet.

"They've gone," she said. "Al's seeing them to the door. They are lazy it seems. Here's some food and water. Stay here until tonight and leave late, just like you arrived."

Ted, Jeff and Brian arrived in Flesherton two days later. Samantha and Brent James did not object when asked to look after Brian.

"We're the poster family for fostering." Samantha laughed. "We are the whole Huron Children's Aid. We even took your sister in this week."

"Where's she now?" Jeff asked.

"She rode towards Irish Lake and then to Southampton."

Jeff hurried to get back to his beloved Jani before their next baby was born. The new information went to Chester with Ted who eagerly headed to Meaford.

Brian Young watched his new friends disappear down the street into a misty rain. He had bonded with them but now had to learn to trust new people. His sombre mood fit the gloom of the day. He missed his family.

Chapter Twenty-eight

Dodger carried Brandi out the farm gate. His head was down against a warm drizzle blowing on a brisk easterly breeze. Brandi waved farewell to her hosts and turned west. Her wide-brimmed hat shielded her neck from the dripping rain. The horse's hooves sloshed where puddles had formed on the broken asphalt.

Her destination made Brandi apprehensive. The people at the farm warned her, "these folks are strange and don't let their words seduce you".

Their only other advice was to head north-west and not to go too far south of the village of Chatsworth. North and east of highway ten, people were solidly in the Huron community, but the southwest was in flux. PLM patrols often travelled away from the river.

Irish lake appeared as a patch of blue between the trees. The road descended, taking her close to a little body of water, a puddle compared to Georgian Bay. Everything appeared normal enough, and the rain stopped. A brightening sky lifted her spirits.

Blue wood-smoke curled from a stainless steel chimney. Brandi turned Dodger into an asphalt-paved driveway and dismounted, tying her friend to a decorative lamppost beside an unkempt flower garden. The big horse immediately explored the fare, choosing flowers for fodder. Brandi knocked on the door.

"Well hello sister," a gaunt, jolly face appeared at the door. The man flung it wide open without hesitation and no hint of suspicion.

"Come on in. What's your name, girl? I am Joshua." The little man, for indeed he only seemed five feet tall and dwarfed by Brandi, spoke in a friendly avalanche of words. "Is that your horse?" It seemed a silly question with no one else around, but Brandi did not dwell on it.

"I am Brandi Sh… " the girl began, but Joshua cut her off.

"No last name," he said suddenly serious. "What we don't know we can't tell. We won't tell lies."

He poked his head out the doorway and looked around as if someone might be watching.

"We don't want to be involved in whatever happens. Come in, Brandi, come in."

Brandi stepped through the doorway, wishing she had secured Dodger out of sight. The room might have been a living room at one time but someone had set it up for a meeting. Three rows of chairs faced a lectern. A large portrait of a young bearded man with long brown hair and wearing a white robe dominated the wall behind the podium. Even though she had not attended church, Brandi recognized Jesus dominating this makeshift sanctuary.

A woman appeared through a curtained doorway.

"I'm Sister Ethel," the woman said, extending a hand.

"I'm Brandi," she replied somewhat nervously despite the pair's disarming smiles. They led her to a kitchen illuminated by large windows. The clouds had parted, and sunshine struggled through. Ethel offered hot tea. Brandi found the taste pleasing. The warmth eased the dampness from her ride. Warm buns appeared, as tasty as the tea.

"What brings you this way?" Joshua asked. "But don't tell us anything you don't want repeated, especially nothing dangerous."

"I come from north of here," Brandi accommodated the man by being vague. "I'm travelling to meet people, see what is happening and let people know we have an organization to help if necessary. We especially want to learn new skills and finding those who can teach them. We share the skills with anyone who needs the help."

"You're a Good Samaritan." Ethel said. "Isn't that exciting, Joshua?"

"Very Christian," the man replied without irony. "We don't need help. We're in the end times so no use worrying. The Lord is our Saviour." He smiled, at peace with his future. "We can share our faith with you though and anyone else you might send this way. The true believers will find the sure way to paradise."

Joshua preached, but it did not sound like a sermon. The couple attracted Brandi who expected to hear more about their faith. This would wait until the evening as chores called everyone away.

Brandi settled Dodger into the garage and found loose hay and a water bucket. She learned that a patrol from the south had confiscated the missing automobile, but the pair showed no bitterness.

The chores comprised tending a large vegetable garden of potatoes, carrots, beans, peas, onions and fruit laden pear and apple trees. Chickens scratched beneath the trees. Ducks scuttled about a crude waterside shed.

"Brother Jones up the lake on the other side has pigs and sheep," Joshua explained. "We planted oats and barley up there. Starving to death isn't the same as being raptured." He chuckled, pleased with his joke.

"We aren't sure when the end will be. The Bible says we won't know beforehand. The signs are all around us now."

Brandi helped the couple weed their garden. It seemed a hopeless task, but after a few hours, they had made actual progress. The plants struggling in run-down soil did not have the healthy look of most gardens in Beaver Valley. Her explanation of humanure and other nutrient saving system horrified the couple, condemning the idea as sinful. Brandi found their outdoor facilities disgusting and would have preferred hanging over a log in the bush.

"Let's go fishing." Ethel rose from the lunch table. The meal had been simple, but deliciously satisfying. "Joshua has to prepare his sermon. We can catch supper."

The pair paddled to the middle of the little lake in a small, old, wooden rowboat. Years of neglect in the weather had perished the leaky floorboards. Plastic tubs for bailing prevented floundering. Brandi noticed a large boat with a huge outboard motor on the far shore and horribly out of scale for the lake. Ethel noticed her gaze.

"Those folks thought everything bigger was better." The woman remembered old times. "They annoyed us by blasting around the lake, scaring the fish. They went away right after the tribulation began. Those people were not believers."

Ethel fell silent. The boat's owner had killed his family and himself. The woman's sadness hinted at the story, but she suddenly brightened.

"Here, let me hook that worm for you."

It was a pleasant afternoon. Brandi had fished little and delighted at snagging a nice bass: "perfect for supper" as Ethel described it. The little craft rocked as the women shifted their weight and bilge water sloshed around their feet. The warm sun dappled on the surface, dancing off little waves stirred up by a north-west breeze.

They landed several fish, and even though the woman preached for much of the time, Brandi would cherish those few hours of pleasant relaxation, a fine introduction to an activity she would use to feed herself many times in the future. The woman said it would be good to stock more fish into the lake. Brandi promised to find out about fish and if anyone could provide fingerlings. The contradiction between preparing for the end times and the desire for longer range planning went unmentioned.

A satisfying supper of fish and potatoes preceded several locals arriving. Three families of believers lived at the lake. The only other resident was a reclusive man on the opposite shore who cooperated with the others but forcibly rejected their faith. One family comprised a mother, father, three young children and one grandmother with the other a family of three.

Everyone crowded into the makeshift sanctuary. One man played the guitar. Ethel performed credibly on a piano. Although taken aback by the standing, stomping and arm waving, not to mention the chanting in strange languages, Brandi enjoyed the music and the enthusiasm.

She wondered about issues of faith. They intrigued her. Brother Joshua preached, full of passion and exhortation, about the end times and the coming of their Lord with responses of "amen" and "hallelujah" from the faithful. Gradually, Joshua built up his theme, encouraged by the congregation, until he reached his final thundering statement. "Those who do not believe will languish in hell forever."

Brother Joshua stepped back from the small dais, and the piano sprang to life with the guitar following, leading another vigorous round of choruses. Once the last bar had sounded, everyone milled about in fellowship. Smiles and friendly faces pulled upon the girl's heart, and she felt close and comfortable with these folks. The throng seemed to be genuinely happy. Brandi wondered if that happiness could spread. In the aftermath of refreshments and visiting, Brandi's enthusiasm led her to repeat something she had heard years before.

"Reverend Wright said after the economy crashed it seemed we had already entered hell. He thought the Bible had lots of suggestions on how to avoid hell but none on how to get out once we were there."

Brandi laughed, seeing the irony Al Wright had intended. The response dismayed her.

"Who is this Reverend Wright?" one of the lay people enquired abruptly.

"He's the United Church pastor in Weyburne."

"Those back-sliding sinners, they're gay-loving, sin-loving reprobates who will suffer eternal damnation!"

Brother Joseph thundered his condemnation to the approving assembly as he consigned Al Wright to hell.

Brandi fought back tears and bit her tongue. Al and Ester Wright were her friends, people she loved and respected. She could not understand how someone who preached love could condemn another to death without ever knowing them. Her ignorance of the scriptures prevented her from arguing about who the Christian creed said was supposed to exercise judgement. Survival instinct silenced her as she struggled to smile.

The evening could not end soon enough. Brandi refused an invitation to sleep in a guest room, saying she always slept with her horse.

In the pre-dawn darkness, with a fresh cool north-west wind on her face, Brandi led Dodger from the garage and walked him silently on the grassy verge to the concession road. Once out of hearing, she swung deftly onto her friend and headed north, trying to ride away from sadness and disappointment.

Chapter Twenty-nine

"I felt sad leaving Irish Lake. The folks there seemed like such nice people, and thinking back I know they were honest and firm in their faith. I am glad I wrote a thank you note. They had lost perspective, I think. I owe them a debt. They were the first people to get me thinking about faith, and what motivates and strengthens people. Later, when I confronted other spiritual responses to life, especially the native ones, it helped me to want to search out and understand. Their judgemental condemnation of Al Wright, someone I knew was a good man, planted a firm resolve in me not to judge anyone. I intended to go back to Irish Lake to learn more about how their beliefs gave happiness, however, I never returned or learned their fate."

From: "Conversations with Brandi Shadly," in the "Voices of the Founders," series by Erin Thomas

As always, riding on Dodger lifted Brandi's spirits. Once they had travelled well away from Irish Lake, she rested Dodger and consulted her map in the light of early dawn. Traverston, an abandoned hamlet on her map, lay on the way to Townsend Lake, a larger body of water than Irish Lake and a thriving agricultural village. It represented the most southern extent of Huron Territory.

After a two-hour ride, Brandi turned up the short roadway through Traverston. As the houses came into view, she expected resting Dodger and watering him by the brook while she ate lunch.

"Who're you?"

Two armed men jumped onto the small bridge leading to the village.

"Brandi Shadly, from Kimberly," she noted the red "H" on the breast of their combat fatigues, Huron fighters.

"What's the password?" The man was abrupt.

"Beaver Cleaver," Brandi replied without laughing, too young to know the origin of the passwords and only thought they nicely rhymed. This the least secure password only changed every six months, and known to anyone travelling out of their locality. Security patrols returning from the south required three passwords.

"You're okay." Brandi walked Dodger to the other side of the creek and dismounted to let Dodger drink.

"What are you doing way out here?"

"I'm travelling around, meeting people to see how they're doing. We're assessing educational needs and trying to find people with skills to teach." Brandi followed the men to a small shelter hidden in the trees.

"You surprised me. I didn't think anyone lived in Traverston."

"This is a forward watch-post. Our job is to spot hostiles and report back. If you had not looked harmless, you would never have known we were here."

The man leaned his rifle against the wall and drank from a small flask. Brandi enjoying her water-skin, dug bread and boiled eggs from her pack, and wondered if he meant they would have stayed hidden or she would have been dead.

"You need to be more careful, young one. Hostile patrols are around. You can't assume anywhere is safe." Brandi silently accepted the scolding. "See where your rifle is?" he pointed. "You left it on your horse, no good to you over there. It should always be an arm's length away."

Brandi retrieved the Savage and ammo pouch.

"Where're you headed?" The man marvelled at the brave girl making such a ride.

"I'm going to Townsend Lake, eventually to Southampton, back through Owen Sound and along the bay." Brandi finished her lunch.

"That's a big ride, impressive. You'll find Townsend okay, nice people and they serve a great fried-fish dinner. Head north-west from there; don't stray too far south. I would head right to Chatsworth and then angle over to the lake well back from the river. It's a long week's ride." The men walked her to the horse. Dodger reluctantly followed her lead to the road, and she swung into the saddle.

"For God's sake, be careful." They spoke in unison. Brandi nodded.

The sound of hooves faded. The pair returned to an endless card game. A sketch of two men and a rider on the bridge lay on the table.

The encounter with Brandi would become a topic of conversation wherever the two went. Soon, many conversations would compare notes as growing numbers of people recounted meetings with the lone girl on the horse. People would examine drawings hung in public places, hoping to find their meeting with the scribe notable enough for public display. Many proudly kept Brandi's drawings in their homes.

It took Brandi three weeks to reach the Southampton area near the mouth of the Saugeen River. She spent most of the trip visiting small farming enclaves and helping for a day while everyone exchanged stories. In an era of little news, Brandi's accounts of the liberation of Flesherton made a big impression. Many people had friends and family affected. She found people willing to travel to Kimberly for training. Many children lacked any education. Brandi's trip prepared the way for a network of home schools and hectic weeks at Kimberly.

Dodger faithfully carried Brandi through regions more-populated. The country remained open territory with both Huron and hostile patrols wandering back and forth, guarding against an attack across the informal boundary of the Saugeen River.

Dodger picked his way gingerly along the broken surface of the road. Brandi trusted him to take the safest footing and concentrated on her surroundings. Clouds filled the sky, but with a westerly wind, she did not expect rain. The brightening horizon promised a night under the stars.

"Whoa! Dodger," Brandi yanked on the reins; Dodger snickered in protest. He seldom felt any urgent guidance. Brandi focused her binoculars on the road ahead.

"Yes, there!" she held the glasses steady, "I see them." She developed a habit of talking aloud when by herself. She believed it interested Dodger. Deep down, she felt lonely, and the sound of her voice comforted.

An armed group approached, luckily on foot less than a kilometre away. Dodger wheeled about. A rifle bullet went past to the left harmlessly into the trees.

Stay north, away from the river, Brandi was angry with herself. She had wandered too near the Saugeen. Another shot rang out, closer.

Dodger cantered along a diverging road towards a thick bush. Brandi used the trees as a screen and swung across a field beyond the woods, exploiting Dodger's speed, wanting to be out of sight before the patrol reached the field. Shrubs covered the abandoned meadow. It would be difficult following her through the mess of vegetation, although the horse left a path of crushed weeds.

Dodger made good time despite small willows slapping his flanks and stinging Brandi's legs. She decided, if she survived, she would get some leather, riding chaps. They reached a crossroad and turned north.

Patrols from the south seldom went over five kilometres from the river. She hoped they would soon lose interest. From a small grove of trees, Brandi watched seven fighters enter the field. They stopped just into the scrub and seemed to debate. The leader's binoculars swept past Brandi without a pause. The rest of the force rested and had lunch.

Brandi followed suit, sitting astride Dodger as she ate, keeping a wary eye on the distant field. The pursuers finally turned back in the direction they had come. She let them disappear then led Dodger to a stream for a much-deserved drink.

"I guess you're the smart one." She hugged the horse's neck. His ears perked up. Brandi thought he had nodded in agreement. She giggled, letting the tension escape.

Chapter Thirty

"That young girl... that young Brandi... changed my life. I had despaired and lived day to day. That wasn't me, but it seemed hopeless. Then she came wandering in with that big horse and some new ideas and enthusiasm. I'm near the end now, but these last few years have been the best of my life. It seems this was why I lived."
From: a note from Corrine Wilson to Stan Gregson

Brandi broke camp after a wonderful night beneath a canopy of stars. Her narrow escape had driven her north, and she found a secluded spot near the eastern shore of Aaron Lake. It seemed prudent to keep the lake between her and the river. Southampton lay at the Saugeen's mouth where the stream emptied into Lake Huron, but she was uncertain of the boundary. She had not risked a fire and shivered in the damp air. Camping beside water had the disadvantage of heavy morning dew.

To reach Lake Huron she headed north to the old highway and then west. By late morning, she reached the native nation of Chippewa Hill.

The community seemed desolate and abandoned, and despite the bright sunshine, raised a feeling of depression. Brandi's spirits fell at the signs of suffering and retreat. Dodger's hoof-strikes echoed from crumbling buildings, their paint peeling, windows and shingles missing and some doors hanging angrily on one hinge.

The smell of wood-smoke became strong and a small plume rose from a chimney. Dodger happily turned into a gravel driveway covered in a jumble of vegetation. Someone had tried to groom the walkway. A weedy vegetable garden occupied the front yard. Brandi knotted the reins to the house's electrical standpipe leaving Dodger lots of fodder to nibble. As Brandi searched about for a water bucket, the front door opened. An older, native woman peered around the jamb.

"Hello, my dear," her voice was tired but firm and clear. "Come in. It's nice to have a visitor."

People eager to hear fresh stories always used similar words.

Her new friend was Ojibwe, her age un-guessable, and though tall the woman stooped slightly. Her old, clean clothes fit properly with signs of repair. Moccasins protected her feet although rubber boots and a set of work boots stood in the entrance hall. She walked with a slight limp as she led Brandi into her bright kitchen. A kettle steamed on the wood stove. Heat smothered the room despite an open door and window.

"Have tea, my dear." She poured the tan coloured liquid into a tourist mug that bore the words "Sauble Beach" above a brightly coloured umbrella stuck into rolling sand. The woman filled her mug. A spoon of maple syrup followed. Brandi mimicked her host producing a sweet, tingly taste, warm enough and satisfying.

"Spruce tea and syrup," the woman said at last.

"It's delicious," Brandi replied. "We use white pine and rose hips."

"I am Corrine Wilson. Where are you from?"

"I'm Brandi Shadly, from Kimberly near Flesherton."

"Do you know Chester Amik?" Corrine sipped, "haven't seen him in years."

"Do I know him? I live and work with his girlfriend." She giggled at her description of Karen.

"Yes, Karen I think her name is. She's a good woman." Corrine opened a pouch and extracted papers and tobacco. She rolled a cigarette with well-practised fingers and offered the makings to Brandi.

"No thank you, I don't smoke." Brandi smiled and remembered her father's disused pipe. Corrine opened the stove door to insert a long sliver of dried wood. A puff of pungent blue smoke rose above the table.

"I have a good supply of tobacco," she said. "There're lots of cartons of tailor-made. I like to save the matches for when I need them. My brother ran the tax-free smoke-shop and tourist trap over on the highway," she drew in a lung full of the smoke and exhale.

"Once the tourists stopped coming, he drank himself to death guarding the store. I inherited the stock."

She sounded matter of fact. Brandi saw pain in her eyes. They sat silently until the woman's tea and cigarette ran out. Corrine replenished both and Brandi a refill.

"Most of the people disappeared the first winter. Some took off with the loose cash. A lot of good that would have done them… money is useless. They probably tried to get to the Big Smoke, Toronto," she blew a perfect smoke ring to punctuate the statement, then coughed and smiled.

"Many of The People headed there. Some went north up the Bruce. There isn't much here to help us live. The communities up there can fish and hunt. Maybe I should have gone too, but I do okay here. I've not lived Indian for many years and don't think I can start now."

Corrine laughed and coughed again, stubbing the cigarette out, with a decisive motion, into an old tea saucer.

"Some youngsters went down to the Grand River to join up with the Mohawks to fight the whites all around there. Oh, I am sorry," she paused as if embarrassed. "I haven't seen them since. I'll make lunch soon. Do you mind fish and potatoes? I caught some trout down in the river. Come, I'll show you around."

She abruptly rose and limped to the open door. They reached the backyard food garden.

"How do you care for all this yourself?" Brandi began pulling weeds as she talked. Corrine joined in the work.

"I share this with two other ladies who stayed. They live over there. We're considering moving in together this winter, not sure it would work. We annoy the hell out of each other." Corrine laughed and coughed again.

"One is my half-sister, and the other is my father's sister's husband's cousin, or so she claims. That one turned up two years ago saying she lost her status card. We told her it don't matter a damn. Helping would be all the status she'd need." Corrine laughed. "She plays the guitar so gets bonus points. Winters here are long and snowy."

"How have you planted this?" Brandi stared at the arrangement of plants. Three varieties were growing from mounds that filled most of the garden except for rows of potatoes, carrots and beets.

"This is called the three sisters," Corrine replied. "It's a traditional native way of planting corn, beans and squash together. In the old days, it came from trial and error. Scientifically, beans climb the corn and fix nitrogen, squash shades out the weeds. It works. I rotate beans through the potato patch for the same reason." Corrine had obviously received an excellent education. Her occasional slips into slang and poor grammar seemed to be deliberate.

"We use manure and our waste, after it has composted," Brandi said, adding the native technique to her list of technologies to support.

"You use your poop?" Corrine seemed taken aback.

Brandi repeated the now familiar explanation, and it excited Corrine. She pointed to her smelly latrine at the back of the yard and made a face.

After an hour of weeding, Corrine made lunch. Brandi found water for Dodger, storing his saddle in the unused garage. Her rifle still slung over her back. If Corrine noticed the weapon, she had not let on.

After lunch, Corrine took Brandi to the river, and they spent a few hours catching fish. Once again, as on Irish Lake, Brandi enjoyed the activity and whooped in delight after catching a nice fat sucker.

"It's a bottom feeder," Corrine explained. "I call them *Pisces politicus,*" She roared at her joke but calmed to explain it to Brandi. Latin and scientific nomenclature had not been part of the Brandi's schooling.

Corrine's explanation led into her personal history. She had graduated from university and worked as a biologist for the federal government on native fishing quotas. Corrine had retired just before the crash.

"I didn't even get my first pension cheque before Harridan cancelled them," she sounded bitter, but then laughed. "I have little of a complaint." Brandi had heard more horrible tales. Still, her brother's death weighed heavily on Corrine's heart.

They were cleaning their catch when someone banged on the front door. Brandi un-shouldered her rifle and slipped in a clip. Corrine went to answer and did not seem concerned. Loud, friendly chatter reached the kitchen. Corrine returned with a large man in a threadbare OPP uniform, his own rifle slung over his shoulder. His hand instinctively found the weapon when he saw Brandi's rifle.

"Brandi, this is ex-constable Stan Gregson. Stan, this is Brandi, my new friend."

"Hi," Brandi slipped the clip from her weapon and leaned it against the wall extending her right hand.

"Nice to meet you," Stan shook her hand vigorously and put his rifle away. "The horse caught my eye, and I came to see who was here. I keep my eye on the old gals up here. I tell them I'm looking after them, but I'm afraid they'll stage an Indian attack."

They laughed. Corrine shot a make-believe arrow from an invisible bow at the constable.

"He just comes up here for baccy and fish." Corrine mimicked a thick native accent uttering a string of Ojibwe words she later loosely translated as: "The white men can't tell the worm from the fish but smell tax-free a mile away."

"I've tried to get these gals to move into town." Stan got in a word. "They're stubborn. They think they're going to inherit all the land from Sarnia to Little Current. I tell them they can't even run Chippewa Hill when nobody is home. These university types think they know it all." Stan winked at Brandi and sipped the tea.

"Cops," Corrine sneered, "they're useless without a doughnut."

"Where did you say you're from?" Stan tapped a briar pipe into the saucer and filled it with tobacco. Corrine laid a flame to it and ignited a cigarette. Smoke filled the room. Brandi happily stayed by the open door.

"Kimberly, originally Weyburne. We had to run for it."

Stan had trained with Stevie Hunter, and he knew Willard. The news of Stevie's murder saddened Gregson.

"Like Stevie, I refused to go south," Stan said. "I still function as a constable, but there's no need for regular policing here. We worry about those guys at the nuke station. I watch and try to make people feel safe."

"You're Jeff Shady's sister? I met Jeff during that Flesherton business. My group linked up with him south of the town. I heard he and Ted Macedo had some big adventures as commandos. It sounded like fun to me but a young man's game."

"I have to go." Stan hugged Corrine. "Come to town tomorrow Brandi; I'll show you around. Ask for me at the bridge barrier."

He retrieved his rifle. Brandi admired Stan's solid quarter horse. The animal seemed eager to get home and moved off without encouragement. Horse and rider disappeared. Dinner was fish, much the same as lunch.

"I'll get Beth to bring over a chicken." Corrine reassured Brandi fish was not her only source of animal protein. "It's her turn to kill a bird."

The three women had a schedule for dealing with meat and other foods. Corrine would deliver a fish to each of her friends tonight and in the future would get a chicken or other edible in return. They would occasionally kill a lamb or kid goat to share and trade meat with others. The arrangement confirmed what Brandi had found elsewhere. Survival and cooperation went hand in hand. Corrine emphasized no one kept score. They would take care of each other if needed.

"Gifting is The People's way," she said.

***

"I was just a dumb cop. Sure, I was honest and did my job, which seemed to be one of dealing with drunks, punks and skunks. Few natives were my friends. Most of the ones I met considered me the enemy. Corrine Wilson was different. She lived in town but cared about everyone up on The Hill. She was on a committee trying to help all the young, but especially those kids up there. It wasn't surprising she stayed. For me, well my family liked it up here and so did I. When the orders came to report to Toronto it was easy to quit. The past few years proved perhaps I'm not dumb after all."

From: "Conversations with Stan Gregson," in the "Voices of the Founders," series by Erin Thomas

The bridge appeared through the rising morning mist. Brandi had made an early start after a breakfast of tea and cornbread with Corrine. She would spend the day with Stan, returning to Chippewa Hill before dark. Corrine had enticed her with the promise of a chicken dinner.

A guard-post defended the north end of the Saugeen River Bridge. The typical zigzag design roadblock interrupted the road itself with the fortifications facing town. Two armed men watched Brandi approach.

Brandi dismounted and walked Dodger. A rider could be intimidating. A walking approach doubled as a cavalry handshake.

"Good morning, I'm looking for Stan Gregson."

"You're early for him." One guard laughed. "Have a hot drink with us. Stan should be along soon. I guess you're the Shadly girl?"

"I'm Brandi Shadly. Your set-up is impressive."

"This is the unofficial border between us and the south," the man waved at the river. Brandi began sketching the scene. "Southampton is an open town. Everyone comes and goes easy; some live in town, others are from up behind. The other side has a checkpoint south, towards Port Elgin. The guards are employees of the nuke station. Our spies watch their barrier and theirs here in town watch us. We get along okay, and a few are our neighbours. If the Tim's on their side were still open, we would all gather there after our shifts." He laughed.

"Everyone benefits from the port. All the PLM stuff comes in at the nuke plant jetty or from the south, but we trade here for everything from ammo to coffee from the USA."

"Good morning," Stan's voice came from behind Brandi. "I see you've settled in." He poured a muddy, ground-filled coffee and strained it through his teeth. "Ugh!" Stan gasped. "This is your worst one yet, Will."

"You're welcome." The man poured a mug of thick brown drink. "No one calls me Tim."

"They're recruiting again." Stan said. "Has anyone asked you yet?"

"Nope, I don't plan to go," Will spat coffee grounds.

"Me neither," the other added.

"A few signed up. I hope we don't shoot each other."

"The local guys are okay," Will said, "but outsiders from Toronto are real bossy types."

"Yes," Stan confirmed, "more fighters are moving up to Goderich. Something's up."

"Too close," one man checked his rifle. "I don't like it."

"Come with me, Brandi. There isn't much to see, but I want you to meet people who sum up our problem."

Brandi led Dodger beside Stan. They ambled across the bridge and a few blocks down the main street. Stan pointed out abandoned businesses. Weyburne was a bedroom community dependent on commuters. Southampton depended on tourism, but the town had the same suffering appearance as Weyburne.

"Here we are." Stan stopped in front of a large church of the austere, factory-like red brick-veneer design of the late twentieth century, with a soaring steeple topped by a huge Christian cross and a parking lot for several hundred vehicles. A large residence near the church blended with the main edifice, both surrounded by immaculate mowed lawns and perennial beds flowering in the morning light. It starkly contrasted with every other place Brandi had visited.

Two people swept the expansive parking area. Smoke rose from a chimney on the residence. Stan knocked as Brandi secured Dodger to the lawn side of a low wrought-iron fence. The big horse bent to explore the meagre offerings of the closely clipped grass.

"When we leave, I want your opinion of this place." They waited.

"Hello Stan, I see you've brought a visitor." A middle-aged woman held the door open. She smiled from a gaunt face above a frail body. In the warm summer morning, she wore a thick sweater over a heavy house dress. She had tied her greying hair in a tight bun beneath a plain white scarf.

The pair followed into a roomy entranceway leading to an impressive spiral staircase. The polished, wooden floor supported an expensive rug, a settee and an antique coat rack made from dark wood.

The space conveyed an overwhelming impression of solidity and importance. Light gleamed from highly polished wood, highlighting a large open Bible sitting on a small table, its gilded letters shining from the pages. Beyond a large parlour archway, women cleaned, polished and arranged fresh-cut flowers. She ushered them into a book-lined study.

"Hello... hello, welcome... welcome!" A large man rose from behind a massive rosewood desk. "Is the sanctuary being cleaned today?"

The dispirited woman nodded and disappeared through a side door.

"I'm Reverend Rush, young lady, Arthur Rush. It's nice to see you, Stan." They shook hands and sat in oversized chairs. The furniture in the room perfectly matched the pieces in the entranceway. "Are you coming to our services this week, Stan?"

"Now Art, you know where I stand," Gregson frowned. "Brandi's a visitor. She's from Kimberly touring for the Huron Council. I thought she should meet the important people in the community."

Stan winked at Brandi who did not comment on her friend arbitrarily giving her official status. She travelled for the HEI, not Council, but Stan knew Rush would show more respect to an official representative.

"The Lord blesses us with your visit," Arthur smiled.

Brandi cringed, remembering similar words at Irish Lake. The girl could not reconcile these opulent surroundings with the simple, rude house occupied by believers at the lake.

"Come, let me show you around."

Arthur Rush ushered them out. For an hour, the man walked them through the buildings and grounds, emphasizing the care and work of the believers who maintained everything "in God's service". Brandi saw twenty adults and children labouring to keep everything perfect.

Contrasting perfection, a ramshackle vegetable garden lay unmentioned, in the shade at the back of the property. Brandi wondered why they had not used the sunny front lawn to grow their food.

Back in the study, they drank cold, weak tea but no food. The expensive china matched perfectly. They barely finished the uninspiring refreshment when the reverend abruptly stood and offered his hand.

"Goodbye, it's a busy day for me, many things to oversee. I'm sorry for those imperfections you saw. I must make sure they do the work right."

Rush scowled as if shortcomings reflected badly on his ability as a pastor. Brandi had seen nothing to complain about, other than the vegetable patch.

Rush guided them to the door. Someone had moved Dodger onto the sterile, crumbling asphalt driveway. She hugged her horse's neck, slipping him a handful of oats as she and Stan made their way back to the road.

"Quite a place, eh," Stan's tone was sarcastic.

"The building seems too important." Brandi glanced back. "They don't look healthy, overdressed. Hungry people feel cold even on a hot day."

"Exactly," Stan replied. "They're obsessive about the facility. This was the biggest church in the area with two thousand members. Most died or left. Many quit the congregation, but Art has a following that bring food to the few working here. They would starve to death otherwise and probably will in the end."

Stan seemed matter-of-fact. Brandi understood he predicted a slower version of what had happened in Weyburne. Many had slid into depression, losing touch with reality once their world collapsed. It amazed her that these folks had lasted six years.

"That building cost millions to build. They defaulted with the bank." Stan wondered at the fragility of what once seemed so strong.

"They had cash on hand to pay the mortgage for a few months of the first year. In the end, the bank closed. They lost all their cash."

Stan spat, perhaps in disgust or perhaps to eliminate the lingering taste of the unsavoury tea.

Brandi tried to understand. While those at Irish Lake emphasized people's spiritual condition, the ones in this place emphasized the condition of the physical buildings. She found it hard to see any unity in faith between the two groups. It all depressed her.

Brandi produced a drawing depicting the church building looming large with a wide expanse of the parking lot in front. Many people, deliberately drawn to a smaller scale, stood on the empty pavement. A diminished cross peeked from behind the massive gable of the church.

Chapter Thirty-one

"Heroes come in surprising shapes and sizes, perhaps we all were heroes, but I count my failures too highly. I know, Barry Young and his family are heroes. If we still erected statues, they would have one. Your drawing of us all on the church steps will have to do, although perhaps you could have made me less noble and more humble. I framed the picture and displayed it in the entranceway to the sanctuary. When I am gone, and the church building is closed, please find a safe home for it. The Young's deserve the honour."

From: a letter written by Reverend Al Wright to Brandi Shadly. The Brandi Shadly Archives.

The bright, mid-summer, morning sun washed the front of the extensive church building in Weyburne. Paint peeled from the cracked wooden trim and mortar had broken away from between weathered red bricks. Unkempt strips dominated by wildflowers replaced decorative gardens, once tended with love. Mullein stalks' yellowing flower spikes guarded the flanks of the crumbling weather-bleached concrete stairway below the entrance. Brown, wooden doors hung wide open in welcome; however, no one greeted visitors.

A family ascended the steps. The parents were middle age, serious and determined. A young girl of about ten held the woman's hand.

"Why are we coming here, Daddy?" the girl pleaded. "We've never been to church."

"We're new in town, sweetie. It's a way to meet people." Barry Young smiled at his daughter.

"Can we stay and live here forever?" The girl seemed hopeful, desiring stability after the uncertainty of their recent life, moving from place to place, sometimes hastily. She had lost many friends and now found it hard to get close to anyone but her family.

Her brother had gone away, and she did not know where or why.

He's gone off to fight. He'll die. One of her playmates in Orangeville had said. It scared Melissa Young, and she often cried.

"Maybe we will," Jennifer answered. "I've met a couple of friendly folks. The railway will need bosses here, after the fighting." Her throat tightened. Jennifer Young feared for Brian, but for now, he lived somewhere safe.

They passed through a small anteroom. The table that normally held pamphlets, the service bulletin, money appeals and other essential congregational communication, stood barren save for a thin layer of dust. In the tranquil sanctuary, a woman at a battered upright piano at the front of the room softly played old Christian melodies with some notes slightly off key. Now useless organ pipes stretched silently across the front wall of the sanctuary.

Several people occupied pews near the front. The Youngs made their way up the right-hand aisle. Barry, clutching a hymnbook, guided his wife and daughter into the last empty pew on the left, the fourth from the front. Some of the congregation turned and smiled. No one paid closer attention than the pianist. Ester did not miss a note, her fingers finding the familiar keys, as her eyes followed the family into their seats. After finishing the hymn, she wrote on a slip of paper, placing it on the pulpit. The music resumed.

Precisely at eleven, Reverend Wright entered the sanctuary from a small door to the left. Al walked deliberately to the pulpit and set a small bundle of papers on it. He had noted the strangers in the fourth pew. The slight nod from his wife confirmed his suspicions. Al examined Ester's note and paused for a few seconds.

"Good morning." Al intoned in the worn, customary greeting. The sparse congregation echoed these words with the voice of an elderly lady trailing the others by a couple of syllables. "There's a slight change in next week's first hymn, number 406 in the blue hymnal."

This conservative congregation had never warmed to the more current red hymnal sharing the racks behind each pew. Al walked to the wooden notice boards at the right-hand side of the nave. One board displayed the numbers of the three hymns and the Psalm for the day's service while the other gave warning of the next week's songs. The Reverend replaced the first number on the second board with "406".

No one thought much of this event. Barry Young did not relate the first number of the hymn to his position in the fourth pew. In the same way, no one would consider the rose Mrs Wright would entwine in the handle of the side door to the sanctuary as any more than a decoration. A certain night visitor would understand. The door remained unlocked as it had been all the years since the day after the collapse.

"Let us pray." Al Wright's voice had lost none of its ability to dominate a sanctuary. In private, he sounded nervous and uncertain. Barry opened the hymnal and found a slip of paper at the first hymn of the day. Glancing about to make certain all eyes were closed in prayer, he bent forward as if tying his shoe. The paper slipped easily between his foot and the leather upper, disappearing deep into the shoe. He had noted several groups of handwritten letters covering one side of the paper along with a small "x o x". Barry's smile shone through his fear.

The congregation rose for the first hymn, number 277. The congregation sat after a tuneless struggle to follow Mrs Wright's lead. Barry Young slipped a folded piece of paper into the hymnal at 277. He wondered if James Bond had ever used a church as a message drop and hoped his coded information would help.

Al Wright continued with the formalized liturgy, unaltered for decades. Scripture reading, prayer and another hymn lead to the central focus of the meeting. Al Wright delivered a sermon of sacrifice and benefit exemplified in the saints and Christ. By the end of his monologue, he inspired and somewhat reassured the Young family. The worshipers sang the final hymn with much more gusto. In normal times, Al often quipped that people sang the last hymn faster to get to the coffee and dessert.

"Welcome to our church." Al shook hands with the Youngs.

"We know you're new in town, with the railway," Ester smiled. "Come over for tea tomorrow evening."

"That would be lovely," Jennifer Young replied. "If Barry's not home too late, we'll be there."

As the family descended the steps, ominous clouds floated overhead. Rumblings from behind the building portended a storm to come.

Jennifer Young loved to sing and looked up the hymns for the next week. The first line of the first hymn read: *Oft in danger, oft in woe*. She had a tear in her eye, her heart in turmoil as they made their way home.

Barry had the slip of paper with the jumbled letters tucked into his shoe.

Chapter Thirty-two

"I plan to come back soon." Brandi swung up onto Dodger.

"Thank you for your encouragement. You lifted me up." A warm smile formed on Corrine's face. "And thank you for this."

Corrine's left hand saluted with a rolled-up sheet of drawing paper. Brandi had drawn a picture of Corrine fishing in the Saugeen River with her two friends. In the background, at the top of the hill, Stan Gregson sat astride his horse, watching over them. To the right, a female figure wearing a wide-brimmed hat galloped away on a huge horse. Brandi also had a portrait stored safely in her folio of Corrine portraying her clear eyes and dominating smile.

"One minute, I almost forgot." Corrine pushed her hand deep into the pocket of her well-worn fishing jacket. She retrieved a brightly coloured scarf and a pouch of tobacco. She spread the cloth on the ground with the corners at the four compass ordinates and poured a few grams of her precious flake amongst the colours. Corrine paused briefly, staring at the arrangement and then added more tobacco. She passed her hand over the little pile, palm down and then folded the corners of the scarf precisely into the centre, tying the resulting corners into a knot.

"Take care, my nimise," Corrine lifted the little bundle to Brandi. "This will keep you safe and me in your heart throughout your life's journey."

Brandi swung Dodger onto the roadway towards Owen Sound. She waved over her shoulder before disappearing behind a grove of aspen. The girl puzzled over the meaning of "nimise" and the gift of tobacco. She had become used to saying goodbye and learned to focus on the next destination. Her rewarding week at Chippewa Hill made her linger enjoying Corrine's company until they had weeded the garden and built a composting toilet. The road called her.

Owen Sound made a notable impression as Brandi approached from the west. The old town snuggled in the valley at the head of the long finger of water of the same name that extended from Georgian Bay. Tree-lined shores embraced the blue with many subtle greens. A stiff breeze came down the bay, waving the tree limbs as if greeting Brandi.

Brandi guided Dodger down a rough roadway, avoiding the broken asphalt. The streets kept their pavement. The locals wanted to avoid muddy paths for as long as possible.

There would be time enough to find the mayor of Owen Sound and honour Chester's request that she make a courtesy call. Evening's approach and the long ride in the summer heat left her tired. She camped beside a little stream with water to drink and bathe in to soothe her road-weary body.

***

The small procession climbed a long hill into the brilliant August sun rising above the horizon. Brandi sat astride Dodger, walking easily beside a large wagon drawn by a pair of heavy Belgian geldings. The wagon carried only a spare whippletree. Two men occupied the wooden seat, bobbing up and down on leaf springs as the wheels jolted over uneven asphalt. Another Belgian, a large mare in full harness, quietly trailed, tethered to the rig.

Brandi had paused in Owen Sound for a week. The mayor had received reports about her from the pickets near Irish Lake. Her reputation as an artist had preceded her, and the man insisted she draw a portrait of him and his family. Brandi produced a satisfactory rendering of the mayor, his wife and their three teenage girls.

Brandi had never encountered someone who had the mayor's inflated view of himself. She did not like his demanding self-importance, although the man was quite personable in other ways. She included a small protest in the drawing. Brandi portrayed the family in their flower garden with a hint of the ground beneath their feet. On closer inspection, one could see the head of an earthworm gasping for air under the mayor's shoe. Never the wiser, he proudly displayed the image in his office. If anyone noticed the joke, no one dared to tell the mayor.

It had been a week of talking and drawing as Brandi earned her keep. She now accompanied the mayor to retrieve useful equipment for reverse engineering from the county museum. They especially had their eyes on a ground driven horse-drawn manure spreader and weaving and spinning equipment. Owen Sound had mechanical shops to build improved versions of traditional technology.

Brandi watched the mayor and decided people were too complex for simple likes and dislikes. He was a good organizer with the ability to lead people to work together. Brandi tolerated his self-importance. In these times of strife, everyone had foibles.

"I noticed a squad of armed men forming up on Tenth Street," Brandi had diverted Dodger around the force in the pre-dawn shadows.

"We're sending reinforcements to Southampton," the mayor replied. "Our friends over the line are telling us some serious fighting units are moving closer. We want to make sure they don't catch us by surprise."

"They seemed friendly down there," Brandi thought of her new Southampton friends, and the simple relationship they had with the residents to the south.

"The bunch in Southampton and even Port Elgin are fine. They're just ordinary folks. The people at the nuke plant include really mean fighters sent from Toronto. The locals on their side don't like them."

"Couldn't we just go down and take it over before they reinforce?"

"We wouldn't want to stir them up. They could hit us hard if provoked." The team turned west to the museum.

He continued, "we would not have been this stable if so many had not died or left," he paused, pondering his words, "but we have a fighter shortage because of it, and the PLM outnumbers us. I am not sure we'll survive."

"Yes, we have gathered into small groups trying to survive," Brandi thought of her precious family at Longview, "but it's a struggle to get enough to eat."

"We've all lost weight," The man smiled and pointed to his waist. Brandi noticed his pants, tucked in as if they were several sizes too large. The tailoring was professional.

"Will you send out more patrols?"

"It would be better for you if you didn't know the answer, travelling about as you do, if they captured you. It would be safer for us in case they tortured you."

"Is there a lot of material to salvage?" Brandi changed the subject from personal danger. Her close escape haunted her.

"There's a ton of great stuff!" The mayor exclaimed. "The problem is Jenkins, the curator. He thinks the artefacts belong to him personally. That's why I wanted you to come. The guy loves talking with new people. He worked great with tourists and other visitors and seems to wait for the tourists to return. I think the crash loosened a screw in his head."

The mayor's companion echoed the laugh.

"You might divert his attention while we work. We would take the stuff anyway, but this will be easier on him. He means well, but lives in the past."

Brandi remembered many in Weyburne avoiding reality, and she thought of the Southampton parishioners preserving the church building.

The group stopped in front of large impressive doors overlooking an empty, dusty parking lot. The trio climbed the concrete steps.

"Have some more tea, my dear." The man leaned over the low coffee table and poured tea into Brandi's cup. Paul Jenkins curated the museum and archives. He had long, grey hair neatly combed and trimmed. In contrast, a salt and pepper unkempt beard covered his face. Bright grey eyes twinkled above the beard. A friendly smile gave the facial hair a life of its own.

They sat in stuffed chairs on one side of Paul's elegant office. A grand, redwood desk dominated the room, facing large doors to the waiting room. Solid glass formed the two outer walls, bathing the room in natural light and meeting in a corner softened by a long coarsely woven banner hanging from the ceiling with the trailing end folded on the thick carpet. The motif woven into the cloth depicted the county history from native culture to industry. The folds on the floor cut an automobile in half.

"How long have you been here?" Brandi liked Paul.

"Thirty-two years," his mind wandered back, "of fun." He paused in happy memory. "My wife and I live over the road." Jenkins glanced out the window. "She has been a rock for me. Melanie's an artist. She sculpts and paints." Brandi's ears perked up.

"I would love to meet her."

"They think I am crazy." He said, looking directly at Brandi. The sudden change in subject startled her. Brandi's mind had wandered off in a reverie about learning from another artist.

"I don't think I'm nuts," he smiled, "but they think I've snapped and love these objects. These people mistreat the collection. The artefacts have become useful, not just curiosities, but they need to respect the history and understand. Some folks are careless and superficial. I give them a hard time just to make them think." He leaned back, contemplating Brandi.

"That's understandable. The Institute is trying to revive useful things from the past, to know what's valuable and what's useless."

"What's the Institute?" Paul looked interested.

Brandi spent an hour explaining their endeavour in Kimberly. Jenkins showed enthusiasm and their discussion turned to creating an Owen Sound campus at the museum. The prospect excited Brandi. She thought of doing the same with Corrine at Southampton and had planted the idea. It would hinge on the security of the territory.

"We're ready to go." The mayor walked in without knocking, not apologizing.

"I'll say goodbye for now." Brandi smiled. "I'll stay here tonight and leave for Meaford tomorrow."

"I hope you take care of that stuff!" Jenkins demanded.

"Say hi to Chester for me." The mayor ignored Jenkins, but he would see Amik long before Brandi.

Chapter Thirty-three

Matt Long peered through the window of the church side-door at movement in the street. Matt held his breath, hoping his fighters, hiding in a backyard across the street, would remain patient. He could not tell if the lone figure stumbling down the empty roadway was a drunk wandering homeward, or a clever watcher staking out the Reverend. The figure turned the corner, disappearing towards the downtown. Matt breathed easy but waited, his hand nervously fingering the thick folded paper containing a long coded message from Barry Young.

At last, Matt joined his comrades. They slipped through the south of town towards tree cover and their trek westward. They skirted well away from the town centre, scurried over the main street, into a protective alley and crossed the new railway. The gleaming tracks, polished by train wheels lay barely visible in the dark of an overcast night. Matt did not like these excursions into town now that the railway had brought more activity. Matt hoped to be far away before the light of dawn could betray them. Morning found them walking through a light rain, well west of Weyburne.

Once he decoded the message, Matt rushed alone on foot to the Huron Territory. The situation was urgent. Huron needed to prepare.

Active PLM security forced Matt to go well west before heading north. Even then, he barely avoided hostile patrols. Matt's next attempt at evading security forces ended dishonourably in a backyard in Flesherton. He used all of his skill to enter the town unseen. He had not counted on the vigilance and cleverness of Huron security.

"Lift your arms where I can see them." The command was harsh and came from the shadows beside a big house Matt had believed abandoned. "Put the rifle down real slow and no sudden moves unless you want to meet Winchester." The voice chuckled. Matt Long did not laugh. "Hands on your head, who are you?"

"I'm Matt Long from Weyburne, looking for Jeff Shadly." There was no reason to lie, and Matt knew he had reached friendly, if not somewhat dangerous, territory. "I have important news about the PLM."

"If you know Jeff, he must have given you a word."

"Beaver Cleaver," Matt replied, un-nerved by the sound of someone approaching from the opposite direction. Hands forcefully patted him down, taking his pistol and ammo along with the long knife from his boot.

"He's sure got a lot of protection," a woman's voice next to his ear startled him.

"It's dangerous down our way." Matt wanted to look at the new person but knew enough to stare straight ahead. He would have used the same technique and would not have wanted to see any spontaneous movement. They removed the papers from his pocket.

"Please don't lose those." Matt was worried. "I have to show Shadly."

"Knowing the word got you a meeting with the boss. You'll have to sit it out for a bit."

She pulled his hands behind him and firmly snapped a pair of metal cuffs onto his wrists. They escorted Matt towards a checkpoint on the main road. He had diverted into the yard to avoid this barrier and now realized the access had been easily available on purpose. Legitimate travellers would walk up to the checkpoint while dishonest ones would try to avoid guards. Matt forgot he was in friendly territory so he spent uncomfortable hours cuffed and confined to a musty room.

"Don't worry, Matt, even Robin Hood got caught a few times." Jeff teased as the guards removed the cuffs. Matt flexed to relieve the stiffness.

"I was stupid. I shouldn't have snuck in."

"I am glad it happened. It was an excellent test for our system." Jeff looked at the two guards who had captured Matt. Everyone was sharper because of the rumours of enemy activity, but these two were some of the best. Both had recently graduated from Roger LaFarge's course. He had heard good things about them. The two were meeting Jeff for the first time. His reputation as the best of the commanders had grown, and everyone knew his name.

"Where can we talk?" Matt asked.

"You can use the office in here." The woman guard opened a door. "We will leave you in private."

"Stay," Jeff said. "Ask me later what you can repeat."

The two young fighters had just learned why Jeff was such a popular leader. He always showed trust and confidence in people, something he had learned from Roger. People had to prove him wrong.

Matt spread the message onto the table and read from memory. Jeff needed no more.

"Can you get a message to Kimberly, to Chester Amik?" Jeff put his hand on the shoulder of one young fighter. "Tell him there is urgent information from Weyburne, and we need all the decision-makers in Owen Sound. The code word is rocket. Make sure he gets word to Roger LaFarge. We're leaving for Owen Sound." The guard left on the run.

"Let your group know," Jeff turned to the remaining soldier, "there's great danger. No patrols are to go past our safe points. Please get Matt a horse. We'll leave at daylight."

It took time preparing the horse, and the local commander needed a briefing. Matt found the James house and hand-deliver an envelope to Brian Young. It contained a decoded message carefully scribed by Brenda. The young boy read the message and hugged Matt. He read the words again and cried. Matt brought the first message Brian had received from home since his exile.

Jeff and Matt arrived in Owen Sound at dark. Matt dozed in the saddle the last few kilometres. The two weary riders slipped off sweat-lathered horses in front of the mayor's office. Even though they longed for a rest, and Matt had been awake for almost thirty hours, Chester's motorcycle and a truck from Meaford told them everyone was waiting.

As the pair entered the office, the sound of a radio greeted them. An alluring female voice filled the room, broadcasting from the PLM radio station in Toronto. She bragged about the virtues of the government, and then fell into an invocation of the listeners' patriotism, asking all to do their duty to achieve the coming grand victory. The one piece of actual news said all males over the age of twelve were to report to their local army headquarters. A shocked look passed amongst the listeners. Once the station had reverted to stirring music, in this case, an old ice hockey fight song, they turned off the propaganda.

"Yeah, we will rock you too, ma chère." Roger frowned at the mute radio receiver.

"Okay, young man, what's this flap all about?" The mayor of Owen Sound assumed leadership. No one argued. They were on his turf.

"This is Matt Long bringing critical news from Weyburne. We have a firm attack date and the outline of their plan."

"What's the date?" the mayor sounded excited and afraid. The twenty people in the room sat in silence. These individuals did not make useless chatter. The code word "rocket'" meant immediate danger.

"It's October fifteenth," Matt laid his messages on a table. "Our information comes from someone risking their neck. That's the date of the major offensive, but we have to worry sooner. They plan to skirmish at the beginning of September, in just two weeks, intending to destroy our patrols and grab people along the border for information."

"Where are they attacking?" Several people asked.

"They're assembling three forces, one at Collingwood, the main one at Orangeville and one split between Kincardine and Mount Forest. The major thrust is from Dufferin. The other two will contain and then advance once the primary force has reached Owen Sound."

"How strong are they?" Chester glanced at the map.

"About two thousand fighters will be in Dufferin and half that on the flanks. They have to wait until after the harvest to have enough soldiers. Their best forces are trying to capture Windsor. They suffered losses against the Mohawks near Brantford and ran into stiff opposition near London. The PLM controls highway eight all the way from Waterloo to Goderich. It appears they know little about us except what rejected refugees may have said and don't expect a problem with Huron Territory."

"We should've killed all the rejects." Many shared the sentiment.

"We couldn't." Chester was not happy revisiting this argument. "If we act like them, then why fight?" The argument ended.

"A ground force in Dundalk patrols out about five kilometres." Matt returned to his information. "They have already laid tracks to a few kilometres north of Weyburne and will be at Dundalk near the end of September. The advance party is building a camp for the principal fighting force that will move up from Orangeville once the railway is operational. It's lucky they have so few fighters."

"We are short too." Chester looked grim. "Disease decimated the big cities and probably germ warfare. I'm afraid they'll use it on us."

"What do we do?" The Meaford mayor asked.

Discussion ranged from surrender to save lives, to launch a pre-emptive attack. The mayor allowed some free-ranging discussion before bringing order to the room.

"Surrender isn't an option. They're murderers and will kill us too."

"We're too weak for a head-on fight." Roger LaFarge was no coward, but saw no point in suicide. "We need to disrupt and weaken them. When war comes, our only hope is to flank them, get behind and kill as many as possible. We will lose many lives."

"There are other groups we're in touch with," Matt spoke up. "We can run an effective guerrilla campaign and spread it wider. They'll use up fighters guarding supply lines. They'll murder some locals, but if it comes to a fight, a lot of us are going to die, anyway."

"It would be better if we wait until a few days before the attack, so they don't have time to make adjustments or murder scapegoats. It might delay things, and the closer we get to the winter weather the better off we'll be, for this year anyway," Heads nodded agreement.

"They depend on motorized transport, a scratched up air force and technology giving us something vulnerable to attack." Roger walked to the map. "Somewhere along here," he ran his finger along the electrical transmission corridor, "we need to blow up pylons and cut their power. We can blow a bridge or two on the railways too. Matt, how are they supplying Collingwood and Goderich?"

"They depend on rail for both." Matt walked to the map. "We have friends to the south who can derail a Goderich train if necessary. It takes time to fix a wrecked track. We have nothing on the Collingwood line but could put a train into a swamp near Weyburne. They depend on trains. The roads and the trucks have fallen apart. Their vulnerability is depending on the nukes, northern hydro and Niagara for electricity. My group will blow the Bruce line, but can't do much more. We just need explosives."

"We can," Roger took over. "There's a sub-station at Essa where the lines from the north come down, east of the old army base where I trained. The railway to Collingwood goes through a big swamp near there. I'll take a force and blow them both. The rulers there are allies of the PLM, but not the genuine party and much weaker and less organized. We can do it easily, and I know the area."

"I was going to veto your going anywhere," Chester commented, "but you're best one for the job. You're the CIC. We need your replacement."

"Helen." Roger did not hesitate. They appointed Helen with a nod.

"One more problem," Matt said. "They have infrared vision stuff, building watch towers and manning them with night observers."

"That's a bother, but there are ways around them." Roger did not like being inferior in technology but had learned many tricks. "If it's necessary to attack, sneak up close in the daylight. At least the field is even, and we might get lucky and have heavy rain, snow or fog. Military class stuff is excellent, so we by-pass these strong points if possible. The reality is they have more men and technology than we do. We need help."

"We need a miracle." The mayor looked despondent.

Matt slumped into a chair, fast asleep. The meeting ended, leaving the details for tomorrow.

"Shadly, your sister is up at the museum." The mayor escorted Jeff to a billet. "She's leaving for Meaford tomorrow."

"I'm glad she's safe." Jeff yawned deeply. "She must have covered a lot of ground. Brandi's braver than I am, riding out on her own. I guess I'll see her at home."

Jeff dropped onto his bunk, fully clothed and fell into a profound sleep. The mayor departed, pondering Shadly's remark. This young man had a growing reputation for courage and initiative, but he thought his sister was braver.

Chapter Thirty-four

"We rode along the high road from the Grey museum towards Meaford in warm air and a clear morning sky. Whenever we glimpsed the lake, the summer haze blended the water and sky. I felt lightness in my spirit on the last leg home. Even though I enjoyed the challenges of my time away, I had not realized how much I longed for my family and my friends. Dodger seemed to share the exhilaration and stepped lightly along the rough pavement. It would have been great to see Jeff and Matt. If I had known they were close, I would have stayed, but I would have missed the wonderful exhilaration of the ride. It would have been impossible had I known of our terrible danger."

From: "The First Days" (The Journals of Brandi Shadly, Vol. 4, p 117)

"Hello, Miss Shadly." The familiar voice surprised Brandi who had become used to meeting strangers.

"Hi, JJ," Brandi slipped from Dodger and led him towards the blockade. "You surprised me. What are you doing up here?"

Brandi had arrived at the intersection of the highway and the road to the Meaford training camp. A new guard post and barrier blocked the roadway. Several young people laboured, building the barrier and digging trenches. JJ Smithson had stripped to his waist with military fatigue pants hanging from suspenders, over the tops of rough, handmade boots. Hours of fieldwork had strengthened and tanned his once emaciated body.

"There's a big flap on." JJ nuzzled Dodger's nose. "A week ago they ordered us to report here to build defences. Yesterday, a runner came down from Owen Sound, and Helen and Ted took off in a big hurry. Jeff called a meeting. All the big shots are up there. The runner told us the PLM is going to attack."

"When?" Brandi's heart hammered in her chest.

"The rumour says late fall," Brandi followed JJ to the trench he had been digging. "We're here for a week and then back to harvest. Everyone's training. Longview has an escape plan. From what my family experienced, we should stand and fight, even if we die."

"When did you grow up so fast?" Brandi frowned at the boy who was not yet fifteen years old but talked like a veteran. He could be a seasoned fighter sooner than anyone would want.

"I'll see you at Longview. I'm helping with the harvest. It'll be nice to be near everyone." Brandi's light mood had changed to fear and worry. She swung onto Dodger and headed towards town. JJ Smithson rammed his shovel blade into the hard clay, resuming his urgent work.

"I told Jeff I wanted to be a soldier like him," JJ muttered to himself, throwing a shovel full of red clay onto the pile, "I bet he never dug holes." Smithson did not yet associate shovels with the glamour of soldiering.

The road paralleled the lakeshore and gave horse and rider a cool, following breeze off the water. They soon reached Meaford's quiet downtown. Dodger's steel-clad hooves clacked along the hardtop, echoing from the buildings. Many of the structures stood derelict interspersed with some carefully kept. She tied Dodger at a water trough in front of the old town hall. Dodger licked up a handful of oats as Brandi walked to the old war memorial and stared at the names of men and forgotten battles. A young girl stepped out of the building.

"This is old-home-week for me," Brandi smiled and climbed the steps to hug the girl. "Steph, you're the second Longview person I've met today. What're you doing here?"

"I'm at the hospital apprenticing with Doc Adams." Stephanie returned the hug. "Everyone has been thinking about you... and worrying I might add." The girl held Brandi at arm's length, hands on her shoulders.

"You look alive enough to me."

"So do you," Brandi reflected Stephanie's cheerful smile. All the sad shadows from long ago lay buried deep. "How long have you been here?"

"Kathy Nelson and I came up a couple of weeks ago. She returned to Longview, but I'll be here until winter. They excused me from the harvest.

Doc is sending someone down in my place with the proviso of bringing back a bag of potatoes and some live chickens. He said, ' Longview's getting a bargain. You'll be worth a chicken coop when I'm done. '" The girls laughed.

"Warren used to say doctors would soon work for chickens and potatoes." Brandi giggled. "He was right."

"Seriously, I am learning to stitch up wounds and make and administer analgesics along with other medicines. Kathy already taught me lots. Doc says I'm almost ready to be a quack like him."

"I'm hungry," Brandi interrupted. "Have you eaten?"

"Nope, but I'm heading back to the hospital for lunch. Come with me. They have a big pot of fish stew on the go. A couple who used to run a pub are now helping run the hospital. They're superb cooks."

Stephanie Hunter led Brandi up the hill. Townsfolk still referred to the place as the new hospital even though it was many decades old. Dodger walked along quietly, occasionally pulling at the lead, trying to reach a tasty weed in the cracked pavement.

There was no sign of the doctor and his wife who partnered in the operating room.

"A young boy came in, trampled by a horse, Steph said. They're in surgery doing their best to save the lad's life. Farm and wood cutting accidents have replaced car crashes as the major cause of injury and death."

Stephanie had mentioned Brandi before. Almost everyone at lunch knew of her trip and her efforts at connecting people. Brandi surveyed the dining room, pondering the role this place had in the territory's educational future. Something different in the look of this group bothered her. She eagerly consumed a delightful concoction of pickerel, potatoes, greens and several herbs blended into chowder, augmented by brown bread. The doctor solved her puzzlement.

Doc Adams was a middle-aged man with short-cropped greying hair. He was tall and slim as was common with almost everyone these days. Wire-rimmed eyeglasses perched easily on a sharp nose. He had shaved cleanly. Brandi suddenly realized this was true of all the young male medical trainees in the room. Beards had become common with men Brandi could not remember seeing a clean-shaven face in several years. Shaving made it easier to have a hygienic environment with no facial hair. None of the old technology making hospital beards possible survived. Doc Adams was adamant on this point.

"Are you a new student?" the doctor sat opposite Brandy. A tall, thin woman eased down beside him. His physician wife would be considered beautiful in any circumstance, with blond hair just greying and soft facial features. She looked tired as she ate her chowder.

"No, I'm just a traveller passing through, borrowing stories to tell at my next stop." Brandi smiled. She heard Adams was a good man but had never met him.

"This is Brandi," Stephanie spoke over her water cup.

"We expected someone more mature." The doctor half stood and extended his hand across the table.

"Don't take me the wrong way, but Stephanie isn't the first one here to tell your story. Jen and I stitched up a farmer from below Priceville who sang about you. We imagined a sage in a white robe the way they talk."

"I am just a girl trying to learn the territory." Brandi blushed. "I try to keep my mouth shut and my ears open."

Jen Adams left the table and returned with a large sheet of paper. Brandi recognized it. The grey tone was an artefact of her papermaking process. Jen spread a drawing of a man labouring over a horse-drawn hay mower on the table.

"You'll be happy to know; he'll be okay. He had a nasty cut from one of the sickle blades. This's why we need these young folks trained. This man travelled a long way to get help. He lent this to us," Jen went on, "said he'll be back after the harvest with some grain to pay us and get it back. You've made a big impression, young lady."

"I don't feel like I have done much. People seem to like a stranger dropping by, listening and telling news."

Brandi stared at her work noting a flaw here and there but satisfied people appreciated her visits.

"I hope I can keep travelling and do more to connect people. There are many stories, and folks seem isolated and sad. You have a much more important job."

Brandi glanced around the room. Everyone had finished their lunch and listened. "I see the need. You have a lot of work to do here to fill it."

"As you just said," Adams looked kindly, "people are hurting inside too. They need you to patch that up. We fix the body. You fix the soul. Come, I'll show you around."

The quick lunch break surprised Brandi. Everyone appeared to be tired but ready to go back to work. The students formed a pack behind the doctor. Brandi trailed. Stephanie walked to her right. Jen Adams disappeared down a darkened hallway.

"Jen has gone to check our little fellow." Adams turned towards the group. "It looks like he'll pull through, but it'll be touch and go for a bit."

"Is he in much pain?" Brandi remembered bruising her hand pounding clay. Even though unbroken, it hurt badly.

"We have painkillers," Stephanie spoke, drawing a frown from Adams. "Don't worry doctor," she added. "You can trust Brandi."

Adams led them on without comment, leaving Brandi to wonder about the exchange. After an hour visiting patients suffering everything from broken bones to a severe case of poison ivy, Doc Adams opened a door into a large laboratory.

Several men and women sat at benches processing various liquids. A glass jar of brownish powder sat at the end of one bench. One worker filtered dark liquid through a glass funnel.

"Repeat nothing." Adams frowned. "This is a sensitive operation, our heroin and morphine production lab."

"I don't see why it's such a big secret."

Brandi only had drug experience with over-the-counter painkillers and a brush with marijuana. She could not put this into perspective.

"They used these for fun and self-medication. People get addicted. If your social therapy doesn't reduce people's mental suffering, they turn to stuff like this. If people knew about this, someone would try to steal the drugs. We already have a problem with alcohol and marijuana abuse. This stuff would be worse."

"How do you use it?" Brandi sniffed the powder.

"Either by mouth or injected," Stephanie said. "It's hard to control the strength. We injected the little guy this morning to relieve his severe pain, but Jen will give it in water when he can swallow."

"There's a war coming. We need lots of this. I hope we get enough." Adams evaluated the amount of powder and the volume of liquids. "I'll show you what's outside."

He opened a steel door into a courtyard. The hospital building formed three sides and the old ambulance station completed the quadrangle. Corrugated steel closed the gaps. Poppy plants in the late stages of flowering or seedpod formation filled the yard.

"See here," Adams lifted a stalk with round green seedpods at the top. They had scored each pod with a cutting blade. A white liquid oozed out of each incision.

"We cut them, let it dry, and then scrape the paste off. This is our second crop. We want to select the best plants but so far haven't been able to figure out which produce the most. If we win this coming fight, we might get a few years to work on it."

The talk of the looming conflict rekindled the fear that dogged Brandi since she had met JJ. She shivered.

"How much can you get from this crop? It seems small."

"We have a couple of hectares of the old golf course. No one goes there anymore, and the ground is good. We hope to get many kilos of opium. It will be a start."

Despite his positive words, Adams seemed doubtful. "We need antibiotics but making them is much harder. There isn't enough time, and there aren't enough trained people."

"We have a garlic crop growing for an antibiotic, and it has nutritional benefits. In the old days, I prescribed a pill. Now it's a clove of garlic."

"Why don't you get Kathy to grow poppies at Longview? It is a secure place, and I know Dad and the others would guard it." Brandi felt, despite the uncertain future, it was better to plan than to worry.

"Kathy has had us growing garlic for a couple of years." Brandi paused for a moment thinking about the word "us". She considered herself a resident of Longview even though she had lived away for several years.

When Brandi and Stephanie left the hospital, late in the afternoon, she carried a half kilo of poppy seeds.

"Where are you staying tonight?" Stephanie lived at the hospital.

"I wanted to visit the Davids," Brandi let Dodger nibble some grass, "stay the night and head to Thornbury. This war talk has me upset. I would like to get to Longview. Come and meet the sailors? You might even get a ride on their yacht."

***

"Sorry, we can't stay home and visit." Jane David opened the door, the rusting hinges squealing into the cool morning air.

"We arrived unannounced; it's no problem." Brandi shivered as a cool north-west breeze tugged at her shirt with the first hint of summer's end, although lately summer lasted into October.

"We have to catch this wind down to Thornbury and then run up the peninsula on an easterly. We owe a load to Wiarton and at least want to get safely tucked into Colpoy's before there's a big blow."

John swung his nap sack onto the boat. "We can't run to Collingwood. Our friends there warned us off. Something big is going on there." John climbed aboard.

"I'm sorry you can't sail with us." Jane hugged Brandi.

"Dodger wouldn't like the ride." Brandi laughed.

"We'll see you this afternoon." Jane glanced at the harbour entrance.

"Here," Brandi reached into her drawing folio and pulled out a sheet of paper, "I drew this last night while you three were partying."

Brandi had decided, after her last stay with the Davids, she should avoid too much alcohol, but the sailors had plied them with their usual good wine. Stephanie had succumbed and suffered. Brandi handed the drawing to Jane. It depicted the Davids on their boat with the jib stretched out full of wind, John pulling the mainsail up and Jane firmly in control of the wheel. In one corner, Brandi had inscribed:

> *There be many a reef*
> *And many a shoal*
> *But fair freshening winds*
> *And the north-star true*
> *Will guide this vessel*
> *Safe home with you*

Jane hugged Brandi tightly.

"Farewell, my dear. Jeff's sister has a poet's heart."

She slipped the bowline and stepped onto the boat. Brandi and Stephanie watched as the sailors expertly tacked out of the harbour. When all they could see was the main mast sticking up above the breakwater, the two women turned away. Brandi went to collect Dodger. Stephanie struck off up the hill to another day of learning.

A few hours later Brandi again chatted with Jane David. The fast boat had preceded the girl by a couple of hours and held goods from the busy Thornbury market for the run up the peninsula.

"Let's walk around." Jane took Brandi's arm and guided her away from the boat. Several vessels sat in harbour including a steel-hulled monstrosity decorated with peeling paint and rust.

Brandi was more interested in the rough-looking man on the upper deck. A scraggly beard hung down over a singlet that might have been white but now resembled the boat itself, smudged and dirty. A long-gun of some type leaned against a bulkhead; however, the fellow seemed relaxed. He rested one foot on a lower steel rail and one arm on the weathered, wood top-rail. His other hand gripped a corncob pipe protruding through his beard and emitting puffs of blue smoke. To Brandi's discomfort, he leered at the two women.

"Don't worry about him," Jane responded to Brandi's comment. "That's the Yankee Trader. They're a rough bunch but no threat in the harbour. They seem to think we might rob them. Violence is common on their side of the lake. They visit once a month. We have ammunition and oil from them on our boat."

On market day in Thornbury, wagons and stalls surrounded the major intersection and spilt east over the bridge and down to the harbour in a hodgepodge of styles and colours for enclosures and awnings. Many had salvaged camping structures or innovated from scrounged materials.

One stall had multiple coloured fabric walls and roof. The weaver spun at wheel behind a table covered with rolls of fabric. Her cloth ranged from plain tan to complicated coloured patterns. A treadle powered the wheel as the woman fed fibre from a large bag through her hands. A wooden spindle received fine yarn.

"Hello, Brandi," the woman did not slow her work. "What do you think about the cloth over there?"

Brandi lifted a roll of material wound tightly around a table leg. The fabric felt smooth and fine.

"That's linen," The woman stopped spinning. "Once I learned how to spin it fine enough I could raise the thread-count on my loom. I love working on flax more than any other fibre. I can't find enough customers who know how to make clothes but I know a woman who makes shirts, pants, skirts and coveralls. Maybe you could order some."

Brandi suddenly felt the dilapidated look of her patched and frayed salvage clothes.

"I need flax," the woman went on. "I hoped Longview had some today, but they aren't here. Remind them they have a customer in Thornbury." She returned to her wheel.

"There's no money here." Jane directed Brandi to a stall offering flour. "The closest to cash is a personal pledge of labour or goods. We see many systems."

"In Thornbury, they call it ' the chips' and use bits of board and a sharp point to write their name and how many hours of labour or how much they are pledging. Someone has to witness it to prevent counterfeiting. People even trade the chips. If you pledged a day's work for flour, you might earn your chip on someone's farm. Once you deliver on your pledge, you get the chip back and can reuse it." Jane opened her shoulder bag and showed Brandi a wooden chip from someone named Rusty.

"Rusty got some fish from us and pledged a half day's work. He has a reputation as a hard worker, and we'll likely trade this for something next time we're here. At another port, we need real goods to trade. These IOUs aren't much good outside here."

Jane stopped and looked at Brandi. "You have quite a reputation already. The word around is you always earn your keep with work, and you chase people's boredom away. Your IOU would be good everywhere, but they might hang it up as a keep-sake."

Brandi blushed. She thought of herself as a simple person doing a simple job, not skilled like the weaver.

"So much depends on people's reputation and trustworthiness." Jane turned back towards the wharf. "John and I have noticed a growing honesty and desire to cooperate. There are still loners who think they can cheat people or not do an honest day's work. Most people quickly learn if you don't give you don't get. If you're reputed lazy, your chip isn't worth much. People work hard to keep their reputations intact. A few people pledged more days of work than were in a year. Honesty is the real currency. Conforming has become important. I hope that won't mean people resist innovation or not tolerate differences. For now, it helps to fit in."

Back at the sailboat, Brandi missed what Jane noticed. The wind had dropped. A dead calm hung over the harbour. "There's going to be a change in the weather." Jane waved at her husband who had arrived from some other mission. "We want to catch the easterly as soon as it blows. A storm can come in quickly, and we want to run up on the east wind before it turns into something big. It depends on when the breeze comes back. Maybe we'll get to The Sound before dark if we are lucky. We could sail all night as long as the stars are out, but there are no lighthouses. We don't like to risk it."

"Hello, Brandi," John David smiled. She could smell beer on his breath. He did not appear to be drunk.

"John has been at the tavern schmoozing with the crew from the Yankee tub." Jane glanced towards the big boat. "We know these guys aren't above a little piracy and would rather not be in the same waters as they are. John tried to find out when they planned to sail. We would prefer a few hours head start on a good wind. They aren't too fast but could ambush someone or catch up on a light breeze. What's the word, Captain Jack?"

"Oh, Delores," John hugged his wife, "my love for you knows no end. Come to my cabin."

"Cut that out, you old fart! Do we sail or no?" Jane gave Brandi a frustrated look.

"The captain's getting drunk and doesn't plan to leave until tomorrow when they will have following waves. They have to fix a shaft coupling, so they may be another day. It looks good as soon as the wind comes back." He glanced at the sky, noting the clouds. "We can go as soon as the flag lifts off the pole."

They said goodbye for the second time in a day. Brandi headed up the street leaving the two bantering about whether they could reach Havana before the hurricane. Some people Brandi simply liked. The Davids were two of those special ones.

Dodger waited patiently in the shade of a large willow tree where Brandi had left him water and food and found a little boy waiting for her beside the horse. In exchange for his self-appointed guard duty, Brandi gave the lad a nice bit of bread from her pack. He mumbled his thanks through a full mouth as he headed in search of another opportunity.

Hunger is still around. The thought lingered.

She saddled Dodger, wanting to be at the barrier before dark.

Dodger carried Brandi towards the frontier on old Highway 26. The escarpment dropped sharply to a tree covered talus slope. It angled to a narrow plane extending only a few hundred meters to where the lake washed against it, forcing travellers to confront the defences directly.

A garrisoned wall forced all visitors along a side-road to the main checkpoint. Kathy, Harold, and John had travelled this route some years before. Shadow shrouded the steep hillside as the setting sun struggled against the corner cliffs of Beaver Valley.

Troops built impediments along the road from Thornbury. They had fortified the bridge on the river with a thick wall of sand and timber at the west end. Workers had altered buildings along the road as part of the defence and levelled several. Brandi could not see the explosives under the bridge or the charges buried where an attacking force might take cover. The untrained girl considered the preparations formidable, but those in charge of military operations understood how thin and perhaps futile the defences would prove to be. Still, they kept at the work.

She paused at the entrance to the refugee and garrison camp on the old golf course short of the actual border. Most of the grounds grew food. Sporting enthusiasts preserved a short four-hole golf course next to the old clubhouse. They applied the same technique used in Weyburne, mowing with grazing sheep and goats, contributing to the camp's food production.

The enthusiasts insisted they were playing the pure game, on pasture as the Scots had invented it. Brandi had never played golf but could see why her mother insisted on serving her regular security duty at the twenty-six. Sharon discovered the course on her first assignment and her clubs, which she had stubbornly carted along on the escape from Weyburne, now remained to be shared in the old facility.

Brandi passed near the course where several players relaxed in the late-day sun. Everyone had a rifle on their handcarts. Brandi resolved to do another: "Mom is golfing" drawing of her Sharon standing on a green aiming her .22 at a stubborn ball that refused to drop into the hole.

She encouraged Dodger into the camp. Soldiers hurried everywhere. The barracks had expanded into the former refugee camp, which had moved to the opposite side of the golf course. The old clubhouse hosted the military command. Brandi stopped to ask about pitching her camp.

"Well, if it isn't the clay pigeon!" The familiar voice stopped her beside an old truck.

"Hi, Jim," Brandi smiled down as Jim slid from the driver's seat. "Did they need a new outhouse built?"

The banter between the two had once been merciless. Both of them had suffered withdrawal from this comic relief because of Brandi's long absences from Longview.

"If I'd known you were coming, I would have whipped up a little palace." Jim took her hand, and she slid down to give him a big hug. "We miss you at the farm. Here, I'm building bridges that collapse easily or we will blow up."

The carpenter looked sad. Jim explained they were building anti-vehicle trenches and installing crossovers so they could booby-trap or remove.

"We don't think they have any military vehicles or armour. If they do, those will just roll over us, but we hope we can stop civilian stuff. Crews are on every back road doing the best they can." He led Brandi into the headquarters, and soon she had settled for the night.

The late night at the Davids caught up to Brandi. She normally woke with the first sounds of the birds before the sunrise and would have had her fire lit and spruce or rose-hip infusion simmering to ease the morning chill. The morning in the twenty-six encampment dawned differently. A more human sound roused her long after sunrise.

"Damn!" The expletive wandered through the morning shadows. Thudding sounds reverberated through the woods not too far from Brandi's campsite.

"Nice shot," the second sarcastic accompanied the fading sound of the ricocheting ball. "I think you only missed that pine tree." Laughter mixed with energetic profanity.

Brandi had made camp in trees not too far from the first tee of the golf course. Some early morning players became her morning alarm. As her tea warmed, she placed fresh water for Dodger with a portion of oats. Her practised hands felt up and down his legs, pausing over a few healing wounds.

"You'll get a little rest soon, Sweetie." Brandi hugged his neck. Her next destination would be Longview. Dodger would have a pleasant time in the barn and pasture, visiting the workhorses. Don Hunter would be there, and he could tend to the horse's shoes and feet.

"Good morning, Pigeon." Jim seemed serious. "Have you eaten?" He made room for the girl at the wooden table in the mess tent. "Let me get you some breakfast."

"I had my usual tea, bread and smoked pork." Brandi accepted a clay mug. Handley went to retrieve food.

"You look skinny." Jim sat beside her as he placed a plate of eggs, thick bacon, and bread in front of her. "You got to be strong if you are going to wrestle a bear."

"I won't be fighting with any bear, Jim."

Brandi ate with gusto and did not tell Jim she ate well with her many new friends along the road.

"We had some excitement last night." Handley sipped his tea. "Refugees staged an unusual arrival, washing ashore in an open boat. It scared the hell out of the watch. They thought it was an invasion."

"Where did they come from?" Brandi pushed the empty plate aside, washing the lingering bits down with her warm tea, eager for a good story.

"The other side of the bay, above Parry Sound trying to make Collingwood using a provincial road map for navigation. They ran out of fuel, and the wind brought them here. They were lucky on two counts, avoiding capture in Collingwood, and they washed up here before the wind picked up. There's a big wind blowing, out of the east, and the waves are pounding down there now."

Brandi remembered the Davids had wanted to run up to Wiarton before this easterly hit. She hoped they made it.

"I'd like to hear their story."

"You can ask Richard. Here he comes." Jim waved towards a man in his fifties by the tent door.

"Good morning, Jim, hello Brandi." Richard brought his tea to the table.

"I don't think we have met." Brandi sized up the older man. She heard stories about him from Jeff and her Mom.

"I heard you were here. Not much escapes my attention, and you have a reputation. There has been some buzz." He sipped his drink and frowned. "I am sorry you won't see your brother. He's going south."

"I just missed him up at Owen Sound," Brandi fought back a fleeting fear for Jeff's safety. "I was hoping to see him at the Longview harvest."

"We have to do without him," Jim intervened. "We're hoping we'll finish the harvest before the fighting."

"Helen's in command of all defences," Richard looked relieved. "Roger is training men for his own mission. She'll be here next week to complete our defences, but they are more worried about the high ground. They say the major attack will be from Dufferin along highway ten. We have to hold this line as long as we can." He finished his tea and retrieved a refill. "We have increased our strength to over fifty at a time here and more on an hour's notice. Patrols are out constantly and see more counter patrols from the hostiles. We captured a group that got too close. Those guys fought a bit, and we killed one of them before the rest surrendered. Their commanders seem to be zealots, but most of the fighters are unmotivated mercenaries or draftees."

A soldier thrust a clipboard in front of Richard. He nodded. The man left, recruiting people from the tent.

"We are sending all the refugees further back, most to Owen Sound. They are in no shape to fight or work. If we lose, at least the PLM won't round them up like cattle."

He seemed resigned the poor odds. Brandi changed the subject.

"I hear we have refugees off the bay." Brandi toyed with her hat.

"Yes," Richard scowled. "They went into the cold water and nearly drowned. There's a baby, and we aren't sure it will survive. They're malnourished and the kid's weak. Kathy came from Longview."

234

"Can they talk?"

"You can have a chat with two adults. It might do them good. Visit me after and tell me what they say. If we lose, we fighters will need to retreat, maybe up north. The PLM won't show mercy. I'll send one here." Richard flashed a thin smile towards the girl. "It is nice having you here, Brandi. You Shadlys have a knack for motivating people."

"I am off too," Jim stood. "I'll see you at the harvest."

"Yup, Jim, I'm leaving tomorrow morning. I hear there's a pile of clay waiting for me."

They laughed; Jim rushed off, and Brandi began drawing a little boy with a piece of bread in one hand while Dodger nuzzled his neck.

"Are you Brandi Shadly?" A thin, tired looking woman interrupted. She brushed unkempt dark hair with her hand and looked to be in her forties but shocked Brandi by revealing her age as twenty-seven.

"I'm Theresa Dubée," the woman extended her hand. "You don't look like these military types." Theresa's name was French, but she spoke with no accent. Brandi considered her own appearance as they shook hands. She knew she must be a sight with long, light hair under a wide-brimmed straw hat, a plaid work shirt overtopped by bib-overalls tucked into worn riding boots. Brandi hoped she had washed the smudges from her face.

"Technically, we are all fighters," Brandi smiled to reassure Theresa. "At the moment, my job is to visit people to assess needs, encourage and listen. Did Richard tell you I wanted to hear your story?" The woman nodded. "Have you eaten?" Theresa shook her head.

Brandi fetched eggs, toast, bread and goat's milk. Theresa ate silently. When she stared at her empty cup, Brandi refilled it, and retrieved tea for herself and Theresa.

"It was horrible!" Theresa shuddered, finally talking, "the trip, the boat, the cold water." She trembled.

"How's the baby?" Brandi hesitated in asking.

"I came from the hospital, and I'll get back as soon as we're done. She's weak. There's a wonderful doctor helping, but she's concerned."

"Kathy's the best," Brandi replied. "Where are you from?"

"West of Sudbury, we've been travelling for a couple of weeks. Thank God it isn't black fly season, but the mosquitoes ate us alive." Theresa refilled her comforting teacup.

"We were on a farm trying to make a go of it when thugs attacked and threw us out. It's the same everywhere along the Trans-Canada. There's lots of fighting and no law. Gangs occupy any place with decent farmland.

Everyone wants those places. The Spanish River valley, Beaver Lake, Chelmsford, Noelville and any place with farms have these groups on them. Some are fighting with the Indians too. They have nothing and seem to want to take it all back. I hate those bastards!" The woman's loudness drew glances from others in the tent.

"Why do you hate them?" Brandi had heard racist mutterings on her travels. Not everyone saw natives like Chester and Corrine as friends.

"They sat on their asses taking our tax money before, and now they act like we owe more. They were the first ones who attacked. We chased them away." She laughed.

Brandi thought of Chippewa Hill, an entire community nearly wiped out, and of her friends there and Chester. The old relationship between Canada and the natives had resulted in a lot of disaster and resentment. Its shadow would linger for a long time. She ignored this issue and left Theresa to Chester. Perhaps he would win her over.

"Is the PLM up there?"

"Those idiots have reached Sudbury and control of the radio. They think they'll get the mines and paper mills working with slave labour but so far, nothing. We hid from them when we were on the move. I wasn't kidding about the slaves. They have the railway open between Toronto and Sudbury. Another group holds the line past there and the PLM isn't yet strong enough to defeat them."

Theresa used good grammar. She had graduated from the local university and planning a career in business when the financial crisis hit. This appeared to be another inconsistency. Racism usually came from ignorance with the university crowd more open and cosmopolitan. Brandi suspected the woman's attitudes came from a deeper place.

"It took two weeks to sneak down to Parry Sound. We stole a boat, thinking we had enough gas to get to Collingwood. We ran out and drifted for over a day. It got rough yesterday, and we nearly filled with water. The waves got bigger. I thought we were goners. We could hear the waves crashing on shore and swamped. Your people saved us. I am glad I didn't see the guns until after."

Brandi recalled her fleeing armed men and sympathized. Theresa had reached her limit, eager to get back to the baby's fight for survival.

After they parted, Brandi searched out Richard. Based on the refugee's story, the north would not be a peaceful haven. Brandi changed her plans and immediately took Dodger down the back road to Longview.

Chapter Thirty-five

"Warren and Brandi were my heroes when I was nine. Warren knew so many important things and was patient. He turned me from a little girl who liked plants and animals to a serious learner about them. He taught me how to consider the needs of Mr Smithers and how my keeping him for my pleasure would be selfish."

"Brandi gave me hope and inspiration. She had gone off to learn, and she did important things. If she could be so important and smart then, I thought, any girl could. I love them both."

From: a letter by Megan Lefevre to her Aunt Karen upon learning she would go to the HEI in Kimberly to study. - HEI General Archives.

Children's laughter greeted Brandi as she turned Dodger into the Longview lane. Splashing and shouting drifted up from the river. Dodger stopped on the bridge, and Brandi watched the carefree fun. Behind her, at the old swimming hole, water overtopped a low weir. A large wooden turbine sat against the base of the dam. A wooden shaft and pulley poked from the free end of the structure. High on the riverbank, a small shed hid other apparatus. A continuous belt completed the drive system, but today the machinery sat silent. She noted a gantry with a large double fall pulley for lifting the turbine free from the dam in the autumn, safe from the spring flood.

The late afternoon sun settled into the west. Shadows crept over the valley, and soon the muddy riverbank lost its warming glow. The children felt the chill and clambered up the embankment. Don Hunter and Muffin Costello had joined the youngsters as lifeguards and helped young Joseph up to the flat ground, his legs eager to try but stiff and limiting. Brandi slipped from Dodger to receive many hugs and tickles.

"We have to get back." Don smiled at Muffin.

"Yes, the horses need a little attention." Muffin added, smooching Dodger's nose. "I hope you have been a good boy." She added with a kiss.

"He's been great," Brandi called out to the retreating pair of wranglers. They were taking a long way through a field of ripe flax.

I don't think they are checking the crop; she thought to herself with a chuckle before turning back to the clamouring gaggle of children.

The youngsters had grown. Joseph was bigger, although his upper body seemed oversized on his spindly, damaged lower limbs. Despite his weakened legs, he wore bathing shorts without shame. His limitation had achieved unnoticed acceptance. Joseph's halting gait matched Brandi and Dodger. Her slightly bowed "cowboy" legs and the unsuitability of riding boots to the rough gravel surface slowed Brandi. The group climbed the slight incline towards the growing cluster of Longview buildings.

"We grow up faster than trees." Megan held Brandi's hand as they walked. She sounded serious. The girl carefully observed the meter high saplings Warren and Willard had planted a few years earlier.

"How old are you, Megan?"

"I'm nine." She said proudly. "I'm to be a naturalist." She said the word so precisely it startled Brandi.

"Where did you learn about naturalists?"

"Warren told me." Megan looked at her hero. "I think he's the smartest man in the world."

"Isn't your Daddy smart too?"

"I love him," the little girl was serious, "but Warren is smarter than Daddy. You are too." Brandi blushed at Megan's definite opinion.

"Warren knows everything." Megan persisted.

"No one knows everything." Brandi was hoping to give Megan perspective. "Harold and Kathy know lots of things, and your Dad and Willard. We know different things, so does Warren, but not everything."

"He knows everything we need to know… now." Megan peered up into Brandi's face as she emphasized the word. Brandi abruptly stopped walking to gaze down on Megan, for the moment, speechless. Brandi realized most of them had known more of what they wanted to know and less about what they needed to know. Warren understood many things they now needed to know to survive. Her lips broke into a huge grin.

"Sweet Megan, I've travelled for weeks, met many good people and learned, but I came back to Longview for you to teach me a big lesson."

She knelt down, her dusty, faded coveralls protecting her knees from the stony roadway and hugged Megan. A memory stirred Brandi. Long ago, someone hugged her like this... who? The happy memory teased, out of reach in her mind's shadows. Brandi's eyes moistened.

Light banter filled the rest of the walk. Megan happily showed the other children fading summer flowers, brown weed-seeds and butterflies flitting in the sunshine over the drying flaxseed pods and finding isolated flowering wild-lettuce or late bellflowers sticking up through the crop.

Joseph hummed an unfamiliar tune. Years later, he would play his song to ease Brandi's sadness. He would remind her of this walk, of this instant that flooded his heart with the song, this flash of complete happiness.

Brandi enjoyed the children's excitement, but she pondered her newest lesson. She knew the substantial contribution Walt Lefevre gave to Longview. Her father, along with Walt and Willard had come together to form a wonderful team, leading the farm forward as a great example for the valley. It amazed her that Bill, who had no local friends before the crisis, bonded with men he had not known until necessity brought them together. Brandi hoped the threat of war would pass, and she could watch this bond grow.

Leadership stayed with Brandi as she settled in after supper to tell her stories. When most of the others had gone to do evening chores, the girl raised the issue. She sat on the old porch with Sharon, Tina and Debbie.

"I have a question," Brandi sat on the top step and looked up towards the others. Her back rested against a weathered post of paint-flecked, grey wood, cracked with age, supporting the overhanging roof.

"What's on your mind dear?" Sharon looked down at Brandi. Her gaze lingered on Brandi's eyes and saw deepening maturity. The child-like sparkle had changed into something calm and deep. Her little girl had become a woman.

"How does Longview work? How are we led?" Brandi had not considered the issue before Megan's insightful comment. Supposedly resting, each of the women did some hand chore. Tina was shucking peas, Debbie darning and Sharon, always the bookkeeper, worked on tomorrow's labour roster. The harvest would begin at first light. Across the yard, chickens squawked as they claimed their roosts. The lilt of a piano drifted from the parlour as Joseph played a restful melody. Brandi sighed, content, at home.

"I think," Sharon began slowly, "we are all, men and women, equal. We share ideas and work out what is best. There's no one leader."

"The children are growing into it as they mature." Debbie looked up from her work. "Don and Stephanie fully take part when they're here, and JJ sits in on our discussions. He's learning fast even though his father still thinks he's V-P sometimes." The women chuckled. "Jim's coming along and has a knack for organizing."

"I would call us new-age tribal." Tina looked thoughtful. "We aren't patriarchal or matriarchal but something else, something new. Maybe we just have the right mix. Others have different approaches."

There's so much more to consider. Brandi tested ideas against ones she encountered on her travels.

No one duplicated the Longview system. Elsewhere, other solutions seemed to work, including decision-making by a single forceful leader. She did not know which ones would endure. This issue became another detail to consider as she met new people.

Walking to her loft above the tack room in the deepening evening shadows, she wanted her comfortable bed. Brandi detoured to check Dodger. As she turned the corner of the barn, a rustling came from the shadows. Embarrassed, Don Hunter and Muffin Costello released each other from a fervent embrace.

"You caught us," Muffin smiled. "Don't tell Ma or I'll get a licking." They all laughed.

"I'm happy for you." Brandi's felt genuine joy, remembering her times of loneliness. "I guessed it down at the bridge."

"Are we that obvious?" Don blushed.

"Yes!" both women exclaimed at once.

"When are you making it official?" Brandi wanted to spread the news.

"Not until after this war." Don said. "They'll post me somewhere after harvest. You two will be out there too."

"They will send someone during harvest to train us to kill with our hands." Muffin did not sound pleased.

"What are your plans after?" Brandi tried to turn to happier thoughts.

"Little Jake will get the ranch when Dad and Mom are too old. He met a girl from Markdale and brought her to the ranch. I want to make my way and can; now they have lots of help." Muffin gazed at her lover. "Don and I hope to start a ranch after the fighting."

"There are vacant farms up on the high ground east of here." Don glanced over the valley towards the cliff. Dusk was rapidly claiming that confining lip of the valley.

Brandi hugged them both.

"Can you check Dodger tomorrow? I think he needs a hoof trim and new shoes. There is a little nick on his right foreleg. I treated it with garlic but not sure it's okay."

"Already looked at him," Muffin replied, her voice happy after sharing her secret. "He's a little sore in the withers. We'll re-shoe him. He'll be fine, but a rest here will do him good."

Brandi left the two in the shadows and went to bed.

***

They noticed Jeff's absence in the grain fields. Longview could not easily replace his sure quick hands and muscular arms on the scythe, but a mower drawn by a fit and strong Belgian horse worked the barley field with Walt bouncing on the spring-steel seat.

The scything crew spent the first day in the flax crop and laid a large area flat. A small group, mainly children pulled flax out by the roots in one corner. The technique was experimental to see if this made a difference in the fibre quality for the weavers. They devoted only half a hectare to this exercise. If it proved superior, Longview would harvest all flax that way. Flax and hemp fibre had become popular commodities as salvaged garments wore out and tailors needed additional sources of cloth.

Making clothes from "patch cloth" with useable portions of worn-out clothes cut into squares and sewn into garments, filled part of the gap Walt called it the "rag doll look". With hotter summers, people did not see wool as a desirable option.

On the second day, as the mower headed into the first oats field, the rest of the workers divided into two groups. One brought in the dried barley; another gathered flax. A horse-drawn side-rake alternated between both fields, keeping ahead of the stookers. Over a dozen field-workers and six horses made up the day's effort. The bulk of the harvest would sit in the barn for later processing, but two other groups threshed both crops. Workers from Heathcote and a few from Thornbury earned grain. Several fulfilled obligations from Chips traded to Longview. The market struggled to establish the value of work in grain. A farm overpaying hurt other farms; underpaying lowered worker's effort.

They had improved technology with hand-driven threshing and winnowing boxes whirling away on the barn's forecourt. Barley straw stacked in beehives stored the material for animal bedding.

Megan, with her eagle eye, carefully separated longer, stronger stalks. She learned to make hats and wanted the best straw. Megan had calculated a naturalist would not have a lucrative career and needed some way to support herself and contribute.

Children carted flax straw near the river and dumped it into clay-lined retting ponds. No one wanted the fetid process close to the dwellings. Jim had built a shed near the ponds for breaking, scutching and heckling. The weaver suggested spreading flax straw onto a field for open retting, having read it produced better fibre. This autumn of crisis made it uncertain anyone would benefit from the harvest.

Helen brought combat trainers to Longview. All available people over sixteen years of age would report for duty in early October. Children, twelve to sixteen would do support, transporting material and perhaps bring the wounded back for treatment.

They took several workers at a time to coach in shooting and hand-to-hand fighting. Brandi shot well, and soon her ability with her hands and a knife matched her shooting skill. She hoped never to need these tools, but it gave her confidence.

The training slowed the harvest and led to an argument with a promissory worker who thought the training should count towards his labour commitment. The trainer had to remind the fellow of his security obligation. He wore a sullen expression after that but still contributed an honest day's work. Walt endorsed the man's wooden chip stating he worked hard making his labour easier to trade in the market.

Despite long days, Brandi set aside each evening to draw and write. She worked furiously to record the Longview harvest.

Brandi left two images at Longview in the ever-expanding art display in the parlour. One drawing depicted Megan, smiling and examining a butterfly on her finger held in front of her nose. The other image was of JJ Smithson, leaning on the gatepost watching down the lane as if on guard. The distant clouds formed the faint outline of Jeff Shadly's face.

"It sucks!" JJ's voice startled Brandi. She paused her efforts at freeing a stuck threshing box and looked into JJ's flashing eyes. He had returned from a hard day of loading stooks.

"What sucks?"

"Everyone gets to fight, and I have to stay home."

"You're only fourteen," Brandi stated the age as if it explained away all of his feelings. He had an early growth spurt, making his body bigger and stronger.

"So what, I can fight like the rest. All I do is dig holes, and they get to shoot at people."

"Is shooting people good?" His eagerness concerned Brandi.

"Jeff does." He sounded defiant.

"Did Jeff tell you he enjoys killing?"

"No, but he's a big-time soldier and gets to do stuff."

"Did you know, Jeff has never actually shot anyone? The closest he came was putting a warning shot into a tree above someone's head. He's my brother. I know he doesn't want to kill anyone." JJ seemed crestfallen.

"He gets to sneak around and stuff. I'm stuck here guarding the chickens."

"First, he's almost ten years older than you, and secondly you are guarding your brother, Mom, the kids and everyone's livelihood. It's important. If the enemy breaks through, you'll get to shoot soon enough."

Brandi jammed her screwdriver into the stuck straw, freeing it in one vicious lunge. JJ's lament had made her confront the closeness of the fight and her fear for their future and Jeff's safety. He would soon wander enemy territory. The winnowing box became the victim of her dread. Later, she heard JJ talking to his brother and Billy.

"You guys can help. We have to protect Mom."

JJ's mom was able and willing to shoot PLM fanatics.

Chapter Thirty-six

"What's going on?" Barry Young and Mike waited on the station platform in Weyburne to catch the work-train north, watching a few hundred soldiers boarding boxcars.

"I didn't think the attack would happen until we had more troops." Barry worried he had passed on wrong information and the PLM planned a surprise attack.

"They're going the other way, back to Toronto."

The PLM fanatic sported an armband bearing the broken maple leaf symbol, and Mike had no skills except as a political watchdog over Barry Young. The man did not trust Young but feigned friendship. Barry saw Mike as a godsend who could not keep his mouth shut.

"They tried to kill the leader, but thanks to God, he survived."

"Who did it?" The news excited Barry. It suggested instability and less government unity than the radio pretended.

"When the police forces, the true patriots took over from the traitors they allied with biker gangs and destroyed most pretenders. These bikers tried to take over and wounded our leader while he heroically fought them. Many patriots died. Some traitor cops were bikers, and we captured a couple of them." Mike flashed a ghoulish smile.

"Their bodies are hanging from lampposts on University Avenue. They died a slow death kicking and screaming." Mike cackled. "It sure taught them a lesson."

"Good!" Barry pretended enthusiasm to hide his horror. "Why are troops going there?"

"They have a problem with biker sympathizers, but we'll wipe out the murderers. We should never have trusted them. The Special Security Battalion is rechecking all the cops to make sure we got them all." He shook the hand of a soldier he knew.

"Give them hell, Roy!"

It did not appear Roy shared Mike's enthusiasm as he climbed into the freight car.

"We had bikers up here. Did you know?" A diesel locomotive hooked up to the line of cars with a loud bang and clanking.

"We eliminated them yesterday. A squad from the city took them into the bush. They dug their own graves," Mike snorted loudly, "crying, begging for their lives."

Barry continued to pretend enthusiasm; however, he pondered the men unenthusiastically boarding the train, questioning the commitment and capability of those teenagers. The train rolled out of the Weyburne yard and disappeared beyond the feed mill.

"This leaves us short of workers," Barry said. "There's about five kilometres of track to build, including the Dundalk loop. We finished surveying the Dundalk camp but needed those soldiers to build it."

"They told me this would take a week or two and then we will have them back." Mike seemed confident, "but it holds us until well into October. Even then, it will take weeks to bring up the troops. It's going to be hard to attack before winter, but we got to while the planes can fly."

Young knew they relied on airplanes for observation and bombing from a runway using the county road east of Dundalk. He would build a spur track to bring in fuel tankers. The PLM had light, single-engine planes supporting two large helicopters capable of carrying fighters. They would drop commandos behind the lines. High winds and snow would ground them. The war had to be over before the end of November.

The Sunday following the departure of the troops, Barry left a long coded message in a hymnal. The PLM power struggle gave short-term relief to Huron Territory.

The revolt in Toronto took longer than Mike predicted. The bikers had the backing of some former elite and organized crime. For a few days, this dissident group controlled the radio station. The speakers hanging on a lamppost in downtown Weyburne fell silent. Angel issued an order not to listen to the broadcasts and thought it necessary to come to town in the first week of the insurrection to rally the local population.

Dressed in an immaculate light-blue business suit and a stylish hat, Angel wore a broken leaf symbol armband that became distracting to the crowd. He had not fastened the sash properly and frequently adjusted the loop. PLM flags and banners, all bearing the same red maple leaf and black slash through the middle, flanked Angel. He delivered a long speech from the steps of the town hall, extolling the virtues of the PLM, demanding solidarity and patriotism and detailing the gruesome fate of the opponents. He noted the supreme leader had survived and directed the fight against the murderous insurgents from his hospital bed. Angel did not hint at his ambition of becoming the supreme leader. The captive audience showed little enthusiasm for his shouting from the steps.

Angel's wife accompanied him to town in a small procession of cars and security vehicles. Her red Mercedes convertible glistened in the street as she remained in the driver's seat, smiling and waving while her husband harangued the crowd. She viewed the throng as her adoring subjects. The woman, healthy and well fed with impeccably coifed blond hair showed no sign of her age. A sparkling necklace complemented her neat fall suit.

The women in the crowd, attired in thread-worn dresses or serviceable work clothes, stared at the woman with emotions ranging from envy to hatred. All the onlookers suffered from an uncertain diet and the hard work of day-to-day existence. The self-appointed first lady of Dufferin seemed oblivious to the condition of the people. Only Mike, standing as close as he dared beside the shiny automobile looked admiringly at the Mrs. Angel.

Black-uniformed, armed men mingled with the crowd. Eyes watched for disrespect from the darkened town-hall windows.

Angel did not wait to meet his subjects, appearing to be nervous of the crowd. The delegation sped away, leaving a cloud of dust. His subjects watched the retreat with silent, staring eyes.

The sixth anniversary of the global collapse came and went without fanfare. Most people ignored the date in the rush to complete the harvest, while the young had no memory of any other life. In Kimberly, Warren Dunne, Jean Bennett, and Maud Dillingham marked the occasion by reminiscing over Warren's delicious fruit wine.

"I'm almost happy." Maud smiled over her glass.

"It has a pleasant taste." Warren stared at his glass, swirling the dark contents. "This is one of my genuine pleasures." He smiled at Jean.

"As you age, you become more like a child." Warren repeated an aphorism, but felt its truth. He thought less about the cares of the world and more of his personal space in it.

Laughter tickled the silence as children played in the autumn-dressed gardens. Late afternoon shadows descended the western slope and shrouded the valley floor.

"If it weren't for these aching bones I'd be running in the weeds myself," Warren frowned, deep in thought.

"Speaking of running," Jean read Warren's mind, "do we make a run for it if the fighting goes badly?"

"We are all on someone's list of fugitives," Maud sighed. She had pushed her darker thoughts to the recesses of her mind, but the stress of the latest threat made them impossible to ignore.

"I saw how Angel works. They'll have detailed records. If they win, they'll be trying to find us."

Maud looked sad. She loved Kimberly and the fellowship of the Institute. She did not want to leave.

"The news isn't encouraging," Warren patted Maud's hand. Her fear matched everyone's. He sipped more of the wonderful wine.

"Their radio claims a glorious victory. The recordings of confessions and screams for mercy were unnerving."

The availability of electricity allowed radios at this end of the valley letting them to hear the Toronto propaganda radio. Some technically competent people up the hill at Eugenia monitored the radio for useful information. People claimed the security group intercepted shortwave and cell phones. These rumours had masked Barry Young's efforts. Only the leaders knew how much they could hear.

"I'm scared," Maud twisted her fingers.

"Where can we go?" Jean would be happy anywhere with Warren.

"Winters are horrible up the peninsula," Warren laughed. "I think we could stay as left-over workers from the resort. Can they recognize us?"

"They would bring Al Wright up here and torture him until he betrayed us." Maud was more sad than bitter. Suddenly, she found the wine less tasty. "They block the way east, and the radio says they aligned with the military in Ottawa."

"We can't put Al into danger, he's innocent, but we don't know if he's still alive. Evy really was the last spy in Weyburne."

"We should head up the peninsula and hope for the best. Maybe we'll cross to Manitoulin." Jean had decided. The others nodded.

Brandi, fresh from the Longview harvest, climbed the broad plank steps and drew a chair to their table. She declined Warren's offer of wine and sipped Longview water. She hoped it would not be her last taste of the familiar liquid.

"It is nice to be home." Brandi felt two homes in her heart.

"We missed you, my dear." Warren took more wine. "We hope to hear good stories."

"I have a few days." Brandi removed her straw hat, rubbing the chafing line made worse by the harvest.

"We must make a liner for your hat." Jean dabbed salve from a pocket pouch onto the reddened skin. "This has aloe in it and should help."

"Thank you, Jean. Megan is making me a new hat. She has many interests. Hats are one. Warren, she says you'll turn her into a naturalist."

"She loves nature," Warren's face shone as he thought of his protégé. "That snake business sealed the deal. She loved the animal and was not selfish in releasing it. I thought it impossible, but the snake bonded to her. It's never far from her."

"Her mother says, butterflies kiss her, bees never sting."

"I won't be here long," Brandi frowned. "They mobilized everyone. I'm to record things and fight if necessary. I must make paper and go up to Flesherton. If I pack up my journals and other drawings, will you please take them if you have to move?" There was a slight tear in the girl's eyes. "I'll separate anything that the PLM might use to hurt people. If they are going to capture you, destroy it all."

Brandi gave Warren a small box of green-headed matches once popular in recreational camping.

"Helen gave me my orders. I am to record the fight. I can do whatever I want, but she gave me these matches. She said if I was going to be captured to burn everything in case they used my records against survivors."

"It sounds bad," Jean seemed shocked.

"They must finish laying the last bit of track to Dundalk and that's less than ten kilometres from our nearest barrier. They'll attack soon."

The news depressed everyone. The jug of wine sat empty, and the air felt chilled. Warren did not feel like moving anywhere. The wine, low in alcohol with no sugar to boost fermentation still induced lethargy. The group sat quietly as the autumn shadows engulfed them.

Chapter Thirty-seven

Two green-clad figures, concealed by thick spruce, hugged the damp, bracken littered ground. Both swept binoculars over a wide scrub-filled field. Dusk drew shadows deep into the forest. Beyond the expanse of scrub-willow, artificial lights revealed frantic activity at the end of the rail line at the aerodrome and fuel storage. The tanks Jeff and Ted had found empty where now filled with diesel oil, kerosene, and high-grade gasoline to power land vehicles and aircraft. A rail tank-car sat on a siding that Barry Young had completed before the end of October.

"I would love to put an incendiary into that fuel." The woman said.

"We don't have any." Her companion replied watching a guard patrol with a large dog. The stout leather lead testified to the animal's strength.

"We can't get near enough either." She panned her glasses to the right towards the town of Dundalk and a large tent encampment. Smoke poured from chimneys, where soldiers lounged.

"They're assembling a larger force in Orangeville. It would take them a half day to get up here. Whoa look, behind the tanker car," the woman focused on the spot.

"What is it? I can't see it all."

"Looks like a battle-tank to me." The man could see a gun barrel poking from the tarp, hinting of what lay beneath.

"I only see one. We need to find out if more of these are somewhere down the line." The man grunted in reply.

"Oh oh, we got to run! There's a patrol coming right at us." They crawled back a few meters and then jumped and hurried back towards their supporting patrol. The observation tower equipped with infrared sensing technology had spotted them. Barely a hundred meters away, six heavily armed fighters, and a dog hurried directly at their hiding spot.

The pair ran through a swamp, safe from bullets. The sounds of the barking dog and pursuit grew loud. After a fear-filled dash, they crested a small hill into a thick cedar bush, stopping some meters in to take up firing positions. They waited. Twelve fighters of their support patrol had spread out on both sides of the ridge, concealed by bracken and twigs. The forward slope was a narrow clearing offering an excellent field of fire. Fingers tensed on trigger guards. The pursuers burst into the clearing.

The first shot killed the dog cleanly. A volley of bullets cut down the pursuing force. Their bodies lay silent, only a few meters from the nearest defender. The ambushers waited, listening for a support force. After a few minutes, the commander approached the ghastly scene. Two fighters flanked her, watching for movement in the quickly fading light. They were confident. PLM commanders hated to send large groups into the bush at night. They did not have portable infrared vision and had learned from experience, Huron forces were excellent night-fighters. Several PLM patrols had disappeared. This added one more to the list.

"Check the bodies," her command was unnecessary as her squad of battle-hardened veterans performed the routine. At least a half dozen of their friends had died in the past two weeks. The fight was personal. None felt any revulsion at the sight of dead enemy fighters.

"Look at the uniforms." One fighter examined a body. "These are the elite."

"I think they've smartened up." The two original observers had returned to the hill. Both had been in Jeff Shadly's training cohort and were some of the most experienced and respected members of the force.

"They've figured out conscripts would rather surrender. They're only sending trusted ones out now."

"Yeah, that's how Jimmy and Shelly died," the speaker continued, rifling through a body looking for useful items. "They got too used to a patrol just surrendering, and a squad of fanatics surprised them."

"The tip-off is the kids," one man, who had finished rummaging a dead man's pockets, stood and stretched. "If there's no one under twenty, they are fanatics. Not one of these guys is young."

"Yeah, they haven't had time to turn the kids into little Nazis." The woman spat into the wet bracken.

"Too bad about the dog," another man looked sad. "I hope, when this is all over, I can get a dog." He had shot the animal.

"Get yourself a sheep farm and a little collie." The woman smiled and raised a water bottle. "You'd make a great shepherd. I love sheep."

She flirted even while surrounded by death.

"I've never even touched a sheep." The man replied. As an ex-PLM conscript, he had surrendered easily and joined the Huron forces.

"When I surrendered, I just hoped to survive and get back to Hamilton, but this could be a nice place. Sheep farming," he looked at his female comrade.

They finished the deadly work. Except for the stout boots, the victors left the corpses where they had fallen fully clothed. The Huron force took weapons, maps and notebooks and closed the victims' eyes leaving no sign of indignity to the bodies. The opposition could not accuse the Huron forces of barbarism. It could reduce the PLM's ability to stir up hatred; however, these fanatics already seemed a lost cause.

Throughout October, activity had increased along the frontier. As November approached, the fighting became intense. Probing attacks against the barriers tried to discover their strength. Huron lost excellent fighters, but in this stage of attrition, they killed or captured many more PLM soldiers.

When Helen received news of the armour, she called her ex-Canadian Army friends together to work out countering tactics. They concluded the PLM must have found an old Leopard tank at Base Borden. All the modern vehicles had been in Quebec, New Brunswick, or deployed overseas. This tank threatened Huron's fixed barriers.

No one had recently served at Borden and did not know how much ammunition might be available for the beast, or if the PLM had anyone who knew how to utilize armour.

As standard procedure, a protective force of infantry should accompany the vehicle to oppose attacking infantry who might have anti-tank weapons. In the end, attacking with infantry was the only tactic Helen could employ. If the PLM had more tanks, that might be insurmountable. It would have been nice if the patrol had captured at least one of their pursuers alive.

Chapter Thirty-eight

"LSZHXMMZKFCCPMU"

"What does it say? Is there anything from Brian?" Jennifer Young leaned over Barry's shoulder as he deciphered the message. They had found this single line waiting for them at the church service.

"It says: ' how many tanks '," Barry squinted at the paper in the dim window light, "nothing about Brian."

Barry looked crestfallen. It devastated Jennifer.

"I don't know how you could let him go." Jennifer accused.

"We let him go." Barry corrected. "If you had said no, it would not have happened. If he had stayed, he would be up at Dundalk, poorly trained and expected to die for the PLM. Brian would be more scared than he must be now, and we would be too."

"Still it hurts." She seemed resigned; the bitterness remained.

"I've only seen one tank," her husband changed the subject, "but no one has talked about it, not even mouthy."

Barry had several disparaging nicknames for Mike. He had developed more disdain for the PLM stooge as the line neared completion. The fellow had demanded even more effort from exhausted workers.

"I'll try to get information from Mickey Mouth. We'll be up there planning the track north of Dundalk."

"They are confident they'll win," Jennifer fretted. "I hope Brian is out of the way of the fighting."

"I'm sorry to say; I don't see how they can lose." Barry had come to terms with a long future serving his PLM masters. "Unless our friends have thousands of fighters and suitable weapons, they'll lose. There're two thousand PLM soldiers up here, at least this one tank and a few aircraft."

"One thing," Barry looked at Jennifer, "we must pass on any news quickly. You'll have to take the message directly to the Wrights and tell them it has to get to the fighters."

Barry never knew Matt's name or location. It was safer for everyone.

The next day Barry took the biggest risk of his life. He asked Mike a question. "What good is one tank?"

Barry Young gave the impression he solidly supported the PLM. The two men stood at the junction where the spur line to the little airport and fuel depot split off from the mainline. The central track ran through the remnants of the town and stopped past the former feed-mill.

"Too bad we don't have more, but it will scare the bastards." Mike laughed. "I am not supposed to know this; they don't have a lot of ammo, but it will bash through the puny blockade."

Barry pretended disinterest and examined a material list for the next phase of the job.

"We're going up highway ten with the tank and the troops." Mike relished his self-importance and thought he was losing his audience. "We plan to spread out once the force passes the defences and kill the rest. Commandos will land behind them from those helicopters. They're only farmers with shotguns, a real bunch of rubes."

"I understand nothing about fighting." Barry thought pretending ignorance would cover up his interest. "It sure looks like we have superb commanders." He turned back to his papers. "I wish I knew when we'd get the next steel and start north again."

"They tell me we'll get to use the trains for material in a week." Mike was full of himself, proud he knew more than Barry who was technically his superior. "We don't think those outlaws have any deep defence. Once we break through, we will get some troops for labour and start building again. This fighting is just a bump in the road." He glanced up the line to the makeshift bumper at the end of the line.

"We'll keep going until we can't work the frozen ground, but they want the line open by the spring ice break-up in Owen Sound harbour. After the last troops come up this weekend, there will be one more shipment of supplies and a gasoline tanker the following Monday. The next train will have flatbeds of steel rail. The attack will start the day after the fuel arrives. It'll be over in a day. We'll be in Owen Sound by Christmas. Want to bet?"

"It's almost seventy-five kilometres. It'll freeze up before we get there. You're on!"

Barry wagered one of his wife's home-cooked meals. This attracted Mike since he thought Jennifer was good looking and he might try to make a play for her. He was always on the prowl for willing women and felt certain she would want someone more important than her husband, especially someone as important as he was. Mike wondered how he could eliminate Barry once he did not need his engineering skills.

The next evening, Jennifer went to the prayer meeting with two pages of coded message tucked into her bra. She left it in the clothes' basket in the manse's bathroom.

Early the next morning, Al Wright made his customary stroll out to the west of town. The guards no longer took any note of his comings and goings. Neither did they pay more than a nodding glance at a roughly dressed man who followed Al by a few hundred meters.

Although this person appeared the part of one of the town drunks, including the stumbling gait of the partly intoxicated, he served angel and came from the cohort of astute agents who infested Weyburne and the nearby countryside. The real drunks formed the largest part of the spy network, but during the day, Angel assigned people who were more reliable.

In the late October mists, Al examined the abandoned house at the bottom of the fifth line. A pair of keen eyes watched from the obscurity of the sugar bush at the top of the slight rise in the road.

Al circled the decaying building, and disappeared from the watcher's view for five minutes before reappearing and struggling through the overgrown yard to the roadway. Al's cane made an impromptu scythe, and he came close to toppling to the ground.

At last, Al made his way over the old highway with his cane countering a slight limp. In the intersection, he prodded an interesting stone with his stick, picked it up, examined the rounded granite erratic, and he noted its unique red appearance. Al placed the overgrown pebble onto the ground. The observer, shivering somewhat in his flimsy disguise did not notice that the stone now sat a meter closer to the abandoned house.

Wright headed home, pulling his coat tight against a cool, easterly breeze. He whistled an old hymn and sang the words to himself.

Workman of God, O lose not heart,
But learn what God is like;
And in the darkest battle-field
Thou shalt know where to strike.

They may not learn about God from this, Al thought, *but they'll discover more about the devil. This one's for you, Evy.*

Matt Long had not waited once he decoded Barry's message that he had retrieved from the abandoned house. He rode hard from Kingscote and turned up the seam between the PLM's Dundalk patrol area and that of their Durham garrison. For a few hours each day, no one watched this route. Matt made good time and arrived in Priceville by the Thursday morning.

After decoding the message, Jeff and Ted saddled their horses. The trio retraced Matt's route, riding hard. They had been preparing to join Matt for attacks on the power grid, but now they had a new target. In the dark of the Friday pre-dawn, the trio rode into the Kingscote compound. Jeff and Ted settled into the main meeting room. Matt stumbled in, suffering the effects of having had only a few hours of rest. The dawn showed past the open field to the east.

"You fellows made good time." Brenda put a cup of steaming tea in Jeff's hand.

"We were ready to head here when Matt arrived," Jeff wanted to discuss the new plan before turning in. "We derail that fuel train and have until Monday, but we'll need to scout out a suitable spot and get set up before then." He spread his map on the table. "We want it heading downhill into a curve." They examined the map and tried to remember the route through the county.

"There's nowhere south of Weyburne," Matt said, "but just to the north, there's a downgrade to a curve over a culvert. The engine will plough into the soft muck so that the driver won't suffer too badly."

"It's too near Weyburne," Ted worried. "They'll hear it and be on us pretty quick."

"It'll be quiet, no explosives. We'll spread the track so the wheels jump off and then blow the gasoline after it wrecks. They usually have a troop car at the end of the train. We'll have to shoot it out with the guards. They won't hear anything in town until the explosion. Most PLM fighters are up in Dundalk. I plan to circle back towards town after and hole up in an abandoned house. They'll likely look for us along 89 west, expecting us to run away. I doubt they'll search in town. If they have tracking dogs, it'll be a problem."

"We won't get out of this without fighting," Jeff frowned. "Can we take a larger force and make it a fight?"

"A dozen besides us is all we can muster." Matt looked at Brenda. "Brenda's taking the rest to blow the transmission line coordinated with the job over in Simcoe, one a.m. on Tuesday, twelve hours after our attack."

"We can't move the transmission attack," Jeff scowled. "Roger has already left and should be in place by Monday. He doesn't know the timing of the PLM attack."

"Does he have a way of tracking events?" Matt wished they had shortwave communication.

"They have a crank radio," Ted pulled one from his pack. "To monitor the spew from Toronto just in case something useful gets mentioned. I doubt they'll report us blowing the train, and even then, he wouldn't change his plan."

"Okay, so we can't count on any distractions. We'll be the only show in town for half a day. Here's my plan."

Early on Monday, several men sweated in the cool October air, unbolting two track joints where the rails curved sharply to the left. Others used large railway pry bars to extract spikes from the sleepers.

"Damn these spikes are hard to move." A large man with muscular arms hung from the end of a long steel bar while the claw slowly withdrew a spike. Despite a cold October wind and light rain, he had stripped to his waist.

"Yeah, the wood is new, but the bolts come easy because they haven't had time to rust." Jeff grinned as he pulled the last bolt clear, throwing it into the bush. "They won't be using these again."

"Just two more to pry out, Bob." Jeff surveyed the work. "We need to move the track three inches."

An hour previously, the group had lain in the trees, frustrated not to shoot as the last trainload of soldiers sped to Dundalk. The tanker train trailed, but they could finish their work in time.

"They inspect the track in the morning," Matt said. "They think we only work at night."

"Won't the engineer spot this and stop?" Jeff looked at the top of the hill towards Weyburne.

"You and I are going to distract him." Matt said. "We're going to be about two hundred meters up the line and stand and wave our rifles at him. He'll look long enough to miss his reaction time, if he spots the break. The guards shouldn't see us. Ted and the others will shoot if needed."

Matt and Jeff waved their rifles on cue and hit the ground before the train's whistle cried alarm. The engine slid sideways off the roadbed, and with a sickening, strangely muffled thudding, and clanging nosed upright into the soft peat bog. The steel undercarriage ploughed a deep furrow through the swamp throwing poplar and tamarack trees aside. Black muck spewed high into the air, splattering the engine chassis. The heavily laden tanker car followed the locomotive into the ditch. It neatly twisted into the left-hand side of the engine and pushed it into a sharp lean. The train only had two cars, and the trailing gondola car flipped up onto the top of the tank car and rolled off on its side spilling the six guards along the opposite bank of the roadbed, finally stopping at right angles to the track, almost at the nose of the locomotive. The air brakes hissed angrily as they lost pressure. For a moment no one moved, mesmerized by the mayhem.

The attackers charged the wreckage. One team retrieved the engineer and brakeman. A squad of riflemen approached the gondola car and checked the spilt human contents. The car crushed two men as it landed on top of them. A third soldier's body lay bent at a crazy angle. Two of the rest were unconscious but not badly hurt. The last man moaned loudly in the ditch. The commandos dragged him, with his unconscious companions a few hundred meters away from the scene. Fighters tried to interview the conscious survivor while others collected weapons and gear. They laid the engineer and brakeman, unconscious but alive, with the others safely away from the coming blast.

Ted and Jeff examined the tank car. They decided not to use explosives but opened a valve to let the gasoline flow. Ted had steel cased bullets and once more would get the satisfaction of setting off a spectacular explosion. If two shots did not start the fire, Jeff would creep close and throw a torch into the volatile fluid.

Ted only needed the first shot. He fired from about three hundred meters giving his friends time to disappear behind the hill into the grey October afternoon. A massive column of black smoke reached into the sky, and Ted and Jeff joined their fleeing comrades.

Several trucks sped out from town. Matt had predicted correctly, and the emergency force came up from the south. Matt hoped his luck would hold as they waited for the other attacks to distract attention as the commandos began a nervous wait in a large house surrounded by trees,

At precisely one in the morning, blasts a hundred kilometres apart lit low autumn clouds with bright flashes. One set of explosions happened northwest of Orangeville toppling six transmission pylons in a cacophony of crumpling steel. Brilliant blue flashes turned night into day as power lines shorted to ground.

At the nuclear generating station hugging the shore of Lake Huron, the lone reactor online scrammed in unnerving blaring enunciators and flashing warning lights. Emergency venting systems failed. The shrill blast of steam venting directly into the air from the turbine loop sounded as far away as Tiverton and became an eerie, lamenting proclamation of the end of Ontario's nuclear era.

The other explosions decimated the Essa switchyard, with secondary blasts and a huge orange fireball enhanced by blue flashes. The sound deafened. Six packages of military explosives demolished three energized transformers and two huge circuit breakers. The sixth charge immobilized the emergency backup generators for the control system. Far to the north, all the way to the Moose River, water gates that controlled the flow through turbines slammed shut. To the south, massive circuit breakers opened, isolating Niagara Falls, its large turbines suddenly shut down as lines went dead. The Ontario electrical grid had become fragile. The commandos had killed much of the system for good.

Roger LaFarge grinned, swearing loudly in French as he watched the results of his handiwork. The two security guards lay unconscious and bound just beyond the danger zone. His commandos cheered and quickly melted away, heading west. It had been a tense expedition, but security had been light once they passed the frontier along the escarpment. No one had imagined an organized attack this far into PLM territory.

The sixteen soldiers worked their way into the bush. Later, a wooden railway bridge on the Collingwood line splintered into pieces as carefully laid packages of military explosive did their work. The force retreated by the road north of the old military base and hoped to gain the escarpment by noon and cause mayhem near Weyburne before returning to Maxwell. The Huron forces needed Roger's group as a necessary reinforcement.

In the darkened house on the edge of Weyburne, fourteen men sat silently and listened to a radio playing softly. The rambling propaganda diatribes had given way to softer music with occasional advertisements for the golden future promised by the People's Liberation Movement.

Three minutes after one in the morning, the radio fell silent. Lights at the Weyburne rail yard went out. The cloudy October sky had no moon, and no starlight softened the unforgiving blackness. They cheered quietly. The grid had died, and they hoped this would end the search for the train wreckers. The dictatorship planned to attack at dawn.

Chapter Thirty-nine

"I don't like this quiet." Helen peered down Highway 10 towards Dundalk, a few kilometres south. "It looks like the railway and the grid attacks delayed them."

She retreated to a bunker hidden in the trees with the sound of distant shooting from the left flank. No one took much notice. Skirmishes had been going on for weeks although this sector had become deathly quiet.

"They're coming!" A calm voice rose from the barrier as a red flare from one outpost hung high in the early morning sky. Red meant they had spotted the tank.

Helen ran back to the line appreciating the cloudy weather and the light westerly wind. There would be no sun in the defenders' eyes. Helen prayed the patrols would avoid death and harass the enemy's rear.

"Ready on the smoke," she shouted. "Dave, you're in charge, don't light the smudges until they shoot or get to a hundred meters. If the tank shows up, light them. We'll wait on the right flank for the smoke and then move into them. Make sure no one shoots blindly. Let the bastards come out so you have a target to kill."

Helen hurried off with a dozen fighters trained in hand-to-hand combat. They would attack the tank and to take on infantry. She fingered her pack containing several bottles of gasoline and double-checked the flare gun in her webbing. It was a primitive weapon, but they had no grenades. The others carried similar kits. Someone must get the tank. She would try first, if she lived.

A large passenger helicopter noisily sped by a kilometre to the south, out of range of the barrier. Several ineffective shots rang out from the defenders below the highway.

The force had no time to lament the escaping helicopter. Two small, fixed-wing planes roared up the roadway. Each craft spewed bullets, and as they passed overhead, a canister detached from each plane. Several defenders return fire with no effect. One of the Huron force lay dead behind the line. The canisters struck the ground well past the barrier, exploding in spectacular fireballs, makeshift gasoline bombs producing more flame than blast. Smoke from the gasoline fires drifted over and obscured the barrier.

The flat, rising whistle of an approaching artillery round preceded a shell passing overhead as the boom of the tank cannon reached their ears. The round sailed beyond the barrier, landing near the aerial-bomb explosions. A few seconds later, a second round arrived. The gun crew had overcompensated. This shell bounced off the asphalt in front of the barrier, hitting the timber facade dead centre. The explosion did a credible amount of damage to the wooden cribbing and stone rubble but did not breach the wall. The fighters crouched behind the barrier, shaken but unharmed by their first ever bombardment.

Helen, although not an artillery or armour expert, decided the round had been high explosive only, not armour piercing. If the bounce off the pavement had made the projectile tumble, it would have reduced its penetrating effect. Another round skipped in and exploded near the first crumbling the installation even more. They had not designed the barrier to resist explosive bombardment. It would not last long at this rate.

In the seconds before the second round, Dave gave the order to ignite the smoke fires. Flares sailed into piles of green brush and old crankcase oil, gasoline and a mixture of tires and other garbage. Acrid grey and black smoke rose in front of the defence and drifted on the slight westerly breeze into the faces of the approaching force. Smoke from similar smudges to the rear, upwind of the barrier drifted eastward and gave more cover. The tank fell silent, blinded by the smoke.

Helen heard the approaching armour through the smoke and blew her whistle. A dozen commandos walked into the haze well to the south of the roadway. The smoke confused the approaching forces in the scramble of brush, trees, and rocks. Trap mats woven from saplings and barriers of sharpened stakes would slow the attacking force.

Helen's tight group swung towards the road. The menacing sound of the approaching battle-tank echoed through the bush. Neither side wanted to shoot blindly. Everyone welcomed the protecting smoke; however, unfortunate attackers coughed and noisily stumbled through the brush. The Huron commandos dispatched the enemy with knives and resumed its manoeuvre. They ignited more smudge fires along the way adding to smoke that hid them from infantry guarding the tank.

Obviously, the PLM intended to breach the barrier with the tank and only skirmish on the dangerous treed flanks. Barry Young's messages suggested the fascist believed the opposing Huron force was weak and did not have experienced leadership. The commandos reached the highway and waited for the tank as it approached blindly through the smoke.

Helen had a simple but dangerous plan and gave it less than a twenty percent chance to succeed, zero chance if the tank crew and infantry had experience. Her force would take a position behind the tank, matching its pace. One group would use their knives to kill soldiers escorting the tank. A second cohort carried automatic weapons, ready to fire if the numbers of enemy fighters overwhelmed the first line. They wanted to delay shooting as long as possible to avoid the attackers returning fire through the smoke. Few would survive a blind onslaught of bullets no matter which side fired. They hoped stumbling over dead comrades would make trailing attackers scared and confused, but they knew nothing of the experience and toughness of the enemy and their reaction to the dead.

Helen planned to climb onto the tank and find an opening, smash a bottle of gasoline in the interior and fire her flare gun into the vehicle. It had worked well in practice. If she died, other commandos would attempt the same manoeuvre.

The commander grabbed a handhold and pulled herself onto the slow-moving tank. Through the haze, she saw the tank commander peering into the smoke from the open turret hatch, trying to find the barrier. He obviously felt safe because there had been no shooting and suffered the rookie's overconfidence of being in a powerful, well-armed vehicle. The hatch partly obscured his head. Helen scrambled forward and smashed the butt of her flare gun into the man's temple. His blank eyes stared as his body crumpled down the hatchway, already dead from her blow.

The gasoline bottle smashed on the interior floor with a crash barely audible above the vehicle's engine. Helen fired the flare gun into the interior, rewarded with a popping sound as the heavy body of the tank muffled the explosion. She pulled back, too late. Heat and flame engulfed her extended hand. Sudden pain staggered Helen, but she used her left hand to throw another gasoline bomb into the blazing tank before jumping off. The tank moved on. The screams from the interior fell silent.

"Bingo!" she cried out the code for success. Except for constant coughing in the acrid smoke, it was the first audible voice in the incident.

"Throw your gas bottles into the smoke and fire the flares at them." Helen commanded through tears of pain and two shrill blasts from her whistle signalled retreat. Blinded by the haze, Helen hoped her little band followed at right angles to the road. The plan said to head away from the road until they hit clear air before turning through the defences. Defenders would shoot anyone coming out of the smoke.

The tank rumbled on, carrying the remains of the dead crew towards the barrier. As the threatening hulk emerged from the smoke, the gunners behind the defences cringed in fear. When they saw the flames and smoke pouring from the open hatch, they regained composure. Shadowy figures appeared behind the tank, and the line erupted in rifle fire. The leading attackers crumpled, and screams of pain came from deeper into the impenetrable fog. A fusillade of poorly directed fire burst from the obscuring smoke hit several defenders and all ducked down allowing the flanking fire to carry on the fight. The tank rumbled into the barrier and heaved up slightly before it stopped with its tracks grinding ineffectually against the weathered asphalt.

"Get to the sides, out of the way. That thing is going to blow!" The defenders scrambled sideways dragging their fallen comrades with them.

With the ceasing of direct fire, several of the attacking infantry reached the wall and cautiously tried to find targets. A hand grenade flew over the barrier onto the Huron side only to explode harmlessly in the vacated area. Ammunition within the tank ignited, but the blast was not as large expected. The machine contained few explosive shells, but the explosion killed PLM attackers within a few dozen meters. The stunned battlefield became silent save for the screams of the injured and the sound of the burning vehicle.

Shocked fighters on both sides struggled to control their emotions. The wall had protected all the fighters on the defending side deflecting the blast and debris up into the air. Falling material badly injured two attackers. Moans and screams rose from the Huron side. Sparse gunfire came out of the smoke, but there seemed to be no direction. Helen ordered a cease fire to save ammunition. A strange silence descended over the battlefield.

An hour had passed from the time the red flare had risen into the sky. Several ambulance vehicles came up to within a few hundred meters of the front. Stephanie Hunter was one of the driver/medics, and the medical crew treated a few dozen injured. Another group retrieved the dead. Helen nursed her burnt hand, sitting on a truck step waiting her turn.

"Have you found Dick and Peter?" The commander called out to one of her commandos.

"They didn't make it." The woman was teary-eyed. "They are over there." The young woman nodded towards the enemy side of the line and hurried on. Helen noted the bloodstain beneath the girl's knife sheath. There would be lots of healing needed later. Helen grimaced as a hand touched her injured limb.

"We had to come the long way around." The medic spoke as she examined Helen's wound. "There is fighting this side of Flesherton."

***

"Let's go! They need us at the high school." An armed boy shouted as he rushed up the hill carrying a rifle much too big for him towards the sound of a helicopter.

Barely sixteen, Brandi thought.

She un-shouldered her rifle and pursued the eager youth.

Brandi saw the helicopter lifting off from behind the old school as she topped the ridge. Clouds of dust flew despite the damp autumn conditions. Gunfire from the building threatened Huron forces in nearby houses. PLM commandos had taken control of the rambling shell of the high school. Bullets spattered dirt to her left, the first time death had come so close. Brandi hit the ditch, trembling beside a fighter. The aircraft roared away.

"There're eight of them." The soldier focused binoculars on the building. "They made a big mistake going in there, but had no choice. I think they planned to land in the parking lot and head into town to surprise us. Our squad here waited to reinforce the barrier and surprised them. They dropped right into us. The pilot nearly crashed as he jerked her around behind the school. The helicopter took some hits. Guess we didn't hurt him too bad. He got away."

"How's it at the barrier?" Brandi thought they might have to run for it. The town residents had already fled.

"We heard explosions." The man said. "It must have been artillery or the tank."

"What can we do here?" Brandi awaited orders.

"Just keep your deer gun ready and shoot at anyone who comes out of the building. I'll try to find you a buddy. We should be in pairs."

The man crawled to the rear. She cautiously peered through the hedge. Friendly shooters occupied the hill east of her and above the highway in the old motel. Someone in the school returned sporadic fire. The main doors of the school hung open with no sign of human activity in the darkness. Another fighter crawled up to join her.

"We have the place surrounded and outnumber them." He adjusted his weapon, an AK, and settled in. "You'll have to use that hunting rifle if they don't get too close. This thing isn't that accurate at that range." He rubbed his weapon.

"Is there a plan?" Brandi was nervous.

"I don't know, but we need to get them out of there before dark, or they might get away. I'll watch for a bit. You can relax."

The sound of an enormous explosion came from the direction of the barrier. The startled pair thought the worst, not knowing the battle-tank had exploded against the blockade. Brandi checked for an escape route.

Nothing happened for two hours. There was an occasional shot from Huron fighters drawing return fire. Two trucks racing from the direction of the barrier broke the routine. Everyone checked their weapons, but Helen jumped from one vehicle. She nursed an arm in a sling but distance hid the pain in her eyes. They saw Helen directing a squad of fighters into the bush with the obvious plan to approach the building unseen. A runner circled to talk to all the firing positions.

"Don't shoot into the building," he told Brandi and her companion. "These guys wear light desert camouflage, and we are all in forest green. Shoot if they come out firing. Helen's commandos will go inside and try to flush them out."

He hurried away. Brandi could see nothing. After half an hour, three shots inside the school then quiet, and then shouting, but the distance muffled the words. Finally, light clad figures emerged through the broken front door. They did not have their hands up but walked slowly with their arms tied firmly behind their backs. Seven captives materialized, followed by a squad of five dark clad fighters, rifles at the ready. A whistle blew, and Helen came around the corner from the far parking lot with of the rest of her commandos.

"I missed all the fun," Helen said to Brandi as they gathered in front of the school. "This damned hand." She waved her damaged arm in the air.

"Helen, don't you think blowing the tank was enough for you?" One commando teased.

"I'm the boss. I should take the risk." Helen spoke from years of service in the old Canadian Forces where good people led from the front. She remembered too many incompetent commanders she had suffered under.

"They killed the commander," Helen continued. "He refused to surrender even after we had four of his men tied up. They made the mistake of separating with no one watching their backs. It's an extensive building, and they tried to defend all sides, disgusting poor tactics."

That their Commander-in-Chief risked her life to destroy the tank horrified the Huron leaders. They did not like her explanation, "they used their best weapon at the start, and we had to do the same", but understood. None of the grateful community would think that Helen bragged.

The PLM did not follow up the Flesherton raid. They had not expected opposition from the Huron defenders. Plans had called for the main PLM force to arrive at the town shortly after the little assault force had landed. The prisoners' orders were to kill Huron fighters with no mercy as they retreated.

A similar force had attacked Maxwell in a bigger disaster. Huron fighters shot the helicopter down after it dropped off the raiders. Unfortunately, two Huron fighters died with many wounded. Everyone in the attacking force had died. Throughout the eerily quiet afternoon, the Huron forces prepared for another assault and endured growing rainfall.

***

"What the hell's he doing?" Jeff hissed as he, Ted and Matt surveyed the train wreck. Distance hid the sounds of the major battle to the north.

"I think he's checking the track spacing." Matt took his eyes from his binoculars and glanced around. He did not want a patrol sneaking up on them. They lay in the dead goldenrod soaked by a light mist. The rest of the force formed a rear guard. Jeff felt exposed.

"Where's Young's buddy going?" Ted watched Mike walk along the tracks towards town. The sniper swept his glasses along the right of way and stopped to examine a red car with a blond woman standing beside it.

"That's Angel's wife," Jeff said. "She ogled the men when I worked up there. She likes to watch men work."

"I think the guy smells fun." Ted chuckled and thought of Helen and then frowned with worry. "I can get them." He fingered his sniper scope.

"That won't delay the work." Matt would love to see the whole Angel family pay. "I would rather shoot the guards, but Young is in the way."

The work crew comprised a dozen workers, a handful of armed guards, and a large diesel-powered boom crane on railway bogies with a diesel-electric yard engine. Workers hooked up chains and slings to lift the twisted gondola car off the right-of-way. The railway had brought a heavy crane north from Brampton.

The bodies of the two guards remained beneath the wreckage. No one appeared to be worried about the dead. Persistent mist falling from low, grey clouds slowed the work. A strengthening wind now blew from the east.

The diesel came to life with loud rattling and a puff of black smoke, drawing tension into the heavy cable-fall on the boom. Then, the work paused. There seemed to be an argument between Barry Young and an armed guard. The guard gave Young a dismissive wave and issued a muffled order. The diesel screamed to life and the gondola car lurched sideways, mangling the bodies and then rose clear. Barry Young walked to the rear of the engine and vomited.

"We know what that discussion was about." Matt seethed. "Young has a conscience. Ted, if we get a shot, that armed guy's your target." Ted did not need encouragement.

"Young's too close." Jeff said.

"We'll wait for a bit and see what happens. The other guy seems to be well away from any work." Matt glanced at the tête-à-tête taking place at the red car. "I guess she wants it." He returned his attention to the work. "We're getting lucky too. Jeff, call the others up here."

Barry Young had recovered his composure and headed up the line stopping every few meters to measure the track gauge. He had found an excuse to extract himself from the grizzly developments at the derailment. Behind him, the workers finally dragged the bodies clear and righted the overturned car. A chain sling snapped on the second lift attempt and delayed the work, allowing Young to put a hundred meters between him and the crash. The delay allowed Matt's force to deploy in a firing line stretching towards the swamp.

"Fire at the guards only," Matt's whispered order travelled mouth-to-ear down the line. "Wait until Ted shoots the guy by the crane."

"It will be one shot," Ted said. "I don't do torture."

Matt nodded; happy he worked with principled men.

The one sided engagement lasted thirty seconds. The only returned fire came from two of the guards, poor targets on the opposite side of the roadbed. They fired a few wild rounds and then hid with the work crew.

Barry Young hit the ditch when the firing had started. The red car fled towards town. Mike ran wildly down the tracks away from the fighting towards Weyburne. Ted's target lay crumpled onto the tracks beside the now suspended gondola car that hung unmoving, with only the sputtering sound of idling diesel engines breaking the silence.

The raiders ran through the swamp, turned north over the old highway and crab-walked up the fifth line ditch until trees obscured them. They took to the roadway and ran to the point of exhaustion. A grove of heavy cedars gave them cover to rest their aching lungs.

A few kilometres away, another incident guaranteed no one would bother chasing Matt's force. As the red car sped out of Weyburne, heading to the safety of the hilltop enclave, several bullets riddled its left rear quarter panel and flattened a tire. The female driver, smart enough or scared enough, kept going and sped up on three good tires with smoke and rubber flying from the destroyed wheel. A reluctance to shoot unarmed civilians spared the woman. A trailing car of armed bodyguards ended in a blazing wreck with both men dead.

"Good work, guys." Roger LaFarge had enjoyed this minor incident almost as much as the destruction at the electrical sub-station. Roger did not have any Weyburne people in his forces, and no one knew the woman. Someone driving a fancy red convertible must be the enemy. Inadvertently, this incident would divert PLM forces into guarding Weyburne.

"Okay, we had our fun," Roger expected a response to this attack. "We're going to where we can be of real help."

The raiders headed up the old highway before turning west along the first side road and then north up the third line. They did not hurry. Roger knew it would take the enemy time to muster a reaction.

They had destroyed two outposts on the way down to Weyburne; he was certain there would be more enemies on the roads. Roger and Matt's forces were only a few kilometres apart but unaware of each other.

"Where's that shooting coming from?" Roger cocked an ear to the west. Faint sounds of gunfire came through gently falling snow. "I don't like it. The damned noise will alert anyone along here."

Roger hid his force in trees while he pondered this fresh problem. The shooting sounded much more than a hunting party and lasted about ten minutes. Roger got his men back onto the road, heading north. There were only a few hours before nightfall, and they would not move in the dark on this unknown ground. The weather turned nasty. It would be twenty-four hours before Roger learned about the mysterious shooting.

The weather determined the outcome. Rain turned to light snow driving on a strengthening easterly wind. As the storm increased in ferocity in the afternoon of the aborted tank attack, it sucked in cold air from the arctic, thrusting it beneath moist air from the south. White flakes changed into slushy snowballs and finally back to rain, not the life-giving variety, but a harsh, super-chilled onslaught coating every surface with a glistening, thickening layer of ice.

The Witch of November stalked the Great Lakes basin, arriving on the first, ferocious, and surly, as if angry at having missed Halloween. Then she lingered.

If they had still been available, satellite images would have identified the large blocking high-pressure system in the Atlantic holding the storm in place, pumping moisture from the Gulf of Mexico over the harsh belly of the arctic front. The barometer on the wall at Longview plunged. In the tropics, this would have been a respectable hurricane. Over the lakes, it wreaked havoc from Sarnia to Ottawa and beyond. As the ice built up, the steady easterly wind pushed against trees, towers, poles, and buildings and in the night these failed. Fallen trees and poles clogged roads and streets. The towers of high-voltage lines crumpled. Through the first day of the storm, Matt and Roger struggled towards Huron territory.

"Can you see anything? This damned ice is bugging me." Matt squinted from glistening trees, watching the road behind.

"Too much rain... this wind in my eyes isn't helping," Jeff grunted. His force had taken cover on both sides of the road. Evergreen trees, their branches bent low from the weight of ice, hid the fighters. They had gone to ground after the rear guard rushed up to say someone followed them, betrayed by voices through the crinkling of windblown, ice-covered trees.

"There!" Jeff pointed down the road as two shadowy figures emerged from the rain. The tailgaters walked, staggered abreast on each side of the road.

Trained fighters, but in whose army, Jeff wondered.

"Let them come. I think that one on the left is Randy from Meaford, but I am not sure. Let them get close." Jeff released his rifle's safety.

As the point men approached the ambush, the main body emerged from the obscuring rain about a hundred meters behind. "That's Roger

LaFarge in the lead." Jeff slipped his safety back on and called out, "Who goes there?" The lead men hit the ditch; the rest scattered at the sound of Shadly's voice. "Password," Matt let Jeff do the talking. He seemed to be sure.

"Lost sheep," The simultaneous reply came from both point men.

"Mother Goose," Jeff replied and stood up, as did the two in the ditches. Soaked and cold fighters greeted each other on the roadway. Two of Matt's force struggled from the trees with a makeshift litter carrying a body wrapped in a tarpaulin.

"What happened?" Roger could see the sadness in Matt's eyes as his gaze followed the stretcher detail.

"A roadblock surprised us yesterday afternoon, this side of Weyburne." Matt sounded tired. "Richard died before we saw them. Then we wiped them out. We would not leave him for the vultures. He has a wife and kids. We walked all night in this mess. There are too many enemies around, and we figured the gunfire would attract them."

"It must have been your shooting we heard." Roger put a hand on Matt's shoulder. "We were on the third line about that time. Let's move. We need a dry place. Let my guys take Richard. You all look beat."

Roger's men were not much better off, but they had had a few hours' rest in a barn. The group struggled to a barrier east of Maxwell. By late afternoon, everyone found a comfortable spot in an abandoned church. A good roof was a godsend, and before long, the village garrison had organized blankets, food, and hot tea for the shivering fighters. A wood stove provided drying heat. The force hunkered down. Everyone had stories to tell. Roger LaFarge took a night's rest and then struggled to Flesherton for a war council.

Freezing rain fell for three days. By the time it stopped, the PLM encampment at Dundalk was a morass of ice, mud, and misery. The tents had collapsed. Morale had evaporated on the first day of fighting when they lost over three hundred fighters. The storm sapped the remaining fight out of the thousand troops who huddled in the remnants of the camp. The major encampments at Goderich and Collingwood and the multitude of outposts all over southern Ontario suffered similar fates.

The panic at the shooting incident involving his wife led Angel to demand troops. The force commander refused, and an ugly argument followed. Orders from Toronto to protect the Angel family resolved the confrontation. Thinking themselves the lucky few, two hundred fighters went to Weyburne to protect the Angel enclave. Those left in the misery of the forward encampment envied the ones sent to the rear, but these fighters found conditions worse than at Dundalk. It took days of stealing food before they found any comfort at all. Supplying this contingent increased the misery and resentment of the local population.

Weyburne became a microcosm of the spreading discomfort and discontent in PLM territory. The radio broadcast appeals for calm and later, threats as the PLM worked to restore electricity. These broadcasts were the first sign things had changed.

"We will deal with the criminals and traitors," became a common theme on the airwaves. Radio reports verged on hysteria. Huron listeners guessed Toronto, and other cities were in turmoil.

The hint of other problems crept into the broadcasts. There were references to the loss of pressure in the natural gas system. At first, everyone thought of electrical failures at the pipeline compressor stations. It soon became apparent the supply from the west had stopped flowing. Chinese invasion forces on the North American west coast had fought their way east of the mountains and stopped shipments of natural gas, wanting to send the gas to a desperate China. Ontario would never again use natural gas.

The population knew none of these details during this November of misery. The disappearance of much of the PLM force gave Huron a clue. It went south to control the unruly population and marked the start of what people called the "wooden winter". A desperate population clear-cut trees. Losing his beloved urban forest in Toronto saddened Warren Dunne.

Huron suffered. There had been little electricity and no natural gas, to begin with, but the Institute and the listening post at Eugenia lost power for a week. Severely wounded fighters from the first days of the campaign died because ice isolated the hospitals in Meaford or Owen Sound; however, many more fighters lived because the fighting stopped. The potential for gunshot wounds gave way to the reality of broken bones as people fell on slippery surfaces. Falling trees injured a few people, and the ice collapsed an abandoned arena.

When the wind finally swung to the northwest, driving snow-squalls from the cold air blowing over the warm lakes covered the ice. Mounting snowdrifts made movement difficult or impossible. The fall campaign ended. Everyone hoped there would be no fighting in the winter. Huron needed to restore itself.

***

"Here is what we know so far." In the first week of December, Chester Amik chaired a meeting in the Boardroom of the Grey County Museum. "The PLM recalled most of its forces to the GTA. The listeners in Eugenia have pieced together a picture of insurrection and desperation down there."

"What about our borders?" The mayor of Owen Sound asked the urgent question.

"We're not completely safe," Helen stood. "We have intercepted a few patrols. Perhaps it's just the bad weather, but they've pulled back into safer garrison positions in Dundalk and Collingwood, and have abandoned the transmission corridor to Bruce since the ice storm and our commandos destroyed the line. At Weyburne, the bulk of the force is in the enclave east of the town. The rail line is on hold."

"I heard something is happening at the Bruce nuke station." The Meaford delegate asked Helen.

"Stan Gregson is here. Stan, can you enlighten us?"

"I can try." Gregson did not like speaking in front of a large crowd. The newly formed Saugeen Authority had appointed him spokesperson. He patted his shirt looking for cigarettes and matches but then realized this was not Corrine's kitchen. "I took a Skidoo down to Port Elgin to meet the operations manager for the generating station," Stan paused thinking he sounded too formal. "This guy said the PLM have abandoned the Bruce generating station. The destroyed transmission line has made the plant useless. He said the only electricity the PLM have is from Niagara, but they're trying to repair the line from northern Ontario. The other nukes shut down, and they can't restart the reactors. They're short of engineers."

Jeff Shadly sat against the wall, feeling sad and wondering if his grandfather was involved. Sharon had last talked to her father three years ago, before they left Weyburne.

"Good God," someone cried. "Are the nukes safe?"

"The managers say yes," Stan continued. "The storm damaged the plant, but they shut it down and can unload the fuel from the last two reactors. They assured us there's no danger."

"They have always lied before," a Councillor muttered.

"Look, we have to trust them. No one else can do it." Stan glanced around. "They want to join us," he finally said, bracing for more hostility.

"Great!" the Owen Sound mayor surprised Stan, "the more, the merrier and they're skilled folks."

"They're skilled in obsolete technology," Chester said. "The nuclear fuel is one of our biggest problems after the PLM. I say we support these people." Everyone agreed. No one else could prevent a nuclear disaster.

The meeting directed Stan to hold preliminary talks with the nuclear managers. They also welcomed the membership of the fledgling Saugeen Authority into General Council as they now called themselves.

"One last thing," Roger LaFarge rose from the corner of the room. "Many guys died and suffered wounds this fall. There's lots of grief. Many of us have religious faith, and even if people don't have a church, we need to help folks heal." The room echoed in agreement.

"It's Christmas. When we all go home, we should organize get-togethers or religious services, so people don't feel alone."

Roger sat, and the room lay silent for a few moments. Everyone remembered home and loved ones and fallen comrades. They left determined to gather, celebrate their good fortune, and heal some of the sadness.

Chapter Forty

"Mike has a person coming up to help. They need a place to stay, and there are no hotels. He asked if the guy could bunk with us." Barry Young stamped snow from his boots.

"Mike gives me the creeps," Jennifer frowned. "I bet this new guy will be just as creepy." She shuddered at the thought. Jennifer had never told Barry she had held off Mike's suggestive advances.

"I know this guy." Barry smiled. "He was one year ahead of me in school and played clarinet in the engineering band. I don't think he's a creep, unless he has changed. He was a radical back then. Rob was an engineer who thought about politics."

"We don't need him here," Barry continued. "They want to park him somewhere safe until they resolve the trouble down there. Rob has an important job in the PLM industrial structure, and Mike thinks having him here will be good for his career. We'll find out when Rob gets here but say nothing. Times have changed people."

Robin Bossley arrived on the next supply train. Rob seemed to travel light or did not expect to stay long. He carried only a backpack and a clarinet case.

"Hello, Barry," Bossley smiled and shook Barry's hand. "I'm glad to see you have climbed the corporate ladder," Rob seemed to joke.

"I'm glad you stayed out of jail." Barry turned. "This is Jennifer, my wife and our daughter Melissa." The man's firm handshake impressed

Jennifer Young, and he reinforced the feeling when he squatted down to look Melissa in the eye to shake her hand.

"How do you like it in the boonies?" Rob asked.

"I have a friend here now," Melissa replied seriously, "and we don't move anymore. I miss Brian."

"Who's Brian?" Rob asked.

"He was my big brother. He died in the fighting." Melissa began sobbing. Tears welled in Jennifer's eyes. Barry choked a whisper into his wife's ear, "We must tell her." Jennifer nodded. Rob felt the emotion.

Somewhat subdued, they left the makeshift railway platform and headed into the village. Snow swirled about their feet. A chilly wind drifted white rills over the rails. The locomotive whistled as the train headed to Dundalk.

"I didn't mean to make her sad." Rob was defensive as he sat by the warmth of the wood stove in Young's kitchen. Jennifer placed corn muffins and hot tea in front of him.

"She misses her brother." She looked away to hide her tear.

"I guess you've suffered a lot." Bossley ate the warm offering and sipped the strange brew. He was used to real tea brought in from somewhere. The evergreen concoction was a novel experience. "I've no family to lose, and my girlfriends don't miss me much."

Jennifer looked at him closely, hoping he was not a pervert. He seemed harmless enough. She went off to find Melissa and let her in on the secret. The couple had delayed telling their daughter the truth, to protect her and themselves, but her startling revelation she thought Brian dead was too cruel to continue. Jennifer took a gigantic risk that would lead to fear-filled moments. In the end, serendipity surprised them all.

"What makes you so valuable to the PLM?" Barry tried to be neutral but could not avoid making the initials of the government sound like a curse. Rob noticed.

"I'm a crazy guy who liked steam power," Rob sipped tea and watched Young. Both men felt each other out. Bossley wondered how much of his feelings he should reveal in these dangerous times.

"They think diesel power will become limited and want to convert the railway to wood and coal. I know little about steam turbines, but I love the old piston technology. I was working with a railway preservation group. It was a lot of fun until..." Bossley's voice trailed off. Barry waited.

"Well, anyway, I had a name in the establishment because of my artsy connections, and someone remembered me. The PLM drafted me. We have shops and engineering facilities in Hamilton. They have grand railway plans. It's too violent there right now, so they are hiding me out in a safe place. Here I am, and by the way, I liked you in school, but you were too damned serious." Rob laughed, and Barry joined him.

"You were too much a character." Barry looked at the doorway where he could hear Jennifer and Melissa sobbing. "You smart guys bugged me. You had lots of fun and still pulled top marks. I envied you." The sounds from the other room became subdued.

"By the way, who pulled the subway power switch?" It had been the mystery of the Toronto engineering crowd for over sixty years.

"That was before our time," Bossley sighed as if cheated out of some special fun, "but medical students caused everything bad." He winked.

The silly old rivalries and myths were long gone, along with the university. The men had much in common. Their humour and inquisitiveness made them friends. Mike dropping in often to suck up to Bossley cause the only shadow.

Barry showed Rob the operation, even trekking to Dundalk. Jennifer's trust took longer to build. Their guest won her over by participating in the makeshift Christmas celebrations at the church. They served no food except thin cookies, tea, water, and cider. They filled the time with singing and socializing and only a brief message from Al, delivered to a receptive congregation. Jennifer noted Rob sat quietly with a serious expression. She decided he too guarded secrets and loss.

When Ester played the piano, Rob changed. He took his clarinet to follow along with Ester through the standard repertoire of carols. The man was indeed a fine musician and did not seem to be snobbish towards Mrs Wright who was simply a competent church piano player. The pair led the crowd in song after song. In the end, Rob swept Mrs Wright from her feet and hugged her tightly; a second hug for Al and Rob packed the clarinet away. Bossley and the Youngs headed home.

"Melissa says Brian is on the other side," Rob Bossley remarked casually as the three adults sat for a Christmas breakfast of oatmeal and raspberry preserves. Jennifer and Barry Young's startled, fearful glances betrayed the truth.

"Oh, don't worry, I am no PLM stooge," Rob smiled. "She said I was a nice man and glad I came to visit. I don't think you have to worry about her telling anyone. After she told me, I told her never to tell anyone again. She understands the danger, and so do I."

"They would have drafted him. He had to get to safety." Jennifer wanted to convince herself as much as Bossley.

"Sending him up there would seem like from the frying pan into the fire, wouldn't it?" He zeroed in on the logical inconsistency of the story. "I bet there's a better reason. And just how did you get him there safely?"

Bossley smiled. It was not the sinister, "I have you now" smile a cop would use, but that of a child who had just figured out how to fit some blocks together.

"Barry, I've seen how you two love Melissa, and I would guess you feel the same for Brian. It would have to be serious for you to risk him leaving. You don't have to tell me, and we can drop it right now, but I do like you. I could help when it's time for him to come home."

Jennifer smiled at the thought of Brian being home and then leapt to her feet to be busy with some dishes to hide her anxiety. Barry trusted Rob and told most of the story, except for the spying part.

"So what else have they got on you?" Rob was cynical. Everyone in authority had a devious purpose. "Are you spying for the other side?"

Jennifer stifled a gasp. Barry glanced nervously at the door as if expecting a squad of Angel's secret police to come charging in. The look was a confession. Bossley's grin expanded. "That sounds like fun!" The man exclaimed with youthful enthusiasm. "Can I play?"

"What?" Jennifer and Barry exclaimed in unison. "Play at what?" Barry hoped to divert his old acquaintances train of thought.

"Look," Rob continued, "I have access to lots of people and hear lots of things. I have to know a lot about their plans to do my design job, so I get official stuff. There's valuable news I could pass on."

"Let's just assume it would be a good idea. What kind of news?" Barry played along while saying as little as possible, still convinced this conversation would get them all jailed, tortured and killed.

"I can let you know everything from whether the trains are on time to who is screwing whom. Maybe your friends would like a list of names of all the insiders so they could hang them if they ever catch them." He made a twisted smile as if he was serious about the idea.

"Seriously, I have friends who are doing insider jobs or are sleeping with someone who is. These folks brag about what they know. Before I leave, I'll tell you the considerable amount I know. What do you say?"

"I always like to know what's going on," Barry said cautiously.

"You always were a cagey one, Young. Not trusting anyone is smart these days." Rob smiled again as if life was a big game. "Don't tell me anything about what you might do with the information. How can I get it to you?" Rob held up his mug; Jennifer gladly poured more tea.

"One locomotive driver is a good friend and will bring me packages safe and sound if you can get them to him." Barry refilled his cup. "You need to code it?"

"The first thing I'll do is send you some real tea and coffee." Rob had acquired a taste for Jennifer's tea but liked the real thing. "We'll use the book of words trick."

"What the hell's that?" Barry had not heard of it but not want to share Matt's code.

"I'll send you a package with your friend. I'm guessing he comes to the Hamilton yard since it's the only place we service locomotives and rolling stock. We're the rail hub at the moment." Rob organized his explanation. "I'm always poking about in the yard. No one will take much notice of me. The package will be a book. Likely no on will steal books. I'll send some you would want to read, anyway. Inside the covers, I'll write unbroken rows of numbers. These will be page numbers, and the number of a word on the page grouped in sevens. The first three will be the page number. The next two will be the line number and last two the word on the line. It won't matter what book it is. Put the words together, and you'll have the message. You can send me messages the same way. No one is paying much attention to me. I avoid political ambitions. Politics can get you killed."

Rob seemed serious as if he had seen it firsthand, but then he brightened. "I'm careful whom I sleep with."

The tension broke. The Young's trusted Bossley. "This Mike guy seems to give you more attention than I get." He was serious again. "Don't trust him. He's ambitious. Kissing my lowly ass is a good indicator. Guys like him will do anything and hurt anyone to get ahead. Be careful. If we get through this alive, tell me what's going on up here."

"Where the hell did you learn the book trick?" It impressed Barry. "Everyone learned codes but me."

"You won't remember a good-looking literature student from Vic who was my lover." Rob had a longing look. "She liked my clarinet." The Young's saw a forty-year-old man giggling with teary eyes. "She taught the code to me and left messages in books in the library. She would give me a note with the book's name and a bunch of numbers. I had to get the message, or we wouldn't make love, excellent incentive. Those librarians wondered why an engineering student frequented the literature stacks."

They said no more about Rob spying. The PLM extended Rob's stay because losing energy supplies had weakened them. Supporters became opponents with power struggles at the highest level and violent street riots. The lack of control delayed plans to push through to Owen Sound. This information ended up in a hymnbook.

The Youngs bid Rob farewell at the end of January. Melissa had an especially big hug for her departing "Uncle Rob" under the watchful eye of Mike the stooge. Rob Bossley's stay had convinced the ambitious man Barry had important allies in Toronto and Mike should keep him as a friend. He heard Bossley was important to the higher-ups in the PLM, and so Barry Young became his link to the seats of power. They watched in a raw wind as the train rumbled backwards towards Orangeville. Barry completed the siding track with a second switch into the mainline. The engineer could then be at the front of southbound trains.

Chapter Forty-one

"Riding home on the hay wagon after the Christmas celebration was one of those golden, perfect moments. I was sitting beside Mom and the girls. I'm sorry I can't remember where you were sitting. The sky was beautiful, and I was full of the warmth of an evening spent with everyone. I have been happy many times in my life, that was one of the best, and when I wrote Silver Clouds."
From: a letter by Joseph of Longview to Kim Handley (shared by permission)–Erin Thomas

Christmas celebrations in Huron Territory were more subdued than in PLM controlled areas where there they did not honour the dead or wounded. Instead, the leaders heaped blame on those who had allowed the defeat. They organized Christian ceremonies as elaborate political events as government members made a great show of attending, with security forces spread inside and outside every place of worship.

The grandeur partly offset empty stomachs and unheated homes. Conditions became as bad as they had been during the height of the chaotic fighting before the PLM won the day. It did not help that they had curtailed religious freedom, banning. Islam and other faiths outright, while Judaism felt under siege. Minority Christian sects were less controllable but unofficially suppressed, becoming the focus of smear, and vandalism aimed at solidifying the main denomination whose high priests claimed the supreme leader had been chose by God to lead the faithful.

The services in Huron centred on remembrance and sacrifice. Lacking traditional pastors, lay leaders officiated at most services. An exception to the lack of pastoral leadership occurred at the enormous church Brandi Shadly had visited in Southampton. Pastor Arthur Rush staged an elaborate service hoping to bring more parishioners into the fold. A candlelit procession highlighted the service with the faithful few performing admirably as a choir. Without electricity, the organ could not function, and they sang a cappella. Residents, eager for positive celebration, flocked to the service. Everyone felt uplifted.

The day after the service, a large sign on the main church doors puzzled passers-by. It read, "Closed for repairs until further notice." When touring the building after the service, Arthur Rush noticed melting snow from the worshiper's feet had stained the floors. The damage to his beautiful hardwood horrified him. His faithful parishioners laboured on Christmas Day to clean and polish floors. The church hosted no more public gatherings.

***

The Shadly family gathered at Longview for Christmas. The fighting had traumatized everyone. A small service in the Heathcote Hall attracted most of the residents within practical riding distance. Joseph's teacher, "the piano playing church lady", led the services. She found a second piano and she and Joseph played together, inspiring the congregation. The duo had rehearsed and found that experience more uplifting than the service itself.

The service began with sombre prayers for the dead and music. Joseph had not yet discovered "Hymn to Freedom". The fine old tune would become his favourite and by default the anthem of the territory. It would have suited the mood of the attendees. Several participants read scripture, and one grieving widow, a young woman with three small children, read a tribute to her husband, killed in the fighting at Maxwell. Everyone shared her grief. Jeff Shadly read the names of the dead and wounded from the valley. Thankfully, it was a short list but had a great impact and followed by deep and heartfelt silence.

Brandi Shadly's heavy heart needed comfort. Help seemed to flow from the gathering, healing and soothing her sadness. She once again pondered the role of faith and the power in the gathering of like-minded people. It reflected a need to feed something beyond the body. In her hurt, she recalled the words of Doc Adams; *people are hurting inside too. They need someone like you to patch that up.*

Brandi was full of questions. People had showed a need for something deeper. Corrine's offering of tobacco was one example, but so was Al Wright's steadfast faith in his beliefs. She had seen examples of faith that led to bad things; Brandi wondered if there could be a balance. Certainly, when faith became organized, it seemed to become corrupted. She had learned enough history to see how like-minded people could justify doing horrible things; however, this Christmas gathering showed the benefit of spiritual sharing.

The crowd sang with gusto and reverence and drifted home after treats and happy fellowship.

They returned to Longview on several wagons. Puffy silver clouds decorated the sky, lit by a waning moon and hurrying on a brisk north-west wind. The moon seemed to scurry in the opposite direction. Above the head of the valley, the bright starlight of Sirius guided the way.

Brandi rode Dodger and accompanied the overloaded vehicles. In the nearest wagon, Joseph and his sisters, Hope and Grace bundled against the cold and snuggled against Ellen. Brandi watched Joseph's smiling face, staring at the sky, his lips moved as if singing. In fact, the young boy composed a new song, full of the happiness, pleasure and the sense of belonging the evening had given.

Brandi looked skyward, following Joseph's stare, and the clouds mesmerized her. Each sped along, changed shapes as they flew, shone silver in the moonlight, full of promise, and they cast no shadows.

The End

Continued in: The End of Shadows, After the Last Day Book Three

Chapter One

As you know, we closed the old building a long time ago. It is just a skeleton now, with only the concrete and steel standing. There is some talk of salvaging the steel for the Hamilton mills. The room where you held the founding meeting has gone, along with Granddad's office where you first met him.

Your depiction of the event and the signatures look even better now, framed under glass in our timber and stone meetinghouse. They hang

above the Chair at the front of the Council Assembly Hall. I know my grandfather was not a formal delegate, but I smile every time I see him in your drawing. Thank you for including him. He was proud of that. Your portrait of Chester is still on the one side, but you may not know the Council recently ordered your self-portrait placed beside his. It is one of you on that big quarter horse from years ago.

We get many visitors, and I tell them the story of the first convention and the founding of Huron. We show your notes and other drawings, and I always read your last line aloud. Thank you for your kindness and for making this so real for my family and me. I know, to you, this is now a place of sadness.

From: A private letter to Brandi Shadly from Paul Jenkins III, then custodian of the Huron General Council meeting hall and offices. He is the grandson of the late Paul Jenkins, the original director of the museum.

They gathered in grief, full of uncertainty and fear, but they did a good thing.

From: "The Founding of Huron" (The Journals of Brandi Shadly, Vol. 6, p. 112)

Note: the Truth Talker Players re-enact portions of the Huron Founding Convention as recorded by Brandi Shadly. Their performance is part of the opening ceremony of the annual council meeting held each March.–E.T.

"Conditions are changing, and we need to get organized." Chester stood at the front of the auditorium of the old museum near Owen Sound. His voice filled the room. He gazed out over an audience of about one hundred delegates from the various villages and other watershed organizations. It was especially pleasing to see the delegation from the lower Saugeen watershed, including his old friend Corrine from Chippewa Hill. The melting of the snow pack had finally allowed for this conference. Chester had been organizing the event since Christmas. Late winter proved the best time for meetings, allowing for travel yet not cutting into the farm work.

www.ingramcontent.com/pod-product-compliance
Lightning Source LLC
Chambersburg PA
CBHW071424200726

48294CB00002B/502